Give Me Peace

M.K. Harper

ISBN-13: 9798358229884
ISBN-10: 1477123456

Cover design by: Art Painter
Library of Congress Control Number: 2018675309
Printed in the United States of America

To growth.

Foreword

Please note that while this story does touch on darker subject matter, the meat of it revolves around the MFC and the relationships she builds with her harem. These guys are all in from the get-go (mostly), and eager to help their leading lady heal from the trauma she's endured. Plainly put, they're cinnamon rolls. You'll even find some laughs to balance out the tougher parts. If you're looking for an uber-dark romance, this book will likely miss the mark for you.

With that said, I hope you'll give these characters a chance to win you over. Happy reading!

Prologue

Saylor

I've come to learn that our hardest and happiest moments usually happen within the span of a few seconds. Whether it's good news or a brash decision that holds life-altering consequences, we rarely see it coming. But it's the tough ones that stand out the most. They make an impact. There's no time to brace or prepare yourself—mentally or physically. It just happens. All you can do is pick up the pieces and move forward as best you can.

Twice now, I've been blissfully unaware of that impending transition from happy to not.

I was ten the first time. Mom and I had gone to church that morning, something we didn't get to do very often because of her hectic work schedule. After that, we stopped by the local mall for some food court pizza, browsed a few stores, then headed home. It'd been a perfectly normal day, but on the drive back, Mom switched lanes to pass a bus. That was it—our moment. A simple act that held no pretense of danger until it did.

Unbeknownst to either of us, a car had stalled

in the middle of the road while attempting to make a left-hand turn. The blind spot the bus created prevented us from seeing it until it was too late. We smacked the back of their Buick and bounced across the median, narrowly avoiding oncoming traffic, before the blunt force of a tree brought us to a stop. Our final destination? The front lawn of the DMV.

Oh, the irony.

I'd been so shocked, the first thing I did was spin around and look back at the place we'd just been chugging along, our car intact and the day unruined. I was convinced I'd hallucinated the whole thing, despite the pungent scent of deployed airbags and seatbelt burn stinging my chest. But there it was—the scene of our accident unmissable. The other sedan was completely spun around, facing the opposite direction, and produce littered the road. For weeks, remnants of bright colored fruits and vegetables could be seen every time we drove by.

We'd gotten lucky. Our injuries were superficial, but being a nurse, Mom insisted that we get checked out. Aside from a sore foot, she was fine. While scrambling to hit the brake, she somehow tore straight through the side of her strappy new high heel. As for me, I had some aches and bruises, but nothing that warranted further treatment. The passengers in the other car were relatively unscathed as well. All things considered—it could have been a lot worse.

The next day, we stopped by the junkyard to assess the damage. Mom's Camry was totaled—a loss we couldn't afford to eat being a one-income household. I could see the worry in her eyes as we gathered our personal belongings, and I wished more than anything that I could go back in time and prevent the wreck from ever happening. A few extra seconds at the mall would've made all the difference, but what's done is done. Sadly, no one has figured out how to rewrite history yet.

We struggled to make ends meet for a while, but Mom never let on how dire our situation was. She didn't have to, though. I was a curious and perceptive kid; I could tell we were stretching pennies. Ramen noodles made a frequent appearance in our dinner rotation, but things slowly returned to normal. Her shifts at the hospital lessened once the overtime wasn't needed, and life went on.

Four years later, on May 23rd, 2017, it happened again. I've replayed that day a thousand times trying to make sense of it, but I doubt I ever will. I was walking home, frustrated and embarrassed, when that bright red pickup slowed beside me. I didn't question the offered ride, not when the person driving was as familiar to me as my own name. They'd been a staple in my life for as long as I could remember. I was hot, and the sour mood I'd been in only made it worse, so I graciously agreed.

But for some reason, when I slid across that torn bench seat and pulled the door closed, a niggle of unease brushed against my senses. I turned to look back at the patch of sidewalk I'd just been standing on, that same disembodied incredulity I'd felt the day of the wreck making my brows scrunch in confusion. Nothing about the two situations was remotely similar, but maybe I knew I'd think back to that moment, wrack my brain endlessly for an explanation as to why someone I've known and trusted for *years* would do what they'd come to do.

Steal me.

Lock me away.

Hurt me.

Or perhaps, some sense of foreshadowing took place, and deep down I knew the girl I once was ceased to exist the second I accepted that ride. I grew more wary with every mile, and despite knowing that something wasn't right, I kept quiet. That sixth sense everyone talks about tried to warn me, but I stupidly ignored it. I brushed it off as paranoia, convinced there was a reasonable answer for all the questions I couldn't bring myself to ask.

Like why we passed my street.

Denial held me tightly in its clutches. I was mute and immobile, too scared to speak up, while hoping it would all be chalked up as an overreaction later on. I never reached for the door handle or tried to make a run for it, but maybe if I would've listened to that intuition a little sooner, I might have had a chance. I realize now that any attempt to get away would have been futile. I'm positive he had backup measures in place should I have tried anything, but I regret not fighting back. At least if I had, I wouldn't feel culpable in my own kidnapping.

I tend to bite my tongue, choosing silence over the possibility of ruffling any feathers. Mom says I'm a peacekeeper, constantly downplaying my own feelings in place of everyone else's. Truthfully, I just hate confrontation. And what could possibly be more confrontational than accusing someone of something, especially if you aren't certain of the circumstances? It's a flaw of mine—*likely fatal*—but the needle he jammed into my thigh effectively wiped away any naivety I had left about his motives.

When I finally woke, I was in a dimly lit room that looked on the verge of collapse. My eyes were so heavy, it took me longer than it should have to fully take in my new surroundings. A single lightbulb hung from the ceiling, flickering in and out, the faint hum of electricity agitating my tender brain. The air was stale and cold, giving everything a damp feel, and the twin bed I was lying on had definitely seen better days. But the rusted sink and toilet situated in the corner of the room had my heart racing. For some reason, seeing those everyday necessities made the panic I'd been purposefully avoiding surge to the forefront.

I stumbled to my feet, eyes bouncing from one thing to the next. A worn, built-in bookcase was stocked with a few bottles of water, some off-brand protein bars, crossword puzzles and VHS tapes. A stack of clothing was folded at the bottom of the bed. Hygiene items—a toothbrush, toothpaste, and an old bar of soap—were placed on the edge of the sink. Lastly, a box TV was mounted near the ceiling, similar to an outdated classroom setup. The combination of those things, of what they meant, made me so lightheaded I had to brace my hand against the wall to keep from falling over.

He's had this planned for a while. It wasn't a

spur of the moment decision. Based on his level of preparedness, taking me was a well-thought-out process. This room has everything needed to keep me contained.

I've never been outspoken. Just the thought of causing a scene or being an inconvenience makes me anxious. I was taught '*you catch more flies with honey*' and I've made it a point to apply that to my everyday life. I'm nice to everyone, even when they aren't nice to me. The whole reason I'd been walking home that day instead of riding the bus was because I had, once again, tried to be friendly with the boy who'd bullied me since grade school.

And look where it got me.

As my new reality set in, politeness went out the window. I screamed for help, banged my fists against the steel door barring my freedom. But it never budged, and my pleas fell on deaf ears. The rest of the room might have been in shambles, but it was obvious my only means of escape was a recent addition. A definite upgrade from the original. All I managed to do was bruise my hands and drain what little energy I had left. Eventually, the adrenaline faded, leaving my throat raw and body trembling. Cold and scared, I huddled in the corner of the bed and silently cried myself to sleep.

The sound of the lock disengaging sometime later made my eyes snap open. By the time he cleared the door, I was already begging. Tears fell once again, or maybe they never stopped. I pleaded with the man that coached my t-ball games and hosted the annual Easter egg hunt. The pillar of our community who radiated trustworthiness. And like the flip of a switch,

I watched someone I didn't recognize in the slightest emerge from those cold black eyes of his.

I didn't know that person. He might share a face with someone I *thought* I knew, but I couldn't rationalize the two of them being one and the same. His massive hand snapped out and gripped my hair, yanking me forward without an ounce of care. My sobs grew louder as he used his free hand to pry the bookshelf from the wall. A second later, an even worse sight than my current predicament greeted me.

It was pitch-black, so dark I couldn't see an inch in front of my face. The lack of sight made me even more frantic. Given the option, I would have rather known what was coming, even if I couldn't prevent it from happening, than be kept in a heightened state of suspense. I was shoved inside the hidden space, my knees connecting with the raw dirt roughly. Instinctively, I searched the ground for something —*anything*—to use as a weapon, while crawling as quickly as possible away from the man behind me.

A clicking sound caused me to freeze. I blinked rapidly, trying to get my eyes to adjust. In the next breath, a light was turned on, the sudden change in brightness making me wince. A lone beam shone on a threadbare mattress a few feet in front of me. It was stained and frayed, several springs poking through here and there. To the left of the light, a flashing red dot drew my attention. The pieces began to click, the image they formed making me fight for air.

A camcorder.

It was old-school, a relic of the past that

wouldn't leave a digital footprint the way a phone might, but I recognized what it was. Whatever he planned to do, he wanted video evidence. Bile rose up my throat, the burning sensation a blip in comparison to the hysteria threatening to overwhelm me. I'd barely had a chance to process any of it when my nightmare come to life stepped back into view.

I screamed—*again*—the sound echoing throughout the small room and making my ears ring. I've never *heard* fear before. Never felt it become palpable. But I did that day. It was a living, breathing entity sharing the room with me. My life was normal. Not once had I been put into a situation where I felt that my safety was threatened, especially by someone in a position of power. The obliteration of that innocence hurt like hell.

Try as I might, I couldn't fight him off when his hands began to wander, pawing at my clothes with vigor. I slapped and kicked, but my sad attempts were useless against his larger frame. I watched in horror as my favorite outfit was torn from my body. Piece by piece, they fell away—a pale pink top, white scalloped shorts, and lastly, my plain white bra and panties.

I prayed it wasn't real, squeezed my eyes shut so tightly, white dots danced behind the closed lids. I needed it to be a dream. A horrible, therapy-worthy nightmare that I'd wake from at any second. As my hands were pinned behind me, any hopes of that faded into nothing. He dragged me to the mattress and tied my wrists together, using enough force to make my fingers tingle. To add more terror to the mix, a thick scrap of fabric was placed over my eyes to blindfold me.

My naked body was completely exposed to him and whoever else might one day bear witness to this depravity. He fondled my breasts, his callused fingers pinching my nipples and causing me to cry out from the pain. I thrashed, gave everything I had to try and make him stop, but eventually, the numbness set in. Survival mode took over. I shut down and ignored what was happening to keep myself from shattering.

He moaned at the agonized sounds I made, and when he'd finally gotten his fill, the camera was switched off. I have no idea how long he violated my body for, it could've been minutes or hours, but my chest ached from the onslaught. He hadn't touched me below the waist, and for that, I was grateful, but I was scared to know how long his refrain would last. I'd been so certain he was going to take a part of me I would never get back.

I was innocent, my basic understanding of sex mostly in regard to reproduction. With Mom's job, we never skirted the topic. But it was always discussed in clear and concise, anatomically correct wording. I didn't *know* sex. Why would I, I was fourteen? I'd barely had my period for a full year.

As I was lying there, slumped against the wall with my hands bound and eyes covered, a sob worked its way free. He'd been quiet, not a single word spoken since he first offered me a ride. No matter how many times I asked why he was doing this or begged for him to stop, he refused to speak. He gave me no answers or inkling of his motives. In a broken, scared voice, I cried for my mom.

And for that, he beat me within an inch of my life.

His heavy boot slammed against my side, the hit so brutal it knocked the breath out of me. Over and over, he dispelled his anger through kicks and punches, until I was nothing more than a broken, curled-up ball, my blood and dignity mixed with the dirt beneath me. I was covered in bruises, the purple and black splotches lingering for weeks after the fact.

To my absolute horror, those trips behind the bookshelf became routine. Once a month, he'd come for me, and so long as I was good and didn't anger him, he'd let me out right after. But on those few occasions when my body refused to just sit there and take what he was doing, when I'd fight against the inevitable, he'd leave me there. For hours, sometimes a full day. The dark, combined with the absolute silence, was cruel in its own right.

Aside from dropping off food and water, and occasionally restocking my hygiene items, I never saw him outside of those dreaded visits. He was always silent, and only provided enough to sustain me for a few days at a time. I'm not sure if the psychological torture was intentional, but it worked. I was kept in a constant state of dread, wondering if the next time would be the last time. The food he gave me was barely nutritional, and more often than not, expired. But it was food. Every time my stash would start to dwindle, the paranoia would set in.

I'd ration my meals down to bites, just in case he didn't come back before I ran out. I think he took a sick sort of satisfaction in making it known, without ever needing to say it, that he held my life in the palm of his hand. In more ways than one. He could stock the room with a case of water or a jar of peanut butter, but that'd be too much of a kindness. Whether I continued to breathe was completely reliant upon him. The constant fear of starvation left me stressed, but nothing was more worrisome than what he planned to do with me next.

I always knew things would escalate. By my guess, I'd been there a year when it finally happened. Time had been hard to keep track of when there was no sense of day or night. He'd come for me, the visit starting no different than the ones before it. I'd grown used to him groping my chest, but when his dirty hand slipped lower, my vision blurred. For the first time in a long time, tears filled my eyes. I'd done everything in my power to mentally prepare myself for that moment, but once faced with it, I crumbled.

He'd been extra rough, tweaking my nipples so hard I couldn't help but whimper. I tried to hold it in, knowing it only spurred him on. He fed off my emotional pain just as much as the physical. The moment his greedy hand ghosted between my legs, I think another piece of me died. Every time after that, he pushed for more. The day his thick finger finally forced its way inside of me, I sobbed for hours. His assaults became relentless, each session going longer than the last.

When he made me orgasm for the first time, I was horrified. It was humiliating, and I felt so betrayed by my own body. My response was natural, but it didn't make me hate myself any less. He licked the tears from my cheeks while chuckling at my distress. It was my lowest moment to-date. Every muscle went limp, my fight and will to live being ripped away from me. He loved that, knowing I'd been broken a little more.

Later that night, when he finally let me go, I tried to touch myself. I thought if I could take back control, be in charge of my own release, that it wouldn't hurt so bad. I couldn't do it, though. The second I felt a spark of pleasure, all I could think of was him and the undeniable truth that he officially owned something of mine I had never willingly given.

Honestly, it's no surprise I finally snapped.

Over the years, I've been given a front row seat to inhumanity at its finest, and I just couldn't take it anymore. Two days ago—or maybe it was three—I completely lost it. It's hard to gauge how long it's been when I'm surrounded by darkness, the constant silence my only companion. Truthfully, I didn't think I still had any fight left in me. But I just couldn't do it. I couldn't walk into that room, my feet carrying me there without protest, and subject myself to another debasing round of torture. He's taken too much already.

Something clicked, and I realized that I would rather die fighting, than risk losing anything else. So when that lock twisted and the door swung open, I lunged. Teeth bared, arms swinging blindly, I gave it everything I had, determined to make it through that opening before he could close it. It was a stupid idea. There was a reason I hadn't tried before. I'm small, but compared to him, I may as well be ant sized. Foolishly,

I thought his bigger build meant he'd move slower.

I was wrong.

He caught me instantly, snatching me back by my hair. A scream lodged itself in my the throat as a chunk was ripped from my scalp. I bit and kicked, but he only laughed, tossing me across the room as if I weighed nothing. I hit the floor so hard, I swore I felt my brain rattling around my skull. He pounded the defiance right out of me, then dragged my half-conscious body behind the bookshelf, closing me inside the hidden space without a backward glance.

And now I'm paying greatly for my error in judgment.

My ribs throb in tune with my head, each hit still fresh and vivid in my mind. Everything hurts. I'd cry if I wasn't so scared the effort would bring me even more pain. Considering how dehydrated I am, I doubt I could form a tear if I tried. The hunger pangs have gotten so bad I'm dry heaving. The last thing I ate—an overripe banana—has long since faded from my system. I can't help but think that this is it. He's finally going to kill me, or let nature take its course and do his dirty work for him. I've never been left for this long, and a small part of me welcomes whatever comes next.

I'm so tired—the kind that can't be fixed with a good night's sleep or a hot meal.

Luckily, the oversized shirt I'd been wearing is still covering my body. He was more focused on beating me for my disobedience and escape attempt than getting off, but the thin material is doing little to ward off the chill. I haven't been warm since the day he brought me here, but this room, with its dirt floor and cinderblock walls, has always felt so much colder. I think it's a combination of the evil acts that take place in here and the shitty state of disrepair. Either way, I can't make the shivering stop.

It's completely black, something I should be used to by now, but being robbed of a sense only heightens all the others. Every sound is amplified, my own breaths creating an echo. The tattered fabric of the mattress feels like knives against my battered skin. It's a special kind of torment, to not know what's in front of you or about to happen. I swear something brushed my leg earlier, followed by a scratching noise a few moments later. A mouse, maybe? The old me, the one who secretly slept with a dozen stuffed animals and still watched the Disney channel, would've squealed and scrambled for the highest surface I could find. This me? She might be desperate enough to eat it.

As I lie here, my eyes wide open but unable to see a thing, I try to think of something good. It's a game I've played for a while now, a way to keep myself grounded. When something awful happens, I list a reason to be thankful. Because even though I'm living any sane person's version of Hell on Earth, I make it a point to remind myself that it could *always* be worse. I've been through the bad, learned what to do and what not to do, and eventually found a place in-between that allows me a sliver of sanity.

So, morbidly, I stay grateful for the things that haven't happened, instead of mourning the things that have. It's sick, this psychological warfare that's been waged. The idea that I could be thankful to this man for a single thing makes my skin crawl. How fucked is it that I'm appreciative he's yet to fully rape me? I know what the statistics say. Most girls who've been in captivity for as long as I have don't make it out alive. And when they do, they aren't really living. They're shells of who they once were, too broken to ever function normally.

I'm scared this might be the end of the line for me, because at what point does the damage become too great? You can't glue something back together when you don't have all the pieces. And that's exactly what he's done—slowly stolen parts of me so that I'm impossible to repair.

And the worst part—*the absolute worst part*—is that I have zero hope of ever being found. In the beginning, I entertained the thought. Fantasized about what it would be like. But I knew reality was worlds away from those silly daydreams. Because the man who took me all those years ago is no stranger. Unfortunately for me, he's loved by our town and the last person they'd ever suspect.

He wears a mask, a damn good one too, but I'm intimately acquainted with the monster he conceals beneath it. He's not at all who he portrays himself to be. Some upstanding member of society, sworn to protect and serve its citizens. In fact, he's the exact opposite of that, and I don't think I'll ever be free of him.

Chapter One

Lochlan

Leaning back, I scrub a hand over my face, exhaustion wearing me down quicker by the second. I've spent more time in my office this past week than I ever have. Initially, when the twins splurged on this overpriced chair, I'd been pissed. We can't afford to spend frivolously. At this point in the game, preserving our funds is crucial, knowing we'll need every cent in the long run. Yet here I sit, appreciative of proper lumbar support at the ripe old age of twenty-eight.

Building a business from scratch, much less a private security and investigation firm, is no small feat. The idea took root when I was just a kid, but never in my wildest dreams did I imagine that we'd be where we are today. We're still small fish in comparison to other agencies, but we're doing it. We're making a difference, and that's all I've ever wanted. We don't need the notoriety or recognition that other groups chase. Our success is measured in something far more valuable: the closure we've given to families, albeit bittersweet at times. I love my job; I love this company we've built. But some days, it feels like I'm selling a part of my soul when we're forced to take on the flashy, big-name contracts.

The washed-up celebrity who hires us to make himself look good, as if he's someone important enough to warrant a security team. Or the kid of some uber-famous asshole, who just has to have the full college experience—paparazzi be damned—and needs a tail to keep them in line. Those grate against everything I envisioned when starting SOTERIA, but they're necessary in order to keep the bills paid. They allow us to funnel money into the cases we're actually interested in.

This week, however, I've caught myself wondering why in the hell we accept some of these clients. Not every situation is life or death, and most of the time the guys are happy to slip away for a bit and recuperate, especially after wrapping up a particularly difficult investigation. But on occasion, we'll take on a shit piece of work, and I start to question if they're even worth the money we'll make. Kade has made it known, no less than a couple hundred times, that his current clientele falls into that category. He's a good kid, if not a little short tempered, but this woman he's been assigned to is pressing every button he has—all at once. I wouldn't be surprised if a complaint is lodged against him after everything is said and done. Kade isn't the greatest at filtering his thoughts, so God knows what the prick has said to the teeny bopper he's babysitting.

I have a mound of paperwork to catch up on, half of it being outstanding invoices for customers who've yet to settle their fee for service's rendered, and all I want to do is crawl into bed and sleep for a month straight. It's always the pompous pricks, the gaudy types who flaunt their wealth, that we have to track down for payment. Glancing at the clock, I groan at the late hour. I'm too old for this. Deciding now is as good of a stopping point as any, I stand and stretch the tightness from my back.

The house is quiet as I make my way towards my bedroom. With Kade gone, it's been all work and no play. If Roan is up, he's likely in the gym, working through whatever's keeping him awake in the first place. The twins are probably out cold, preferring to keep as close to a normal sleep schedule as possible. And if one is done for the night, you can bet the other is too. Kash doesn't sleep well without Krew close by.

I can't count how many times they've been needed for days on end, getting little to no rest while living off of energy drinks. Hacking their way through code and combing the dark web, chasing one lead to the next. Those two are invaluable to SOTERIA. We're a ragtag bunch, but we're family. We all have different reasons that led us to this point in our lives, some darker than others, but I couldn't imagine my life without those four. I toe my door closed with a sigh, too exhausted to bother with a shower.

Tossing my phone on the nightstand, I strip and climb into bed. *So good.* The second my head connects with the pillow and my eyes shut, sleep overtakes me. It feels like seconds have passed—*goddamn seconds*—when the buzzing of my phone wakes me. I swear to Christ, if it's Kade calling to complain some more I'm going to fire him. The illuminated display reveals an unknown number. My body is so weighed down and tired, it takes me several tries to swipe my finger across the screen. When the call finally connects, I grunt out a greeting.

"Calloway."

"It's Denvers." I'm instantly awake, fully aware that he wouldn't be calling in the middle of the night unless it was urgent.

"What's happened?" I head for the bathroom to splash some water on my face. The likelihood of this concluding with me going back to bed is slim to none. Silence greets my question, so I pull the phone away to make sure we didn't get disconnected.

"Denvers? You there?" He clears his throat, an audible sigh coming through the line.

"I need you in Lyola."

"Lyola?" I parrot, knowing it sounds familiar, but unable to place it.

"Laiken County, Calloway." I freeze, my heart battering against my ribcage. I have to lean against the counter for support, my free hand gripping the edge so tightly, it sends pinpricks through my fingers.

"In regard to?" I feel certain I know, but I'm going to need him to clarify.

"We've got a lead. A solid one." I close my eyes, relief flooding my system. A lead is far more preferable than a body. "A woman by the name of Sheena Wilcox phoned in the tip just a bit ago. She's a CNA at Lyola Assisted Living. It seems one of her patients has been going on for a few days now about this girl that's living under her porch." Confusion swamps me, my eyebrows scrunching together as I try and make sense of Denvers statement.

Her porch?

"The old lady is a stroke patient, so they'd written it off as crazy talk. Ms. Wilcox said she never fully recovered after the last one and her mind's not quite right. Until.." He stops to take a deep breath.

"*Until?*" I snap hotly.

"Until the patient gave a name. *Radley*. She kept saying '*that Radley girl*'." The rest of my strength evaporates as I slump to the floor.

Is this real?

"This shouldn't need to be said, but it's a long shot. The likelihood of this turning up anything is low, but it's more than we've gotten in years." I'm nodding my agreement, as if he can see me, completely lost for words but so fucking hopeful it hurts.

"I think this should stay between us for now. Bring Roan if you need to, but it'd be best to keep this quiet until we know more." I hate keeping anything from my team, but I understand Denvers reluctance to sound the alarm so early.

"Yeah," I finally manage to speak. "I think that'd be wise." But what we're both not saying is who, specifically, needs to be kept in the dark. "It'll take us about three hours to get there, maybe less at this time of night."

"I should arrive before you. Might have enough time to scope out the place and get local authorities on site." Denvers doesn't seem too thrilled by that idea. He has jurisdiction, as the case went to him not long after Saylor went missing, but it's always easier to play nice when you're on someone else's turf.

"One more thing, Lochlan." My spine straightens at the use of my first name. "The patient that offered up the information? She's the mother of the county sheriff. He's lived with her all of his life."

"Fuck," I groan, thumping my head against the vanity.

"Fuck is right, son. Even worse, the CNA said that he visits his mother nearly every day, but hasn't been in since Friday."

It's Tuesday.

"I'll get there as quickly as I can." I hop up and end the call, knowing there's nothing left to discuss and time is of the essence. I'm yanking on a pair of slacks a second later, pocketing my phone as I rush around the room. Grabbing my duffel, I hastily pack a few days' worth of clothes. My perfectly pressed, color coordinated shirts are ripped from their hangers without a care, zero thought going into matching anything. There's no way to know how long this will take, but I won't be leaving town until we've scoured every inch of that godforsaken place.

We're on borrowed time. For all we know, the fucker's been tipped off already. The fact that he's changed his routine, missing visits with a mother who's clearly in poor health, doesn't bode well for us.

By now, he's had plenty of time to flee with Saylor, or worse. I can't think about the worse. Pulling my cell back out, I send a quick text to Ro.

Be ready in 10. Pack for a week.

There's no need for me to elaborate. The guys know by now that when they get this type of message, it's go-time. I'll fill him in once we're on the road. In two minutes flat, I'm entering the kitchen and firing up the Keurig. The clock on the microwave reads 2:42. It's going to be a long night, and an even longer day. Tightening the lid on my coffee, I sling my bag over my shoulder and speed walk to the garage. As expected, Ro's already there, his own bag resting by his feet as he leans against the front bumper. I hit the unlock button and toss him the keys, quickly sliding into the passenger seat.

"Just us?" Roan grumbles, the low cadence of his voice making the words nearly indiscernible.

"Just us," I confirm. "I didn't want to wake the twins. You know Kash would never get back to sleep. I'll reach out closer to sunrise." Ro hits the button for the garage door, the modern lift barely making a sound as it rolls upward. While he gets us on our way unnoticed, I plug in the coordinates that Denvers sent. Roan gives the screen a cursory glance as he steps on the gas, the driveway rapidly fading behind us.

"Pike's Bay?" Ro questions, spotting the neighboring town on the map before I can hit '*go*'. "Kade?"

"Not Kade," I answer robotically, pulling my spare laptop from the backseat. "Saylor." I whisper her name, too afraid to say it out loud and make it real. I've both dreaded and longed for this day. Ro still heard me, if the white knuckled grip he has on the steering wheel is any indication. I quickly summarize the call from Denvers, explaining the urgency of the situation. A hundred and seventy-six miles has never felt so far. It may as well be on the opposite end of the country. Fidgety as hell, I settle in for the longest drive of my life.

Chapter Two

Lochlan

The first time I ever stepped foot into Pike's Bay was three years ago. Ro and I were following a lead on the disappearance of a politician's daughter. Her cellphone had pinged off a tower just before Laiken County, so we'd questioned the locals, hoping someone might've seen or heard something useful. The only thing we managed to find was Kade.

He'd been a right asshole, shoving a crumpled manilla folder in my face, insistent that we look at the information he'd gathered on a local girl that'd been missing for two years. I'd been impressed with his effort and the thoroughness of his knowledge. Something about the desperate way he angrily demanded our help gave me pause, made me want to help him in whatever way I could. To this day, I still don't know the full story, or why he's taken it upon himself to bring Saylor home, but Kade's dead set on trying his damndest. His devotion to the cause has never wavered, but it begs the question—*why?*

He didn't have the means or resources for a

proper investigation, and while I couldn't promise we'd ever find her, I did offer Kade a job and the chance to help others in the same predicament. He jumped at the opportunity to get out of Pike's Bay, and even though it was an adjustment, we eventually found our groove. It wasn't always easy, but we click more days than we don't. He's our brother—in all the ways that count—so it didn't take long for his personal crusade to become our own.

We studied everything he had on her, and the twins did what they do best and filled in the missing pieces. There was hardly anything. Nothing, truthfully. Not a single lead or clue as to what happened on the day that Saylor went missing. With no starting point, I decided to reach out to the agent assigned to Saylor's case. From there, our connection with Denvers was born. He was wary at first, not wanting to jeopardize any potential evidence, but he came around. Not that it did us much good, as he had fuck all too. He promised he'd never stop looking, though. And one more person out there searching, was one more that wasn't.

Our working relationship progressed over time. We've built a lot of trust between us these past three years, and I know he's just as eager and hopeful as we are that this will pan out. Saylor's grown on each of us, beyond just the loyalty we feel to help our friend. It was impossible to not get wrapped up in the blue-eyed girl with the button nose. Her pint-sized frame was enough to send our protective instincts into overdrive.

She has fire, though. I've seen it a few times in

the home videos we've been given access to. Saylor's a champion for the underdog, always standing up for the weak and bullied. I can only hope she found some of that fight she reserves for everyone else. That she's somehow still alive, and we aren't headed towards a devastating conclusion.

"How the fuck is this possible? We pretty much ruled out she was still in the area after..." Ro trails off, his jaw clenched so hard I can hear his teeth grinding together.

"I don't know," I sigh, leaning my head back against the seat. "The only thing I can come up with is that it was a distraction tactic. He made us think she was long gone, sold to some fucked up billionaire with too much money to spare and a taste for depravity." I try not to think about it, not wanting to relive what we'd seen, but the memory is forever etched into my brain. While we'd found no trace of her initially, a few months after the twins began their search, they stumbled across our first piece of evidence.

It was a picture of Saylor, her hands bound behind her back as she knelt on a dirty mattress. She'd been blindfolded, but there was no mistaking it was her. Her naked body had been offered up for anyone to ogle, covered in bruises and small abrasions. From what we could tell, it'd been taken shortly after she was kidnapped. We were years late in finding it, and never came across another. That left us with two possible outcomes: she was already dead, or she'd been sold.

Being so close to the coast, it made sense. It would've been too easy to traffic a young girl with that sort of access. The deep recesses of the internet are a vile place. Saylor's photo had been discovered in a '*meat market*', an opening bid of five hundred thousand attached to the image. Not once did we think she was one town over, right under our fucking noses. It makes me ill to think we might have failed her so epically.

Even with the information we gained, we never stopped searching. Kash and Krew have single-handedly wiped out a multitude of trafficking rings and flesh auctions, combing through each one for any sign of Saylor. It's messed with their heads, all the twisted shit they've seen, and those two have enough baggage as it is. There was only so much we could do with no new information, but that doesn't stop the guilt from churning. I'm trying not to get ahead of myself, knowing there's no guarantee that this will go in our favor. It could be another dead-end, just some old lady off her rocker. But my gut says it's more than that.

God, I hope it's right.

Shaking the negative thoughts away, I refocus my attention on learning as much as I can before we get there. Laiken County is made up of three towns, a whopping two hundred-and-eight square miles combined. Pike's Bay is where Saylor and Kade grew up. The other two—Lyola and Sesley—are just a smidge bigger. The basic information I'm able to pull up tells me that Sheriff Liam Price resides at 8037 Sebastian Avenue. The same address is listed for his mother, the actual owner of the home. Clicking over to Google Earth, I zoom in and scope out the property.

It's a small house, with wood panel siding. While certainly less common due to the climate of the area, it's not unheard of. It makes sense now, that they'd have a porch to match instead of a concrete patio like most stucco builds. From what I can tell, the only other structure that's visible is a tiny tool shed that might fit a lawnmower, but not much else. I'm not sure what the plan is once we arrive, seeing as there's not much to search, but at least we know where to start looking.

My phone dings from the cup holder. Absently swiping the screen, I see a text from the same unknown number Agent Denvers called from earlier. He must be between phones, using burners in the meantime.

Just got word that local deputies are enroute to do a welfare check.

"Goddamnit!" I slam my fist against the door, frustration simmering beneath my skin as I take in the remaining time on the GPS.

"What?" Roan glances over, his probing gaze focused on me instead of the road.

"They've sent units to the sheriff's place for a '*welfare check*'." Ro swears, pressing harder on the gas as the reality of how poorly this could go starts to set in. "We've still got half an hour. All we can do at this point is hope they don't have too much of a head start. Denvers shouldn't be far behind them." I hate everything about this situation. All of the unknowns. I don't know what to expect from the rest of the department, if Price's deputies are going to go to bat for him or happily hand him over. It's difficult to have faith in any of them when the man in charge is such a steaming pile of shit.

Allegedly.

It feels like ages before we cross into Lyola. Roan flies through town going twenty over the posted speed limit, but we roll straight on through without any fanfare. It takes us another ten minutes of navigating back roads before we reach our destination. I'm holding my breath as we pull into the driveway, immediately noting the three cop cars already present. A blacked-out suburban sits front and center, giving me hope that Denvers made it here first. I don't trust them, and unless they give me a reason to, that tune won't be changing. Ro slams his foot on the brake and throws the SUV into park. He has his door open and feet on the ground before I can even blink. Tossing the laptop aside, I quickly hop out and join him at the front of the vehicle.

"Keep quiet, and don't piss them off." Ro grunts but doesn't agree. I wouldn't expect anything less from the giant fucker. Two deputies break apart from the group and walk towards us, preventing me from saying anything more.

"Gentlemen, is there something we can help y'all with?" An older, overweight male is the first to speak. His sidekick looks underage and seconds from shitting his pants.

"They're with me." Denvers makes his way around the guard patrol, earning himself a sneer. He doesn't give the deputy a chance to respond, just nods his head to the side, gesturing for us to follow him. As soon as we're away from prying eyes and have a semblance of privacy, he starts updating us.

"Got here just before they did. Gave me the same rundown I was given earlier. They're here to execute a welfare check since the sheriff has been MIA. Last known sighting was after work on Friday, when he stopped by the nursing home. He failed to show up to work Monday morning, and after numerous attempts to reach him went unanswered, they finally received the go ahead for the search. So far, there's no indication that they know anything about Saylor or the tip from the CNA, and I'd like to keep it that way. The less they know the better."

I nod my agreement and ask, "What reason did you give for an FBI Agent being here?" Denvers smirks at my question.

"I didn't. I'm not required to tell them anything. I'd planned to as a courtesy, but *that* unpleasant fucker pissed me off." Ro snorts at the pointed look Denvers aims at the one who greeted us, clearly appreciating the pettiness.

"They're doing a sweep of the house right now," Denvers states, his arms crossed and eyes laser focused on the other deputies still lingering outside.

"They came in awful heavy for something that should be rather simple," Roan remarks, his stance a mirror image of the agent standing between us. His statement is followed by silence, the three of us too busy scanning the darkened house and the men stationed around it. Every so often, a light will switch on in one room before being flicked off a moment later, the process repeating itself as they search the rest of the space.

Ro is right, though. There's about four too many men here. Maybe it's coincidence, a result of who the welfare check is in regard to, but the sun has yet to even rise and these boys are raring to go. Laiken County is fairly small, and communities like this tend to be tight-knit. Until I know with absolute certainty the type of men we're dealing with, my guard is sky fucking high.

"Is Sergeant Hannigan here?" I question Denvers.

"Retired about a year ago." His answer surprises me. Mainly because this is the first I'm hearing of it. Hannigan had been our local point of contact. He'd taken the initial statement from Saylor's mom and filed the missing person's report. We didn't really have a reason to reach out, considering the case had been turned over to the FBI long before we came into the picture, but he'd introduced himself when we were in town three years ago and offered his assistance should we ever need it.

I grunt and glance to the side, still keeping a close eye on the house. My hands are in my pockets, but my weight keeps shifting from one foot to the other. This is taking too long, and while I'm typically a patient man, that's not the case today. One deputy in particular, the grimy wanker who'd approached us when we first arrived, keeps glaring in our direction. They whisper amongst themselves, then three of them break apart from the group and move towards the front, leaving the young one to stand guard by the back door. I shift forward, trying to make my approach as unassuming as possible.

Roan and Denvers move with me, apparently as fed up as I am. We spread out, not wanting to draw attention to ourselves, but the young deputy keeps bouncing his eyes between us suspiciously. As soon as we're close enough, I casually scan our surroundings.

"Long night, am I right?" I try to make small talk, hoping he'll let his guard down enough that he won't spook once I start looking around. I'm done waiting for whatever clearance they plan to give when it's not actually necessary, and the last thing I need is for some trigger happy fucknut to shoot me. He gives a noncommittal response, but I'm too busy eyeing the porch to pay attention, searching for anything that looks out of place.

It's a deck, really—no bigger than eight feet by eight feet. It sits so low, there's barely and inch between it and the ground, leaving no room to wedge a flashlight underneath. But the front side of the house only has a concrete stoop, so this has to be what the old lady was referring to. I can hear the other deputies moving around inside, but I couldn't care less. I glance at Denvers, and with a nod for me to go ahead, I drop to my knees and carefully run my hands along the planks.

"Hey!" The kid pipes up, his voice cracking with nerves as he attempts to be assertive.

"Don't you fucking move," Ro spits, but I block them out and continue feeling my way around. We have seconds, at most, until the others finish up whatever they're doing and make it back out here, and I really don't want to deal with the headache I know they'll bring. When I feel like I've touched every inch of the deck's surface, I climb to my feet and start pace. Palming the back of my neck, I stare at the sky, longing for some sort of clue or sign. The first rays of dawn are starting to peek through, but the new day brings no renewed sense of hope with it. Instead, defeat washes over me.

We can't be this fucking close, only to walk away empty handed. Even if we don't find Saylor alive, her remains would be better than nothing. It guts me to think that way, but we need closure. Kade especially. He's burning the candle at both ends, trying to balance his everyday work with this inexplicable need that's eating him alive.

This case has followed us for three years, a permanent fixture that we devote as much of our free time to as we can, and Kade will never stop. None of us will. But he deserves peace. I hate that he lives with this torment, that he feels like it's his sole responsibility to unearth the truth and find answers. Most of all, I hate that I don't understand *why* he feels this way, and it makes me livid to think that I might have to break the news of another dead-end to him.

Squaring my shoulders, I scrutinize the space once again. I'll get an ax and hack it to pieces if I have to. One way or another, I'm going to find out what's beneath these boards. Denvers is cussing up a storm, his frustration bleeding over as he comes up short as well. I'm pondering the logistics of hulking the damn thing straight into the air, when something leaning against the house catches my eye. *A tire iron.* Almost directly beside the door. Cocking my head, I contemplate why I find it, along with its location, so odd. Walking over, I lift the tool, causing the green-as-baby-shit deputy to flinch. I roll my eyes, but say nothing to dissuade his thoughts.

Scrubbing my foot across the deck, I turn in circles to try and gain a different perspective. To the left, just in front of where Ro stands, a deviation in the pattern of planks makes me pause. The gap is slightly bigger in one spot, which could be from a knot in the wood, but the closer I look, my fingers trailing over it curiously, the more I'm convinced it's from something else.

Like an iron bar being wedged between the boards.

Without wasting another second, I shove the tip into the groove. It slides in perfectly, making chills dance along my spine. I shout for Denvers as I push downward, the boards rising easily and without much effort. Six planks lift together, the larger grouping making the hidden passage practically invisible. They line up seamlessly, and if we hadn't known to look here, I'm not sure we would have noticed anything off about it.

"Holy shit," Roan sputters, rushing forward to grab the hatch. The muscled prick doesn't stumble once as he tilts it open and leans it against the house. "Gimme that." Ro yanks the flashlight from the pale-faced deputy, whose eyes are bugging out from the hole that just appeared. He shines it down, but the only thing that's visible is a cylindrical shaft with a ladder attached to the side. Impeccably timed, the other deputies stumble out the back door, stopping short as they try to avoid the empty space where the deck used to be.

Chapter Three

Lochlan

"What the hell is this?" The man that greeted us shoves his way through the group, speaking with a heavy dose of hostility. "Parker, you good for nothing fucker. What part of keep the scene clear did you not understand?" he barks at the rookie they left behind to keep an eye on us, but Denvers steps forward and interrupts the asshole before he can add anything else to his tangent.

"Actually, you're the one who needs to clear out." He slaps a search warrant to the man's chest, who studies the piece of paper intently, his jaw working back and forth in anger. I get why Denvers played his little game, allowing these guys to think they had any power while we sat back and observed. Those first few minutes were crucial.

It gave us the opportunity to get a read on the situation while they were still oblivious. We have no idea if Price was working alone or not, and as expected, the second the deputy fully grasps the severity of the situation, he shuts down. The switch to him guarding his thoughts and emotions is damn near instantaneous, and who knows if that's because he's genuinely shocked by the circumstances, or if it's just a ploy to cover his own ass. He nods, handing the warrant back to Denvers before gesturing to his men to move aside.

"I'm going down there." I point to the shaft, making my intentions known. I can see that Denvers is about to protest, but I'm not backing down. "You can either join me or shoot me, but one way or another, that's where I'm headed." He huffs at my dramatic declaration, but fuck anyone who thinks they're going to stop me. We both know that bum knee of his can't handle such a steep decline, so that rules him out.

"We have procedures that need to be followed, Calloway. Protocols. You're here because of me, which means it's my ass on the line if you go in there all gung-ho and compromise a possible crime scene." He gives me that look, the one other agents cower from and find intimidating, but my Nan was far scarier, so it doesn't faze me. When I do nothing more than hold his stare, refusing to back down, he groans in exasperation.

"Start climbing down," he huffs in annoyance. Thank fuck, because the self-control I pride myself on is rapidly dwindling. I slip around Denvers, maneuvering my body into position.

"Loch," Ro calls out gruffly. I sigh at his hesitancy, knowing he's worried about what I might find, but it needs to be me. There's no way I'd send him in after everything he's been through. Besides, I need to see it for myself. Whatever *it* may be. I want to be sure that nothing is overlooked and every detail is catalogued.

"I'll be fine, brother." I quickly but carefully move my feet down the rungs of the ladder. At roughly fourteen feet, the shaft bottoms out and I hit solid ground.

"Toss me a flashlight," I yell. The words have barely left my lips when Ro sends one flying. I catch it easily, spinning around to face the narrow hallway behind me. The walls are made of raw, dirty sheetrock, and a few paces down I find a solitary door. I twist the knob, but of course it doesn't budge.

"Fuck."

It's heavy duty, definitely not original based on the rest of the space. It's framed in a block of cement, the hinges bolted in securely. Based on the looks of it, this was a storm cellar at one point, which means there's likely no entrance from inside the house. I backtrack to the shaft.

"There's a door, but it's locked. I need something to pick it with, or hell, a cutting torch will do." Denvers calls out to the deputies, asking if they have anything that might assist the situation, but I guess no one's jumping at the chance to help.

Fuck this place and fuck these people.

"Move back, Loch," Ro orders, giving me no time to object. His big ass drops straight down, barely touching the ladder at all. I step into the hallway just before he crushes me. "Pieces of shit. I'm gonna burn this hellhole to the fucking ground." He storms past me, nearly flattening me along the wall in the process. And then he kicks the ever-loving shit out of the door. Foot planted flat, he pounds against the steel barrier, making the ground vibrate beneath us. After several failed attempts, he switches to his shoulder, ramming it so hard, I'm shocked he doesn't break a bone.

"Give." *Slam.* "You." *Slam.* "Fucking." *Slam.* "Asshole!" Roan bellows the last word, throwing his entire body into it. The concrete crumbles, the door flying open as one hinge finally gives, causing it to sag from the other still holding it up. Light floods the hallway, and for a second, I just stand there, too stunned to say or do much of anything.

Crazy motherfucker.

When my feet finally get with the program , I step inside to join Ro, who flew in with door. He's dusting himself off by the time I reach him, both of us scanning the small room for any sign of life. It's filthy from years of neglect, but there's a half-empty bottle of water laying on the floor. I pick it up, twisting it to read the expiration date.

Over a year ago.

A twin-size bed is pushed against the wall on my left, and to the right sits a sink and toilet. They're completely open to the rest of the room, not a shred of privacy in sight. I frown, the scene before me painting a grim picture. All of the things I dreaded are present, but there's no sign of Saylor. I brush my fingers over the bedding, then turn towards the bookshelf to do the same. I'm reaching, desperate for some sort of sign that she was here. At least then we'd have a trail to follow. But there's nothing that screams anyone, much less a teenage girl, has been here recently.

Just as I'm about to turn and call for Denvers to send someone to comb through the place, a tiny keyhole inside the bookshelf snags my attention. My gaze drops to the ground, noticing the faint arc where the concrete floor has been worn away. I wrap my hand around the edge of the built-in and give it a good yank, but nothing happens. Ro stops his own exploration once he sees what I do. He repeats my exact movement, but the bookcase still doesn't move.

"I'm getting real fucking sick of playing what's behind the door," he huffs.

I snort, deliriously tired and holding onto hope by the skin of my teeth. At least this one's made of wood and looks just as decrepit as the rest of the space. Instead of using brute force this go round, Ro snatches up one of the bigger pieces of broken concrete and bangs it against the keyhole. It takes a few tries, but the wood around it splits and the locking mechanism falls to the ground a second later.

Resting my hand on his shoulder, I gently push him behind me. A pit has formed in my stomach, and I feel certain that whatever's waiting for us, it won't be pretty. I ease the door open, slowly revealing the space beyond it, and flip the flashlight back on, instantly wishing I hadn't. A pained sound must escape me, because Roan surges forward just as I stumble back, both of us colliding with a grunt. The sight before me is so heart wrenching, I can't process what I'm seeing.

She's here.

Curled into a ball on that piece of shit mattress, the same one she'd been photographed on by the looks of it, Saylor's petite form is engulfed by a dirty, blood-streaked baggy t-shirt. But the thing that has my breath suspended, my heart slowing to a nearly nonexistent thud, is the utter stillness. She hasn't so much as flinched, and Lord knows we made a lot of racket with our entrance. I take a cautious step closer, praying to every entity out there that we didn't get here just a little too late. Roan sucks in a strangled breath, finally catching his first glimpse of Saylor.

"Oh, fuck," he croaks, clenching his eyes closed before spinning around. He drops to a squat, his hands going straight to his hair as he hangs his head. I knew he shouldn't have come down here, but I can't help him right now. Focusing back on Saylor, I kneel beside her, my fingers trembling as I reach out to place them over the pulse point on her wrist. She's so fucking still, but after several painfully long seconds, I finally feel a faint sign of life. Terrified that I'm imagining it, I stare at her chest until I can make out the slightest rise and fall. It's too far apart, though. Her body is weak and barely hanging on.

"She's breathing," I exhale, but there's no real relief. We need to get her the hell out of here. Roan takes a deep breath and forces himself back to his feet. He stands beside me, warring with his emotions.

"Saylor?" I say her name softly, not sure if I should just grab her and run, or try to coax her back to awareness. "Sweetheart, we're here to help you. Can you hear me?" Nothing. Not a hitch in her breathing or twitch of a finger.

Goddamnit.

I'm afraid to move her without knowing the extent of her injuries, but EMS will take forever, and I'm not sure how much longer she's going to last. I carefully slide my arm around Saylor's back and pull her forward. Scooping her too thin frame into my arms, I hope like fuck if she does come around she doesn't fly into a panic. If she freaks out down here, one or all of us will likely end up hurt.

I nod at Ro to lead the way, and with carefully placed steps, I follow behind him. Saylor's cradled against me, her blonde hair matted and filthy. The weight of her slight frame barely registers. When we reach the shaft, I pass her off to Ro. He avoids looking at her bruised body at all costs, choosing to stare blankly at a spot on the wall instead. I climb up as quickly as possible. Once I'm back topside, I take the few free seconds we have before Ro and Saylor make it out to fill in Denvers.

"Call it in. The old lady was spot on and she needs medical attention. Immediately." Ro pops out before Denvers can even process my words, Saylor's frail form visible a second later. Muffled curses can be heard as he pulls himself up, everyone scattering to make room. The deputies who'd been less than helpful have come closer, their eyes wide with shock. There's this moment of silence, where no one moves or does anything, the gravity of the situation surrounding us all. And then Denvers bursts into action, barking orders and directing us to his suburban.

Ro carefully hands Saylor over once we reach the SUV, his entire body trembling as he takes the passenger seat. I slip into the back, situating myself in the middle of the bench. As she lies in my lap, I carefully brush as much of the grime from her face as I can. The pictures I've seen of Saylor were from five years ago, and while some parts of her look familiar, a lot has changed.

"Five minutes, Calloway. How's she doing?" Denvers questions, his eyes connecting with mine in the rearview mirror.

"She's alive." That's the only response I know to give. He swallows thickly, his eyes darting back to the road.

"Duncan and Woolard were pulling in as we left. The scene's still secure." I nod, grateful we didn't just leave everything to the locals. It's going to be a shitshow trying to weed through the department to see if there's anyone else who's been on Price's payroll for more than just their civic duties. Every case the sheriff worked will now have to be reviewed.

I glance down, in awe of who I'm holding. Grazing my knuckles along her cheek, I let the stress of the last few hours start to fade, and tuck a strand of hair behind her ear. I trace my thumb across her eyebrow, then towards her temple. When her lashes flutter, I focus on the movement. Slowly, her eyes blink open and connect with mine. I've never seen such a pretty shade of blue. Saylor stares at me, but before she even has the chance to be confused, she loses consciousness once again.

I'm snapped back to the present when we come to a screeching halt outside of Laiken Regional. It's chaos as we rush through the automatic doors of the Emergency Department, Denvers demanding a doctor while the nurses and receptionist look on in confusion. And Roan, *fuck*...he looks like he might need to get checked out as well. Finally, someone in a white coat comes to offer their assistance. We follow the middle-aged man through a set of double doors and down a long corridor before we reach an exam room. As I place Saylor on the table, I have to force myself to step away and let the medical professionals do their job.

Denvers relays as much information as he can, giving him the basics of her medical history and the circumstances. I'm only half paying attention to their conversation, too busy watching Saylor, but I can tell the doctor recognizes her name. I have a feeling her sudden reappearance is going to send a shock wave through the whole community. Once they've gotten what they need from us, we're ushered out and directed to a private waiting area meant for family. I take my first full breath of the night, closing my eyes as I sink into one of the chairs.

It takes a while to get myself back together, my nerves well and truly shaken from everything that's happened. Without making it too obvious, I glance at Roan. He's tense, his hands squeezed into fists at his sides. He's exhibiting all the signs of a panic attack, but I know it'll only make things worse if I try to intervene. Denvers steps out to take a call, but I keep watching Ro, choosing to stay silent for the time being. I know he prefers to work through shit on his own, and I have no problem with that, so long as he actually does.

I've known Roan for nine years. Of all places, we met playing a video game. He was seventeen and I was nineteen. For me, it'd been a way to pass the time, something to do to stave off my boredom. But for Ro? He'd found a way to live out his revenge through a computer screen without the added hassle of a rap sheet. We'd been playing together for over a year before he finally confided in me. I learned he was born in Albania, but his family had moved to the States when he was eight. He didn't remember much about living there, and never really knew what made his parents make such a drastic move.

Turns out, his dad had gotten involved with the mafia. He'd accrued debts he wouldn't have been able to pay in five lifetimes, much less one. So he packed up his family and ran. But people who traffic everything from guns to flesh aren't the type of men you walk away from. Maybe if he had handed himself over as payment, they wouldn't have hunted him down and demanded the life of his innocent daughter in return.

Even more fucked up than that, is that Ro's father agreed. He traded his own pathetic existence for his child's. Elira had been four years younger than Roan, but he loved his baby sister fiercely. He'd been her protector from the day she was born, and in the end, her last moments in this world were full of pain and betrayal. I don't think Ro will ever forgive himself for not being able to save her.

Poetically, the Albanians put a bullet through his father's head anyway. They had him hand over his kid, made the entire family watch as she was brutalized, and still took his life after making him believe it'd been spared. It fractured Ro, having to stand there, unable to do anything. His mom disappeared shortly after, her heartbreak turning her into someone he didn't recognize. So, from the age of sixteen, Ro had been on his own, fixing his own problems and making his own way.

For someone like me, his life was unfathomable. Things like that didn't happen in the real world. Those sorts of horrors were reserved for movies and books. I was dumbfounded that no one had intervened. But I'd lived in a bubble. My parents have more money than they know what to do with, but it's never been enough. They've chased career achievements my entire life, and that didn't leave much time for me. I was never treated poorly, just indifferently. But every summer I'd vacation at my Nan's house in the UK, and those trips plenty made up for the lack of affection I received at home.

When Nan died, she willed me everything. Along with the trust from my parents, I was pretty set. I guess my superhero obsession, steady cash flow, and Ro's fucked up childhood somehow led us to talking about what we'd do differently if given the chance. The changes we could make, miniscule or grand. We were still kids when we first tossed around the idea of SOTERIA, but over the years, it started to feel like there was potential for it to become something real. Once Kash and Krew came along, the pieces sort of fell into place.

I've tried to avoid putting Ro in a position like

we were in today. He's come a long way, and the last thing I'd ever want to do is set him back. I'll give him some time to work through his emotions, but I refuse to watch my brother sink himself into the pit of depression he's currently circling. No one deserves that kind of mental torment, least of all him.

Chapter Four

Roan

It feels like the blood pumping through my veins is made of lava, burning me from the inside out. Guilt is a nasty bitch. She's had her claws sunk deep in my psyche for so goddamn long, I'm doubtful I'll ever be rid of her. The pain of losing Elira has dulled over the years. It's not as debilitating as it once was. Those early days, I barely left the bed. I lost all sense of purpose, and a few times, I debated if it was even worth it to keep putting up the good fight. It sounded so much easier to just follow her into the next life.

It will always hurt, but I've gotten better. I've learned how to cope with the loss of my sister, as much as one can. But there are moments, flashes of a memory or physical reminders, like this fucked up night, that suck me right back in, and it feels like the very day it happened. I'm once again that scrawny sixteen-year-old being held by two beefed up criminals as I'm forced to watch the desecration and death of my sister. I'd screamed my throat raw, but it hadn't mattered. Nothing I tried made them deviate from the orders they'd been given.

And like an obsessed lover, grief is always shadowing guilt. I've thought about that day so often, I have it memorized, picking it apart down to the minute Elira took her last breath. I've agonized over what I could've done differently. If I'd taken her for ice cream, then maybe we wouldn't have been home when those Albanian fucks kicked the door in. Or if I had noticed sooner that our father was a shady piece of shit, I might've convinced our mom to leave him while we still had the chance. We could have been long gone by the time his sins came back around, demanding penance for crimes we never committed.

Lochlan Calloway is the sole reason I'm still here. When we first connected, I had no idea the role he'd come to play in my life. I don't think I'd even spoken to another person since my so-called mother decided to bail. Until him. The separation my headset offered helped me let my guard down. He didn't feel real, so I had no reason to filter my thoughts or words. I was a gruff asshole at first, but he never disappeared. Like clockwork, he'd log in daily to the first-person shooter game I'd become obsessed with, and we'd talk about mindless bullshit for hours.

It'd taken time for me to fully open up, but Loch was patient. And when he finally got the full picture, he cemented himself in my life and refused to watch me self-sabotage any longer. I was seventeen and bordering on alcoholic. I'd drink whatever I could find just to numb the pain for a little while. But it always came back, accompanied by a hangover so brutal, I'd rather take an ice pick through the eye. So he got me help.

From the other side of the country, he worked his magic and paid up my back rent. Kept me off the radar of the local Department of Family and Children Services. Loch found a therapist that specialized in post-traumatic stress disorder, and kept me accountable every step of the way. He purchased a condo close by, since we weren't sure where we wanted to plant roots permanently, and as soon as I hit eighteen and couldn't be flagged by the state, I left the shithole my sister died in for the last goddamn time.

Loch became my family, the only one I had left. It made sense to make it official, so I changed my last name to his. We're brothers in every sense, fuck what a blood test might say, and I couldn't stand to be attached to the Ahmeti line another day. I'd been determined to sever any remaining connection to my father. It was unwarranted, but I came to loathe anything Albanian. It was hard not to when the ruthless fucks who ran the country had torn my family to shreds.

Even now, I can feel Loch's eyes on me. Analyzing every tic of my jaw and labored inhale. I've gone through the breathing exercises I've been taught to do in moments like this about a dozen times, but I can't get that image out of my head. I'd sworn we were too late. The broken state of Saylor's body and the knowledge that she'd been enduring who knows what in that pit of fucking horrors for five years, had the walls I've carefully crafted crumbling in an instant.

And the guilt. *Fuck me*. She's been here, only a few miles from where she grew up, all this time. How the hell does something like that happen? There'd been no indication she was even in the country still. In fact, everything pointed to that being the least likely scenario. Yet here we are, twiddling our fucking thumbs as we wait for someone to update us on the condition of the girl we'd all thought was long gone. None of us would ever admit to it, but we never thought this day would come. Not after the twins came across that picture.

"What a fucking night." Denvers sighs heavily as he ambles back in, roughly running a hand through his graying hair as he takes the seat across from Loch. "I hate to leave, but I have to get back over there. I've got several places to visit, one being the nursing home in Lyola. We need an in-depth statement from Ms. Price and the CNA who called it in."

"Do you think the old lady is liable for any of this?" Loch asks, the question catching me off guard. I guess I hadn't really thought about what part the elderly woman might have played in Saylor's disappearance, if any.

"Hell, if I know," Denvers answers. "We have to figure out how long she's known that her son had a girl stashed beneath their porch, and why she's only come forward now. If she had any involvement that could warrant charges, then what? The woman's halfway to the grave as it is. My head hurts just thinking about it." He groans, twisting his neck from side to side to alleviate the tension he's undoubtedly carrying.

I don't envy him, that's for sure. We were fortunate to be a part of executing the search, but at the end of the day, it's him that's left with a stack of paperwork and hammering out the details.

"I wouldn't trade it, though. I hope you boys know that." He gives us both a meaningful look. If he were anyone else, I'd probably take offense to being called a boy, but I know he sees us as the men we are. Despite his best efforts to remain impassive, he's grown attached to us over the years. "I'd write reports and take witness statements every day, for the rest of my life, if it meant we'd get this outcome." Denvers swallows, averting his gaze to try and hide the emotion he's feeling. I think we'd all do that, and then some.

"I gotta run, but keep me updated. I want to know her status as soon as you do." Loch dips his chin in acknowledgment. "I've listed you both as her next of kin, that way the doctor can fill you in."

Shit.

I didn't even think about that. When Saylor wakes up, *because she absolutely fucking will*, her life is going to be in shambles. In more ways than one. Denvers heads for the door after saying a quick goodbye, and Loch stands with a groan, looking dead on his feet and uncharacteristically disheveled.

"I have to get these bloody contacts out," he gripes, squeezing his eyes shut to try and help with the irritation. The guy spent a sum total of twenty-ish months in London, and somehow clung to British slang without ever picking up an accent. It's mostly curse words, but I find it funny as shit. "I'm going to get a coffee or ten. You want one?"

"Yeah. Black will do." He nods, then disappears to the cafeteria to fetch us some caffeine. I doubt either of us got much sleep before we hit the road last night. A quick glance at the clock shows it's only eight-thirty in the morning, so I close my eyes and try to rest for a few minutes.

On top of dealing with everything finding Saylor has brought up, I'm anxious as fuck for someone to let us know what the hell is going on. The audible tick of the second hand is doing nothing to calm my nerves, but before I can get comfortable enough to doze off, the door opens, and Loch saunters back in. His phone starts to ring just as he hands me a Styrofoam cup full of piping hot liquid.

"Shit, it's Krew." Our eyes meet, both of us excited to share the news, while simultaneously dreading the impending conversation. He sits across from me, placing his phone on the small table separating the two rows of chairs, and puts the call on speaker.

"Krew," Loch greets, to which the other man follows with, "Boss Man." It's quiet for a second, neither of them wanting to speak first. I know it bothers the twins when they're left in the dark, but their expertise is more useful back home, with full access to the software required to get us whatever we need, whenever we need it. It's rare for them to do any sort of field work. However, they've made it known they'd still appreciate being kept in the loop. I'm certain finding the house all but empty this morning is the exact opposite of that.

"Sorry I haven't reached out. We had to hit the

road fast and I didn't want to wake you. Denvers called with a lead, but honestly, as hopeful as I was, I didn't expect it to go anywhere." Loch runs his hands over his slacks, his palms slick with sweat.

"Okay," Krew drawls. "And where might you be exactly?"

"We're in Pike's Bay." Not really, but he knows Krew would recognize the meaning of that over saying Laiken County or Lyola. No one says anything, but I can hear shuffling on the other end.

"And this lead…is it for who I think?" Krew's voice has an edge to it now, something only those close to him would pick up on, but otherwise he's as closed off as he always is.

"Yeah," Loch sighs. "We.." he pauses to clear his throat. "We got her."

"What do you mean you '*got*' her?" Krew growls, showing far more emotion than I expected. "Her remains?" I flinch, the thought making my chest ache. But it's a valid question. The twins, especially, know how unlikely it is to recover a missing person after five years. And when that does happen, they've typically been gone long before that.

"No, Krew. She's alive. In a sorry state, but she was breathing when we got her to the hospital. We're still waiting for an update, so I don't have a detailed list of injuries yet." Loch smiles, his eyes looking a little glassy, but who could blame him. He carries the weight of our burdens like they're his own. He's been that person for me since the day he shot my player on a damn video game and I cussed his ass out. But Saylor is a cause we all got behind, and this is going to affect each of us on a personal level.

"Fuck." A whoosh comes through the phone from Krew's exhale. "I have so many questions."

"I know you do, and I promise to answer them all. But right now, I need to focus on what's going on here. I'm not sure how long we'll be, but as soon as I have more info, you'll be the first to know," Loch promises.

"Understood," Krew replies. "And Kade?" he asks, addressing the big ass elephant tiptoeing around us.

"I haven't told him," Loch admits. "He's on the other side of the country, and we both know he'd drop everything to get back here, contract be damned. He'll have a million questions, and I won't be able to give him much of anything until we know more. When there's concrete information to pass along, I'll reach and bring him home." Krew grunts a noncommittal response. It's true, but I'm not sure he agrees with Loch's choice. For that matter, I'm not sure I do either.

"I'll be in touch." Loch waits for Krew's acknowledgement before ending the call. His shoulders are tense again, that weight pressing down once more.

"You sure about this?" I question.

"No," he bluntly answers. "In fact, I'm certain it's a mistake. If anyone deserves to be here right now, it's Kade. But it's my responsibility to ensure that we follow through on our commitments. We're still running a business, and if Kade bails in the middle of a job it's going to tank the reputation we've built. At present, I don't give a flying fuck about that, but then we'd be risking the ability to help other people just like Saylor." When put like that, I can understand the dilemma he's in, but before I can offer any input, there's a knock at the door, bringing a halt to our conversation.

"Mr. Calloway?" The doctor we met in the ER peeks his head in, making sure he's in the right place before slipping inside. Loch and I stand, both of us anxious for news. "I'm Dr. Ashburn. I apologize for how long it's taken to get you an update, but we're a small hospital and currently understaffed."

"No worries. What can you tell us?" Loch cuts in, more concerned with Saylor than small talk.

"Ms. Radley is a very lucky girl." I nearly scoff, but somehow manage to rein it in. I get what he's implying, but it seems insensitive to use that word. "We just got her results back from radiology. According to the scans, she has a few bruised ribs and her left wrist has a hairline fracture. Multiple contusions were notated, as well as several lacerations, none of which required suturing. The patient is severely dehydrated and malnourished. Saline and IV antibiotics are currently being administered, as well as pain medication. We're still waiting on bloodwork, but for any other testing, we'll need Ms. Radley's consent." The pointed look he gives us leaves no room for misinterpretation.

I turn away, staring at a wall of inspirational quotes that are meant to be uplifting, but right now they're just pissing me off. If Saylor's been violated beyond the obvious, there's a good chance she won't be on board with a physical examination. Who'd want to have strangers poking and prodding on them after enduring something like that?

"There were no signs of internal bleeding, but she does have a concerning bruise near the right temple. A concussion is likely, but we'll be keeping a close eye on it to make sure there's no swelling. Right now, the best thing for Ms. Radley is to rest so that her body can begin to heal. She's yet to wake, and it could very well be a while before she does. Do you have any questions?" Dr. Ashburn closes the chart he was reading from and gives us his full attention.

Only a couple thousand.

"Can we see her?" I voice the most important one, causing Loch to stare at me strangely.

"Yes, but we ask that you please respect the posted visitation hours," he requests, though I doubt we'll be doing that.

"Sure thing." Loch smiles, but it's not sincere. And if I had to guess, the good doc is well aware that we plan to follow no such rules, if his sigh is anything to go by.

"Come with me."

He sets a brisk pace as we follow behind him, weaving through a maze of hallways. We pass a nurse's station, a few of them pausing to look at us curiously. I have no idea how much has gotten out about who Saylor is, but I wouldn't be surprised if half the town knows by now. At the end of the hall, we come to a stop outside of room 402.

"I'll leave you to it." Dr. Ashburn places the clipboard in a slot along the wall, giving us a thin smile, then heads back toward the group of nurses who continue to stare and whisper. I take a deep breath and step forward to push the door open, but Loch's hand on my shoulder stops me.

"Are you sure going in there is a good idea?" I understand his concern, appreciate it even, but I need to see Saylor. If for no other reason than to assure myself she's not Elira, that their stories won't end the same. Right now, I think it's doing more harm than good for me *not* to see her.

"Positive," I answer confidently, making sure he knows I'm well aware of what I'm walking into, and the memories it'll likely conjure. Loch bounces his eyes between mine, looking for any sign of uncertainty, but eventually relents. Turning the handle, we step into Saylor's room. When her tiny form comes into view, I take a minute to breathe through the flashbacks the sight of her causes.

The lights have been dimmed, but her bruising is more apparent now that the dirt has been washed from her face. Her injured wrist is in a brace, and there's a dark bruise visible at the top of her gown. *This is Saylor, not Elira.* My sister never even made it to a hospital. I focus on the tubes and wires connected to various parts of her body. She's hurt and it shows, but she'll be okay. She has to be. Loch walks across the room, not stopping until he's beside her bed. Gently, he brushes his hand over the top of her head. I move to the other side, but it's even harder up close. If I could erase every mark from her flesh, I would.

"I'm going to go give Denvers and Krew a call. Will you be okay to stay with Saylor?" Loch questions, his attention already on his phone.

"I'm good. Take your time."

I pull a chair over, not wanting to go too far. Loch exits quietly, the snick of the door closing barely making a sound. And then I stare like a full-fledged creep. I'm so fucking exhausted I could sleep for days, but I can't seem to tear my eyes away from the girl in front of me. I have no idea how much time has passed when, suddenly, one of her machines starts going haywire. I surge to my feet, my gaze tracking every inch of Saylor as I search for the problem. But she's just as still as she was two seconds ago, showing no outward sign of distress. I take off for the door, throwing it open with enough force that it smacks the wall. Thankfully, a nurse is coming out of another room just a few feet away. She startles from the noise, her eyes going wide at the sight of me.

"Something's wrong," I blurt, spinning around and rushing back to Saylor. She follows immediately, the beeping alarm clueing her in to the source of my panic. I'm breathing harshly, my fingers beginning to lose feeling from how tight I'm gripping the bedrail.

"Oh." The nurse huffs a laugh. "Her fluid bag ran out. Let me grab another." She disappears for a few minutes, and I just stand there, blinking like a moron.

Her fluid bag.

"Sorry about that." The woman pops back in, a hesitant smile on her face. She presses a few buttons, then trades the empty bag out for the fresh one. When the beeping is gone, I fold in half, exhaling a ragged breath. With my hands braced on my knees, I close my eyes and count to ten. The nurse observes my entire meltdown, her gaze pitying, but I couldn't care less how pathetic I look.

"We're closely monitoring Ms. Radley's vitals, so we'll know should there be any life-threatening changes." She gives me a sad smile. "But to put your mind at ease, this right here shows you her current heart rate. As you can see, it's strong and steady." My eyes fly to where she's pointing. I vaguely hear her explain what a few of the other numbers mean, but I'm more concerned with the one that tells me the organ in Saylor's chest is thumping properly. The nurse, who definitely thinks I'm a fruitcake, mumbles a goodbye and leaves me to it.

We are so fucked.

This tiny woman has no idea who we are, has zero attachment to any of us. Except, maybe Kade. Yet we know her. Not everything, but enough that we've formed a connection without ever meeting her. Saylor's going to wake up and think we're all certifiable. Shit, maybe we are. Selfishly, I slip my hand beneath hers, wanting to feel the warmth of her skin. She was so cold when we found her. It's intrusive as fuck to touch her without permission, and with everything she's been through, I doubt she'd appreciate it very much. Reluctantly, I pull away. I want to comfort her, but I have no idea how to accomplish that. So instead, I sit and watch as the beats of her heart flash across the monitor.

"You're gonna be okay, Little Fighter."

Chapter Five

Krew

I stare at the black screen of my computer for what feels like hours. If there's one thing I never want to be, it's caught off guard. And right now, it feels like the rug beneath my feet has been yanked away. Brutally and without warning. I pride myself on knowing what's going to happen before it ever does. I'm thorough in my research, mapping out every possible scenario. But it's painfully obvious that I've missed something important. Vital information was overlooked, and it makes me fucking livid.

When Lochlan calls sometime later, Kash is still asleep. Unless we're working a case that's kept us up all night, he's usually the first one up. It's odd for him, but I'm not one to look a gift horse in the mouth. Once Loch fills in the rest, giving me as many details as possible, I switch my computer on and get to work. It feels like a dream that the girl we've been searching for all this time has been found. But the fact that she's alive? I can't wrap my head around it.

I had little hope, none really, after Kash and I found her picture. We kept looking though, praying we'd eventually find another breadcrumb if we just kept at it. But the shit we'd seen in the process made it difficult to keep searching. Brutality has been an acquaintance of ours for a good portion of our lives, but there were times I would come across something so horrific, I'd have to step away for a day or two. It's sickening to know there's a price tag for just about anything. Regardless of what we've been told, almost everything is replaceable, and never is it priceless. People will sell their souls, or someone else's, for far less than you'd think.

The probability that Saylor hadn't been trafficked was so miniscule, I stopped obsessing over it. I still sought her out in every auction we infiltrated, always hopeful, but consciously realistic of the likelihood we'd ever come across her. And I sure as shit hadn't bothered with looking anywhere else, certainly not right in her backyard, so to speak. Somehow, we'd been led to believe she was long gone, sold off before we ever caught wind of it.

It shouldn't have been possible. These virtual markets are sophisticated, run by people who know what they're doing and how to avoid fake accounts slipping through the cracks. Everyone involved is vetted meticulously. I'm booted more times than not, trying to piggyback into their live viewings and sales. We discovered Saylor's bid from a chatroom, one of many, where sick fucks like to go and brag about their latest finds. It'd only been a thumbnail photo, with no information about the final sale. It's not impossible that the man who had her wasn't the one who bought her, but I find it unlikely.

That would be a lot of trouble for someone who lives so close, his accessibility too easy. Not to mention, in no world could a county sheriff afford to even place the opening bid. He never would have made it to the virtual waiting room of the auction, because the organizers wouldn't have granted him access. Your bank account has to be seven digits deep to participate in such hedonism, and you can bet your ass they check.

Which leads me to believe it was all a ploy, because had the listing been real, someone would have bid on Saylor. She'd have gone for far more than the initial asking price, and when whoever won her was deprived of their prize, they'd have come looking. So, Sheriff Fuckstain either got really lucky and pulled one over on some very powerful people, cashing in on a hefty payday in the process, while somehow not getting tracked down for the betrayal, or he has friends in high places who helped him orchestrate the entire thing.

I hate both options.

If it was real, then someone—undoubtedly shitty and evil—believes they are owed one Saylor Radley. And I imagine that they're pissed after being screwed over for the past five years. If it wasn't real, then who the hell does this small-town sheriff know that's been helping him? I click away at my keyboard, rapidly flipping from one screen to the next as I pull up everything I can find on the piece of shit. But nothing of interest pops out at me. He's a nobody. His bank account has been frozen, likely Agent Denvers doing. There's no family listed aside from his mother.

No additional properties.

And that's a whole other can of worms, because where the fuck is he? On paper, Liam Price has no one to turn to. No one who'd stick their own neck out for him, or any off-grid place to hide. Next, I pull his deputies' backgrounds. He worked day in, day out with those men, so they're the closest connections he has. Everything I find, which is fuck all, I forward to Loch.

Pushing back from my desk, I rub a hand across my jaw. I feel like I should be doing more, but there isn't more to do. I hate that I didn't flip that town upside down before ruling it out. I thrive off of getting answers, and I thought I had them. I was certain just a few hours ago that I knew what had happened to Saylor after she was taken five years ago. I couldn't tell you the lead up or the exact execution of her kidnapping, but I was confident in where she'd ended up.

And I was wrong.

This oversight makes me question my ability to be a productive part of the team. It's literally my job to gather intel, to be sure that my findings are absolute in their entirety, and I somehow fucked that up with Saylor. I can't help but wonder what else I've missed. Were there times when I gave the guys' half-assed information? All it'd take is the absence of one minor detail for a case to go sideways. Someone could wind up hurt, or worse, because I dropped the ball.

That's a lot of responsibility, and old wounds make it hard not to question if I'm really the right guy for the job. I might be the most closed off of our group, but it's taken years to get the shit out of my head that'd been beaten into me. We met Loch and Ro at a really low point in our lives. Kash and I had been one more hit away from catching ourselves a premediated murder charge. We'd taken as much as we could, pushed beyond our breaking point, and the only way out seemed to be if one of us left in a body bag. And I had no intention of that being my brother or me.

When our mom met our stepdad, we'd been thrilled. He had money, something we lacked and were desperate for. Not because we wanted a three-story mini mansion or a private school education. Our excitement came from having a stocked fridge and clear tap water. But nothing is free, and the payment for our new luxuries was collected every time our stepfather's temper required an outlet. Kash and I were his favorite punching bag, and as much as I tried to take the brunt of his anger, he took a special liking to Kash's soft demeanor.

Where I'd fight back and hurl insults just as quickly, Kash would beg him to stop. Archie Sellers, millionaire entrepreneur and ruin-er of lives, clearly had a degradation kink. It made him gravitate to Kash, knowing he could break him far easier than me. It wasn't the physical beatings he loved to hand out that fucked me up, though. I could take his fists any day. For me, it was the near constant lash of his words. He loved reminding me, every chance he got, that I was nothing but a waste of space. A failure and fuck-up of the highest degree.

It was easy to brush off in the beginning, but

after years of hearing how worthless you are, how unlikeable, it slowly starts to wear you down. I didn't even realize it at first. I'm not sure when I started to believe him, but Archie's hate had slithered beneath my skin, infecting my body like a slow spreading cancer. By the time it had reached my mind, it was too late. I believed him, as ridiculous as it sounds.

It didn't help that our mother stood by and let it happen, too enraptured by her new life to risk putting a stop to the abuse. She came from money, but our mixed-race father made her family cut ties. The luxuries she was accustomed to suddenly vanished. We'd struggled for years before her cash cow came along, so I guess we were a sacrifice she was willing to make. Like I said, nothing's priceless. The few times Archie beat her too, it was somehow my and Kash's fault. Over time, she grew to blame us. The hits became so frequent, our old bruises wouldn't have a chance to heal before we were gifted a fresh set.

Call it happenstance or divine intervention, but Roan—a complete stranger at the time—witnessed Archie's rage get the best of him. He'd been careful up till then, always keeping a leash on his temper until we were behind closed doors. He was a prominent businessman with a reputation to uphold, after all. But out of the blue, Kash decided he was going to grow a backbone in the middle of downtown Seattle on a random Tuesday. He'd pissed Archie off so badly, he snapped without a second thought to any onlookers. He backhanded Kash so hard, his lip split, causing blood to splatter across the sidewalk.

I'd never seen my brother so murderous, but

it was there that day, shining in his eyes. That dark gaze that matched my own promised death, and I was whole-heartedly on board. Then, out of nowhere, some big fucker stepped in and laid Archie flat on his ass with a swift right hook. It'd taken me a minute to process, but then I folded in half, laughing so hard my goddamn side hurt.

Ro and Loch became a fixture in our lives after that. We had a place to escape to, a safety net and support system. To two fifteen-year-olds, they seemed godlike. I'm certain they hadn't planned to stay in Washington for as long as they did, but they wouldn't leave without us. Kash and I had tried to report what was happening, but we'd been made out to be shit-starters. Money talks, and so does a statement from your own mother refuting your claims.

So we sought justice the only way we could. I breached the multitude of offshore accounts Archie had been amassing, draining each and every one. And as a special little fuck you, we sent all of his illegally earned money to nonprofits for victims of childhood abuse. After that, I gathered as much damning evidence as I could against him—racketeering, embezzlement, even his unpaid parking tickets—and forwarded it to the district attorney. It didn't happen overnight, but Archie Sellers was eventually charged and sentenced to twenty-two years in federal prison.

He might not be there for the reason he really deserves to be, but it's amazing what you can find on the dark side of the internet. There's a whole fucked up world out there, right at your fingertips, if you know where to look. It wouldn't take much to secure a contact in a place like FDC SeaTac, who has a particular dislike for men who enjoy beating kids. Whatever torment Archie's enduring is well deserved, and I hope like fuck it hurts.

I wouldn't change how things happened, but a part of me, some twisted piece that's broken, wishes I could have put a knife through his chest. A couple hundred times. People joke about killing someone, might even mean it, but when the time actually comes, they can't go through with it. Not me; I know I could. After everything I've seen, I wouldn't think twice about ridding this world of the filth inhabiting it. A lot of lives would be saved if we stopped trying to rehabilitate the unredeemable. Tax dollars too.

"What's up, little bro?" Kash saunters in, a lollipop hanging from his mouth and a cup of too-sweet tea in his hand. He was born nine whole minutes before me, a fact he'll never let me forget. I roll my eyes, rocking back against the office chair we paid way too much money for.

"You got that thing going on." He waves a hand in the general direction of my face. "Where your eyebrows scrunch together and make a wrinkle form between them. I can never tell if it's concentration, or constipation." He smirks at the annoyed look I give him.

"Contemplation," I state.

"Oookaayy," he drags out, waiting for me to elaborate. "Is this about our two brothers from another mother, who bailed in the middle of the night without so much as a kiss goodbye? You know those two are connected at the dick and can't go anywhere without the other." Kash flops down, his own chair just a few feet from mine.

We have no room to talk about co-dependency.

I almost laugh, but manage to bite it back. It's true, Loch and Ro are close as fuck, but I feel no jealously over that. As much as I love them like brothers, Kash and I will always be closer, so I understand how the shit they've gone through has made their bond as tight as it is. I'm not even annoyed that they left without giving us a heads up. More like insulted that they thought we didn't know the second they went out the door. Tech is our expertise, including the multitude of security cameras that case the perimeter of the house. It's like they forget we have them. I got the alert as soon as the garage opened.

"Nah. It is about *why* they left, though." I run my tongue over my teeth, lost for where to start. "They found Saylor." *Straight to the point it is.* Kash is spinning his chair around, like a fucking child, when he stops so abruptly, he nearly lodges his sucker in his throat. He proceeds to cough and gag for a good minute before getting his shit together.

"The fuck?" he rasps, his eyes watering from all the hacking. "Like...in what way do you mean *found*?" I see the flash of vulnerability in his eyes, but it's gone a second later. We've both done a damn good job of not attaching ourselves to anyone, the guys excluded. Kade less so than the others, because he's an even bigger asshole than me. While Kash took on the role of being the guy who takes nothing too seriously, always cracking a joke at the worst possible time, I went the opposite direction. I shut down and quit letting people in so easily. I feel shit, I just don't want to. We all cope differently.

"Alive." His jaw drops at my response. It's probably the last thing he thought I'd say. I go over all the information Lochlan relayed, most importantly being that Saylor's stable, but still unconscious. Just retelling the whole ordeal leaves me exhausted, so I can't imagine how Loch and Ro are holding up.

"Shit, man." Kash is pacing, his sucker flipping from one side of his mouth to the other every few seconds. It's a tic of his. When he's anxious or stressed he bites the candy, crunching it to bits, and then it's gone and he's reaching for another to repeat the process. But when his stash is running low, he tries to refrain, which has him bouncing the damn things around his mouth like a fiend itching for a fix. "This is...amazing. But also, crazy. Where's Kade?" He stops moving, his eyes holding mine as he waits for me to answer.

"Loch thinks it's best to keep things quiet for now."

"He *what*?!" Kash sneers. "That's fucked up, and you know it." He points his finger at me accusingly, like I'm the reason behind Loch's piss-poor decision.

"Never said it wasn't, Kash." I stand, glaring back at my brother. "For what it's worth, I don't think he'll keep Kade in the dark much longer. And we both know how unpredictable that fucker can be when shit hits the fan. Loch's not being an asshole for the fun of it."

"I know that." Kash cuts his eyes at me as he resumes his pacing. I sit back down, wiggling my mouse to bring the monitor to life. There's fuck all we can do until we know more, but there is an inbox full emails that need to be gone through. We're at a standstill until Saylor wakes up and can be questioned, and who knows how well that will go over. I doubt she'll be chomping at the bit to detail the past five years anytime soon.

"I'm going to drop the Browns off at the Super Bowl, and then make muffins. With extra chocolate chips," Kash grumbles as he walks away, feeling the need to inform me he's gotta take a shit.

He's going to stress eat his way into a coma one of these days.

Chapter Six

Lochlan

It's been three days, and Saylor still hasn't woken up. The hospital staff is sick to death of us, but there's not much they can do to make us leave. Therefore, they have nothing to threaten us with, so we keep pestering the shit out of every nurse and doctor who comes through the door. We get the same response every time.

It's completely normal.

I don't like it. I'm scared by moving her I damaged something and they didn't catch it. I've spent the last thirty-six hours pacing the hallways and it's making me a cranky asshole. To add fuel to the fire, two deputies have been stationed outside of her room for '*security purposes*'. Denvers is just as thrilled as we are, but there's not much that can be done. It'd be a bit beneath the FBI to delegate an agent to babysitting duty.

A nurse walks in, forgoing a fucking knock, and starts checking Saylor's vitals. I bite my tongue, but it takes effort. She's just as annoyed by me, as I am by her. It's irrational for me to feel so frustrated—seeing as they've done everything they can—but I can't help but wonder if Saylor would be better off at a bigger hospital. With a full staff and newer, state of the art equipment. Or maybe it's just this town and everyone in it that I have a problem with. I want to get her the hell away from here.

"Calloway." Denvers knocks, *like a gentleman*, before I call out for him to come in. I give the nurse a pointed look, to which she huffs at and continues right on with her assessment.

"Got a minute?" He nods toward the hallway once he sees we aren't alone. I hesitate, not wanting to leave Saylor when Roan is still catching up on some sleep in the room next door. The space was empty, but we still had to beg and plead to use it. "She'll be fine." Denvers tries to act put out and annoyed, but I can see the smile he's fighting.

Reluctantly, I get up and follow the agent out, but he doesn't stop right outside like I expected him to. He eyes the deputies, clearly not wanting to talk in front of them either. They're harmless from what I've been able to pick up on, but I still don't like going so far from Saylor. Denvers keeps walking until we reach the stairwell, then proceeds to check that it's empty before he speaks.

"I think we've got all we're going to get from Old Lady Price. It's taken so long to piece together a statement because she isn't always lucid. But from what we've been able to gather, she knew for at least two years that Saylor was there." I think I actually feel the spike in my blood pressure from how angry that makes me.

“Liam has lived with his mother all of his life. She’s never been the picture of health, so it made sense for him to stay close by. Which, apparently, had everyone clamoring about how selfless and caring he is. Not one person we’ve spoken to has had a bad thing to say about the man. He’s perfected this persona he created. Loyal, kind, someone you can call on when you’re in need.” Denvers shakes his head in disgust.

“Unfortunately, the CNA, Sheena Wilcox, wasn’t the only one his mother had been chatting with about their sordid family secrets. Several other workers were given the same story, but blew it off. I think she was telling anyone that would listen, hoping someone might take her seriously. According to Sheena, it’s not uncommon for patients to start spilling their guts when they feel that the end is near. Called ‘em deathbed confessions. A last-ditch effort to get right with Jesus.”

I scoff, refusing to feel an ounce of sympathy for the woman who had the means to free Saylor two years ago, if not longer. I’m not a parent, and may never be one, but I can’t fathom letting my kid get away with something so heinous. Sometimes, you can do all the things you’re supposed to—teach them right from wrong, instill morals—and it’s not enough. Sometimes, people are just evil, no matter how they were raised. But protecting that kind of person, regardless of who they are to you, makes their sins your own. His mother is just as guilty in my eyes, and I’ll die on that hill.

“Why is that unfortunate?” I question, trying to figure out where he’s headed with this.

"Because Liam Price is in the wind, and I'd like to know why. The search of his house showed no signs of a preplanned trip. There's a steak in the refrigerator that expired on Saturday. That tells me he intended to be home, but wasn't."

Meanwhile, Saylor had been eating next to nothing.

"My working theory is that someone tipped him off and he didn't know how much time he had, so he bolted without going home. He even left his laptop, which is currently being picked apart."

My back meets the wall as I take a second to think over everything. Our worries that Liam could be working with someone seem valid now. No one disappears like that, especially when they've got a long-term hostage situation going on beneath their house. Suddenly, a cold sweat washes over me. If that CNA hadn't reached out to Denvers, Saylor would have died. She'd have starved to death, left to waste away until there was nothing left. The thought of her suffering like that makes me physically sick, the cafeteria sandwich I ate earlier threatening to make a reappearance.

"When you find him, I really hope he's hostile. Enough of a threat that you're well within your rights to shoot the motherfucker," I growl, my hate for Liam growing by the second. Denvers laughs, but doesn't comment. That's okay, I know he feels the same way. That badge might prevent him from voicing it, but I know if he has any say in the matter, Liam won't ever see the inside of a prison cell. He'll be too busy taking a permanent dirt nap.

"Last thing," Denvers wavers, his lips pressed together grimly. "Until this is over, Saylor needs to be someplace safe."

"Obviously," I deadpan, confused as to why that would even need to be said.

"I want her to go with you and the guys." I raise an eyebrow in surprise. "Hear me out...I think we both know this case means more to me than just another win under my belt, and it sure as hell means more to all of you." I nod in agreement. "I trust you, and that's not something I'm handing out freely right now. I think the best place for her to be is with you and your team. No one knows who you are, other than an asset of the FBI. There's no connection to your company, and I'll wipe any trace of your names from Saylor's paperwork." He looks at me imploringly, waiting for an answer.

Truthfully, I'd been wondering how I was going to sweet talk Denvers into giving up the address to the safe house they planned to stash her in, cause the likelihood of us walking away from Saylor with no guarantee of contact was...zero. This plan is much more preferable, in my opinion, and I doubt the guys would have a problem with it either.

"Of course," I reply.

"Good." Denvers pats me on the shoulder before pulling the door open. "Let's get back out there." We've barely made it two feet down the hallway when it happens. An agonized scream echoes through the corridor, turning my blood to ice and my feet to lead. I freeze, it's only for a second, but my body locks up tight and forgets how to work. And then it happens again, a wail so broken it makes my goddamn teeth hurt.

Saylor.

I'm running before my brain has a chance to catch up, my body somehow knowing it's her and desperate to fix whatever's wrong. My assumption is confirmed when people start scrambling. Nurses, deputies, the doctor. The door beside Saylor's is thrown open, and Roan comes barreling out, his eyes wild and panicked. It feels like the longest forty feet in existence, but I finally push my way into the room, Denvers hot on my heels and panting like he ran a marathon.

"What the fuck is going on?" I whisper, the words getting lost in the mayhem taking place in front of me. It's chaos. Complete and utter chaos. There's at least ten people crowding the small space, leaving me no clear shot of Saylor. A choked sob cuts through all the shouting, and I swear it makes me fucking feral. Ro must have the same response, because he fists the front of a deputy's shirt, one of the two who'd been posted outside just a few minutes ago, and heaves him out of the way. The moment a path opens up, I push forward, my gaze connecting with those beautiful blue eyes I haven't seen nearly enough of. Saylor's lips part on a gasp as her head swings to the side. I track the movement, finding a nurse pushing meds through her IV line. Seconds later, Saylor's body goes slack, once again lost to unconsciousness.

"What the hell did you just give her?" Roan

storms across the room, his anger so palpable, the nurse backs away with her hands raised.

"It...It's a sedative," she stammers, her response not helping in the slightest.

"The fuck does she need to be sedated for? The goal is for her to wake up!" Denvers wraps his hand around Ro's bicep, attempting to calm him down.

"Sir," the doctor cuts in. "Ms. Radley was panicked. It would've been dangerous to leave her in that state."

"Can someone please explain how this happened?" Denvers demands.

"It was him." The nurse who sedated Saylor points behind me. Slowly, I turn to see who she's referring to. There, against the back wall, is the same asshole deputy we dealt with at Price's house. His glare is prominent and unabashed. "He told her that her mother's dead."

Anticipating my next move, Denvers steps between us, preventing me from assaulting an officer of the law. And thank God for that, because the last place I want to be is stuck in a holding cell.

Chapter Seven

Saylor

A slow, steady beep wakes me, making my nose scrunch in confusion. Slowly, I peel one eye open. It's bright. So bright it can't possibly be coming from the lone light in my room. For a brief moment, I think I've died, and this must be whatever awaits us in the afterlife. I'm not even sad about it; it'd be preferrable to my current existence. And then I blink through the bleariness, noting the crisp white walls and lack of overall grime. The air isn't stale. It smells clinical, like antiseptic. Lastly, I see the cords attached to my chest. The IV in the bend of my arm. The pulse oximeter on my finger.

I'm in a hospital.

The thought hits so hard, it causes me to jerk upright, a movement I regret instantly when my entire body throbs in protest. The pain in my side is so sharp it steals the breath from my lungs. I apply pressure to the area in hopes of lessening the ache, and find a brace covering my wrist in the process. The pounding in my head matches the cadence of my heart, and only gets worse when I try to make sense of what happened and how I got here. Struggling to get my bearings, I search the room nervously, but I'm all alone. My brain is fuzzy, and I have no recollection of anything really. But, oh my God...*I'm in a hospital.* Tears flood my cheeks as a sob lodges itself in my throat. I'm so scared I'm going to wake up and this will all be a dream.

The door swings open, making me flinch. When the privacy curtain is pulled back, revealing a cop, fear encompasses me from head to toe. I want to run, but I doubt my feet would even cooperate. I fist the hospital bedding, my eyes tracking every step he takes, each one bringing him closer and closer. He's big, and has a hard look on his face, and all I can think about is that I want him to go away.

"Ms. Radley." He stops at the foot of my bed, his arms crossed over his chest as he glares down at me. "We need your statement." It's a demand, not a question. He's not asking if I'm ready to talk, he's telling me that I'm going to. I swallow thickly, my eyes pinging around the otherwise empty room. My mouth is so dry, speaking feels impossible. Not that I want to, and especially not to him. On the wall behind him, something catches my attention. I squint, recognizing the logo printed above the whiteboard.

I'm at Laiken Regional.

"Is my mom here? May I see her, please?" I blurt, my wariness getting pushed aside. Surely she's here; this is where she's always worked. My voice is scratchy from disuse, so when he doesn't answer I think it's because he didn't hear me. I open my mouth to try again, but he interrupts before I get the chance.

"Eliza Radley is dead."

A nurse gasps from the doorway, but I say nothing. My mind simply blanks. He's delivered those four words as if they hold no meaning. Just some jumbled letters that state a fact. Like the sky is blue, or rain is wet. When, in reality, they're the catalyst that splinters the last bit of sanity I have left. The world tips and sways, my vision dimming. A scream claws its way up my throat, anger and grief demanding an outlet. Followed by another. And another. Pain radiates from every inch of my body, but it pales in comparison to the damage being done to my insides. It feels like I can't breathe. There's yelling and people moving all around me, but I'm all alone. Noise is accosting me from every direction. It's too much, too soon. *Too loud.*

Across the room, honey-colored eyes meet mine. And then...nothing.

I'm suspended somewhere between awake but not, and for a few precious seconds, I've forgotten all about the reality I've been thrust back into. My finger slides across the soft material beneath me, the feeling foreign but delicious. That simple motion seems to trigger an avalanche of memories. They hit hard and fast, making my pulse race.

Mom.

I press my lips together, choking back tears. Maybe he was wrong or confused. But if that were the case, she'd be here. I tried so hard to convince myself that she would've moved on by now, along with everyone else. I couldn't let myself believe that anyone was still looking, because then I would've had hope that someone might find me. But it was bullshit, a lie I told myself to get through every day that came and went with no one breaking down the door and taking me home. I couldn't be disappointed, if I never expected it in the first place.

I did, though. In the farthest corner of my mind, a little part of me hoped and prayed for this day, and it looked nothing like this. Mom would've been here, her arms wrapped around me tightly as we both cried. She'd still smell like the floral perfume she loved so much, and it might've taken some time, but eventually, things would have gone back to normal. We would've picked up where we left off. I nearly scoff at the ridiculousness of my naivety.

Even if she was here, nothing will ever be the same.

I used to dream about what I'd do if I ever made it out of there. At first, it was all simple things: eat an entire pizza by myself, get an extra-large chocolate shake from Lettie's Diner—brain freeze be damned—and even a promise to finally stand up to my playground nemesis, Havok McKade, whose parents must have had a sixth sense when naming him.

Eventually, those thoughts shifted to things more meaningful. Like tell Mom how much I loved that she made me breakfast every morning before school, even though she'd been up all night from working her shift at the hospital. I wanted to visit my Grandaddy's grave, who'd only passed a few months before I was taken, so I could finally apologize for stealing his stash of Reese's and never fessing up. At some point, the *'if I escape'* game seemed so improbable, all I really longed for was to feel the sun again. To press my toes in the sand at our favorite beach. I wanted the option of sound, laughter and voices. Anything but the silence I'd grown so accustomed to.

Now, I just want my mom.

The door creaks behind me, and I instinctively steady my breathing. I learned a long time ago that feigning sleep is an excellent survival tool. I've yet to open my eyes, too afraid to face the world, but now I want to know who's in the room with me. Just the idea that the cop from earlier might be back makes chills erupt across my skin. Carefully, I lift my eyelids while keeping the rest of my body perfectly still.

Sitting in the seat beside me, is the man with the honey-colored eyes. He's wearing square, black-framed glasses now, but it's definitely him. And he's staring right at me. He sits up straighter when he sees I'm awake, but he doesn't speak. My heart begins to race, because I'm certain I've never met him a day in my life. But he's here. There's an actual person within touching distance. It's so overwhelming, it brings tears to my eyes. I've been alone for so long, the relief of being in the vicinity of someone else is almost too much. My gaze moves behind him, just now noticing there's another man sitting on the floor, his head rested against the wall as he sleeps.

"That's Roan," the stranger beside me whispers. "And my name is Lochlan. He and I work together." I say nothing but quickly scan his outfit. There's no indication that he's a cop, but he could just be off-duty. "Are you in pain?" he questions, a furrow forming between his brows as he looks me over.

Honestly, I feel kind of numb. It could be a side effect of whatever medication they gave me earlier, or maybe I'm so checked out mentally there's nothing left to feel. I shake my head, the slight action barely discernable.

"Okay, that's good." The man, *Lochlan*, runs his palms over his knees nervously. "Would you like for me to explain everything now, or would you prefer to wait?" His tone is soft, as if he's speaking to a wounded animal.

"Now, please." His eyes widen, clearly caught off guard by the voiced response. My throat feels raw, so I doubt I'll be offering any more, but I need to know how I got here.

"Three nights ago, the agent assigned to your case received a call with information regarding your whereabouts. A search warrant was executed at Liam Price's home." I cringe at hearing his name said aloud.

Lochlan continues to explain the events that followed, that it was Liam's own mother who made the claim. That shocks me, because as far as I was aware, no one else knew about me or where I was. *I* hadn't even known where I'd been. He'd drugged me before we made it there. I get the breakdown of how they found me, as well as a list of my injuries. It's a dump of information that leaves me sad and tired.

"That's the CliffsNotes version, but we can go over any details you'd like to know once you're feeling up to it. For now, I'm going to let the nurse know that you're awake." Lochlan gives me a hesitant smile. He looks just as exhausted as me, his brown hair mussed and button-down wrinkled. As he slips away, my gaze connects with the other man's. *Roan*. I'm not sure how long he's been awake, but his eyes are locked with mine. I swallow thickly. While I can't make out any details since the lighting is low, it's obvious, even from his seated position, how huge he is.

Lochlan reappears quicker than I expected, but he's alone. He takes in the scene before him, his friend and I locked in a staring contest, before walking over to help him up. He groans, twisting from side to side. I can attest to the fact that the ground does not make a great bed. They both take cautious steps towards me, but other than a slight tightening of my muscles, I'm not feeling overly threatened.

"Saylor, I'd like you to officially meet Roan." He nods beside him, gesturing to the walking skyscraper. I have to tilt my head back against my pillow to maintain eye contact. "And Ro, this is Saylor." Lochlan smiles, like it's brought him immense joy to finally introduce the two of us. It confuses me, but seeing his happiness, anyone's really, makes me feel a little less hollow on the inside. Coming from someone else, it seems more achievable, a possibility of something I might feel again one day.

"Hey," Roan greets me softly, his voice sounding strained.

"Hi." I mouth the word, but no sound comes out.

"The nurse will be here any minute now, but I wanted to make sure you know that no one outside of the hospital staff, Agent Denvers, myself and Roan have access to this room. Ro here is a brick shithouse, and if anyone tries to get in here, they'll have to go through him first," Lochlan jokes, but I can hear the underlying threat. A string of tension snaps free, easing my mind a little. "Whatever you need, you let us know. If there's someone who makes you uncomfortable, just say the word and they're gone." I nod, my attention going to the female nurse who's pushing a cart through the door.

"We'll give you some privacy." Lochlan moves to leave, but Roan looks like he'd rather have a root canal administered with no anesthesia than follow his friend. His eyes, which I can now see are green, bore into mine, like he's trying to communicate without the use of words. I blink at him, unsure of what he's looking for.

"Be back soon, Little Fighter," Roan grumbles, stomping towards the door but clearly unhappy about it. The nurse shuts it behind him and then pulls the privacy curtain into place.

"Finally." She shakes her head in exasperation. "Those two are pains in the ass, but at least they're pretty." I feel like I should smile, but it just won't form.

"Let's get you upright. That sound, okay?" She hovers beside me, waiting for my response. I nod, albeit reluctantly, as she presses a button to bring the bed to a seated position. "My name is Karley. I worked with your mom a few times." Her smile is sad, but her confession makes me stiffen. Mom floated, going wherever she was needed at any given time, so it's not improbable that their paths crossed at some point.

"Mr. Calloway said he explained your injuries, but if you have any questions feel free to ask them." I'm assuming she's talking about Lochlan. "We removed your catheter a few hours ago, so if you need assistance getting to the bathroom just press this button here." I glance to where she's pointing, seeing a small '*call*' symbol.

"Now, for the most important part..." She reaches behind her, grabbing something from the cart she brought in. "Are you ready for a nice, hot shower?" Karley wiggles a shampoo bottle in her hand and I nearly groan at the sight. She must see the gleam in my eyes because she laughs.

"Thought so, but I need to know that you're okay with having assistance. You won't be able to get all that pretty blonde hair clean with just one hand." I hesitate, having overlooked that very important detail. "This is my job, honey, but the last thing I want is to make you feel uncomfortable." I weigh my options, but the last thing *I* want is to lie here with remnants of the worst years of my life still clinging to my skin.

"I'm okay with it," I answer.

"Alrighty then." Karley holds her hand out to help me from the bed. Pain shoots through my ribs, making me hiss, but we slowly make our way to the connecting bathroom. She turns the water on, letting it heat up as she motions for me to spin around. "I'm going to let you wash yourself while I change your bedding, then I'll get your hair taken care of." She works the ties of my gown free, letting it pool to the floor, then removes the brace from my wrist. With careful steps, I position myself beneath the spray.

It's quite possibly the best thing I've ever felt. For five years, I had to make do with a small sink. The water was barely warm and it was strictly meant for a single purpose: to get clean. It wasn't relaxing or enjoyable. Before, I'd take baths every night, the water so hot my skin would be tinged pink by the time I got out. But I loved it. I stand there for a while, just soaking in the heat. It hurts to run the soap across my body, but there's relief too, as I watch the dirty water swirl around the drain.

"Ready?" Karley pops back in, shampoo and conditioner at the ready. I nod, folding my arms across my chest in order to feel some sense of modesty. She washes my hair twice, working the suds through every strand while being mindful of my tender scalp. The same process is repeated with the conditioner, hopefully loosening all the tangles. Silently, tears slip from my eyes. I should feel traumatized that yet another person is viewing my body, but the dominant emotion tightening my chest is graciousness. I wish it was Mom here doing this, but I think it helps that it's someone she knew.

Karley hands me a towel to wrap myself in, then uses a second one to dry my hair. Lastly, she ties a fresh gown around me, slides my brace on and helps me back to bed. My legs tremble from the small amount of exertion it took to shower, and any pain medication that'd been in my system is quickly wearing off.

"Sip on this." I'm handed a cup of ice water, the straw making it easier to reach without lifting my head back up. "I'll request a dinner tray, but it's going to be liquids only. We don't want to overwhelm your body with too much all at once." Karley pulls the clean blankets over me, patting my hand once she's done.

"Thank you." I force the words out, my eyes burning with emotion.

"No thanks necessary." She smiles and gathers up the old bedding. "I'll have that plate up as soon as possible, and then we'll get another round of meds going." I think I nod, but my eyes are already closing before she walks out. I have no idea what happens from here. There are so many questions I still need the answers to, but they can wait.

"Saylor?" Lochlan softly calls my name. I must have dozed off. He's standing beside me with the tray Karley sent for. "Ready to eat?" I don't respond, but he situates a table over my bed and places the food on top. There's a bowl of broth, a few crackers, and some juice. He takes the same seat he'd been in earlier, then peels back the top of my drink for me. I look around, but his shadow is nowhere to be found.

"Roan's grabbing our dinner," Lochlan offers without me needing to ask.

I feel self-conscious at first, with him staring at me, but I finally dip my spoon in the soup and take a tiny sip. Lochlan seems to relax now that he sees I'm eating. It's not that I'm not hungry, because I am. I'm just not used to normal tastes anymore. Mine has become very singular after only having the same few things for so long.

"Um..." Lochlan starts to speak but pauses to run his fingers through his hair. "Ro and I have been staying in here, at least one of us at all times, but if you'd rather we didn't, that's okay. Neither of us wants to overstep." I'm not sure I fully understand what role they play in all of this, but they haven't done anything to make me fear them. My gut says they're okay and I have nothing to be concerned about, but after everything, I doubt my ability to distinguish good from bad.

"It's fine," is what I go with, because if having them near means no one can get through that door who isn't supposed to, I'll manage. I drink a little more, but I can feel my stomach start to tighten, ready to expel the foreign substance. Lochlan looks like he wants to say something when I push the table away, maybe encourage me to eat a bit more, but chooses to stay quiet.

A few minutes later, Nurse Karley comes back and administers some pain medication through my IV, saying it should help me sleep through the night. One can only hope. My bed is lowered, and though it takes some serious effort and a lot of deep breathing, I manage to turn on my good side. It's the way I've always slept, but it leaves me facing Lochlan and his honey-colored eyes.

Karley leaves with my half-eaten dinner tray, turning the lights down as she goes. Thankfully, there's a glow from the bathroom that keeps the space illuminated. I try to close my eyes, already drowsy from the drugs pumping through my veins, but it's dark and blank when I do. When I'm awake, I can see that I'm no longer there. I know it's real.

"I'm scared to sleep. What if this is all a dream?" I speak my fears quietly, but Lochlan hears me.

"It's not a dream, sweetheart. Put your hand in mine, and anytime you need to remind yourself of where you are, you squeeze as hard as you need to." He lays his palm on the bed, facing up, and waits patiently for me to decide if I want to take it. I bite my lip, wondering if that's something I should try and push so quickly. I haven't touched another person, or been touched without the accompaniment of pain, in so long. My hand shakes with nerves, but I slowly slide it into Lochlan's, until the heat of his skin is warming my own.

"Sleep, Saylor." His whispered command barely breaches my mind before I fade away.

I jerk awake, making my side pinch. Just as I feared, my dreams were plagued with threadbare mattresses and blinking red lights. No one had come for me; it was just a fantasy I'd created in my half-dead state. Before my heartrate has a chance to return to normal, I take in my surroundings. It's completely dark. There's no light from the bathroom, no glow of a lamp. I can't see anything and it's sending me headfirst into a panic attack. But my hand is still wrapped in something warm, so I squeeze, hoping to ground myself.

"Lochlan," I whimper, needing to know with

absolute certainty he's still here. That he's real.

"Saylor?" He wakes instantly, standing so fast something gets knocked over. "What's wrong?" He's feeling around with his free hand, looking for the lamp.

"There's no light," I sob. "It's too dark." Someone mutters *'fuck'*, and then there's another crash. Tears are streaming down my cheeks, when finally, the bathroom light gets flipped on. My entire body sags in relief.

"I'm so sorry, Saylor. I must have switched it off without thinking." Roan stands in the doorway, his chest heaving and eyes full of remorse.

"It's okay." I lick my dry lips and focus on taking slow, measured breaths.

"It's not," he urges, his voice right next to me. I force my eyes open, noting how distressed he looks. "I was half asleep, but that's not an excuse." Lochlan squeezes my hand, his head resting on the side of my bed. I think I took a few years off of everyone's life.

"It really is. You didn't know, but now you do." I think that's the most I've spoken to either of them.

"It'll never happen again," Lochlan promises. I can sense the looming adrenaline crash, so I nod, keeping my hand wound with his. I thought it'd be difficult to fall asleep again, but it's really not.

Chapter Eight

Saylor

There's sunlight streaming through the window when I wake, but it's early. My palm is sweaty from where it's still connected with Lochlan's, and my arm is partially numb from sleeping so soundly in one position. There's a weight over my ankle that wasn't there before, and when I look down to see what it is, I find Roan's arm laid across it. He's slumped over, his body far too big for the chair he spent the night in.

Lochlan is snoring lightly, his breath tickling the inside of my arm. Gently, I try to pull my hand from his so I can go relieve my bladder. I've barely moved when his eyes fly open and his back goes straight. It sets off a chain reaction, causing Roan to do the same. I freeze, shocked by how easily I'd woken them when they'd been sleeping so hard.

"Bathroom," I explain, needing to get there sooner rather than later.

"Right." Lochlan pulls away, giving me space to move from the bed. "Do you need me to get the nurse?"

"I think I've got it," I tell him, but he doesn't look convinced. Other than a little help getting to my feet, I manage to do the rest on my own. I'm wiping my hands against my gown, trying to dry them off as I open the door, but stop short when I see there's a man I don't recognize. My eyes immediately search out Lochlan's for an explanation.

"Saylor, this is Agent Denvers." He waves towards the newcomer. He's older, late forties to early fifties, with salt and pepper hair. His eyes appear kind, along with the small smile he gives me.

"I can't tell you how good it is to finally meet you, Ms. Radley." I take my spot back on the bed, not sure where else to go. "I know we're strangers to you, but it feels like we've known you for some time now. I'm sorry we couldn't bring you home sooner." Lochlan takes his same seat while Agent Denvers grabs the free one, leaving Roan to lean against the wall by the door.

"There's a lot we need to go over, and as much as I hate it, I need to get your account of what happened, starting from the day you were taken." He grimaces, like he knows I'm not ready for this, but he has no other choice. I fist my hand so tightly, my fingernails start to break the skin. As soon as Lochlan notices, he wedges his fingers between mine and twines them together.

"Um," I cough, looking at my cup of water. Roan follows my gaze, then pushes off the wall to bring it to me. His huge hand holds the straw still so I can have a drink. When it no longer feels like I've swallowed sandpaper, I start again. "I missed the bus, so I was walking home. I'd done it plenty of times before. Mom was working the night shift, so I couldn't call for her to pick me up. Sheriff Price offered me a ride. I didn't see anything wrong with accepting; I'd known him forever. Something felt off, but I was too scared to say or do anything. I thought I was overreacting." I have to stop and take a breath. Hearing it now, all laid out, makes me feel incredibly stupid.

"We missed the turn for my house, but I still didn't say anything. I'm not sure when it happened, but he shoved a needle in my thigh. When I woke up, I was already in the room he'd prepared. I never left it, not once. He took me to the one behind the bookcase every month. He'd.." I swallow past the lump in my throat, squeezing Lochlan's hand so hard, I'm shocked his bones aren't groaning from the pressure. "He'd touch me. And I'm pretty sure he recorded it." It feels like Liam steals another part of me with that admission. I'm ashamed, though I have no reason to be.

"Saylor, can you elaborate on *how* he touched you?" Agent Denvers politely asks, but I'd rather drink battery acid than give him every dirty detail of what that man did to me.

"Denvers," Lochlan growls in warning. I have no idea why he's been so nice to me, but I appreciate it more than he knows.

"Okay," the agent concedes. "I'm going to ask this once, and all you need to respond with is a simple yes or no. Do you need an exam or any testing done for sexually transmitted diseases?" I knew where he was going with his questioning, but it still makes me flinch to hear it.

"No." I shake my head. "He never went that far." I leave it at that, hoping he can piece it together on his own. Lochlan is so still, but the muscles in his jaw keep flexing. And Roan suddenly finds the floor fascinating. I look away, blinking back tears. I don't know what they're thinking, or how they view me now, but it can't be any worse than how I see myself.

"Well, I guess that brings us to where we go from here. As of right now, the location of Liam Price is unknown." I jerk my head around, wondering why I never thought to ask if he'd been arrested. I guess I just assumed he was in custody.

"He's not in jail?" I squeak. The idea of him out there, free as bird, makes my skin crawl.

"Unfortunately, the home was empty when we went to investigate. He hasn't been seen since last Friday." A quick glance at the whiteboard shows that it's Friday, the 3rd of June, which means he's had an entire week to put as much distance as possible between him and the scene of his crime.

I'm going to be sick.

"We're going to find him, Saylor. He'll get the justice he deserves." Lochlan's gaze is unwavering.

"Our main priority is ensuring your safety, Ms. Radley. Normally, you'd be placed in a safe house with a handler, but I personally think it would be best for you to remain with Lochlan and his team." I scrunch my nose in confusion.

"I promise we're qualified," Lochlan states adamantly. "We run an entire company that's partially based around security. We wouldn't have made it as far as we have if we lacked the ability to keep our clients safe. You can look us up if you'd like." He slips a business card from his pocket and hands it to me. The front is embossed with black lettering that reads SOTERIA. When I flip it over, I find a link for a website, a company email and phone number.

"We do investigative work as well. Like Denvers said earlier, we might be strangers to you, but you certainly aren't to us. You've had an entire team of men looking for you, Saylor, and that sort of devotion doesn't just stop now that you've been found. It isn't fair of me, but I'm asking you to trust us. There's more to your kidnapping than you realize, and until we've found every person responsible, it'd be smart to keep our circle small." That's vague and filled with insinuation, but I bite my tongue, knowing I'm not ready to hear anything else quite yet.

"Just think it over. We want the choice to be yours, but you have to decide by tomorrow. Dr. Ashburn is planning to have your discharge papers ready when he makes his morning rounds, and I'd like to have you moved directly to the location you intend on staying at until this is all sorted." Agent Denvers stands to make his exit. "You couldn't be in better hands, Saylor." With a nod to the other men, he heads for the door, letting in Nurse Karley on his way out.

"Good morning!" Karley's upbeat and smiling, despite the early hour and dark circles beneath her eyes. "I have your breakfast." She hands me a protein shake. “Drink this slowly.” I eye the chocolate concoction, taking a sniff, though I wish I wouldn’t have. It smells like vitamins.

“I know. It’s not the most pleasant thing, but bland is your best friend right now. It won’t be long before you’re scarfing down a double cheeseburger.” Karley smiles, trying to infuse some lightness. I can’t wait for the day I can eat normally again. Everything I thought would happen if this day ever came has been a letdown. I didn’t get to run to my mom and have her make everything better, there’s no pizza in sight and the closest thing I've been given to a milkshake is this foamy, foul-smelling crap in front of me.

“We’re about to have a shift change, but I’ll be back this evening. I hear you’re blowing this popsicle stand come tomorrow.” She raises an eyebrow in question, but I just shrug. It feels like everything is moving at warp speed and I’ve barely had a chance to process that I’m no longer being held prisoner by a madman. It makes my eyes prick with tears every time I think about it. I’ll never spend another day as Liam’s captive, but it still doesn’t feel real yet.

“There are two ibuprofens here for when you need them. The doctor asked that we start weaning your IV meds.” She holds up a tiny paper cup and places it on the table. “Can I get you anything before I leave?” Karley asks, fixing the bottom of my bedding so it's tucked back in.

“No, I think I’m okay for now,” I answer, taking a sip of the protein shake. I almost gag. It’s not the flavor, but the consistency. She pats my foot and waves goodbye. Lochlan walks back over, having moved next to Roan to allow Karley the space to do what she needed.

"I need to make some calls. Will you be okay here with Roan?" I nod, trying to force down a bit more of the shake, but ultimately choose to set it aside before it makes me sick. "I won't be long." Lochlan smiles, and trades places with Roan.

"Would you like to take these now or wait a while?" Roan's deep timber fills the quiet room as he points to the pills.

"Now, please." I'm not in agony, but I'd like to avoid getting to that point. He cracks open a bottle of water and pours some in the cup I've been using. I quickly wash them down and sip on my drink. He takes the seat Lochlan's been glued to as I get comfortable. I'm not sure what else I'm supposed to do aside from rest. We study each other, but neither of us speaks.

Roan is quite possibly the tallest man I've ever seen. If I had to guess, I'd say he's about six-feet, four-inches. He's broad, like a linebacker. His hair is dirty blond and falls to his shoulders, but he currently has it thrown into a messy knot on the top of his head. His green eyes are bright, but I've noticed they darken with his mood. He should scare me. The difference in our sizes alone intimidates me, but no internal alarms are going off. I feel safe enough to take a nap, so that's exactly what I do.

~

Sometime later, I peel my eyes open and find Roan in the same spot. There's a bag of takeout on his lap and his feet are propped against a bar along the bottom of my bed. He's looking at his phone, the crooked grin on his face making him appear younger. As if he can feel me watching, he glances up.

"Hey, sleepyhead." Roan drops his feet to the ground and leans forward. "You were out for a while." I look to the clock on the wall, seeing we're well into the afternoon. "I told Loch he could get some rest next door, but if you want me to go get him I can."

"That's okay," I respond with a shake of my head. It's apparent neither of them has gotten any decent rest since they've been here. He looks down at his phone again, a short laugh coming from his chest at what he sees.

"Look." He hands the device over. It's a lot sleeker than the ones I remember, and I grip it tightly so I don't accidently drop it. "That's two of the guys we work with—Kash and Krew. They handle anything tech related." Roan points to the screen where there's a video playing of a grown man standing on a dining table, swatting at something with a broom. Sitting on the kitchen counter, watching in amusement, is another man who looks identical to the one on the table.

"That one's Kash. He's terrified of anything scaley, and there's currently a lizard running through the house." I watch as the guy named Kash whirls around, his broom pointed out like a weapon. Poor guy. He's living in the wrong state if he's trying to avoid that particular aversion. I notice a camera icon in the corner of the screen, the current time beside it showing the seconds as they speed by.

"Is this live? Does he know he's being recorded?" I look at Roan, hoping my accusation wasn't as blatant as it sounded. But I know what it's like to be on the other end when you never gave consent to being filmed. Roan smiles sadly, his hand covering my good wrist and giving it a gentle squeeze.

"He knows, Saylor. This is just one of the cameras we have placed around the property, and we were all in agreement to put a few inside. They're only in the common areas, and if they make you uncomfortable, we'll cut the feed if you decide to stay with us. Our job is mostly background work, but there's always a chance someone could harbor a grudge. We know who comes and goes at all times, and that gives us an advantage should we ever need it." I nibble at the dry skin on my bottom lip. That makes sense. And if I'm being honest with myself, it makes me feel a little better to know that if I stay with them, I'd be someplace secure.

"Watch this," Roan says, tapping something on the screen. A second later, sound comes through the speaker.

"Krew, I swear to Martha Stewart, goddess of all things sweet and decadent, if you don't get that spawn of Godzilla out of here, I'm disowning you. We might have shared a womb, but you'll be dead to me. *DEAD*!" Kash waves the broom threateningly at Krew, who's obviously his twin. I feel my lips twitch, the urge to smile so close I can practically taste it.

Krew hops off the counter and saunters toward a corner in the kitchen. He bends and picks the lizard up, but instead of going out the back patio, he spins around and flings it at Kash. What follows next is the highest pitched squeal I've ever heard. Kash scrambles away, but his foot slips and down he goes. He jumps back up, wiggling his body all around while repeating, "Get it off! Get it off!" I giggle, the sound slipping out unconsciously. Roan's eyes widen, his grin filling his whole face as he watches me.

"Hey, Kash." Roan presses and holds another button, activating a microphone feature. "Thanks for the laugh, buddy. Saylor just got to see firsthand how big of a pussy you are." He's smiling, so I know the insult is meant jokingly. Both men whip their heads up and face the camera. The picture is so clear, not at all pixelated, which leads me to believe their equipment is new and likely top of the line.

"Uh," Kash clears his throat, smoothing down his clothes as if they're wrinkled. They're not. "Hi. It's nice to sort of meet you." Kash waves, forcing his voice to drop a few decibels. Roan snorts and shakes his head.

"We'll see you guys tomorrow." He ends the video feed and goes back to munching on his food. I watch longingly as he eats a fry, the greasy smell so good it's making my mouth water. Roan extends the bag, offering me one. "I won't tell if you don't." His smirk is secretive and for the first time, it feels like someone isn't handling me with kid gloves. He's giving me a choice, knowing I'm aware it might not go over well, but ultimately leaving it up to me to decide. I pluck a single fry from his outstretched hand and take the smallest bite. I groan. *God, that's good.* I savor the rest of it, but refrain from eating any more. Roan stares back in amusement, riveted to the sight of me enjoying a damn french-fry. After I finish, he hands me my water, and I down the remainder of what was in the cup.

"That good, huh?" He laughs, the sound making a tiny smile grace my lips. I can't help but run my finger across them, wanting to feel the difference. We're quiet for a while, but it's not uncomfortable. The opposite, really. There's no pressure to fill the silence; I can just be.

"How many people do you work with?" I question after a while, my curiosity getting the best of me. It'd also be smart to get some more information before I have to make a decision about tomorrow.

"There are five of us. Me, Loch, Kash, Krew, and Kade. Kade's currently working an assignment on the west coast, but he'll be home shortly," Roan replies, arms crossed behind his head and eyes closed. He's the picture of relaxation, so he must not be bothered by my inquisitiveness.

"And you all live together? Here in Florida?" That's been my assumption, but maybe I should stop jumping to conclusions. They could be from another state, for all I know.

"Yep." He nods, still looking peaceful as he lounges. "Our main house is about three hours from here, near Pensacola. It's our home base, but we have a condo in Seattle as well. It's only used when we have work in the area."

"Do you always bring your clients home for safe keeping?" I hope that doesn't sound snotty. I'm genuinely curious how this typically works for them.

"Never. You'd be the first. Any protection details we've worked have always taken place wherever the client resides," he states emphatically.

"So why me, then?" I ask the question before I've fully thought it through. The backs of my eyes burn when I remember I don't have a home, so technically, I reside nowhere.

"You're different." Roan stares at me intently, willing me to understand. I look away, the moment too charged for my liking. I don't think it's fully set in how alone I am. I have no family left, not a single person I could call on for a place to stay or a simple shoulder to cry on. Loneliness is something I've become intimately acquainted with, and I loathe it. I think I've been so open to having Lochlan and Roan around because I don't want to be the only person in a room ever again. The door opens and Nurse Karley steps in, looking much more rested than she did this morning. She smiles, a sight that's quickly growing on me, and starts the routine check of my vitals.

"Looking good, kiddo," Karley comments as she writes everything down on the whiteboard. "I have some stuff for you, and wanted to see if you'd like another shower? Things are a bit slow at the moment, so I've got time to help." She glances back at me over her shoulder, so I nod politely.

Roan takes that as a sign to clear out for a while, but sweetly brushes his thumb along the inside of my wrist before walking away. Karley helps me out bed, but it's slow-going now that the stronger meds have been cut back. My ribs feel like they're on fire, and there's a general soreness that radiates from every inch of my body, including my hair. By the time I manage to undress and slip the brace off, I'm trembling and weak.

"Sorry, honey. There's not much we can do for bruised ribs. Compression is no longer recommended, but the anti-inflammatory you've been prescribed will help." I grunt, hoping the hot water will loosen my muscles. Karley closes the door behind her once I'm safely in the shower, giving me a few minutes alone. I close my eyes and lean against the tiled wall, my bad hand cradled to my chest. It feels so good I could fall asleep, but my mind is too chaotic to rest.

I don't know what the right thing to do is. I could tell Agent Denvers I'd rather be placed somewhere official, but then I'd be starting over with people I've never met. Lochlan asked me to trust him, and I do—on a surface level. We put our faith in strangers every day, to some extent, with the expectation for them to be decent human beings. Cab drivers, blind dates...we constantly walk into situations under the assumption that we're in good hands, but there's no certainty.

I never would've imagined that Liam Price was capable of the things he did to me. I know it could've been so much worse, but there's still this disbelief that he harmed me at all. Having my trust broken so brutally, by someone I thought I knew, has left me questioning everything. But I think I'd feel better if I went with Lochlan. I haven't felt panicked around him or Roan, and I might not have the same reaction to whoever would be in charge at the safe house. It could be a disaster.

Agent Denvers thinks this is the best option, and I'm inclined to agree. I just hope this isn't another one of those moments where I'm caving to everyone else's wishes and discarding my own. That girl who aimed to please feels foreign, though. A part of me will always want to avoid conflict as much as possible, but no longer to the detriment of my own wellbeing. I've lost too much to allow anyone to walk all over me ever again.

"You ready for me?" Karley calls out, derailing my inner turmoil.

"Just about." I quickly run the soap over my body, loving how clean it smells. I used to have a stockpile of shower gels, like most teen girls, with every scent imaginable. Seems frivolous now, when I'm thrilled with plain old Irish Springs. Karley helps me with my hair, but I try to do as much as possible, knowing I'll have to figure it out on my own after tonight. Once I'm dry and she's brushed through any tangles, she offers me a pair of scrubs.

"Since you're leaving tomorrow, I figured you'd rather be fully clothed while doing it." She smirks. "This is going to be rough on your ribs, but I sized up so it'll be a little easier to get the top on." We try several different ways of contorting my body, but wind up with me sitting on the toilet as she works my arms through one at a time. I'm sweating once we're finished, making me wonder why I even bothered with a shower.

"I got you some stuff." Karley pulls out a Target bag and empties the contents onto the counter. "There's deodorant, a razor, some shaving cream, toothbrush and toothpaste, and though I wasn't certain of your preference, I decided to grab a few feminine items." She lays out three packages of pads, all in different sizes. One pantyliner, one for regular wear, and the last for overnight. I never wore tampons; I'd been too scared to try them.

"They're perfect," I choke out as tears burn my eyes. I was rarely given anything like this, most of the time I'd have to make something work with extra toilet paper or an old rag. He'd rather I bleed all over myself than allow me any sort of comfort. But at least he wouldn't touch me for a week. Unfortunately, I've never been regular and my periods tend come and go as they please. Most girls dread their time of the month, but for five years, I've coveted mine.

"Oh, honey." Karley wraps her arms around me. It makes me tense, but I don't pull away. She's been nothing but kind to me. "I'll give you a minute." Once she's gone, I wipe the tears from my face and move to stand in front of the sink. With a deep, fortifying breath, I raise my head and glance in the mirror. It's the first time I've seen my own reflection since I was fourteen. I've been too nervous to look. My hair is so long it reaches the base of my spine. It's still wet, so the blonde looks darker than usual.

My eyes are the same bright blue they've always been, a trait I got from a father I barely remember, and my skin is pale from the years I've spent deprived of the sun. I was always tan, having grown up so close to the beach. Mom called me her little gingerbread. It's alarming, seeing this person who's me but somehow isn't. Worst of all, there's a dark bruise along my right temple that spans halfway down my face. I want to scrub it from my skin, but there's a dozen more littering my body that have failed to go unnoticed every time I shower.

Each one is an ominous reminder of what Liam Price is capable of. He's a wolf in sheep's clothing, and he played the part brilliantly. I clear my throat and look away, wishing it was possible to speed up the healing process. I open the toothbrush Karley got me and get to scrubbing. The toothpaste is so minty it makes my eyes sting, but there will be no complaints from me. The tubes I've been using were cheap, and probably expired. After I'm done, I place everything back in the bag and exit the bathroom. Lochlan is back, but Roan is gone. He's setting up my dinner tray, but stops when he hears me.

"Hey," he greets me. "You look like you're ready for your first shift." He nods to the blue scrubs I'm wearing with a grin.

"Well, I can't leave with you guys in only a hospital gown." I attempt a smile in return, but I'm pretty sure it falls flat. I place the Target bag on the floor and climb into bed so slowly, I could pass for a turtle. The ibuprofen has worn off, and all that twisting and turning to get my top on has exacerbated the pain.

"You're going to come home with us?" Lochlan's steps falter, his honey-colored gaze clashing with mine. I nod, feeling mostly confident in my decision. His eyes close on a quiet exhale, and then he smiles. "That's great, Saylor."

We eat in silence. Lochlan's turkey club looks a million times better than my chicken broth and plain toast, but I manage to eat more of my food this time. We've just finished when Dr. Ashburn, who I've yet to be awake to meet, comes in to speak with me. He goes over my bloodwork, informing us there was nothing noted in my toxicology report. Other than an iron deficiency, I'm otherwise healthy. Which is a miracle in itself. Nurse Karley makes her final check once he leaves and gives me my next dose of pain meds. She clears our food trash and promises to be here in the morning so we can say goodbye.

When it's just the two of us again, I press the button to lower my bed. It feels like I've been put through the wringer this past hour, both physically and emotionally. Lochlan dims the light, making sure to leave the bathroom open, and then takes his seat beside me. My eyelids feel so heavy, I can hardly keep them open.

"Sweet dreams, Saylor," Lochlan whispers, sliding his hand beneath mine as I sink into oblivion.

Chapter Nine

Roan

When I make it back to Saylor's room, she's already sound asleep. Selfishly, I was hoping to have a few more minutes with her. Maybe it's because I'm so focused on her at the moment there isn't room for anything else, but she quiets the acidic thoughts plaguing me. I don't feel the constant weight of regret or inadequacy. I have a purpose—to keep her safe—and I'm not going to let anything hinder that, especially my own bullshit.

Lochlan is staring at Saylor, his hand holding hers, likely counting every breath she takes. I'd give him shit for it, but I doubt I'm any better. It's hard to look away from something you've just found, when you'd been convinced it was lost forever. I soundlessly pull up the other chair, prepared to spend another night on hard, unforgiving plastic.

"She agreed to come back with us," Loch speaks softly, not wanting to wake Saylor.

I had a feeling she would, but I'm fucking thrilled. It's not that I don't trust the agents that'd be tasked with looking after her, I just trust us more.

She'd be an assignment to them, but that's about it. And while some people are adamant that feelings shouldn't interfere with your job in this line of work, I wholeheartedly disagree. They might be trained to protect Saylor with their lives, but if they've never been put in a position where they've had to make a decision like that, who's to say how they'll actually respond.

As for me and the guys? I know where we stand. If the choice came down to us or her, it'd be her. Every single time. You do whatever you have to when you care about someone. Saylor staying in our home will keep her safe and us sane. Denvers would've lost his shit on us if she had decided to go the other route. We would've bugged the poor bastard to an early grave.

"Thank fuck for that." I exhale in relief, kicking my feet out to gain a bit more room on my makeshift bed. "She laughed today."

"Really?" Loch turns to look at me, using his finger to push his glasses back up his nose.

"Yeah." I smile, remembering the soft, tinkling sound and the way her face looked in the moment. It's like she forgot about all the bad shit for a second. I want to feed those glimmers of happiness. Until the good outweighs the bad and she no longer has that haunted look in her pretty blue eyes.

"What got that reaction from her?" Loch teases, probably wanting to know so he can recreate it and be the cause.

"Fucking Kash," I snort. "I had the feed up

for the kitchen cam, watching his dumbass prance around on the dining table because of a lizard. Krew threw it at him and the big baby went down. Completely ate shit while squealing like a stuck pig." We both laugh, doing our best to muffle the noise.

"Figures it'd be him," Loch scoffs, but I nod in agreement. Kash has more issues than I've got brain cells, but he's funny as shit and knows how to keep the heaviness at bay. That's something I've always envied about him.

"I called Kade back in." Loch's statement throws me for a second, but I shake off my surprise.

"Did you explain why?"

"No." He drops his head. "His flight leaves at 1pm tomorrow, so he should be home by six. We haven't even explained the situation to Saylor." Loch groans, clearly stressed about the revelations to come.

"In all fairness, there's a *lot* we haven't told Saylor. But we agreed it wasn't the brightest idea to dump everything on her at once. That decision isn't yours to bear on your own, Loch." I grip his shoulder, giving him a good shake. "Let's get some sleep, brother." I change topics, knowing he won't see things that way, no matter what I say. "I mean, it's going to be shitty sleep, but sleep, nonetheless."

"The shittiest," Loch mumbles, his head already laid against Saylor's bed. "I can't wait to kiss my fucking mattress. I'll never take it for granted again."

"Worth it, though." I grin, looking at the sweetest face, content in sleep.

"Definitely," Loch agrees, his snores filling the quiet just a few minutes later.

~

"Ro."

Someone kicks my foot, but it can't be time to wake up already, so I decide I'm dreaming.

"Ro."

The smack to the back of my head does it, and I pry myself up, cracking an eye open to glare at Lochlan. The clock reads 5:32, and I've never hated him more than I do in this moment.

"What the *fuck* are you doing?" I growl, irritated and stiff from being folded over half the night. My hand must have a mind of its own, because it's once again wrapped around Saylor's ankle.

"The goddamn press is here. Denvers just called to give us a heads up," Lochlan whisper-yells his outrage, but it succeeds in waking me up.

"How the hell did that happen?" I carefully move away from Saylor and start stuffing shit in my bag. Snatching our charging cords from the outlet, I hand them to Loch, who's just about finished with his own crap.

"I imagine some asshole leaked that she's being released today, so they're frothing at the mouth to get a fucking picture," he snaps, pissed at the situation and the invasion of privacy. We knew it'd be a circus once the media caught wind of Saylor's return. It's not every day that a kid goes missing for five years and is found alive. This is a small town and word travels fast.

That's why we purposely kept the information about today's exit limited to a small group of people. And one of them fucked us over.

"Denvers has the SUV ready for us in the staff garage. It's basement level and private, so hopefully we can slip out unnoticed." Loch reads the forwarded info from his phone. "Wake Saylor while I go get the discharge papers." He's gone before I can so much as nod. I drop my bag, debating how to do this without scaring the shit out of her.

"Saylor," I whisper, stroking my thumb over her good wrist. I love the feel of her pulse. That *thump-thump* makes me sigh. "Hey, Little Fighter," I try again, and her eyes finally flutter open.

"Roan?" she questions, her voice gravelly with sleep.

"Sorry to wake you, but we have to go." She frowns, rightly confused by our sudden departure. I debate if I should tell her what's happening, not wanting to freak her out unnecessarily, but she has a right to know. "Someone tipped off the local news stations that you're leaving today and they've got reporters posted out front trying to get a picture." She blinks at me a few times, but other than that, she gives no outward reaction to what I've just told her.

"The car's ready to go, away from prying eyes, but we need to move quickly." I hold my hand out to help her from the bed. Once she's steady on her feet, Saylor shuffles across the room, looking adorably rumpled in her oversized doctor getup, and bends to pick up a plastic bag. She hisses at the strain it causes on her ribs, but she's already upright before I can offer to help.

"Ready," she states, just as Loch and the nurse rush back in.

"Saylor, I need you to sign these discharge papers, sweetheart." Loch walks them over to the bedside table and hands her a pen, then shoves them at the nurse as soon as she's finished.

"Lochlan has your prescription, okay?" Saylor nods, her eyes looking a little glassy as she says goodbye to the woman who's helped her so much these past few days. She hands her a pair of flip-flops so she has something for her feet. They speak quietly for a moment, and then Saylor gives the nurse a weak hug, but it still shocks the shit out of me that she's the one who initiates the contact.

Loch and I grab our bags and sandwich Saylor between us as we head down the hallway. A few heads turn our way, but no one stops to ask any questions. I hit the button to the elevator and wait very impatiently as it travels down from the fifth floor. As soon as we're inside, Loch presses '*B*' for the basement, trying to get the door closed before anyone can join us. It spits us out right in front of Agent Denvers, who tosses me the key to our SUV.

"About time." He sounds as excited as I am to be up this early. "Gassed it up for you too. You're welcome." Loch rolls his eyes but mumbles a '*thanks*'.

"Ms. Radley, I'm happy you chose to go with the guys, but if at any point you change your mind, give me a call. Lochlan has my number." Saylor agrees, but all I'm thinking is there's no chance in hell she's changing her mind. I'll buy her a dozen puppies if I have to. Whatever it takes to keep her happy and makes her stay.

Commotion from the side of the building grabs my attention. The entrance to the parking garage is just a few feet away, and the longer we're here, the more anxious I get that someone's going to waltz right in. The last thing Saylor needs is another fucking camera shoved in her face. We say our goodbyes to Denvers, promising to be in touch soon, and then I steer us towards the waiting SUV. I place our bags in the trunk, then open the door for Saylor. She slides across the backseat, but my need to know that she's safe and secure has me leaning over to buckle her in. She flinches at the sudden closeness, and it feels like a shotgun blast straight to the fucking chest.

"Saylor, I'm so sorry," I blurt, backing off just as quickly. Her eyes are bouncing around the cab of the vehicle, like she's searching for the nearest exit.

"What's wrong?" Loch twists around from the passenger seat. I ignore him, more concerned with the tiny girl on the precipice of a panic attack.

"Hey." I lift my hand and rest it against her cheek, hoping I'm not about to make things worse. Saylor goes completely still. "It's Roan. You're okay, but I need you to focus on me, Saylor. Match your breathing with mine." Her gaze slowly clears as clarity creeps back in.

"I'm sorry. I promise it wasn't you," she squeaks, a single tear slipping free. I brush it away with my thumb, giving her a sad smile, because we both know this was my fault.

"You're okay, Little Fighter," I whisper, pulling my hand away and gently closing the door.

For the first hour, we drive in silence. Loch's angry glare practically burns a hole in the side of my head, but I can't fault him for being upset. I'd be pissed at him too if the roles were reversed. This isn't the first time I've dropped the ball, and that sliver of self-doubt I'm so used to feeling tries to weasel its way back in. I've always been a heavy sleeper, which is why it took me a minute to process Saylor's screams when she first woke up and that fuckwad cop was in her room. Then again when I flipped the bathroom light off the other night after taking a piss. I'd been half asleep, but it was my mistake. Regardless of the reasoning.

I'm trying to cut myself some slack. This is new territory for all of us, and no doubt, I won't be the only one who fucks up in the days to come. We need to learn her triggers, but I'm not sure Saylor even knows them all just yet. I have a sick feeling we'll be discovering them the hard way. My fingers flex against the steering wheel, the joints stiff from how tightly I've been gripping it. I keep flashing my eyes to the rearview mirror, sneaking glances at Saylor as she sleeps.

"What was that?" Loch finally asks, his voice flat and cold.

"I wasn't thinking." I shift in my seat uncomfortably. We might be thick as thieves, but Loch has this way of ripping the wind from your sails when he feels like you've fucked up.

"No shit," he deadpans.

"I could hear people talking right outside the parking garage and I freaked out. If someone had walked in on us, God forbid a fucking reporter, it would've been a clusterfuck. I just wanted to get her out of there." I can still feel those claws of paranoia. It has me scanning the mirrors, double checking that we aren't being followed.

"I get it, Ro." Loch exhales his annoyance. "We have to make a point of thinking before we act. Saylor's been fine with the touches we've exchanged so far, but that doesn't mean she's comfortable with anything more. And at any point she could decide she wants *no* contact, and that'd be perfectly fine. She's allowed to change her mind. That girl's owed a lifetime of takebacks." While his words are true, they also make my throat tighten. If I pushed her into changing her mind about staying with us, I'm going to kick my own ass.

"I sent Kash out yesterday to get her some stuff. Clothes, toiletries...those sorts of things," Loch mumbles absentmindedly, his gaze focused out the window, as if he's lost in thought.

"Shit. I'm glad you thought of that." My head has been a jumbled mess these past few days, but I can't believe I overlooked the fact that Saylor has not a single thing to her name. It's going to be an adjustment having her at the house. No one but the five of us has ever stepped foot into our home, and certainly no women. We built that place to be a sanctuary, filled it with everything we could possibly need so that we'd always have a safe spot to land. It represents security and reminds us of how far we've come. If you'd asked me a week ago, I couldn't have imagined ever allowing someone to invade that slice of peace we've carved out for ourselves, but it wasn't even a question with Saylor. For her *not* to be there would feel wrong.

"I figured Kash was the best choice to handle it. You know he has a way with awkward situations," Loch adds, breaking through my train of thought. "Karley gave me her best guess as to what sizes Saylor would need, so hopefully she was somewhat close."

I think about the man-child I've known for eight years. Because this is Kash we're talking about, he probably poured over every detail we have on Saylor pre-kidnapping—all her likes and dislikes—and created a fucking time capsule in her bedroom. I wouldn't be surprised if there's a Justin Bieber poster tacked to her wall, since we know he was a favorite of hers...*when she was fourteen*. There's a good chance that would have her calling Denvers immediately. And sweet Jesus, I pray any...*intimate*...things he bought won't be just as cringey. Surely there's a happy medium between pre-teen and negligées.

Fucking hell.

Chapter Ten

Saylor

The smooth asphalt we've been driving on switches to gravel and rocks me awake. It takes me a minute to remember where I am and how I got here. We're quickly approaching a gate, showing no sign of slowing down, when a beep echoes through the vehicle and the wall of iron slides open. The driveway is long, but eventually the house comes into view. I only have a second to take it all in before we're entering the garage. From what I could see, it's massive. A modern, concrete fortress with a smattering of windows.

That seems to be the theme of the day. Earlier, despite what Roan might think, my panic hadn't stemmed from his nearness. I'd been on edge from the moment we stepped into the hallway. For some reason, it hadn't registered for me that I'd yet to venture outside of my hospital room. I'd felt safe in there, with the rest of the world being held at arm's length. But then we were moving, forced to rush our exit, leaving me no time to mentally prepare.

I'd felt like a spectacle. Every person we passed

eyed me with a mixture of curiosity and pity. The wide corridor began to feel claustrophobic, and I was grateful to step into the elevator for a moment of reprieve. But then we were in the parking garage, and I was surrounded with reminders of how much time I've lost. Everything held a slight touch of familiarity, but it was mixed with new, foreign aspects I didn't recognize. Like with Roan's phone, the cars are different from what I remember as well. They've been given newer body styles and fancy upgrades.

The technology wasn't so advanced that I didn't know of it, it's just improved. The inside of the SUV was shocking, but maybe that's because Mom never drove anything quite that nice. I'd been lost in my head, grappling with the fact that five fucking years have come and gone without me, when Roan scared me. I hadn't seen *him* though, just movement that was directed at me. It could've been a fly, for all I knew. My reaction feels ridiculous now, but at the time, it was real and terrifying. The click of the garage door closing brings me back to the present.

"Ready?" Lochlan asks, a shy smile on his face as he waits for me to exit the backseat. Roan joins us a second later, his hands full with their bags and my gifts from Karley. I nod, walking between the two of them as Lochlan begins to climb a metal stairwell that leads to a door one floor above us. A rush of cool air greets us as we enter the house. I eye the open plan room, noting the kitchen to my left and a familiar dining table a few feet beyond it. Glancing back, I see the camera Roan tapped into yesterday. The one that captured the lizard fiasco.

The living room is to the right. Their sectional couch is gray and u-shaped, with seats so deep I could get lost in it. Mounted to the wall is the biggest television I've ever seen. A noise startles me and I turn to find Roan dropping our things on the kitchen island. Mom would have killed for a setup like this. Their appliances are stainless steel, but industrial scale. The marble counters are a mixture of white and black, and the cabinets are pale gray. It's beautiful.

"Thing one and two, is that you?" someone calls from the hallway straight ahead of us, followed by the sound of a door opening. Roan moves closer, flanking my free side. Impulsively, I grab his hand. Partly because I'm nervous to meet new people, but also because I feel horrible for upsetting him earlier. He looked devastated by my reaction. His eyes find mine, a question swimming in the green depths, but I just squeeze his fingers. His lips twitch, a faint smirk tilting them upwards. Footsteps greet us and I turn to find the two men I've semi-met standing a few feet away.

"Kash and Krew, this is Saylor," Lochlan introduces us. "Saylor, Kash and Krew." He points to each of them, making sure to distinguish who is who, but it's unnecessary. They look identical—same light-brown skin, black curly hair that's longer on top but shaved on the sides, twin brown eyes—but it's clear their personalities are night and day.

"Hey, Best Friend." Kash grins, acting as if we've known each other all of our lives.

"Ignore him," Roan groans.

"It's true," Kash shrugs. "So don't get jealous. Green's not your color."

I'm not sure what to say, so I keep quiet. I'm not as nervous as I was, but it feels weird being in someone else's space. I barely did sleepovers as a kid because I'd get so awkward and uncomfortable. I've never understood the '*make yourself at home*' saying.

"Nice to meet you both," I mutter, not wanting to be rude. Kash gives me another full-toothed smile and Krew dips his chin in lieu of speaking. He's definitely more reserved than his brother.

"Let's give you a tour," Lochlan announces. I release the death grip I have on Roan and move to follow him.

"This leads to the lower level." He points to the first door on the left once we're in the hallway. "That's where you'll find the gym, media room, and firing range." My eyes widen, but Lochlan doesn't stop to elaborate. A little farther down, he points to the right. "This is Kash and Krew's domain." The open door reveals an office of sorts. One long desk stretches the entire length of the front wall, but it's been divided into two workstations. There's a multitude of monitors, some bigger than others, that appear complicated and high-tech. Lochlan moves us along, stopping once we dead end and the hall extends to the right and left.

"Down this way we have my room, the twin's room, and Roan's room." He gestures to the right, pointing out each person's as he goes. He has the one at the end, and the twins are on the left with Roan's across from them. "And over here," he begins walking in the opposite direction, "we've got my office on the end, Kade's room on the right, and yours is here on the left."

Lochlan opens the door to the room he said is mine, letting me walk in first. There's a queen bed on the right wall, flanked by matching nightstands. The comforter is distinctly feminine, and there's a plush rug covering half the floor. To my left I find a dresser, where several empty photo frames sit atop it.

"We all have attached bathrooms." Lochlan slides around me to open the door. It's gorgeous, with a separate tub and shower, but I'm a bit overwhelmed with how nice everything is. I've gone from one extreme to another. "And this is the closet." I glance inside, shocked not just from its size, but by the rows of brand-new clothing, their tags visible from where they hang.

"Uh...," Lochlan pauses, giving me a cautious look. "Kash got you a few things. If something doesn't fit or if there's anything he forgot, just let us know." He rubs the back of his neck, his eyes watching me closely from behind his glasses. I stare at the full racks, thinking our definition of the word '*few*' is *not* the same.

"I did good, huh?" Kash remarks from the doorway, a proud grin plastered across his face. I smile and nod, not wanting to hurt his feelings by saying it's too much.

"I really thought you'd have a Justin Bieber poster stuck to the wall," Roan comments.

"*Please*," Kash scoffs. "He's soooo last season." He feigns a hair flip and struts away.

"He gives me indigestion," Roan gripes as the rest of us head back towards the kitchen.

There's so much left to see and I can't seem to focus on any one thing. With a different view of the space, I notice the built-in electric fireplace beneath the TV. My constantly cold toes practically hum in delight. The kitchen is neat and clean, considering a group of men live here, with only a few extra appliances littering the counters.

"Want to see something cool?" Kash points to the frosted glass door that I assume leads to a patio of some sort. He has a sucker in his mouth and a muffin in each hand, but uses his elbow to hit a button on the wall. Light bursts through the glass, causing me to blink a few times. Once I've adjusted to the brightness, I gasp.

"We're on the beach?" I surge forward, nearly pressing my face to the slider as I soak in the sight before me. Sand dunes and grass somewhat obscure the view, but it's impossible to miss the roll of the waves in the distance.

"Can I go?" I swing around to Lochlan, my pulse thrumming with excitement.

"You don't need permission, Saylor." He smiles sweetly. "You're a grown woman."

Shit. I am, aren't I? Nineteen—nearly twenty—is technically an adult, but I don't exactly feel like one. Besides, I'm here to ensure my safety, not traipse around without proper clearance first.

"I just meant is it dangerous for me to go out there?" I backtrack, feeling silly.

"You're safe," Krew answers in place of Lochlan. It's the first time he's spoken to me. "Our property is secure, and I'll know well beforehand if that ever changes."

"Okay," I quietly reply, hoping I didn't make him feel like I was questioning his ability to do his job.

"Go soak up the sun for a bit, but we have some things to discuss once you're back." Lochlan slides the door open for me, drenching us in the Florida heat.

Walking out, I stop at the edge of the patio and kick off my borrowed flip-flops. The second my toes sink beneath the sand, I sigh with contentment. I look back over my shoulder, seeing all four of them watching me, and attempt a smile. My feet move without command, drawing me closer to my favorite place. When I crest the small hill hiding the shoreline, I nearly cry. If it wouldn't hurt so bad, I'd run the rest of the way. When my feet connect with the waves, I bask in the calmness, feeling truly free for the first time since being found.

After a few minutes, I plop my butt in the sand, mindful of my injuries, and tilt my face toward the sun.

Chapter Eleven

Kash

I give Saylor a good ten minutes to herself before deciding she's had enough alone time. With my rations replenished, I head for the beach and my new best friend. She's sitting, her small form swallowed up by those hideous scrubs, while staring at the ocean. It's a pretty sight, but it's got nothing on her. I pull my phone from my shorts and snap a picture, wanting to capture the way the sun glints off her long blonde hair.

"Hi." I drop down, causing her to startle. It's not that I want to scare her, but I know firsthand what it feels like to jump at every little thing. There's no way past it, only through it. You've gotta grow used to sudden movement and noises, and that won't happen if everyone tiptoes around you all the time.

"Muffin?" I offer, tilting it toward her.

"Thanks."

Saylor takes tiny bites, chewing them slowly. I know Lochlan said she had to ease back into eating normally, but with the amount of sweets I keep on hand, I'll have some meat on her bones in no time. I stay quiet, not wanting to disrupt the peace she's found. I'm happy to just sit here and steal glances of the girl I never thought I'd get to meet in the flesh. It's surreal. I've spent too many nights to count wondering if Saylor was still out there, and if so, what god-awful shit was being done to her.

"Big fan of the ocean, huh?" I ask after a while, desperate to know more about her. The things only she can tell me, not what some file we've pieced together says.

"The beach, actually." She turns to me as she answers, her eyes so vivid in the sunlight. "I'm actually afraid of the ocean."

"You are?" I guess I thought the two were sort of synonymous.

"Yep." Saylor nods, swirling her finger in the sand. "It's huge and scary, and eighty percent of it has yet to be explored. Who knows what's down there? Makes you feel insignificant in comparison. Like a speck."

In no world, in any galaxy, could she ever be deemed insignificant.

"Could be that my dad died out there too," she adds hesitantly. I know this, but only the basics, and I'd rather hear the story from her.

"Yeah?"

"It was a boating accident. I was only four, so I have no memory of it. I barely remember him, much less the day he died. Mom said he'd gone out to fish, but he never came home. The boat was located the next day, but it was empty. There were traces of blood, so they think he slipped and hit his head, then went overboard." She stares at the water, like she's imagining what it would've been like. "They called the search off after day three."

"That must've been hard for you and your mom," I say sincerely, but she only shrugs.

"The few memories I have are vague, so I think I missed the idea of him more than anything. It was harder for Mom. She had to bury an empty casket, accepting that she would never have any real closure."

Shit, that's depressing.

"So, what about the beach makes you love it so much?" I ask, trying to steer us back to a happier topic.

"Everything." Saylor smiles, the sight making my chest squeeze. "The memories, mostly. Mom and I would spend every spare minute we could sprawled on oversized towels or building sandcastles. It's always been a happy place for me."

"Well, it's a good thing you've got unlimited access now." I bump her shoulder with mine. She watches me carefully but doesn't shrink away. "No swimming, then?" I gesture towards the waves.

"God, no," she shivers. "Pools are for swimming. We are *not* at the top of the food chain out there." I laugh, soaking up every bit of this girl I can get.

"My turn," I blurt, making her look at me in confusion. "If we're going to start this best friend thing off on the right foot, it's only fair that I tell you something I love and hate as well."

"Go on, then," Saylor encourages, a faint trace of amusement dancing in her eyes.

"Sugar," I declare. "Love it. Gotta have it. I'll take it in any form, even raw, straight from the canister." She nods, like that makes perfect sense and it's completely normal.

"And I *hate* creepy ass lizards and their slippery little bodies." I shiver like she did, but mine's more of a full-body convulsion.

"Hmm, not sure that one counts since I already knew about it," Saylor jokes, biting back a grin. Fuck, it feels good to be the one helping her escape for a while. I know it won't last, but she's okay right now, if only for the moment.

"You, my little Puddin'-Pop, are absolutely right." I boop her nose, causing her eyes to temporarily cross as she tries to follow the movement. I think I've stunned her, but I hammer on. "Let me expand upon that. My phobia actually lies with all things that aren't snuggly. You got a spider that needs to be squashed? I am *not* your man. If you see a snake, pretend you didn't and never, *ever* tell me about it. If it's an insect of any kind, I can offer you some bug spray, but that's about it. I will, however, bake you some kickass cupcakes." I spread my arms, wiggling my fingers as if to say, *'I'm a catch, huh?'*.

"That's..." Saylor pauses, contemplating her next words as she nibbles on her bottom lip. "That's okay. I can squash your spiders. And snakes? Never heard of 'em. Folklore, I'm sure. As for the bugs, we'll get a zapper, and if that doesn't work, you can hold the hairspray while I strike the match."

I think I just fell in love. Not in a sexual way. God, that's...not something Saylor's ready for just yet. But I'm ass over teakettle for who she is as a person. That's the purest fucking thing anyone's ever said to me, and I think she actually means it. Saylor's the kind of loyal that would risk life and limb to flame roast bugs with me. And if I'm anywhere near that catastrophe waiting to happen, you can bet your ass it'll involve bodily harm. In other words, she's a fucking keeper.

"Deal." I clear my throat of emotion, holding out my hand for her to shake. She wavers but takes it eventually. "Gotta say, Gumdrop. I think I came out on top with this arrangement."

"That's because you're under the impression that I can cook, when in reality, I burn water. I'm going to get cupcakes. That's a win no matter how you look at it." I laugh, rising to my feet when I notice she's preparing to get up. I offer her my hand, but she sucks in a sharp breath when I gently tug her forward. Trying a different route, Saylor moves to her knees first, then slowly gets her feet underneath her. I help keep her steady, but my free hand fists tighter with every pained exhale that leaves her lips. I know all too well how badly she's hurting right now.

I've got x-rays for days that paint a grim timeline of my years spent in hell. Some breaks were clean, while others never healed right because they weren't treated properly to begin with. My right shoulder dislocates far easier than it should from the numerous times it's been snapped out of place. But I'd still add to it, take on all of Saylor's pain, if I could.

"You okay?" I lean down so we're eye to eye.

"Yeah." She nods her head. "I just haven't had any pain medication today. We left the hospital really fast and it slipped my mind." *Fuck*. Her forgetting is one thing, but those two grown ass men know better. And they say I'm the one who doesn't take shit seriously.

"Alright, let's get you inside and drugged so good, you're counting unicorn farts within the hour." I keep my hand on her elbow, steering us toward the path of least resistance as we navigate the thick sand.

"Is there something special about these unicorns that would make me want to count their farts?" Saylor asks, likely to take her mind off the forty more feet we have to go.

"Oh, yeah. They also shit sparkles, but that's a different type of drug, meant for far different circumstances." She laughs, the sound short and sweet, but it hits me right in the feels. When we finally make it to the house, Saylor's panting and sweat dampens her skin. It's been a hot minute since she's been out in the sun. We should've had her put some SPF on. The temperature shift once we're inside is glorious. I walk us to the kitchen, get her seated on one of the barstools, and fix us both a glass of water. Loch and Ro come sauntering in a second later, and if looks could kill, they'd both drop like those bugs Saylor and I plan to barbeque.

"Has the heat made you ornery?" Roan, being the giant, annoying fucker he is, ruffles my hair as he walks by.

"No, the fact that Saylor hasn't had a single thing for pain today has me ornery," I snap, my glare dripping with accusation. They both look at each other, then me. And then back to each other once again.

"What the fuck," Roan demands, while Lochlan asks, "How the hell did we let that happen?" at the same time.

"It's okay," Saylor interrupts, her voice soft and unsure. "It was a crazy morning. No one's at fault." Not true, but I bite my tongue, not wanting to stress her out even more. Apparently, Lochlan has the same idea because he has the pills ready a second later. She needs to eat again if she's going to take those, so I get busy making us a grilled cheese.

"You've only got a few more in this bottle, so one of us will run out first thing tomorrow to get your refill," Loch tells her, watching as she pops them in her mouth and washes them down with the water I gave her. A couple minutes later, I'm plating a perfectly cooked cheese sandwich. I cut it in half, creating two triangles, and move to stand across from Saylor. Placing it on the counter between us, I give her a goofy grin.

"Whatcha say, Sugar-Britches? Wanna go halfsies?" I waggle my eyebrows. She rolls her eyes playfully but picks up her side as I pick up mine. We tap them together in a '*cheers*' motion before taking a bite.

Heaven. Gooey, cheesy heaven.

"Yum," Saylor moans, going in for more. I preen, happy I've contributed in some way. She ate that whole muffin earlier, without even noticing, and it looks like she's going to finish this off too. We'll be slinging back pizza in no time. Saylor thanks me as I rinse the empty plate of any crumbs and place it in the dishwasher. I'm just about to tell her it was no problem when Krew comes flying from our office, hollering for Loch.

"What's wrong?" Ro comes around the corner at the same time. Attached at the asshole, those two.

"Kade just came through the gate," Krew fires off quickly, tossing a bomb at our feet. It's silent for all of a second, then the panicking commences. Meltdowns are always better when we're together.

"Why the fuck is he so early?" I ask no one in particular.

"Because he probably switched his flight so he could get home sooner. I booked it for later to avoid this exact thing, but he's an impatient asshole and he hates California. I should've known he wouldn't stay there a second longer than he had to," Krew gripes while rubbing at his temples. The faint sound of the garage door clicking into place makes us all scatter.

"Come here, Saylor." Roan holds his hand out and guides her behind him. Her eyes are wide with worry.

This shouldn't be happening like this. We were

dumb as shit to not sit her down as soon as they got here so we could explain everything. When the door finally opens, we've formed a wall in front of Saylor, but it'll mean jack shit to Kade. He'd tear his own arm off to reach her, so there's no telling what the scrappy fucker will do to us.

Chapter Twelve

Kade

I've spent five hours on a plane and another two in my car. My ass stinks and I'm hungry as fuck. If Krew thought I was going to spend half my day lounging at the hotel until it was time for my flight, then I've been giving him too much credit in the brains department. And the dude's pretty fucking brilliant. There's no such thing as relaxing if I'm not in the comfort of my own home. I don't know if it was my constant complaining that had Loch calling me back early or something else, but I could kiss the motherfucker for letting me cut and run. These past three weeks have been hell.

The Vantworth assignment was garbage. For nearly a month, I've done nothing more than babysit some rockstar's spoiled, twat of a daughter. The hours that girl keeps are ridiculous, bouncing from one night club to the next. I never did the party thing, so maybe that's why my tolerance for her bullshit was at an all-time low. Who has that much energy? *Coke fiends, that's who.* All I want to do is fall face first into my fucking bed and sleep for a week straight.

Preferably after a hot shower.

Whatever perfume the brat wore is lingering like a bitch. I think it's attached itself to my clothing after being around her for weeks on end. I'll probably have to burn it all. Some days, I really question why I continue to put up with shit like this, but then I think of all I've gained and know I'd tolerate a hundred more Sabrina Vantworth's to keep living this life I've been given. For someone like me, I never dreamed I'd have people I could count on, much less consider family.

No one in my hometown of Pike's Bay ever thought I'd amount to anything. After all the hell I raised, I can't say I'm not shocked by my choice of job either. I've always been the person someone might need protection from, not the protector. When Loch and Ro came to town, I'd been one wrong move from landing myself a plot at the local cemetery. I'd been through some shit over the years, but I think I was at my absolute lowest the day I approached them.

And everything I have now is a product of my regret. The bank account that's no longer at risk of being in the negative, the buttery leather seats of my Audi, the family I've gained. Each one serves as a reminder that our actions have consequences. That there are no do-overs in life. So I spend my days trying to right my wrongs the only way I know how. I see her in every broken girl whose file comes across my desk. She's not just a part of my story, she's *the* story. It all began with her.

For so long, I tried to justify the things I did. I had a shit upbringing, blessed with parents who didn't give one iota about the kid they made. Their only concern was where they'd get their next fix and how they planned to pay for it. It made me an angry kid, so in turn, I took my own issues out on people who were weaker than me. Specifically, one pixie of a girl, with golden blonde hair and magnetic blue eyes.

Saylor Radley.

Just thinking her name makes my stomach twist. It sends a jolt through my body so powerful, my heart forgets the proper way to beat. She was an easy target; the girl who had it all. I'd crawl into bed at night, after searching our cabinets for something —*anything*— to fill my stomach, and let my mind wander. It was the only time I'd allow myself to hope for something more. And then I'd shut that shit down and accept those thoughts for what they were—fantasies.

Saylor had the life I wanted and I hated her for it. Only now, I realize it was never *hate* that I felt. I was just fucking jealous. Her mom would pack her a lunch every day, with little notes hidden inside for her to find, and mine screamed at me for daring to eat the last few stale crackers when I'd been starving. She was carefree and ignorant of the real world. She got to be a kid while I had to grow up way too fast and fend for myself.

I wanted her to feel the way I felt. So I did everything I could to darken Saylor's pristine little world. In grade school, I'd yank her pigtails and trip her on the playground. She'd never rat me out though, even when I'd get caught. Saylor would come up with some reason or another for why she was sprawled in the dirt that wouldn't implicate me. Every single time. She never fought back or mouthed off, and it infuriated me.

By the time we got to middle school, I'd grown fond of verbal taunting. I'd cut Saylor down with my biting words and hateful rumors. I teased her relentlessly, but she never caved. I tried so hard to bury that day, to push it from my goddamn mind, but it wouldn't let me go. It was the first time I'd ever seen a visible crack in the mask she wore. She put on a brave face, acting like my bullshit didn't bother her, but not that day. She wasn't quite so successful in hiding her hurt, and it didn't feel nearly as good as I thought it would.

Saylor's eyes had filled with tears, those crystal orbs betraying her as she fought tooth and nail to appear unaffected. The things I'd said, on the front lawn of the school with everyone watching, will haunt me for the rest of my life. She'd embarrassed me, so I was ruthless with my words. I let her walk away, knowing she missed her bus, and I can never take that back. That's the last time anyone saw Saylor.

At first, I wondered if she'd simply run away. If maybe she was fed up with being treated like shit. But then the days turned into weeks, and the weeks into months, and I knew it went beyond her bully fucking with her head. I joined every search party the town organized. Hell, I even got her picture from the school's website, printed off copies at the library, and slapped a missing sign on every light pole in Laiken County.

I felt personally responsible for Saylor's disappearance. And why shouldn't I? If I hadn't caused her to miss the bus, she wouldn't have been walking to begin with. At bare minimum, I could have made sure she got home safely. But I didn't, and the regret of that is immeasurable. My mom named me Havok for a reason, though. Apparently, I came into the world and fucked everything up the moment I took my first breath. I reckon I haven't stopped since.

The years that followed were dark. I spun even further out of control, lashing out at anyone who so much as looked at me the wrong way. And God help the poor fucker who dared to speak the name Saylor Radley. Everyone in Pike's Bay knew not to breathe a word of her around me. My teenage years were one for the books. I had my ass thrown in a holding cell more times than I can count for sticking my nose where it didn't belong.

I became obsessed with finding out what happened to her. The men whose jobs I was interfering with didn't appreciate that too much, but I wanted answers. It was stupid to think I could figure out what no one else had been able to, including the FBI, but I couldn't let it go. Eventually, I approached Saylor's mom. That was akin to having my knees taken out with a sledgehammer. It knocked me on my ass to see how alike they were. I never expected it, but we grew close. And then I lost her too.

But Lochlan came along, offering me a job, after I had all but accosted him and demanded he take on Saylor's case. It'd been a complete accident that our paths crossed. Then we found that picture, and it's felt like I've been living on borrowed time ever since. I try to avoid these fucked up trips down memory lane, knowing they usually conclude with a three-day bender I can't afford. It's a rabbit hole, and once I'm in, it requires a heavy dose of Prozac to climb back out.

When the driveway comes into view, my mood is even worse than it was. I could go for a pint of whiskey, but a beer will suffice. The gate slides open easily and I creep down the long gravel drive. I wish Loch would give in and have the damn thing paved already. Not all of us drive tanks. When the garage closes behind me, I cut the engine, feeling ten pounds lighter already. I really hope Kash has been in one of his baking frenzies. I've been living off of microwave dinners for far too long.

I shove the door open, dropping my shit to the floor as soon as I'm inside. My keys are tossed on the entry table, though Loch will probably bitch about that later. It takes me off guard when I look up and see the guys standing there, their faces all showing various degrees of concern. All I can think is '*what the ever-loving fuck has happened now?*'. I love these assholes, they're family, after all, but there's not a chance in hell I'm heading out again on some bullshit assignment before I've even unpacked from the last one.

"The fuck are y'all standing there like that for?" My head jerks back with the question. The way they're lined up like they're headed to battle puts me on edge.

"Kade, I need you to stay calm, mate." I snort. Our supreme leader is clearly feeling flustered. He only throws around his English words when he's worked up or nervous.

"Your British is showing, *mate*," I throw back, amused but also wary. There's this morsel of dread in my gut, but it's steadily growing the longer they drag this out...whatever *this* is. I'm half a second from saying fuck it and walking away when Loch says something that stops me dead in my tracks.

"It's Saylor," he rushes out, causing my blood to run cold. "We got a lead early Monday morning. A location."

"Where?" I croak, pushing back the acid sitting heavy in my throat.

"Lyola."

One word. *One fucking word* makes the room sway. I throw my hand out and clutch the counter. There's a roaring in my ears, as if my mind is screaming. I was just thinking about her ten minutes ago. How's that possible? It's like I conjured this moment into being. Or maybe it was a premonition. But it's all wrong. The outcome. The answers. How the fuck was she so close this whole time?

"Did you find..." my voice cracks, but I push on, "a body?" The question tastes like ash on my tongue, bitter and final. Loch's lips press together, his eyes full of emotion as he gives me a small shake of his head. My breath whooshes out of me, because if they didn't recover anything, then there's still a chance she's out there. Before I can ask anything else, Roan pulls a girl from behind his back like he's performing a goddamn magic trick.

My heart's still beating off-key as I take her in. She's tiny. In both height and weight. She's also hurt, judging by the splint on her wrist and the bruises marking her body. It's a horribly inappropriate thought, but fuck she's beautiful. Long blonde hair. Striking blue eyes. My brain stutters, like it's trying to tell me something. *No way*. My eyes are playing tricks on me. They have to be.

"*Saylor*?" My disbelief is evident.

She stares back at me, her small nose scrunched as she valiantly tries to figure out how the hell she knows me. But she does. Some part of her recognizes me and my fucking soul sings. Why isn't she saying anything? Shit, what if she can't talk? Like maybe she regressed from the years of school she missed. I'm vaguely aware that I'm verbalizing these thoughts, in the shittiest way possible, I might add. Fairly certain I use the word '*illiterate*'.

Saylor's eyes widen, my name slipping from her lips as she stumbles back. *Fuck me*. That sweet, innocent voice hasn't changed at all. It's really her. A pitiful laugh tumbles out of me as my eyes fill with tears. I lunge forward to wrap my arms around her, but I only have a second to savor the feeling before she squeals and Roan pulls her away.

The guys are yelling at me, but it's all white noise. I'm not actually hearing anything they say. I haven't even processed what just happened, still standing there like a gaping goldfish, but Ro is kneeled in front of Saylor, whispering reassurances. Kash—goofy, sweet Kash—looks like he's going to pluck my eyeballs out with a dirty pair of tweezers. *And enjoy it*. But I'm more fixated on the way my gruff and hard ass friend has been brought to his knees—literally—

by the pint-sized girl I can't take my eyes off of.

Is she really here?

That thought evaporates in the next second, when Roan turns to me with murder in his eyes. I raise my hands and take a step back, knowing he could put me on my ass if he wanted to. He stalks forward, rage twisting his features, and I'm the sole recipient.

"Are you fucking stupid?" he seethes. My own anger starts to build, more at myself than him. It's obvious I fucked up, but so did they. I just walked into an emotional ambush that they've all known about since *Monday*. Yet no one thought to give me a heads up. From the corner of my eye, I can see Saylor trembling on the couch. It makes me want to kick my own ass.

"Back up, asshole." My voice is cold. The last thing I want to do is throw down with him right now, but I'm feeling a thousand different things at once and his alpha male bullshit isn't helping.

"Enough." Lochlan pushes us apart. We're both breathing heavily and glaring at each other like two catty high school girls. "We have a whole heap of shit to discuss, so if the two of you could put your dicks away for the time being, that'd be bloody fantastic." Fuck, he really is wound tight. Ro and I put some distance between us, but I keep the keyed up giant in my periphery.

"Kash, could you help Saylor get settled? Her meds should be kicking in soon. I'm sure she's tired," Lochlan asks.

"Sound good to you, Best Friend?" Kash looks at

Saylor, waiting to see what she wants to do. She nods, but he approaches her slowly, aware of the cornered animal look she's sporting. More like an abused one that's been held in captivity. I swallow hard and look away, refusing to let those thoughts take root. She's here now. *Alive*. Whatever else happened, we can work through it.

And best friend? I think not, Sir Fuckwad.

The two of them leave, my eyes drinking in every inch of her. It takes herculean effort not to follow, but I've got questions, and these assholes have a lot to fucking answer for.

"Care to explain?" I lean against the wall with my arms crossed.

"I didn't know what we were walking into, Kade," Lochlan sighs. "The last thing I wanted to do was get your hopes up for nothing."

"Right." I nod in agreement, his reasoning sound. "And when you realized it *was* something? Or how about day two or three? What about then? What's your excuse for sitting on the one thing you know that I, above anyone else, deserved to fucking know?" My voice grows with each question, until I'm flat-out yelling.

"Does it matter? It wasn't justifiable. Regardless of how I try to paint it in my mind, it was wrong of me to keep you away." He looks ashamed—as he fucking should.

"You're damn right it was wrong," I sneer. "If it wasn't for me, none of you would even have a connection to Saylor. I'm ground zero, asshole! *Me*,

Loch." I slap my chest to emphasize my point, my anger so strong it's taking every bit of restraint I have to keep my fist from greeting his face.

"I know that!" Loch growls. "If I had told you, you'd have thrown protocol to the wayside and flipped your middle finger at the job you were tasked with. It could've put our client at risk, not to mention the blowback to SOTERIA. I made the right call professionally, but not personally. That's on me. I got you out of there as soon as I secured other arrangements for the Vantworth's."

"So you thought you'd just surprise the both of us?" I throw my hands up. "Because it looked like Saylor had no fucking clue that I'd be here."

"That's why I booked your flight for later, you prick." Krew glares at me. "We planned to tell her before you got here."

Well, that's what happens when you keep secrets.

"There's a lot we haven't told Saylor," Roan chimes in. "She knows her mom died because some asshole cop blurted it out, but she's yet to ask *how* it happened. I think she's aware of how fragile she is at the moment, so she's choosing to stay in the dark for now."

"Start at the beginning." I kick my boots off and take a seat on the couch. "Where'd you find her? How'd you find her? I wanna know everything."

"For the past five years, Saylor has been held against her will by Liam Price," Loch states. I stand back up, the uptick in my heartrate verging on stroke-level.

"I'm sorry, did you just say Liam Price? As in, *Sheriff Liam Price*?" My blood turns to pure, molten lava. Loch nods grimly and I absolutely lose it. "Fuck," I roar, my fist connecting with the wall.

"Kade," Loch warns, glancing towards the hallway.

"You don't understand," I snap, pacing around the living room. "He put me in a fucking jail cell, Loch. Accused me of hindering an investigation. I personally went to every business between the school and Saylor's house and asked if they had security cameras, and if they did, I begged them to let me watch everything they had from that day. Price insisted they'd already gone through it all and there was nothing worth noting. But it was just to steer me away. This whole time, I'd been so fucking close." I drag my hands through my hair, tugging at the ends in frustration.

"How the hell were we so wrong? Where does the picture we found fit into this?" My thoughts are bouncing all over the place.

"We don't know yet," Loch admits. "Liam's computer is currently being analyzed. Denvers is hoping to have some answers within the next few days."

"And Liam?" I question, hoping someone put a bullet through his skull.

"He's MIA. Hasn't been seen since last Friday," Roan sneers.

"You," Kash spits the second he clears the hallway. "Her ribs are bruised, you fucktard." He looks

downright scary, but Krew throws his arm out and keeps him from getting any closer. I'll still lock my bedroom door tonight, just in case.

"Shit." I cringe, the thought of causing her pain making me sick. I've hurt Saylor in ways I'll never be able to make up for, but the man I am now wouldn't harm a hair on her head. At least not intentionally. "I obviously didn't know that."

"She's taking a bath right now." Kash smiles. "I thought she was going to cry when I showed her the jets." He shakes his head sadly. "The shit we take for granted is a luxury to her. That girl deserves the world, and I don't know about you guys, but I plan to do everything I can to give it to her." He's so fucking gone already. A haze of red coats my vision, but I bite back the threat I wanna make.

"I think we can all agree that we should do whatever's needed to make Saylor as comfortable as possible," Loch placates. "We'll have to come clean about everything soon, but I also think we should establish some ground rules." I cock my head to the side, curious to hear what he's thinking.

"First of all, we've never had a woman here. Ever. So, I think it should go without saying that we need to avoid walking around half-naked. No more midnight snack runs to the kitchen in our underwear." Loch looks pointedly at Kash, who meets his stare without an ounce of shame. "No blatantly adjusting our dicks or any other disgusting shit we like to do."

"Farts are a normal bodily function." Kash

sniffs haughtily, slipping back into the jokester role seamlessly. I think we all roll our eyes.

"Saylor's gone five years without any sort of affection." Loch barrels on, ignoring Kash completely. "Touching is iffy for her. Though, she has allowed Ro and me a bit of contact."

"Me too," Kash adds, making me jealous when I have no fucking right to be.

"He..." Loch stops, needing to clear his throat. "Liam didn't rape her, but she was definitely sexually assaulted. That's all I'm going to say on the matter, and only because I think you should be aware of what triggers she might have. A simple sex scene in a movie could send her to a dark place. Just be conscious of the things you say and do. Allow her to be the one to initiate contact, but at bare minimum, give her the choice to decline."

I'm relieved, but shocked. I expected worst case scenario, and now I feel guilty for being glad that it only went so far. It was traumatizing, regardless of the extent, and I wish more than anything that Liam never laid his eyes on her. I've worked assault cases before, but this is personal. It's Saylor. I won't be able to detach emotionally if I see her breaking. I wish I could fast forward and skip all the hard moments, but life doesn't work that way.

"Let's get some sleep." Loch stands, gesturing toward our bedrooms. I head for my bags, feeling beat as fuck. It's barely six o'clock but we all seem eager for an early night.

"One last thing," Ro adds, rapping his knuckles

on the wall. "Keep a light on out here. Saylor hates the dark."

Chapter Thirteen

Saylor

After Kash leaves, I lock the bedroom door behind him and shuffle back to the bathroom. The water is running and filling the tub, but I take a second to look beneath the sink to see if there's any bubble bath by chance. My jaw drops at what I find. There are neat rows of varying products —lotions, body wash, sugar scrubs—everything you could possibly think of. My hand trembles as I reach out and pick one up, giving it a thorough examination. It's like I've never seen soap before.

I check the drawers next, blinking at the items piled inside. There's a brush, leave-in conditioner, hair-ties and clips. So many things, I can't seem to focus on just one. A brand-new straightener sits in the middle one. I trace my finger across the packaging, completely lost for words. In the bottom drawer, I find something that makes my eyes sting. There's an entire feminine aisle in there.

Everything a girl could possibly need—pads of every kind, tampons in all sizes and brands, Midol, even a pack of mini Hershey's. Right at my fingertips.

This is clearly Kash's doing. He didn't know what I'd like, so he bought it all. I wipe a tear away, aware that my bath water is dangerously close to overrunning. I close the drawer and turn it off, contemplating how I'm going to get myself undressed.

Bending at the waist, I use my bad wrist to avoid straining my ribs and grab the back of the top from over my shoulder. I wiggle it off, sighing in relief when I'm met with little to no pain. The scrub bottoms are much easier, and then I take my brace off and place it on the counter. I don't want to, but I glance up and take in the state of my naked body. It's like a car wreck you can't look away from. You're curious, so your eyes are drawn to the sight. But you're also wary, because there's a good chance you'll see something you don't want to.

I didn't even look this bad after being in an actual wreck. My ribcage is mottled with purple and black bruising. The rest of me isn't much better. I'm too thin. My breasts have grown since I was fourteen, but I doubt they're bigger than a B-cup. It's hard not to wonder what I'd look like if I was still the Saylor from before Liam Price got his hands on me. I take a deep breath, and grab a scrub and body wash from the stockpile.

Once my body is fully submerged in the gloriously hot water, I groan loudly. After you've been deprived of something for so long, you kind of forget how great it is. It's probably the brain's way of maintaining sanity. We talk it down, that thing we loved so much, like it's no big deal that we can't have it anymore. Eventually, we crave it less because it's no longer a part of our new normal. But as I sit here, covered to my chin in bubbles, I'm not sure how I ever made it five years with only a rusted sink.

I rub the body wash over my skin, pausing when I see the hair on my legs. *That's embarrassing*. I'd just started shaving the summer before eighth grade. I was a late bloomer, and my hair was fair so it never bothered me. But it wasn't something I kept up with while being held against my will, fearing that every new day would be my last. Not to mention, the razor I'd been so graciously given was old and clearly used. I was scared I'd cut myself and catch something, so it was rarely put to use. Plus, I'd done everything I could to make myself as unappealing as possible. Little good it did.

I pull myself up, dripping water all over the marble tiles, and rummage through the bag of things Karley gave me. One of the guys must have placed it in here while I was at the beach. I find the razor and shaving cream, and slip back in the tub. Ridding my body of hair seems like it should be the least of my worries right now, but I feel dirty. I think I'll always feel this sense of being unclean. There are parts of Liam I won't be able to wash away. They won't fade like the bruises will. Nothing short of a time machine can undo the damage in my head.

I lather my legs and run the fresh blade across my skin, hissing at the few nicks I get. I shave the rest of my body, drain the dirty water, and then refill it. I turn the jets on the way Kash showed me and let my head rest against the edge of the tub. With my eyes closed, my thoughts turn to the thing I've been avoiding for the past hour. Or person, I should say.

Havok McKade.

I don't understand how or why he's here, but it's obvious he knows the men I'm now living with. That he's a part of this group they've created. It makes no sense, and he's the last person in the world I imagined I'd ever see again. To be honest, I assumed everything I left back in Pike's Bay was now a part of the past. From the second we left town this morning, I knew I'd never go back there. There's way too much bad associated with that place for me to ever consider it home again. I have no idea what will happen or where I'll go from here, when it's safe for me to leave, but it won't be anywhere near Laiken County.

I feel tricked, though. They're obviously aware that Havok and I know each other, yet didn't bother to mention that he'd be here. If they know anything about our history, then I'm sure that was intentional. If I had known that he would be involved, I never would have agreed to come here. Lochlan said I'd be safe with them, but I can honestly say that Havok has never once elicited that feeling from me. Even stranger, is the way he behaved.

I've felt anger from him. Envy. Annoyance. *Hatred*. But never has he looked at me the way he did earlier. He seemed relieved, almost happy. To see me, the girl he made a sport out of taunting and ridiculing. But that would be absurd. Havok made it known, in many ways, that he would never like me, though I'd never done a damn thing to warrant his disdain. I have no idea what I ever did to him, and I probably never will, because I plan to avoid him like the plague.

He hugged me.

I'm not sure if my yelp came from shock or the flare of pain it caused in my side. I hadn't even recognized him at first. There was something niggling my brain, but it was my body's response that was the most telling. My spine had tingled in warning, and when he casually insulted me in that way he's perfected over the years, I knew exactly who I was looking at. But gone was the boy I remembered. Havok's hair is silver now, a shock from the near black it naturally is, and his tanned skin is covered in colorful tattoos. He hasn't grown much in height, still hovering around six feet, but he's filled out everywhere else.

He was lanky growing up, and I'd always wondered if that was his natural build or if it'd been a result of his circumstances. I knew he didn't have the best home life. His clothes were always worn and baggy, even on the first day of school when everyone else was sporting new outfits and shoes. Havok is two years older than me, but I had been drawn to him from the moment I first saw him. I'd just started Kindergarten, while he was in second grade. My recess overlapped with his P.E. class, and on occasion they would be on the field that butted against the playground.

Havok was always angry, and for some reason, that bothered me. I didn't like to see other people upset. The day I tried to play with him, was the day he decided to hate me. I've never been the type of person who could brush off not being liked. I want to understand what I did wrong, if I said something rude. So I tried, over and over again, to make nice with him, but it always backfired. It's pathetic of me, but once upon a time, I had a crush on Havok. I naively thought I could fix the broken boy with ice in his eyes, but he proved he never needed saving, and certainly not from me.

The water's barely warm when I turn the jets off and wrap a towel around my body. My fingers and toes are pruned so badly they resemble an eighty-year-olds, but it was worth it. I head to the closet, my eyes scanning the new clothes apprehensively. I feel guilty that Kash went to all the trouble of getting me this stuff. It couldn't have been cheap. I check the built-in chest of drawers for pajamas, but the contents of the first drawer make me pause.

I can feel heat flaming my cheeks as I pull out a pair of panties, one of many, noting the price tag still attached. '*Tuesday*' is embroidered across the front. I grab another pair, baby pink boy shorts, then yank out a lacy red thing that makes me choke on air. It's like Kash decided he'd get a smorgasbord of underwear the way he did the bath and body products. I check the next drawer, discovering a row of bras. They also vary in style and color, and when I check the sizing, I groan, completely mortified. The measurements are spot on.

My shame only grows when I realize I've been around them all day, Lochlan and Roan even longer, without having worn one. Mine was taken the first time Liam ripped my clothes from my body, never to be seen again. I shudder, having to close my eyes and remind myself of where I am. Better yet, where I'm *not*. I quickly look through the other drawers, finding several sets of pajamas. Pulling out a soft cream-colored top and matching shorts, I push the door closed on the closet. Even though my room is locked, it doesn't feel right to dress out in the open.

A laugh burst out of me, the ease of it shocking. I guess Roan was right to question Kash, because plastered to the back of my closet door is a Justin Bieber poster. It's older, from when I was a fan. I doubt the singer still looks the same now. I spend a good five minutes trying to dress myself, a smile tugging at my lips the entire time, and then retreat to the bathroom. I hang my wet towel and slip the brace back over my wrist. It hasn't bothered me too much, only when I twist it a certain way, so maybe I won't have to wear it for too long. I quickly brush my teeth and climb into bed.

I'm exhausted, and I hope between the pain pills and extra-long bath, I'll be able to sleep through the night. I'm nervous for tomorrow. To be around the guys again after feeling like they deliberately kept something from me in order to sway my decision. I've been living in this place of ignorance, by my own choosing, since I found out about Mom. But I need to suck it up and face reality. The answers aren't going to change, no matter how long I put off asking them.

I glance at the door, double checking that the lock is still in place. I feel safe here, but my trust is fragile, and it makes me feel better to know that no one can barge in unannounced. With the light from my closest casting a faint glow around the room, I slowly drift away in the softest bed I've ever slept on.

I jerk awake, my skin slick with sweat and breathing ragged. I can't remember what I was dreaming about, but I know it wasn't anything good. There's an icky feeling coating my body, making me want to rinse off again. I flop against the mound of pillows and will the moment to pass. Thirty minutes later and it's still dark outside, but I can't get back to sleep. My throat is so dry I could drain a well. I debate going in search of something, but I'm nervous to leave my room in the middle of the night. This isn't my house and I feel awkward roaming around as if it is. Ultimately, I opt to tiptoe and pray that I don't wake anyone.

My bare feet hit the cool floor and I shiver. The sound of my lock clicking over is extra loud in the otherwise quiet, making me pause. I open the door just enough to slip my head out. There's no one around, not that I really expected there to be. With careful steps, I navigate the darkened hallway. It isn't pitch black, but I'm not familiar enough with the layout of everything to know if I'll bump into something. Sliding my fingers along the wall, I use it as a guide until I turn the corner down the main hall.

The closer I get to the end, the more visible everything is, which makes sense when I see that the kitchen light has been left on. The next thing I notice is that the refrigerator door is open, making my steps stutter. As if summoned, the person bent behind it rises and looks directly at me. I hadn't made a sound, but he seems keenly aware of my arrival.

"Hi," Krew whispers. I wave, swallowing past

the lump in my throat. His expression is blank, giving no indication of what he's thinking. I worry I've crossed a line, impeded a boundary I'm unaware of but should somehow be obvious. Like *'don't go traipsing around a house that isn't yours'*.

"Everything okay?" he asks, his tone completely neutral.

I nod, then pluck some bravery from thin air and say, "Could I have some water, please?" Krew blinks, my question going unanswered for several awkward seconds.

"Of course, you can, Saylor." He nods for me to take a seat at the island, so I comply and shuffle forward. Krew grabs a glass and places it beneath the water dispenser on the fridge. Sliding it over, he watches as I drain half of it in one go.

"For future reference, you don't need to ask for anything."

He spins around, giving his attention to the spread of food laying on the counter. I watch as he takes a bagel, slices it in half, and lathers both sides in cream cheese. He sprinkles on some cinnamon sugar before popping them in a toaster oven. As he clears away the mess and puts the food back where it goes, I discreetly observe the man I know the least about.

He's different from his twin. Kash is relaxed and approachable, where Krew is standoffish. He's guarded, but not in a rude way. Like he wants to reserve judgment until he knows you better, but until then he has no opinion of you—good or bad. I have a feeling that's my current categorization, but I find no fault in that logic.

The toaster dings and Krew places each bagel half onto a plate, then pulls a jar of honey from their spice cabinet and drizzles some over both pieces. Once he's finished, he places a slice in front of me and leans against the counter. I take a small bite, not wanting to be rude, but I'm surprised to find I actually like it. Krew eats his portion way faster than I do, never speaking a word, but he patiently waits for me to finish.

"You won't always have them," he states out of nowhere, rinsing our plates in the process. I scrunch my nose in confusion. "The nightmares," he clarifies. "That's what woke you, right?" I debate answering because, honestly, I'm not sure.

"I think so, but I don't remember any of it. It was a feeling more than anything," I answer quietly. Krew nods, like that makes perfect sense.

"They fade with time, but there's a good chance you'll never be completely rid of them. When you feel safe again, sleep won't be as difficult to come by. At least, that's how it was for me." He shrugs, like it's no big deal for him to disclose something so personal. "I'm gonna catch a few hours of sleep before this place comes alive. Fair warning, Kash is one of those elusive morning people, so beware. He tends to get restless when he's the only up, and he has no qualms with waking the whole house if it means he doesn't have to be alone." I smile, picturing a fidgety Kash, pacing the floors as he waits for the rest of the guys to finish up their beauty rest.

“Thank you for the food,” I voice softly as he turns to walk away. “Goodnight, Krew.”

“Night, Tink,” he calls over his shoulder, disappearing down the hallway a second later.

Chapter Fourteen

Saylor

"Best Friend."

I bury my face against the softness it's resting on, intent on ignoring the incessant whispering that keeps trying to drag me from the best sleep I've had in years.

"Best Friend..." The voice prods again, slightly louder this time but still somewhat muffled.

"Saylor."

My name is spoken clear as day, the person's tone comically deeper this time. I blink through the sunlight streaming through my window, struggling to sit up as I wipe the drool from my mouth. It was close to four in the morning when I finally climbed back into bed after my impromptu snack and chat with Krew. It didn't take long for me to crash, and it's obvious I slept like the dead.

"Um...just a sec," I force out, my voice raspy and dry.

I peel the covers off and slowly slip from the bed. It sits higher off the ground than the one I had at

Mom's, and with my body still so sore, it makes getting in and out of it a little more difficult. I grab a bra from the closet, not wanting to make things awkward for myself or the guys. It takes me two seconds to realize that there's no way I'm going to get this thing on by myself, and even if I could, the tightness of the band would kill my ribs. I worry my lip, looking over the two rows of clothes for something extra baggy, but nothing catches my eye.

"Best Friend," Kash whines, because who else could it possibly be, sounding as if his face is smooshed against the jam of the door. I move to open it but keep myself concealed as much as possible.

"Hi," I greet softly, causing the man to stumble forward.

"Oh, goody, you're awake," Kash jokes, as if he isn't the sole reason that I am. I roll my eyes playfully, an act that feels foreign, but good at the same time. "I made breakfast."

"Okay." I nod, happy to join him, because it's clear that Krew was right about his brother's need for company. "Can I ask you a favor, though?"

"'Course you can, Sugar Plum." He steps back, his face open and earnest.

"Do you have a sweatshirt I can borrow? I don't want to make things weird for anyone, but I can't wear a bra right now." I think I'm as shocked as Kash is that I managed to articulate my problem so bluntly, but he makes it easy to open up and say what I'm feeling. And it doesn't hurt that he's the one who went and bought it all, so if I have to bring this up with someone, it might as well be the guy who picked said garments out.

"You got it. Be right back," he calls as he walks away. In less than a minute, he returns, handing me a gray sweatshirt.

I politely excuse myself, leaving Kash to wait in the hall, then head to the bathroom. I take care of business, wash my hands and brush my teeth, then toss on the sweater. I snort when I see my reflection. It's practically a dress on me. You can't even tell that I'm wearing shorts beneath it. The image on the front of it makes me smile, though. *Pooh*, the honey-loving bear, is dressed in fatigues, a rifle slung over his shoulder, with *Winnie the Pew* written in the signature character font. From what little I know of him, I'm not surprised in the least that this is something Kash would own.

I grab some socks, the fuzziest pair I can find, and open the door. Kash is casually leaning against the opposite wall, beside Havok's door, not nearly as restless as he was when he'd been whisper-yelling my name just a bit ago. He smiles, big and uninhibited, as he looks me over. I likely resemble a child playing dress up, but beggars can't be choosers.

"Thank you." I motion toward his sweatshirt, giving him a grateful smile.

"No worries. You can raid my closet anytime, Best Friend." He winks playfully and pushes away from the wall. "Come on. Let's go eat before those other assholes wake up and pounce like vultures." Kash extends his hand, and even though it confuses me, I take it.

We're going to the kitchen, so it's not like I could get lost on the way and require an escort. But it feels nice to touch another human being. His skin is soft and warm, and there's no harshness to the way he's holding me. He steers me to a barstool and helps me up, my toes barely grazing the footrest once I'm seated. I think everything in this house is built for giants.

Kash buzzes around like a ball of energy, pulling food from the oven, where he must have left it to warm, and orange juice from the fridge. He takes a plate from the stack he's already laid out and begins to fill it. There's a slice of bacon, eggs, toast, and half a pancake placed in front of me by a happy Kash, grinning proudly for a job well done. I smile, or try to, feeling overwhelmed by the amount of food and the expectation I feel to eat it all so he won't be disappointed.

"Morning," Havok grumbles, sauntering into the kitchen with a slight scowl on his face. "Just to be clear, you suck at whispering." He shoulders past Kash, going straight for the coffee maker.

"Well, I can't be good at everything, that wouldn't be fair to the rest of the world," Kash retorts, hiding his smirk around a mouthful of over-syruped pancake. He looks at my untouched food, then back at me, so I tentatively bite into the toast.

"Good?" Kash asks, arching an eyebrow curiously. I nod and take a drink of the OJ he poured me. Havok hits the button to brew his coffee and then tilts his head, watching me so intensely it makes me squirm. The only attention I've ever received from him has been swiftly followed by a cutting remark, leading to my inevitable humiliation, so it's logical to assume that's where this is headed.

"No, she does *not* find it good," Havok states calmly, taking a sip of his hot bean water. Completely black, I might add. He must like it to match the color of his cold, dead heart. I feel guilty the second I let the thought form, knowing I'm not the kind of person to judge so callously, nor do I want to be. Especially when a part of me has always felt there was something more to the brooding boy who insisted on bullying me every chance he could.

"What?" Kash looks at him in confusion.

"Saylor likes her bacon crunchy, almost to the point of being burnt. And she doesn't eat eggs." I gape at Havok's reply, wondering how the hell he knows those things. "She won't tell you that herself because she's a people pleaser and doesn't want to hurt your feelings." I can feel my cheeks redden with embarrassment as Kash swings his head back around to focus on me.

"Is that true?" he asks, but there's no hint of anger, just genuine curiosity.

"I...I'm sorry," I stumble over my words. "I didn't want to make it a thing after you were nice enough to cook." I could throttle Havok. In my mind, I've kicked him no less than ten times. From the corner of my eye, I see him smirk, as if he knows exactly what I'm thinking and finds it amusing.

"Saylor," Kash says my name softly, moving to stand beside me. He spins the barstool so I'm facing him and takes my hand in his. "If there's something you don't like, we want to know. This is your house too. I swear, nothing you say or do could ever make me upset. I'd feel worse knowing that you ate something just to appease me than if you threw it in my face and said it tasted like Kade's dirty socks." His eyes shine with humor at my scrunched nose. I could've done without the example, but I feel the tension begin to dissipate.

"I'll try to speak up next time," I offer, but history would prove me a liar. Making unnecessary waves is not my forte.

"Good." Kash boops me on the nose, just like he did at the beach yesterday, and takes my food back. I watch as he scoops up my bacon and places it back in a skillet. He cooks it until it's perfectly crunchy, then scrapes my eggs onto Havok's plate. When he brings my breakfast back to me, I'm fighting the urge to cry. I didn't have to ask him to do any of it, he just did. Because he *wanted* to. I give Kash a watery smile, hoping he can sense how much his kindness means to me.

"Oooh!" Kash's fork clanks as he drops it, breaking the silence we'd formed while eating. "I have an idea." He opens a drawer, digging around for a second before he pulls out a small notepad and pen.

"Let's make a list." I watch as he scrawls my name at the top, then adds '*likes*' and '*dislikes*' beneath it. "Crunchy bacon goes here," Kash declares, the tip of his tongue poking out in concentration. "And eggs over here." They're placed in their respective columns, and then the paper is tucked beneath a magnet on the fridge. I blink at it, a mixture of emotions bubbling to the surface.

"We'll leave this here, so if there's something you want us to know, or we should know and you don't feel comfortable outright saying it, you can just add it to the list." Kash goes back to eating, completely unaware of how sweet and thoughtful his gesture is. It takes me a little longer to sort myself out, but I eventually refocus on my plate.

"Morning." Lochlan and Roan step from the hallway, both looking more rested after a good night's sleep. I bite into my bacon, groaning at the crispy goodness. Four sets of eyes watch me as I shovel the whole strip down, barely savoring the taste. Kash spins around and adds stars beside crunchy bacon on my '*likes*' list, then proceeds to underline it. Twice. I laugh, shaking my head at the man as he adds more syrup to his already sopping stack of pancakes.

"You do realize that the syrup didn't disappear, right? It just got soaked up." His finger lands over my lips as he shushes me. Lochlan stiffens, watching me for any sign of distress. I'm amused more than anything, because, as I'm quickly learning, Kash has no sense of boundaries. He's like an overactive puppy who needs constant attention.

"We don't discuss those sorts of things over breakfast, Saylor. It's impolite. I like to save all the diabetes and cholesterol talk for my annual check-up with the doctor," Kash states, sounding dramatically serious.

"Right." I nod, playing along. "Hear no evil, see no evil, speak no evil."

"Exactly!" He snaps his fingers and points at me. "If we don't acknowledge it, it doesn't exist. You just get me, Snickerdoodle." Kash braces his elbows on the counter, his chin resting in his hands, and flutters his eyelashes at me. I look at the other three, wondering if they see the crazy too, or if they've just grown so used to it that they no longer notice. They roll their eyes, but it's clear as day they have a soft spot for Kash and his theatrics.

"Saylor, are you up for having a talk with us this morning?" Lochlan asks, changing the conversation and overall mood of the room.

"Sure," I respond, hoping the slight shake in my voice isn't too noticeable.

Roan gathers the dirty dishes, waving off my offer to help. Before I know it, we're seated in the living room and Krew has joined us. I take one corner of the sectional, while Roan grabs the middle. Lochlan is across from me on the opposite side and the twins are lounging on the floor. Havok chooses to lean against the wall closest to me, his arms crossed and face hard. My palms are damp from nervousness and I can't quit toying with a loose string on Kash's sweatshirt.

"First off, I'd like to say how sorry we are for what happened yesterday. It was never our intention to keep Kade a secret. We had planned to explain everything before he got here," Lochlan admits. "We met three years ago, when Ro and I were in Pike's Bay for a different assignment. Kade approached us and asked for help with your case."

"More like demanded," Krew scoffs. Havok shrugs, neither confirming nor denying the claim.

"We looked over your file, spoke with the local point of contact at the time, Sergeant Hannigan, and ended up offering Kade a job. His need to find you became a focal point for the group, something we all grew fixated with rather quickly. We were able to learn so much about you, through statements taken by the sheriff's department and the FBI, but also from Kade." I feel completely lost. I don't understand why Havok would have been involved at all. It's not like we were friends.

"It took us three months, but we finally found something useful," Krew jumps in. "Given how close Pike's Bay is to the coast, it wasn't farfetched to think that you might have been trafficked." My heart stutters. I'd wondered what everyone thought, what conclusions were drawn, but that had never been one of them. I figured most people assumed I was dead and my body just hadn't turned up yet.

"We found a picture," Kash whispers. When I turn to him, his eyes are glassy and I get the strangest urge to stop them from saying any more.

"A picture?" I question robotically, my brain taking the lead, whether I want it to or not. That internal warning blares to life, begging me to turn around because there's nothing but danger up ahead.

"It was taken shortly after you were abducted. In the room we found you in," Lochlan answers, his honey-colored eyes finding mine.

The camera.

"And you saw it? All of you saw it?" I look at each of them, searching for any indication that I'm wrong, but all I find is guilt. When I land on Kash, his gaze drops to the floor.

"Oh, God," I whisper hoarsely, horrified that they've seen me in such a vulnerable state. Bile rises up my throat and it takes everything I have to force it back down.

"I'm so sorry, Little Fighter." Roan's voice breaks through the static in my mind and I open my eyes, wishing I could erase the last five minutes and not know any of this.

"The image was tagged with a starting bid of five hundred thousand. You were listed in an auction, Saylor. We've been under the impression that you were sold, but it appears Liam only orchestrated it to look that way. No one had any reason to believe you were stateside, much less so close to home. If it wasn't for the CNA who spoke with Liam's mother, I'm not sure we'd have ever thought otherwise." I flinch from the bluntness of Lochlan's words. The picture they paint—my body bound and bared with a price tag attached, giving anyone with enough money and evil inside them the option to own me—has me sprinting towards the trash can.

I barely make it in time, my knees connecting with the floor painfully as I empty my stomach. *So much for breakfast.* It sounds like a stampede behind me, but I pay it no mind. Tears are streaming down my face, and then a sob wracks my body. It hurts to cry this hard, but I can't make myself stop. They just keep coming, forcing their way out.

"Fuck this."

Arms band around me and tug me closer. I bury my face against their neck, but the wetness clouding my vision leaves me clueless as to who I'm clinging to. All I can see is that room, the bright light and recording device. I want my mom. I need her and she isn't here. So, I cry. I cry until I exhaust myself completely and that blackened piece of my soul is nothing but a void.

Chapter Fifteen

Kade

I sit there on the cold marble floor of our kitchen until my ass is numb, but Saylor continues to shake. She finally passed out, but I've been too afraid to move. Her mind and body need the rest too much for me to chance waking her. Just as I predicted, I wasn't able to stand there and watch her fall apart. I risked fucking her up even more by grabbing her the way I did, but I couldn't take those agonized sounds a second longer.

I fully expected her to pull away, but I had to try something. When she pressed her tear-stained face against my neck, everything shifted. That gaping hole inside of me felt a little smaller. Her tiny hands gripped my shirt like a lifeline, and I knew there and then, no matter what it takes, I'll make her forgive me. I'll fix the pieces I broke, because there won't be a day between now and the one I die that's spent without her. Her and I, we're tethered for life, whether she realizes it or not.

"Kade," Lochlan warns as I get to my feet, holding Saylor as tight as I can without aggravating her injuries.

"Fuck. Off," I growl, stomping towards her bedroom.

I would put her in mine, but I think it'd terrify her to wake up somewhere unfamiliar, and it would damn sure torture the shit out of me to have her sweet scent all over my sheets. I kick Saylor's door closed behind me, then gently lay her on the bed. She looks so small, her body barely taking up a quarter of the space with how she's curled in on herself. I want to be mad at Loch for delivering the blow that got her to this state, but it's not his fault. She needed to know, *deserved to*, no matter how difficult it was to hear.

I slump to the floor and lean against Saylor's dresser, never taking my eyes off of her. I hope her sleep is dreamless. She's still as can be, and there's no movement behind her eyelids, so maybe she's at peace. When I walked into the kitchen this morning and found her sitting there in Kash's sweatshirt, fuzzy socks pulled halfway up her calves, I thought she'd never looked more beautiful. I also wanted to rip my shirt off and have her wear it instead. Her hair was mussed from sleep, but those guarded blue eyes still looked at me with a hint of fear, and that alone stole my focus.

I'm sure Saylor has no idea what to expect from me. I've given her no reason to think that she can let her guard down while I'm around, but I'm determined to make things right. I need her. It's irrational and obsessive, but it's not something I have any say in. There's this connection between us and it's uncontrollable. And that's not guilt speaking, because

I've always sought this girl out. Even when my intentions were impure. I'm not sure how much time has passed when Saylor finally stirs, but I stay seated and wait for her to notice me.

She returns my stare, looking perplexed. Probably wondering what the hell I'm doing in her room. Neither of us says a word for a good five minutes; we just watch each other. And maybe I'm the dumbest fucker in the world, but I stand, succumbing to that burning need to be closer, and erase the few feet between us. Saylor rolls to her back as I loom above her, visibly tensing from my nearness. With slow movements, I bring my hand up and brush a stray piece of hair from her face, causing her lips to part on a sharp inhale.

"Hey, pretty girl," I whisper, not wanting to break the bubble we're in. "There's something I'd like to show you. Would that be, okay?" Her eyes dart back and forth between mine, likely searching for whatever bullshit she thinks I'm trying to pull. She nods, but it's clear she's questioning her decision, so I step back and head to my room before she changes her mind. It only takes me a minute to find what I'm looking for, and then I'm back, watching as Saylor situates herself so she's propped against her headboard.

"When you disappeared, I kinda lost it. Felt responsible, and I am to some extent. But it took your mom to set me straight." I take a seat at the end of her bed, placing the box beside me.

"My mom?" Saylor sits up straighter, that button nose of hers scrunching adorably.

"Yep," I laugh. "It was rocky at first. She knew exactly who I was and there was no love lost for the boy who'd put her daughter through years of torment." I smile, but it's chagrined and self-deprecating. "I went to every search party. Posted flyers in all the neighboring towns I could hitch a ride to. And then I knocked on your front door and confessed that it was all my fault. I explained what happened the day you were taken, that I let you walk away." I grind my teeth together, feeling disgusted with myself all over again.

"She slapped the shit out of me." Saylor gasps, her hand going to her mouth. But I just shake my head, a small smile playing at my lips. "I swear, sometimes I can still feel the sting. Tiny but mighty, you Radley women." A faint laugh leaves Saylor, but her eyes are full of pain.

"I kept coming back, even though she made it clear that she had no interest in having me around. I cut the grass, changed the porch light that was blown, whatever I could find to just...be there. It took a year before she ever said another word to me, but all those angry looks and blatant dismissals were worth it in the end." I clear my throat, needing a second to regroup.

"She forgave me. Just like that." I snap my fingers. "She swore it wasn't my fault and begged me to let go of my guilt. It helped, to hear that from the person most affected by your disappearance, but it will never erase the part I played. I'll always feel some measure of responsibility." Saylor has silent tears running down her face, and more than anything,

I want to pull her close and whisper a thousand apologies.

"So, I was there, every day, doing whatever I could to make your mom's life a little bit easier. Sometimes we just sat there, in the rockers on the front porch, without ever saying a word. I'd help her make dinner or we'd sit around and watch old home videos. Whatever she wanted to do. I got to hear a hundred stories about the girl I treated like shit, and each one broke my fucking heart a little more. But I never asked her to stop; I deserved to know *exactly* what I missed out on by not having you in my life. All those wasted years." I shake my head, knowing there's fuck all I can do to change the past, but it doesn't stop me from wishing I could.

"I need you to listen to me very carefully, Say." I slide forward and frame her face with my hands. She breathes heavily but makes no move to pull away. "You did nothing wrong. *Not a damn thing.* I was an asshole kid with a shitty home life and you…you were fucking perfect. You had everything I wanted and I envied you because of it. That still doesn't excuse the shit I did or the things I said. If you hate me for the rest of your life, I'll understand. But I hope you won't. *God, I hope you won't.* I'm a selfish bastard, so even though I don't deserve it, this is me asking for forgiveness. *Begging.* I'm so fucking sorry, pretty girl."

I swipe my thumbs beneath her eyes, clearing away the tears that continue to fall. She doesn't say anything, and the deer in headlights look she's emitting has me pulling away to give her some space. I can only hope that she believes me. I grab the box from beside me and place it on my lap.

"You haven't asked, but I'm sure you'd like to know. Liz had breast cancer. It was aggressive, but she had a chance at beating it. Unfortunately, she declined any intervention."

"What?" Saylor's disbelief is evident, as is the hurt in her voice. "What does that mean?"

"I think she was tired and heartbroken, so she didn't see a point in fighting what she deemed inevitable. Recovery was slim. I didn't know until things were too bad and treatment was no longer an option. I promise you I would've tried to change her mind had I known sooner, which is probably the exact reason she didn't tell me." I regret not noticing the signs I should've picked up on. Liz being tired more often than normal, the drop in weight. I'd attributed the changes to stress from work and Saylor's case growing colder by the day. Not to mention I was living here, three hours away, and didn't see her nearly as often.

"Am I the reason she's dead?" Saylor whispers brokenly. "Why would she do that?"

"Fuck, Say." I wrap my arms around her, hugging her against me. "Shh. It's okay. Please don't think that. Your mom saw firsthand how brutal treatment could be on a daily basis. I honestly believe that was one of the main deciding factors for her. She wanted to enjoy the time she had. Do I think if you were home, if you'd never been taken, that things would have gone differently? Abso-fucking-lutely. Liz would've fought with everything she had because there's no way in hell she'd have ever left you without trying her damndest not to. But that doesn't mean you're the cause for her choice." Saylor sniffles and peels herself away, so I take my place back at the foot of the bed. Her eyes are puffy and red, and I know her heart has taken a goddamn beating today, but I'm hoping I can make it a little better.

"I was there till the very end. I made sure she wasn't alone." Saylor's chin trembles. Maybe one day she'll feel comforted by knowing that, but these truths are too fresh to find any sort of silver lining. "She set aside some things for me to keep, and a letter she wrote to you. Just in case you ever found your way home."

"She did?" Her eyes are bright with hope, and I pray whatever she reads gives her a modicum of closure, healing the parts my words can't touch.

"She did." I smile, feeling grateful that Liz thought to do something like this before she got too sick. "I've never opened it. Whatever she had to say was meant for you alone. But there's something else in here too." I tap the box, hoping like hell Saylor's not going to freak out. I pull back the top and grab the urn encasing her mother's ashes. I've barely gotten it in my hands when she yanks it from me and holds it to her chest, as if it might disappear. Her eyes are closed, a bittersweet smile carved across her pretty face.

"She hasn't been in a box this entire time," I quickly add, seeing how it could look that way. "I've had her on a shelf. Even talk to her sometimes." I shrug at the look Saylor gives me.

"Mom told me once that I better not put her in the dirt with the creepy crawlies. She wanted one of those fancy drawers or to be cremated." Her watery laugh makes my chest twinge, but I follow her finger as she traces the etched design of her mother's final resting place.

"We arranged everything shortly after she broke the news to me. I took some time off and stayed until she passed." Saylor smiles appreciatively, but it's thin. "January 5th, 2021, is the day of her death. So, she's been gone about a year and a half now." I slide the box between us, letting her take the lead on how and when she chooses to go through the contents. I've seen everything but the letter, so I know it'll be emotional for her to reacquaint herself with old items of her mother's and mementos from her childhood.

"Why do the guys call you Kade?" Saylor asks, the question completely off topic from what we'd been discussing.

"I hate the name Havok," I tell her honestly. "My parents thought it was fitting, I guess, since I fucked up their plans by being born."

"I'm sorry. I won't use it anymore." She frowns, looking bothered by my admission.

"It's okay, pretty girl." I grin, not wanting her upset on my behalf. "I don't mind you calling me that. It's more the way it was used, how it was spoken, than the name itself. Like it was synonymous with a curse word. I've never felt that way when you say my name." I can still remember the way her voice sounded all those years ago, the first time she called out to me.

Dainty and sweet. "The guys caught on pretty quickly that I wasn't really a fan and took Kade from my last name."

"That makes sense." Saylor nods.

"I'm gonna head out. I know it's been another shit day, but I'm here if you need me. We all are." I'm just about turn the doorknob when she stops me.

"Thank you."

"For what?" I quirk an eyebrow in confusion.

"For everything. The things you did for my mom. For never giving up on me. The apology." Her eyes are bright with emotion again, but I force back the need to go to her. "It wasn't your fault, but I might've used you as something to bitch about while I was down there." I laugh, my smile wide and genuine, not the least bit offended by her honesty. "And as for everything that happened between us before that day? You're forgiven." She shrugs a shoulder, like it's no big deal to her when it means the fucking world to me.

"You mean that?" I can hear the strain in my voice.

"Yeah. I mean, I always knew this was one of those '*it's not you, it's me*' situations. The '*me*' in that scenario being you." She smirks, a hint of mischief peeking through.

"It was definitely me, Say," I confess, my fucked up grinch heart growing way too big for my chest.

"Let's just start over. Okay?" She wavers slightly, nervously biting her bottom lip. "It's in the past, and I think we could both use a clean slate."

"Hearing that makes me really fucking happy, pretty girl." I wink and pull the door closed, her soft laugh following me to my own room. I could snort cocaine and feel a lesser high than the one I've got from spending a few hours with that woman.

I'm not a soft man. I've never known an ounce of affection outside of Eliza Radley and the men I've come to call brothers, and even then, we're not sitting around, hugging every day while forming a trust circle to share our feelings. It's a sense of belonging with them, a level of comfort I've allowed myself to enjoy. Because I know, no matter what bullshit I pull or how badly I fuck up, they'll never turn their backs on me. That kind of loyalty is rare, and I won't take it for granted.

But Saylor...Saylor feels like home. She makes the years of neglect and misery take a backseat, because she's here now, and everything that happened prior to her is irrelevant. I'm putty in that girl's hands and it fucking terrifies me. She has me completely exposed, offering myself to her in whatever way she'll take me. But that means I'm knowingly putting myself at risk of being absolutely eviscerated if she kicks me to the curb. So, that leaves me no other option but to get my shit together and be whatever she needs me to be.

A best friend.

A confidant.

A goddamn punching bag if that's what it takes.

Regardless, I'll never be the Havok she remembers ever again. If Saylor's going to give me a second chance to set shit straight, then you best believe I'm going to do everything I can to ensure she doesn't regret it.

Chapter Sixteen

Saylor

I stay in my room for the rest of the day. Aside from Kash bringing me a toasted ham and cheese sandwich in the afternoon, the guys don't bother me. I'm grateful for the space. I've spent the last few hours going through the box of belongings Havok had been holding on to, looking at each item with new eyes. These are the only things I have left of my life with Mom. The Christmas ornaments I made her throughout elementary school, a half-used bottle of her favorite perfume, photo albums and videos. I slide out a picture of us from the Valentine's Day before our lives imploded and grab one of the empty frames from my dresser. Once I've secured it, I flip it back over and run my fingers over both of our faces.

We'd been so happy. Mom always said I was the greatest love of her life, so who better to spend the day with than me. Crazy how blissfully unaware we were of the impending doom. Like I said, we rarely see those moments coming. Devastation like that, the sort that tips your world on its axis and changes who you are on a fundamental level, gives no warning. Those particular ruinations like to blindside you.

I would have never imagined that three short months after we'd taken this picture everything would change. Who could possibly anticipate something like that? I got all the same talks most kids did about stranger danger, but that was my downfall. I knew the asshole who thought he could steal me and claim me like a stray he'd found on the side of the road. Every time I think about the interactions I had with Liam Price prior to the day he kidnapped me, I start to feel lightheaded. It's scary to think that some people are skilled enough to pull off the con he did.

I place the picture of us on my nightstand, right beside her urn, then pull the perfume out and uncap the lid. I breathe deeply, smiling at the familiar scent. It feels like she's right here in the room with me. There are several other trinkets inside the box of memories, mostly things of mine that Mom had been proud of—like the participation trophy I got for soccer—but her jewelry might be my favorite. The sentimental pieces she coveted, like a pair of diamond earrings that she was gifted from my dad and their wedding bands, mean far more to me than my grade school artwork. I set them on my dresser for now, keeping them in the tiny duster they were placed in until I can find a safer alternative.

The only thing I don't look at is the letter. I'm not ready to open it. Those are the last words I'll ever get from my mother. And she wrote them to me, the Saylor I am *today*. For a few minutes, I'll still have her with me, but I know it won't be long enough. As soon as I read them, she'll be gone. There won't be any new thoughts or opinions from her, and the current state of my emotional stability is not prepared for that. I need to shore up my defenses before delving into *that*, especially after the whiplash of feelings I've cycled through today.

I place the box in my closet, sans a few things I chose to keep in my room, and head to the bathroom to brush my teeth. I can't believe the day is practically over. It feels like it dragged, but also flew by. I should be concerned with bathing, but I'm too drained to put in the effort it would require. I take the pain meds Kash dropped off with my early dinner and down half my bottle of water. I've grown so used to rationing things that it's causing me not to drink enough, strictly from habit. The last thing I want is to end up dehydrated again.

A sigh escapes me when my sore body meets the cloud-like feel of the mattress. The second my eyes close, thoughts from this morning start pouring back in. Lochlan's words play on repeat, but no matter how many times I force myself back awake, I'm just too tired to ward off the nightmare that awaits me. Eventually, I lose the battle. And as I feared, I quickly sink to the pits of my own personal hell.

I'm back. It wasn't real—not the guys or the hospital.

No one came to save me because no one knows I still exist. I'm just a faded memory that people think about from time to time. That girl who went missing but no one ever found.

"Poor thing," *they'd say.*

And then he's *there—the Devil himself. I can feel the chill of his fingers ghosting across my skin. His hot breath against the back of my neck. Every inch of my body that's been hurt by him flares with pain, vividly reminding me of how vile he is.*

The light is brighter today than it normally is, but slowly, just beyond the glare, faces begin to emerge. They're strangers, men I've never seen before, but they look at me as if I'm a valued piece of real estate. A blank canvas to mold as they please. I try to hide myself, to cover my nude body from the leering eyes that would love nothing more than to break me—mind, body, and soul.

But my arms are held behind me, and no matter how hard I struggle to break free, I'm no match against the man spreading me out to be visually feasted upon by like-minded evil. I scream; with every bit of air in my lungs, I scream for someone to help me.

I'm right here, damnit. How can no one find me?!

I can feel them closing in, those grotesque hands of monsters reaching out to grab me. Instinctively, I know if that happens, I'll be lost forever. They'll take me away, to a place far worse than Liam Price's storm cellar and destroy me in a way that he never did. So, I kick and thrash. I scream some more because I refuse to go quietly.

I can't be here again. I'd rather die than go back to this life.

"Saylor!"

My eyes fly open, panic gripping me as I struggle to get away from the weight holding me down.

"Let go!" I sob, my throat raw and face soaked with tears. I dig my nails against their skin, but it's no use.

"It's Lochlan, sweetheart. You're safe. You're okay," he swears, his cheek pressed to mine. I still my efforts of escape, the fog in my head slowly clearing as I notice the wall of my bedroom. Robotically, I turn my head and find honey colored-eyes filled with sadness. *I know those eyes*. My gaze moves around the rest of the space. Roan is standing at the end of my bed, his hands gripping the footboard with enough force that the wood creaks. Havok and Kash are both pale, looking seconds from throwing up or passing out. And Krew is watching from the hallway, his face as unreadable as ever.

"Oh, God." I pull myself away from Lochlan, wincing at the sight of his arm. "I'm sorry. I'm so, so sorry." I try to scramble off the bed, wanting to get a washcloth to clean him up, but he stops me by wrapping his fingers around my good wrist.

"It's okay, Saylor. I promise." He looks stressed, his eyes roving over my body like he's searching for any sign of injury. "It's over." Those two words make me sob. Lochlan pulls me closer, one hand cradling my head while the other strokes my back. I cry so hard his shirt is soaked within a matter of seconds. It's over *because* of him. When I needed someone to find me, he did. Even in my dreams. They each came running—*for me*.

"I've got you, sweetheart. You can sleep."

"Can you stay? I don't want to be alone," I

mumble pleadingly, my words hitching with every inhale.

"I'm not going anywhere. Get some rest, love." Lochlan presses a kiss to the top of my head as he repositions us. With my ear to his chest, I let the steady beat of his heart lull me back to sleep.

~

I'm drenched in sweat when I wake. Kash's sweatshirt clings to my skin, leaving no room for airflow. I shift—with great effort and way too much pain—and the heat at my back disappears. When I finally get myself untangled from the covers and upright, I look to my left and find Lochlan. He's snoring softly, one arm thrown over his eyes while the other rests across his stomach. As soon as my eyes land on the injuries I caused, a massive wave of guilt washes over me.

I swallow and look away. As I attempt to scoot down the bed, a mound of blankets at the end emits a low groan, making me freeze. It's only then that I notice Roan is sleeping on the floor in front of my bathroom and Havok's doing the same by the door, his head propped against the side of my dresser. Warmth floods me, and not the hot, sweaty kind that woke me. This feels like safety and being cared for. The blanket at my feet is tossed back, revealing Kash. The second he sees me, a huge grin lights up his face.

"Mornin', Cupcake." He stretches lazily, making the most ridiculous noises. Like a domino effect, the other three start to move around too, grunting and groaning, as if waking up is the hardest thing they've ever done. "Since you didn't specify who you were asking to stay last night, and no one was willing to risk losing at a game of rock-paper-scissors, we decided it was an open invitation. So, we all stayed," Kash explains as he climbs to his feet.

"More like they refused to leave," Lochlan scoffs as he slides his glasses on.

"You guys didn't have to sleep on the floor." I wince as Roan cracks his neck.

"Best Friend, this bed barely fit the three of us. Where else would they have slept?" Kash arches his eyebrow at me.

"Um…their own beds?" I answer, but it comes across as a question. They chuckle, like my response is downright comical.

"Yeah, not a chance, Say." Havok winks at me, the simple action leaving me a little off kilter. I think it's going to take me a minute to get used to this new version of him.

"Seriously, though," Kash starts as he heads for the door. "If puppy-piles are going to become a part of our norm, we need to invest in a bigger bed. Like one of those monstrosities that sleep a dozen."

"Kash, the last fucking thing I want to do is share a bed with you. You're a cuddler, for Christ's sake." Roan shivers dramatically. I press my fingers to my lips, holding back a laugh.

"I'd snuggle *Saylor*, you giant beanstalk." Kash gives him a '*duh*' look. "Remember that, Best Friend. Ro-Ro here isn't a fan of cuddling." His wide-eyed front of innocence isn't fooling anyone.

"I'm not a fan of you pressing your junk against my ass, you little fucker. If Saylor needed a cuddle, I'd give her a damn cuddle," Roan declares, glaring at Kash accusingly.

"It was one time. Get over it already!" Kash rolls his eyes.

It's like watching a ping-pong match, but with words. I'm sure there's a goofy grin on my face, but this is way more entertaining than it should be. These grown men are arguing over cuddles. The laugh I've been holding back finally breaks free, making them stop and stare at me.

"I'm sorry," I say, pressing my lips together to try and gain a semblance of control.

"No, you're not," Havok snorts.

"Okay, children. Let's get breakfast started and give Saylor some privacy." Lochlan stands and ushers the guys out. I smile appreciatively because I *really* need to pee. Slipping off the bed, I stop Havok just before he leaves.

"What's up, pretty girl?"

"Do you have a sweatshirt I can wear today?"

Please don't ask why.

"Anything for you, Say. Give me a sec."

He's back in a flash, which my bladder appreciates, and I promise to be out shortly. I do my business, rid my mouth of fuzzies and decide to take a quick bath to rinse the stale sweat from my body. Once

I'm clean and dried off, I slip Havok's hoodie on. It's all black and lands exactly where Kash's did, swallowing me whole. I head to the closet for some clean underwear and lounge shorts, then free my hair from the clip I placed it in to keep it dry. It's going to be gross soon, which means I'll have to wash it one-handed or ask for help. Neither option sounds appealing.

When I get to the kitchen, a plate of food is already waiting at what's become my designated stool. It's a lot fuller this time, with three pieces of bacon, a biscuit, and a sliced-up strawberry. My stomach growls, earning me a wide smile from Roan. He has dimples in both cheeks, but they're only visible when he's really grinning, like he is today. The guys are too busy scarfing down their food to talk, so I start on my perfectly crunchy bacon, humming in contentment.

"So, yesterday sucked," Krew deadpans, making me choke on the food I was attempting to swallow. Roan pats my back gently, sliding my OJ closer as he glares at the other man.

"It's all good, Big Guy. Just caught me off guard." I wave him off and clear my throat. "Uh, yeah. Pretty sucky, if I do say so myself." I nod at Krew in agreement.

"I think, given the circumstances and everything you've had thrown at you this past week, you're doing pretty damn great, Saylor." Lochlan smiles reassuringly, and while it's nice to hear him say that, I don't agree. I have pockets of happiness, this morning for example, but it never lasts.

"Here, here." Kash clinks his glass against mine, his timing impeccable, bringing some levity to the conversation right when it's needed.

"The guys have to run some errands today, but Krew and I will be here. Is there anything you'd like for them to pick up while they're out?" Lochlan asks as he goes about making his second cup of coffee.

"Not that I can think of but thank you." I take another bite of my biscuit, wondering who made breakfast today. The flaky dough is cooked to perfection and practically melts in my mouth.

"Come on, pretty girl. Surely you can think of something. Food, drinks, girly shit." Havok braces his forearms on the counter across from me, his face right in front of mine. I narrow my eyes, but his smirk is light and playful.

"Specifically, what type of '*girly shit*' would you be referring to?" I take another bite of my delicious biscuit as I wait for his response.

"Oh, I've already bought Saylor all the *shits*. Hair *shit*, body *shit*, clothes *shit*, period *s*..." My eyes widen as Kash's verbal diarrhea is mercifully cut off by his twin's hand covering his mouth.

"That's enough from you, brother," Krew grumbles, a look of exasperation replacing his typically blank expression.

My face feels like it's on fire, but Havok looks mighty pleased with himself. Despite this new leaf we've turned over, there will always be a part of him that enjoys teasing me. It's just who he is. Thankfully, it's all in good fun now.

"Your pink cheeks are my favorite," Havok whispers, stealing the last bite of my biscuit and popping it in his mouth.

"You didn't!" My shocked inhale is overexaggerated. "I wanted that." I poke my bottom lip out, my eyes doing that thing Mom used to yell at me for. She hated it when I gave her this exact look while trying to get my way. The guys glare at Havok with murder in their eyes. I watch, in slow motion, as horror and regret wash over his face.

"Fuck, Say. I'm sorry."

"Did you just eat her food?" Kash cocks his head to the side. "Surely not. Right, Ro?" He looks to the man sitting beside me for clarification.

"You're dead." Roan stands so quickly his barstool gets knocked over. Havok bolts, vaulting over the couch, but his lead is dwindling by the second. You'd think his size would slow him down, but Roan's just as fast and agile as the man he's chasing. I spin around, watching as they go round and round. Eventually, Havok gets put in a headlock, his face buried right in Roan's armpit.

"Fuck, man. Have you showered recently?" His muffled words are barely audible as Roan frog-marches him across the room, stopping directly in front of me.

"Apologize," he demands, holding Havok by the back of his shirt like he's an errant child.

"Sorry, pretty girl." His icy blue eyes are filled with genuine remorse.

"It's okay." I shrug and hike a thumb over my shoulder. "There are three more on the baking sheet." Their heads swivel as one, staring at the remaining biscuits in silence. Kash is the first to give in to his laughter, but it doesn't take long for the others to join.

"Oh, you find this funny, huh?" Havok grins. "Let's see how humorous you find it when you've got Ro's pit sweat all over you." He lunges, rubbing his face all over mine and against my neck. I'm laughing so hard it makes my ribs throb, but I can't seem stop. It feels like ages before he finally relents. As I try to catch my breath and wipe my watery eyes, he stares at me, a look of pure happiness in place of the angry one he used to wear like body armor.

"God, I love that sound." Havok frames my face with his hands and plants a kiss on my forehead. It stuns me stupid, so I just sit there and gape after him as he winks and heads down the hallway. Kash's fake gag breaks me out of my daze.

"Here, let me fix it." He takes the sleeve of his sweater and wipes my forehead, dropping his own kiss in place of Havok's. "There. Much better." Kash boops my nose, an apparent favorite of his, and grins in satisfaction.

"Bloody idiot," Lochlan groans, the bridge of his nose pinched between his fingers. I just shake my head, secretly loving all the crazy. This whole morning has felt oddly normal, especially after the nighttime debacle I caused, making me desperate for more stretches of ordinary life.

Chapter Seventeen

Krew

The guys left a while ago, but I doubt they'll be gone for too long. Not one of them had any interest in leaving the house, or should I say Saylor, but Loch and I need to have a conversation with her that doesn't involve anyone else. At least until she decides otherwise. I'd been awake, working through bank statements for a client, when Saylor's ear-piercing scream shattered through quiet. I tore out of my office, nearly busting my ass trying to get to her, but her door refused to budge.

Cursing up a storm, I grabbed the hairpin key that Lochlan keeps in his office and dropped to my knees. My hands shook, but seconds later I managed to feed it through the hole in the doorknob and disengage the lock. It felt like an eternity passed as Saylor wailed from the other side. My focus was singular, so I felt more than heard the guys behind me, each of them just as panicked and restless. Before they could see how unnerved I was, I schooled my expression into something more fitting. Polite indifference is what they were used to from me, so that's exactly what I gave them.

Loch didn't waste any time pushing through as soon as I got the door open. I stood there, frozen in the hallway, as the rest of them stormed in to fight whatever monsters needed slaying. I was stuck in my own head. Saylor's screams were morphing into Kash's, a sound I swore I'd never have to hear again. It wasn't the blue-eyed blonde thrashing and pleading for help, it was my twin. I can't count how many times I was ripped awake in the middle of the night to those same pained cries because I was too late and failed to protect my brother.

It's fucked up how we convince ourselves that we're better, that we've moved past the shit we fought so hard to overcome. I've been fine for years, but one small setback can easily reopen the wound. Unfortunately, no matter how much effort you put into healing the damaged parts, it can take decades to fully scar. Until then, the skin is fragile and a slight bump can rip the scab right off. Before you know it, it's bleeding all over again. I want to cauterize this particular wound so that I can be done with it for fucking good.

And the cherry on top of the shit cake? Kash, who hasn't spent a night away from me since we were kids, chose to sleep at the end of Saylor's bed, refusing to leave her. There wasn't an ounce of hesitation on his part. So, as I was spiraling, needing my brother more than I have in years, he'd been perfectly content to curl around her feet without a second thought. And that scares the hell out of me.

It's clear as crystal he's attached to Saylor. I

have no idea how deep Kash's feelings have grown, but I imagine they're pretty intense if he's able to fall asleep without me in the same room. All because *she* was there. The woman who now holds more power than she realizes. Kash isn't like the other guys. He jokes and fucks off because he doesn't think he's good enough to be anything more than that. He sure as shit doesn't put himself out there with women. My twin has this idea that he's somehow less because he has issues, like his misguided perception of being weak and dependency of me, just to name a few.

But who the hell doesn't have baggage these days? The deprecating shit he thinks of himself is conjured by his own head and the lingering voice of our stepfather. Truth be told, I depend on him just as much as he does me. The only difference between us is that I've grown more hardened by this fucked up world. Yet this pint-sized girl has him wrapped around her finger. The problem with that, is he's not the only one who's staring at Saylor with hearts in his eyes. I'd be lying if I said she doesn't intrigue me too. We've been under her spell long before she ever set foot in this house, but I don't want my brother to get hurt.

I know we'd never cross a line. Not a single one of us would put Saylor in a position that could compromise the comfortability she's slowly falling into. She's nowhere near ready for any sort of intimate relationship, and when that day does come, there's a good chance it won't be with any of us. She needs someone who doesn't have their own trauma to deal with, who can devote their time to helping her heal without any outside factors hindering her from having the best goddamn life. It makes my jaw tic to think of Saylor with some vanilla asshole—for reasons I refuse to explore—but if there's anyone who deserves a happily ever after, it's her.

And where the hell will that leave Kash now that the stupid fucker has went and attached himself to her like a damn leech? Fucked, that's where. Right up the ass by a horse-sized dildo. Lube not included. I've learned to guard myself, but my twin loves too easily, despite having every reason not to. I just hope that he has enough sense to pump the brakes before he's in so deep that he's blinded by everything else. If not, when she walks out that door one day, after all of this Liam shit is put to rest, he might as well rip his heart from his chest and give it to Saylor as a parting gift.

I roll my neck, working the tightness from my muscles after sitting at my desk most of the night. A quick look at the time has me pushing back and heading to Saylor's room. I guarantee those dopey-eyed assholes are already on the way back. It'll be the quickest trip to town any of us has ever taken. I rap my knuckles on her door a couple times, hoping she's not asleep. There's some shuffling from the other side, and then she eases it open.

"Hey, Tink," I greet her softly, keenly aware of the way her skin flushes. I'm sure she wasn't expecting to find me, of all people, standing here. In fact, I have a feeling that Saylor thinks I don't particularly like her. This divide I've erected has been for my sanity, though. It has nothing to do with anything she's said or done.

"Hi." She gives me a sweet smile, her lips curving heavenward.

"Loch and I wanted to talk to you about something. You up for it?"

"Sure."

Saylor follows me next door to Loch's office. I don't bother knocking, knowing he wouldn't be doing anything that would warrant a heads-up before barging in. As expected, the posh prick is sitting behind his desk, those Clark Kent glasses perched on his perfectly straight nose as he reads over a stack of paperwork.

"Boss Man."

I drop to one of the leather chairs that faces Loch while Saylor takes the other. Her gait is timid. It's obvious that she's nervous based on the way she keeps biting her bottom lip and twiddling her fingers. She looks even smaller wearing Kade's hoodie. It makes me want to ease her worries, but I bite my tongue and let Loch take the lead.

"Saylor." My brother by choice grins happily, pushing his work to the side as he leans back to stretch. Lost causes, every single one of them. "I'm going to jump right into the deep end, because I doubt we've got long before the rest of the gang is back. I wanted to get your thoughts on how you feel about speaking with someone, professionally speaking."

"Like a therapist?" Saylor questions.

"Exactly like a therapist," I answer. "I know

from experience how beneficial it can be to talk with someone who isn't connected to you personally. Someone who can give you their thoughts and advice without any bias. But that needs to be a choice you make for yourself, not because you feel forced into it."

"Which is why we wanted to bring it up and let you know that, should you want to, the option is available," Loch explains. "Denvers already sent me the name of a well-respected psychologist. She's worked with patients who've experienced similar traumatic events and even some fellow agents of his dealing with PTSD. She comes highly recommended."

"Huh," Saylor mumbles absently.

"Everything would be done by video conference. You wouldn't have to go anywhere. I can set you up in here, with complete privacy," Loch adds.

"So, no creepy office where I have to lie on a scratchy couch while someone asks me '*and how does that make you feel*'?" Saylor dips her chin, her long blonde hair covering half of her face, but I catch the smirk she's fighting. Loch laughs, his head tipping back from the force of it.

"Christ, woman. What weird experience did you have?" I look at her expectantly.

"Just the one," she deadpans. I blink, wondering why the fuck I thought to say something so blatantly insensitive, but then she snorts. "Guess I picked the stigma up from books and movies," Saylor shrugs.

"Definitely none of that," Loch jokes. "Whatever you decide, just know that you can still talk to us too. If there's anything on your mind, night or day, we're always here to listen. Seeking outside help doesn't change that. We've dealt with some heavy situations, but that doesn't give us degrees in psychology. Ultimately, we just want to give you the best chance at healing."

"Okay," Saylor offers after a few minutes of contemplation. "I'd like to try the therapy route."

"I'll reach out and set something up, then," Loch says, his relief obvious to me but likely not to her. Before anything else can be said, the garage door bangs open. It'll be a miracle if there's not a damn hole in the wall.

"Honey, I'm home!" Kash's loud ass yells. I groan, climbing to my feet.

"C'mon, Tink. I've got a feeling you're the '*honey*' he's referring to." I lead us down the hallway, my eyes widening at the massive amount of grocery bags covering the kitchen floor.

"Are we preparing for a hurricane that I'm unaware of?" I look from one man to the next as I wait for an explanation.

"Yeah, Hurricane Kash," Ro grumbles.

"Listen." My brother pops up from behind the island, sucker hanging from his mouth. "Every time I saw something, I couldn't help but wonder '*when was the last time my Toaster Strudel got to eat that?*'. So, in the buggy it went."

"Toaster Strudel. Really?" I give my quacked-out twin a long, hard look. Searching for any lick of sanity still bebopping around that head of his.

"It was on the brain." Kash taps his temple with his finger. "Look, Best Friend. I got us every flavor!" He holds up several boxes of the frozen pastries, a stupid grin plastered across his face.

"You bought all of this because of me?" Saylor whispers, looking slightly horrified by the thought.

"No." Kash's eyebrows draw together indignantly. "Kade did." He points to the man clomping in with more bags in his hands, his black Doc Martens haphazardly laced, as usual. "Why spend my money, when I can spend his?"

"Don't look so horrified, Say." Kade drops the load he was carrying and ruffles her hair. "I'm sure it won't be long before you're sprinting around a Target, competing with Kash in the '*who can spend the most*' department."

"Unlikely," Saylor retorts. "That would require money, of which I have zero. And this..." she spins in a slow circle, taking in all the bags. "This looks like it was really expensive, Havok." Her voice gets fainter with each word. It also doesn't escape my notice that Kade seems completely unfazed by Saylor using his first name.

"Yes, you do," Kade states, tucking a piece of hair behind her ear. "You have money, pretty girl."

"What?" Saylor's nose scrunches in that cute fucking way it does when she's confused.

"The work I did around the house for your mom helped up the resale value. After it sold and the remainder of the mortgage was paid, there was still a decent amount left. I saved it. Opened a separate account to stash it in just in case this day ever came. As soon as I built up my own savings, I had Krew invest some of your money a little at a time, but never more than I could compensate for in case it ended up being a loss. Luckily, that didn't happen. How much is it sitting at currently?" Kade looks to me.

"Just shy of two hundred grand," I answer.

"Two hundred thousand?" Saylor's eyes are wide with shock, her lips parting like she wants to say something, but no words come out. For a good minute, she just stares at the two of us. Eventually, her teary gaze lands back on Kade. "You did that for me?" In the otherwise silence, her emotional whisper is heard by everyone.

"Didn't I tell you that I'd do anything for you, Say?" He tilts his head, looking at Saylor with complete and utter adoration. Like I said, it's going to be a fucking shitshow when this blows up in all of our faces. She blinks through the tears that are desperately trying to fall, then steps closer and wraps her arms around his torso. I think we all quit breathing for a second as we witness Saylor freely hugging Kade, her tiny fists gripping the back of his shirt. His chin rests on the top of her head as he holds her, his eyes closed in contentment.

"You can do whatever you want, Say," Kade tells her. "Pay for school. Buy a car. Donate it, for all I care. You'll be taken care of, regardless. Long after that bank account is empty."

Smooth-talking fucker.

"I don't even know what to say." She steps back, swiping a finger under her nose. "Thank you."

Saylor turns to look at me. Her steps are hesitant, but she slowly closes the space between us. Reaching out, she takes my hand in hers and gives it a gentle squeeze. A goddamn lightning strike would've been preferable to the reaction it causes inside of me. My brain is screaming '*Abort!*' but my body has other plans because my fingers force their way between hers until they're twined together.

"You're welcome, Tink."

And down goes another one.

"Okay. Feeling a little jelly," Kash pouts, breaking up the moment.

We separate, both of us walking over to start unloading the stupid amount of food they bought. If we didn't have Roan, I'd be concerned that it might go bad before we could eat it all. But that overgrown fucker is a garbage disposal. Not to mention, half of it is junk and Kash will have no problem hoovering it down.

"Why are there so many pizza rolls?" Loch asks, holding up two family-size packs.

"Because you can't have movie night without proper snacks. Duh." Kash rolls his eyes. "Let's pop those babies in the oven and then we can decide what to watch." He pulls out a baking sheet and slides it over to Loch.

"Anything but *John Tucker Must Die*," Ro huffs,

tossing the empty bags into the trash. “I’m not watching that shit again.”

“It’s a classic,” Kash gripes. “And it has an all-star cast.”

“It’s a chick-flick,” Ro deadpans. We stare at him, then at Saylor, who’s definitely a chick. She raises her eyebrow but says nothing. This girl knows how to bring a man down, that’s for sure. The shit she pulled at breakfast was pure gold. A mumbled ‘*fuck*’ leaves Ro, making me grin.

“What would you like to watch Saylor?” Loch questions.

“A comedy, maybe?” She looks unsure, like she doesn’t want to choose something that everyone else might not like. Probably doesn’t help that half of what she’d be interested in Ro just shit on. Idiot. I glance at the giant, obtuse wall of muscle and glare at him pointedly while mouthing ‘*fix it*’. Kash grabs every sweet imaginable and drops them on the coffee table, then comes back for the chips. He’s gonna send us both to an early grave. Him from clogged arteries and me from worry.

“Let’s go check out our movie options, Little Fighter.” Ro nods for her to follow, and together they start perusing the digital library we’ve amassed. By the time we’ve plated the pizza rolls and grabbed a few drinks from the fridge, everyone’s claimed a seat and the TV’s paused on the opening credits of whatever they agreed on. Saylor’s tucked in one corner, her legs folded beneath her with a blanket over her lap. Ro’s to her left with Kade on the opposite side. And there on the floor, right below her, sits my Saylor-obsessed brother with a Twizzler hanging from his mouth.

"So, what are we watching?" Loch sets the food down, but quickly makes a plate and passes it to Tink.

"We let Ro decide." Kade grins, pressing *play* on the remote. "He chose *Legally Blonde*." Decidedly of the chick variety. I nearly snort.

"Love a good movie about perseverance and overcoming obstacles. Elle Woods is a trailblazer," Ro grumbles, arms crossed over his chest as he nods a couple of times for emphasis. Swear to Christ, the man must have researched the movie as fast as he could because there's not a chance in hell he's watched it. He likely saw pink and thought '*that'll do*'. Those are absolutely Google's words, but maybe there's hope for the big dummy after all.

Saylor giggles through most of it, munching on a bowl of popcorn and the candy Kash keeps passing back, but her eyes get heavy halfway through. She's out cold ten minutes later, her head resting on Kade's shoulder. We stay seated, watching the movie for a while longer, because apparently, we all like chick-flicks. Kade lifts Saylor once we get everything shut off and the food taken care of. With her cradled in his arms, he nods goodnight to the rest of us and heads toward their rooms.

Kash stays in ours, surprisingly, but barely sleeps. I'm not sure that any of us do. At least not well. We're too busy anticipating a scream to ever drift off fully.

Chapter Eighteen

Saylor

I have no recollection of coming to bed last night, but when I peel my eyes open my cheek is pressed against something hard. I turn just enough to figure out what I'm lying on and find an arm full of colorful tattoos. I have zero doubt whose body said appendage is connected to. And to my absolute horror, I've drooled all over him. Using the sleeve of the sweatshirt I'm still wearing—his, no less—I slyly attempt to wipe it away, refusing to look behind me and see if he's awake.

There were lots of things I envisioned doing to Havok McKade as a form of payback for all the years of torment he put me through, but slobbering on him had never been one of them. His arm is likely numb from me sleeping on it all night. It takes me a minute to roll over, since I can't put any weight on my injured wrist, but once I'm facing him, I find his sleepy blue eyes fixated on mine.

"Hi," I whisper, enjoying the peaceful moment.

"Hey," Havok replies, stretching his free arm to the side. "Not gonna lie, I was kinda worried you were going to freak out when you found me here. I tried to lay you down and leave last night, but you latched on and wouldn't let go. I planned to slip out a bit later but must've fallen asleep."

"It's okay," I reassure him. Maybe I should be more concerned about why I slept so great with him next to me, but I feel the safest when I'm not alone. "I didn't have any nightmares."

"Yeah?" He looks relieved. "That's good, Say."

Who the heck is this man? Havok looks even harder on the outside than he did the day I was taken. His features are more defined from age and his skin is covered in artwork. I imagine that this is what women refer to as a *'bad boy'*. Yet he's softer than I've ever known him to be. Finding out about the money he kept safe for me and the lengths he went to, without knowing if I'd ever have any use for it, leaves me speechless. It's mind blowing to think that this is the same person who made me dread going to school.

It's a morbid thought, but I can't help but wonder where Havok would be today if I'd never been taken. Would we have called a truce? Would he have felt bad for everything he put me through and apologized? Or would he still be the same angry boy who hated the world and did everything he could to make the rest of us as miserable as him? I hate to think that I was the catalyst for such a visceral change in him, that seems a bit self-centered, but I'm fairly certain my abduction was the turning point.

"What are you thinking about so hard, pretty girl?" His thumb rubs between my eyebrows, smoothing out the line I'd caused with the direction of my thoughts.

"Just that I really like this version of you." I smile, hoping he doesn't take that as an insult.

"Me too," he replies softly, his blue eyes looking even brighter from the sunlight flooding the room.

"Shit, it's almost lunchtime," Havok comments as he taps his phone. "You need anything before I go shower?"

"No, I think I'll do the same." I pry myself up, allowing us both to move. "Actually, could I get another one of these?" I pinch the fabric of his hoodie.

"Sure thing, Say. I'll leave it on the bed for you." Havok winks and walks out the door.

I gather some fresh clothes and head for the bathroom. My hair definitely needs to be washed, so this should be fun. I turn the shower on, opting to go with the easier option, and quickly undress. There's already shampoo and conditioner placed on a tiled inlay, so I only have to snag a bottle of body wash from under the sink. I choose a new scent, still floored by the fact that I have so many choices, and slip beneath the spray, closing the glass door behind me.

The water pressure is perfect and feels heavenly on my shoulders. I tilt my head back and let it soak my hair. My wrist is still tender, so I try to do everything one-handed, but it's difficult. I end up squirting the shampoo directly on my hair, hoping I got the amount right. Based on all the suds, I went a little overboard. It takes me longer than it should, but once I've got it rinsed, I leave the conditioner to sit while washing off. My bruises have mostly faded to yellows and greens, but they're still prominent.

By the time everything is taken care of, it feels like I've been in here for ages. With a towel wrapped around my body and head, I ease the bathroom door open to make sure Havok isn't dropping off the sweatshirt I asked for at the most inopportune time. The room is empty, but my eye catches the navy blue fabric tossed on my bed. I quickly grab it and close myself inside the foggy bathroom to get dressed. I chose a pair of black gym shorts today, not that it really matters, since I'm sure they won't be visible.

When I get the blue sweater on, it makes me scoff. This one's even longer, ending right at my knees, so I'm doubtful that it's Havok's. Written across the front in gray lettering is SOTERIA. I remember that being the name of their company from the business card Lochlan gave me at the hospital. I'm standing in the middle of my room, trying and failing to run a brush through my hair, when there's a knock at the door.

"Come in," I call out, hissing as I hit a tangle.

"Best Friend," Kash says as he walks in, giving me one of those lopsided grins of his. "Ro made me run the beach with him this morning so I wouldn't wake you. It was torture, Honeybun. Absolute torture." The back of his hand is splayed across his forehead like he might faint.

"I'm sorry." I scrunch my nose in agreement. "Cardio is pretty brutal."

"Not the running." Kash waves his hand

dismissively. "It was torture to be kept away from my favorite person for half the damn day." His smile is full of mischief, and I can't help but swat his arm playfully.

"Let me help with that. Looks like you're struggling." Kash takes the brush before I can protest and swirls his finger, telling me to turn around. He starts at the ends of my hair and slowly works his way up, each stroke soft and gentle. I barely even feel it when he meets a knot. It's so calming I close my eyes, thinking of the way my mom used to do the same thing when I was a little girl. After he's brushed through it several times, Kash runs his fingers through the strands.

"All done," he whispers by my ear. I turn back around a give him a grateful smile.

"Thank you." I toss the hairbrush in the bathroom and search my closet for some socks. Their floors are tiled and my toes get cold really fast. When I'm ready, Kash and I head toward the main part of the house. Lochlan is sitting on the couch, his laptop placed on the coffee table in front of him as he works on something. Havok and Roan are in the kitchen, but Krew is noticeably absent.

"Cereal?" Havok offers, his mouth full of Cocoa Puffs. He pushes an empty bowl and spoon in front of me and nods to several boxes lining the counter.

"Sure," I answer, glancing at my options to see which one looks the most appealing. I go with Lucky Charms and take the milk Roan pulls from the fridge for me. "Yum." I savor the first bite, loving the little pops of sweetness from the marshmallows.

"Sorry about that," Havok says, gesturing to my overall appearance. "This brute decided it was his turn to donate a sweatshirt and cut me off when I was bringing you one of mine. It probably stinks." He smirks at Roan. Without thinking, I pull the collar to my nose and take a sniff. Definitely doesn't.

"Smells good to me," I reply with a shrug, going back to munching on my cereal. Roan shoots Havok a smug grin, like he's bested him somehow.

"Hey, Saylor," Lochlan interjects, so I spin to give him my attention. "I need to ask you something about what we discussed yesterday. Would you prefer we talk privately?"

"Um." I look at each of the guys, not seeing a reason to keep it from them. I'm not ashamed of the choice I made, so it really makes no difference to me. I assumed they were already made aware. "No, here is fine."

"Okay. Well, Dr. Kerrigan just emailed and she has an opening at two o'clock due to a cancellation. I know it's last minute, but she wanted to offer the spot to you first."

"Oh." I bite the inside of my cheek as my heartrate begins to climb. A quick glance at the clock shows the appointment slot is only thirty minutes from now. So, *really* last minute. But maybe this is the perfect scenario, where I have no time to stress or talk myself out of it. I'll never *want* to pick apart the last five years, but I know I need to. "Yeah. I'll take the opening." I grimace but square my shoulders.

"Let's go ahead and set everything up, then." Lochlan closes his laptop while I take my bowl to the sink and rinse it. Roan tries to grab it, but I manage to get it in the dishwasher before he can. I stick my tongue out, making him grin and shake his head at me.

"Proud of you, Little Fighter," he whispers as he places his hand on the base of my neck and tugs me closer. He drops a kiss to my temple, and for some reason, it makes me tear up. It's silly to be this scared, but it terrifies me to bring everything to the surface again after trying my hardest to banish it to the farthest recesses of my mind. I doubt Roan would be very proud if he were privy to my current thoughts, but it still feels nice to hear. I give Havok and Kash a wobbly smile, then follow Lochlan to his office.

"You can sit here." He pulls his desk chair out and places his laptop in front of me, the blank screen coming to life after he taps a few keys. A video icon appears with a link at the bottom showing my name, along with the date and time for the meeting. Above, it reads '*click to join*'. "When two o'clock rolls around, all you have to do is tap this and Dr. Kerrigan will be added to the video call. The guys and I will to stay clear of this part of the house, so nothing either of you says will be overheard. Do you have any questions?" Lochlan looks at me, his honey-colored eyes observing every nervous twitch I make.

"I don't think so," I answer, but even though I can't think of anything I'm still feeling woefully unprepared.

"Here." He bends down, pulling out a bottle of

water from the bottom drawer of his desk. "Just in case you need it."

"Thanks." I take it with shaky hands.

"You're going to be fine, sweetheart," Lochlan tells me, his hand sliding under mine to give it a reassuring squeeze. "If at any point you need to stop, that's perfectly fine. I'm going to go, but whenever you're done, come find us." I nod, my throat feeling too tight to form words. As soon as the door shuts behind him, I stare at the clock and watch the minutes tick by, one by one. I focus on that and that alone, so there's no room for me to start overthinking. When it's two on the dot, I take a deep breath and click the link. It chimes for a few seconds before the video connects and a brunette woman, who looks to be in her thirties, fills the screen. She's classically pretty and her smile puts me at ease.

"Saylor," she greets me. "It's so nice to meet you. My name is Danielle Kerrigan, but you can call me Dani or Danielle, if you'd like." Her eyes are warm and welcoming.

"It's nice to meet you too, Danielle." I smile, at least I hope that's what I'm doing.

"I know the basics of your case, but first I'd like to hear how you're feeling about today's meeting. I know it was sprung on you at the last second, so it's understandable if you feel ambushed or unsure."

"I'm nervous to talk about what I went through. Dreading it, actually. Yesterday was a good day, and I don't want to go back to feeling overwhelmed by grief. I've been trying to ignore it and live in the moment, though I doubt that's healthy." My voice cracks as I rush to articulate my thoughts, but a heavy exhale leaves me when I manage to say what I needed to.

"That's understandable. And healthy is relative. What's best for you now, might not be the same thing you need a month down the road. If, at this moment, what works for you is to focus on the present and not the past, then that's what we'll do. As long as you plan to address those hard topics at some point, I find nothing wrong with the way you're coping," Danielle states emphatically, leaving me stunned for a second.

"How about we discuss your current state. Do you feel safe where you are?"

"Yes," I respond instantly, knowing it to be true without needing to think the question over. "The guys have been great."

"I'm glad to hear that." Danielle nods thoughtfully as she repositions herself.

"And your sleep and diet? I know those things might seem trivial, but they definitely factor into your stress levels."

"I'm eating more every day, but it's been a process since my body isn't used to so many options. I've tried to ease my way in, and it seems to be working so far. Sleep isn't the greatest. I've had a few nightmares," I explain. "They tend to happen when I've been upset or dwelling on things during the day, which is why I've been keeping my head in the sand."

"That makes sense." Danielle taps her pen

against her lip. "What's it like to be a part of the world again? Are you finding it difficult to acclimate or connect?"

"It's confusing, I guess. Things have changed, but not enough for it to feel like I've time traveled to the future. I wish there were a handbook to tell me what happens next," I joke. "I haven't really been around anyone, but I've been okay with the guys."

"Well, I'm happy you have them. It's important to have a strong support system. As for adjusting to your new normal, I'd suggest taking things one day at a time. This won't be a sprint, Saylor. Honestly, not a marathon either. More like a cross-country trip by foot that might have some surprise stops along the way. And that's okay, because every step forward is progress, no matter how far the finish line is. I think it would be good for you to make a checklist of all the things you wanted to do, but weren't sure you'd ever get the chance to. Maybe add some stuff that the woman you are *now* would enjoy too. Because you're alive Saylor, and the possibilities are endless."

"That could be fun," I voice quietly, wiping at the tears building along my lower lashes. We chat a bit longer, keeping the topic light and menial. It's a nice segue into building trust with her so that when the time does come, it won't be as difficult to open up and bare my darkest secrets to her.

"I'm excited to hear what you come up with. How about we meet at the same time next week?" she asks while thumbing through her schedule.

"Sounds good."

"Perfect. I very much enjoyed our talk today. I'll see you next time, Saylor." Danielle grins and wiggles her fingers in lieu of waving.

"Bye."

I return her wave and hit the *end call* button. Slumping against Lochlan's office chair, I take a few minutes to process our conversation. It went nothing like I thought it would. I'd been so worried she would pry until I caved and blurted everything out, but it was the exact opposite of that. Danielle was respectful of my feelings and didn't once push me to talk about anything I didn't want to. I fully expected to leave this room a blubbering mess, but the only tears I cried were because her words made me feel hopeful. I twist the top off the bottle of water Lochlan gave me and drink it greedily. As soon as I leave his office, I can hear the guys laughing and joking. When they come into view, I stop to take in the scene before me. Kash and Roan are playing a game on the TV, their hands making karate chop motions as they jump around.

"Fuck off! It's not natural to be that quick when you're tank sized." Kash shoves him in the shoulder, but he barely moves.

"Tink." Krew appears beside me out of nowhere, causing me to jump. My hand goes to my chest, but he only startled me. I didn't for a second think I was in danger or worry about being hit. It makes me wonder if I'd be as trusting with anyone else as I am with these men. And why the heck it's so easy with them. "Ready to watch my twin make an ass of himself?" Krew smirks. I look back to find Kash wrestling with Roan. I can tell it's going nowhere fast. After toying with him for a few minutes, Roan seems to be over their little game and pins him to the ground. Using a t-shirt Havok tosses him, the two of them to tie Kash's hands and feet together while keeping him on his stomach.

"Hey! We agreed to no more turtling!" Kash shouts, wiggling around like a roly-poly.

"Turtling?" I whisper.

"Yeah. 'Cause he looks like a turtle that's stuck on its back," Krew explains, a slight laugh leaving him as he watches his brother attempt to free himself.

"Oh, look. Say's here." Havok grins.

"Best Friend!" Kash yells. "I require your assistance." I walk closer, stopping a few feet away, and assess the situation.

"You're really in a bind, huh?" I ask, pointing to the twisted-up shirt holding him hostage.

"Did she...was that a pun, pretty girl?" Havok swivels his head around to stare at me, then folds over laughing. The others follow suit, but I step forward and begin untying the man who's deemed himself my best friend. His limbs flop to the ground as soon as he's free. I hold the fabric, giving it a hard look as my mind brings me back to a time when I had something similar binding my hands and covering my eyes. I blink, swallowing past the lump in my throat, and remind myself that this isn't the same. It was a joke. Kash is fine. I'm perfectly safe and no one here would ever do that to me.

"Hey." Roan slides in front of me, his size

blocking out everyone else. "I didn't think. I'm sorry, Little Fighter. I keep messing up, but I swear I'd never do anything to hurt you."

"I know," I tell him, having to crane my neck back to meet his eyes. "You're not messing up. I'm just sensitive."

"No, you're trying to heal from something traumatic. Seeing reminders of said trauma doesn't help the cause. I'll do better." I nod, knowing it's pointless to argue. "Can I give you a hug?" I practically faceplant against Roan's chest, inhaling his scent and letting it block out the memory of being there. Instead of mildew, I'm surrounded by spicy hints of his cologne. He holds me until I'm the one to pull away.

"Who's down for another movie night?" Krew asks, glossing over my mini meltdown. I'm more than happy to move on and act like it didn't happen. Everyone agrees, so we settle in with a load of blankets and start a marathon of *Harry Potter*. We eat and laugh, then eat some more. I'm not sure who falls asleep first, but we end up crashing on the couch. Thank God it's massive.

Chapter Nineteen

Roan

My body is stiff as fuck from sleeping in a seated position for half the night, but damn if I was going to move. Saylor's tiny feet are laid across my lap. I've had my hand wrapped around one or the other, my thumb softly stroking the side of her ankle any time I feel her move. She's stirred once or twice, but one of us has been there to reach out and calm her before it got too bad. It's still dark, just past 4am, when I extricate myself from the impromptu slumber party.

My mind is restless. I've been dozing on and off, but haven't slept more than an hour at a time. It's not uncommon for me to be up and down throughout the night. Sometimes, I spend hours in the gym trying to tire myself out, eager for the inevitable crash. I've been so wrapped up in Saylor, worried about how she's doing and what she needs, that I haven't really had the time, nor brain power, to obsess over Elira the way I usually do. That's a mindfuck in itself.

My sister has always been my driving force. To do better—*be* better. Now here's this woman, occupying all of my free time and taking up residence in my thoughts, leaving little to no room for anything else. It's a different type of guilt. Like I've somehow forgotten or replaced Elira. I know it isn't true. I'll never forget my baby sister or the hell she endured. I just don't feel as consumed by it, and that's bothering the shit out of me.

Kade and I fucked up last night. We shouldn't have joked about tying Kash up like that. I noticed the second Saylor slipped away, lost to a memory she shouldn't fucking have to begin with. We were careless. But damn if she didn't pull herself out of it all on her own. She came to me, even after I'd been a part of the problem, and pressed her face to my chest like it was the only place she wanted to be. I would hold that girl forever, but I've never been more proud of her, seeing her take the comfort she needed and then strengthen her resolve.

Saylor is a lot fucking stronger than any of us give her credit for. If I'd been through the shit she has, there's a good chance I'd be holed-up somewhere, refusing to interact with the rest of the world. But not the five-foot-nothing pixie who's healing more and more every day, and she doesn't even realize it. Saylor has this idea that she's meek—maybe a bit of a pushover—but she's assertive when she needs to be. She's the perfect balance of soft and hard, and every time she lets go and her laughter fills the room, I swear it's like a shot of sunshine straight to my fucking nervous system.

I make a quick trip to my room to change into some gym shorts and a t-shirt. It's early as hell, but I know I won't be getting any more sleep. As quietly as possible, I slip out the patio door and make my way towards the beach. The air's still cool, but it won't take me long to work up a sweat. As soon as I reach the packed sand, I take off in a brisk jog. I've never been a runner, but there's something calming about being out here all alone, nothing but the sound of the ocean for company.

We're the only house on either side for a good mile. When we bought this land, it'd been the last piece available for purchase. Some old-money Floridian acquired several plots because he didn't want anyone to build right on top of his estate. He sold a few pieces off a while back and we were lucky enough to snag one. Thus far, it's been the perfect setup, not having some nosy ass neighbor in our business on the regular. When I finally make it back to the house, I have to take a second to catch my breath. With my hands braced on my knees, I drag in deep, steady pulls of air.

It's silent when I step inside; everyone's knocked out still. Kash has candy wrappers strewn across his chest, likely sleeping off a sugar crash. Saylor is exactly where I left her, but Krew's slyly taken my place. His hand is resting on her calf, blanket pushed aside so his skin is touching hers. As much as he tries to pull away, it seems he's just as fucked as the rest of us. Kade's slumped in the corner, and Loch has claimed the other side to stretch out. With the shape of the sectional, it's basically three long couches that form a U. Krew thought it was unnecessary, especially since we have the media room downstairs, but I bet he's happy we have it now. I shake my head, a smile curving my lips as I think about how easily Saylor fits with us.

I make a beeline for the shower, eager to wash the sweat from my body. My thigh muscles are going to hate me from the torture I put them through this morning. I don't usually run for as long as I did, but I got lost in the rhythmic thump of my feet and the quiet nothingness inside of my head. I shower, dress in some sweats and a plain white tee, then throw my damp hair up to keep it out of the way.

The first sign of sunlight is peeking through the windows when I walk back out. Kash is usually up by now, so I'm shocked to see he's still sleeping. Like a fucking rooster, he rises with each new day and proceeds to wake the whole goddamn place with his racket. Where Krew is content to keep his own company, Kash thrives on interaction. He doesn't do well when he's left alone, so as much I might want to strangle the fucker when he interrupts the rare sleep I do get, I understand that it's not something he does to be annoying. But the other hell he causes? Definitely intentional.

I head to the kitchen, planning to get some food going. After the junk we ate last night, we could do with something more substantial to even out the scales. I grab some diced potatoes from the freezer, toss them in a mixture of seasonings, and stick the baking sheet in the oven. The biscuits Saylor loved so much go in as well, and then I start frying the sausage. I've been cooking since I was a kid, not really having any other choice but to learn or go hungry. The guys caught on pretty quickly, even Loch, who'd been used to having a private chef for most of his life.

As soon as the meat's done, I crumble a few pieces up and place them back into the pan to make sausage gravy. Hopefully, it's not too greasy for Saylor to handle. I know her stomach is still sensitive and trying to adjust, but just like everything else she's been dealing with, she's doing far better than I thought she'd be at this point. It's been little more than a week since I kicked that fucking door in. It feels like so much longer, though. When everything's done, I start making Saylor's plate first. I can see the sleepy fuckers rousing, but my Little Fighter is still down for the count.

"Goddamn, that smells like heaven," Kade mumbles as he climbs to his feet unsteadily. His eyes are closed as he walks to the kitchen, but his nose leads the way.

"Only you could take the Lord's name in vain while comparing something to Heaven." Loch sits up, elbows braced on his knees as he scrubs a hand over his face. Kade grunts, trying to take the plate I'm making, but I swat him away. I've already put him on his ass once for taking Saylor's food, and I won't hesitate to do it again.

Krew stretches out, glancing to where his hand is resting on Saylor. The moment awareness filters back in, he jerks it away. What a dumb fucker. He can play unaffected all he wants, even try to put distance between them, but it'll be pointless. If I have anything to say about it, she won't be going anywhere. Kash grumbles from where he's passed out, but eventually rolls over and pushes himself to his feet. Both him and his brother follow Loch and start shoveling down mounds of food before I can even get Saylor moving. I walk over, squatting beside the couch, and lightly brush my finger over the bridge of her nose.

"Little Fighter." I speak quietly, trying to draw her awake gently. She flutters her eyes, slowly coming around and giving me the sweetest fucking smile.

"Good morning," she whispers groggily. "Something smells good."

"I have a plate ready for you. You hungry?" She nods, so I hold my hand out to help her up. She stretches, wincing a little at the pull it causes on her ribs. I steer Saylor to the kitchen, get her seated, then slide her food and morning pain meds over.

"You made biscuits and gravy?" she gasps, looking like a kid on Christmas morning. "This was Mom's favorite." I expect her to get emotional, but she just grins, more nostalgic than upset.

"I might've grown up in Washington, but the mouth of the south here taught us a few secrets." I wink, pointing at Kade.

"It's her recipe, Say." He looks up, giving her a sad smile. *Well, fuck.* Kade's always been tight-lipped when it comes to Saylor. We never understood his obsession with finding her. Outside of sharing a hometown, there'd been no obvious link connecting the two. There's a lot he's never told us, but his closeness with Eliza Radley was never a secret.

"Seriously?" She returns his smile, but it's fragile.

"It definitely wasn't my shitty mother that taught me how to cook," Kade jokes, trying to lighten the mood.

"I didn't realize you weren't from here," Saylor says, giving me a questioning look and redirecting the conversation. She takes a bite of her food and groans. It's an indecent fucking sound, and I'd bet my left nut that every one of us just popped a semi. She's the center of attention, but not for the reason she's thinking. Saylor's ignorant of the affect she has on us, and we're dirty bastards for looking at her with any sort of interest.

"No," I answer, clearing my throat while searching for something else to focus on besides the way she's licking her fork. "I was actually born in Albania, but moved to Washington when I was a kid."

"What?" Saylor drops the silverware she was assaulting, causing it to clatter against her plate. "How did I not know that?" Her brows pinch together.

"I guess it just hasn't come up before now." I shrug. "I don't usually talk about my life before the guys."

"Oh." Saylor resumes eating, but it's obvious she's biting back a million questions. "I feel like all of you know so much about me, but I barely know a thing about any of you." She nibbles her bottom lip nervously, like she's worried it's somehow crossing a line to want to know us better.

"You're right," Loch says, rinsing his plate and placing it in the dishwasher. "It's not something we've done intentionally. I can't speak for anyone else, but

I'm an open book. Anything you want to know, you're more than welcome to ask." He smiles, arms and feet crossed as he leans against the counter.

My skin tightens at the thought of spilling my life's story to Saylor, but I know if she asked, there's no way I'd deny her. It terrifies me that she might see me differently. That she could confirm all the insecurities I fight to overcome every day. The dark thoughts telling me I failed the one person I should have protected above all else. A knife to the jugular would be less painful than to have Saylor's eyes cloud with judgement and disappointment every time she looks at me.

"Are you from Washington, too?" she questions, taking the opening Loch offered.

"I was born in Upstate New York, but spent my summers in London visiting my Nan. I moved to Washington when I was twenty because that's where Ro was," he responds. Not for the first time, I remind myself of how lucky I am to have someone like Lochlan Calloway in my life. I should send the makers of that stupid video game a damn fruit basket or something.

"We're from Washington as well," Krew cuts in. "We met Loch and Ro when we were fifteen. Moved in with them when we were legally allowed to, and then made the jump to Florida about six years ago." Kash is quiet, letting his brother speak for the both of them. I think we can all agree that our personal shit —*the painful shit*—should be discussed with her one-on-one. It's hard enough to open up without the added pressure of an audience.

"And you know how they found my sorry ass," Kade adds, grabbing Saylor's empty plate along with his.

"Wow. How did you even meet Roan if you guys lived on opposite ends of the country?" She tilts her head to the side, her nose turning up in confusion as she ponders the logistics of us stumbling across each other from thousands of miles away.

God, I love it when she does that.

"A video game," Loch answers simply, laughing at the surprised look on her face. "We played together online, got to talking and never really stopped."

"That's...not what I was expecting," Saylor laughs, earning a smile from each of us at the lighthearted sound.

"So, I know Havok is twenty-one, but how old are the rest of you? I feel like that's a question I should have asked by now." Saylor plants her elbows on the counter and rests her chin in her hands, her feet swinging back and forth as she waits for our responses.

"I'm twenty-eight." Loch smiles tightly. He's practically sweating bullets, worried how she might feel about their age difference.

And why might that be, you cocksucker?

"Twenty-six," I tell her, tugging on the hem of my sweatshirt she's wearing.

"We're twenty-three." Kash grins with the admission. "But I'm nine minutes older." Krew rolls his eyes, more than used to his twin's need to tack on that bit of information every chance he gets.

"And now you're the baby of the group instead of me," Kade jokes, ruffling Saylor's hair to further prove his point. She looks thoroughly unamused, but he just grins, as if he finds her annoyance cute.

There's a lull in conversation, so I start cleaning up the mess from breakfast and run the dishwasher. I'm just about done wiping the counter down when the mail we picked up the other day catches my eye. It's usually junk, but the edge of a postcard peeking out from the pile makes me pause. I toss the rag in the sink and dry my hands off before grabbing it. The front reads, *'Greetings from Fargo, North Dakota'*. I wrack my brain, trying to remember if we've had a client anywhere near there recently, but no one comes to mind. I flip it around, thinking it might've been placed in the wrong box or something, but stop short at the name it's addressed to.

Saylor Radley

In the blank area to the right, *'see you soon'* is scrawled in red ink, a sequence of coordinates just below it. I think I blackout for a moment. Pure, unadulterated fear seeps from every pore on my body, closely followed by rage. Loch catches my eye, having picked up on the sudden shift in my emotions, but I look to Saylor and shake my head. His back straightens, a look of worry flashing across his face before he schools it. The last thing we need is to freak her out.

"I'm going to go take a shower if no one needs me for anything right now?" She slides off the stool, looking between us for an answer.

"You're good, sweetheart. Take as long as you want." Loch smiles, and off she goes, her tiny little feet padding across the tile floor. As soon as we hear the soft click of her door, he rounds on me.

"What's wrong?" I hand him the card, my jaw clenched too tightly to respond.

"Fuck," he swears angrily. "What the hell is this?"

"What's happening?" Kade questions as the twins close in. Loch hands it over so they can see for themselves.

"The fuck?" Kade whispers, his eyes flitting over the writing, trying to make sense of it.

"How would anyone know that she's here?" Loch starts pacing. "Denvers said he was going to scrub any connection that Saylor has to us. Other than being listed as her next of kin at the hospital, there shouldn't be a link."

"It's not foolproof," Krew answers. "And I think you're forgetting that there were plenty of people who saw the both of you with her. Not just during her stay, you left together as well."

"Goddamnit." Kade grabs the back of his neck, his gaze fixed on the ceiling.

"This is why we have a P.O. box. The house is listed under the trust, so theoretically, it shouldn't be possible for someone to trace it back to us," Krew offers, but words like '*theoretically*' and '*shouldn't be*' aren't really working for me at the moment. Loch pulls his phone out, swiping through it quickly before placing it against his ear.

"Denvers," he greets. "Gonna put you on speaker, but I need you to keep your voice down."

"What's going on, Calloway?" His words are clear, just loud enough for us to hear.

"We received a postcard addressed to Saylor. I'm sending you a picture of it now." Loch snaps a photo of both sides, then texts it to him. The vibration sounds through the line a second later.

"Jesus Christ," Denvers sighs. "When?"

"We picked up the mail two days ago, but I just noticed it this morning," I answer with a wince. He grunts, but doesn't chew our asses out like I expected him to.

"Have the Wonder Twins ran these coordinates?" Denvers asks.

"Negative. We wanted to call you first," Loch tells him, cutting off whatever smart remark Krew was gearing up to make.

"Looks to be a wooded area along The Red River. I'll touch base with local authorities and have them check it out. Keep your phone on you," Denvers demands, hanging up without so much as a goodbye.

"I'm going to see if Saylor wants to spend the day at the beach. She needs to be away from here whenever he calls back," Kash rushes out. "I don't want her to overhear anything by accident."

"I'll go, too," Kade offers. "Meet you out back in a few." The two of them head in their respective directions to get changed. If anyone can keep Saylor occupied, it'll be them.

"Let's hope she's up for it," Krew chimes in. He must be blanking on the way Saylor's eyes lit up when she realized the beach was basically her new back yard. Of course, she's fucking up for it.

Chapter Twenty

Saylor

There's a light tap at my door, but I'm still wrapped in my towel, trying to figure out what to put on since I forgot to ask one of the guys for another hoodie. Mindful of my lack of clothing, I peek my head out to find Kash grinning back at me.

"What's up?"

"Whatcha doing, Best Friend?" he asks, a hint of laughter in his voice.

"Um...trying to find a shirt?" I answer. Kash makes a choking sound, likely as uncomfortable as I am.

"Oh." He's quiet for a second, but then clears his throat and says, "Would you like to go to the beach?"

"*Yes!*" I answer way too quickly, my excitement taking over before I can rein it in. Kash just chuckles, his brown eyes twinkling with amusement.

"There are a few bathing suits in your dresser, but wear whatever you'd like. I'll be in the kitchen when you're ready."

As soon as I hear his footsteps retreating, I close the door and scurry to my closet. Shorts and a t-shirt would be my preferable go-to, but it'd be nice to feel normal, at least for a little while. I check the top drawer, and sure enough, there they sit. There's a white bikini, to which I instantly veto. It's way too skimpy and my current state of paleness would make me look transparent if I attempted to wear something so light. Next, I find a black one-piece. It covers all the right places, so I decide to try it on.

I'm not the least bit surprised to find it fits like a glove, and it wasn't as hard to get on as I thought it'd be. Still feeling marginally underdressed, I grab some black gym shorts and pull them on as well. I can't really do much with my hair without the use of both hands, so I grab the flip-flops Karley gave me and head out.

"Ready to go?" Both Havok and Kash are waiting by the patio door, one bouncing around like an eager puppy who's been locked in a crate all day, while the other looks slightly annoyed by the hyperactivity. They've already filled a bag with beach towels and snacks. Obviously, the house is too far away for Kash when he might require sustenance immediately. I smile, shaking my head at the man.

"Yep," I reply, putting the poor guy out of his misery.

"You want your hair down, or would you rather have it up?" Roan asks, walking over from the living room.

"Up would be better, but…" I trail off, lifting my

bum wrist in the air as an explanation.

"C'mere." He pulls me closer, then tugs the tie from his own hair. "Flip over." I do as he says, biting back a smile as he gathers my blonde strands near the top of my head. Roan tilts me up and wraps the elastic around the ponytail he's formed, gently tightening it when he's finished. I look back at him, something akin to awe making my cheeks flush. He chuckles, dropping a kiss to my temple.

"Have fun, Little Fighter."

"Smooth fucker," Havok grumbles, jerking open the slider.

The other two are nowhere to be found, so I follow Kash and Havok to the beach. The waves are calm today, the water crystal clear. There's no yucky seaweed clinging to the shoreline; it's the perfect time to visit. Kash drops our bag and lays out a towel for each of us, then hands me a bottle of sunscreen. I lather it on without protest, because Lord knows I'll bake myself crispy otherwise. Once it's dry, I take a seat and slowly lie back. I can't help but think of how badly it hurt to even walk through the sand last time. I'm still sore, but every day I feel a little better.

"Sucker, Pumpkin Doodle?" Kash waves the candy at me.

"I'm good. Thank you, though." I smile, turning toward him slightly, but the sun's too bright to meet his eyes.

"So, how'd yesterday go? Anything you want to talk about?" Havok asks, leaning back on his elbows beside me.

"It was okay," I answer. "Danielle thinks I should make a list of all the things I want to do, but didn't know if I'd ever get the chance to."

"She gave you homework?" he jokes, but it makes me laugh.

"Yeah, I guess she did since she wants me to discuss what I wrote down next week."

Kash snaps his fingers, like a lightbulb's gone off inside his head. "Be right back!" In a flash, he sprints towards the house. Havok stays quiet, so I close my eyes and listen to the waves crash against the shore. Next thing I know, Kash is flopping back down, barely out of breath.

"Okay, let's hear it. What's the first thing?" I look over, eyeing the pen and notebook in his hand. "Tell us what you want to do, Best Friend." His eyes are wide with excitement.

"Um." I tap my chin, trying to think of something. "Eat pizza?"

"Okay." He nods and writes it down. "What's another?"

"Eat ice cream?" I scratch my head.

"Got it. Now something that *doesn't* involve eating," he orders, giving me a mock glare.

"I..I guess I'd like to get my GED." Admitting that comes with a heavy dose of insecurity, not because I think it's somehow less than the high school diploma I should've gotten, but because I know it's not an easy test, and I have no idea where I stand with my education. Luckily, school was pretty easy for me and

I typically tested ahead in my classes. But I've missed vital years of instruction.

"Yeah?" Havok grins. "I think that's awesome, Say."

"Alrighty. Next up. What's it gonna be, Best Friend?" Kash wiggles his pen at me, eagerly awaiting the next thing he can add to the list.

"Learn how to drive," I tell him, because really, how the heck does one acquire independence when you can't get from point A to point B without needing a chauffeur? He writes it down quickly, peering at me expectantly as soon as he's finished. My cheeks hurt from how hard I'm smiling.

"If I do get my GED, I'd like to take college classes."

"*Please*," Havok scoffs. "*If*, pretty girl? We both know you'll ace it. You've always been the smartest person in the room, at any given time." He winks at me, but I swear a ten-ton stone has lodged itself in my chest cavity. I didn't feel very smart in that cellar. No matter how many times I brainstormed or tried to fight my way out of there, Liam was always one step ahead. I certainly wasn't the smartest person in the room then. As if he can sense the dark direction of my thoughts, Havok slides his hand closer and links his pinky with mine.

"Maybe one day.." I pause, mulling over my words. "I hope to have a career I love. A family." Conveniently, I leave out the fear I'm harboring about my own worthiness. The apprehension I have that a future partner might see me as dirty or damaged goods. Those aren't attractive qualities any man would desire.

"You've already got a family," Kash states, looking me dead in my eyes. There's a hint of hurt in his voice, but I don't think he understood that in the context I meant it.

"You're right." I smile, waiting for his chocolate gaze to lighten, along with his mood.

"Okay, that's a good start. We'll stick it on the fridge and add to it like we do the other one." Kash flips the notebook closed and tosses it aside. "Who wants to have a sandcastle building competition?" He waggles his eyebrows, completely ignoring Havok's groan of annoyance. Reaching behind me, he whips out a bucket of beach toys. I squeal, the excited noise uncontainable. They laugh at my over-the-top reaction, but I'm too busy inventorying the goods to be bothered.

"Snagged these bad boys from the garage when I went back for the pen and paper," Kash explains.

"Why do you even have them in the first place?" I ponder.

"Why do you think?" Havok cocks his head to the side. "For our man-child, of course." Kash flips him off as he dumps the bucket, handing me all of the pink toys before splitting the rest between the two of them.

"Okay, thirty minutes starts...*now!*" Kash starts slinging sand everywhere, barely giving us a heads-up that it's go-time.

I wiggle off my towel, claiming a bare spot as

my own so the guys can't encroach on my territory. They have no idea how many times Mom and I did this very thing. I briefly mentioned it to Kash, but I don't think he understands how seriously we took our castle building. Even one-handed, I'm determined to best their amateur skills. I grin, digging my fingers beneath the sand until my arm is completely buried, then push it through the other side to make a bridge. Shovel in hand, I form a circle, extending the moat until an island takes shape in the middle. From there, I construct the castle itself. Using the two pails—one bigger, one smaller—I begin erecting the turrets.

Right when Kash calls a five-minute warning, I haul myself up and head for the water. I'm too focused on my own build, so I have no idea how theirs are coming along. I fill my bucket and walk as quickly as I can back to my nearly finished masterpiece. Despite my best effort, the water only soaks into the sand. I growl in frustration but spot some seashells a few feet away. Scattering them around the edge, I decide the moat is currently experiencing a drought.

"Time!" Kash screeches, scaring me half to death. We step back to view our work. "Well, it's clear my Jujube will be taking first place." I fist pump, but only a little. My ribs are starting to ache from all the moving around.

"Say, who's second?" Havok questions.

"Uh..." I freeze, not wanting to be the one to decide. "It's a tie?" I analyze both castles, though I'm not sure you could call them that. Kash's has a bit more shape, whereas Havok's is nothing more than a couple of lumps. No rhyme or reason. They look eerily similar to...

"Are those boobs?" I point, blurting out the accusation. Havok folds over laughing as Kash rears back in shock.

"You dirty bastard! Grounds for disqualification. I win!" Kash dances in victory, but who knows what moves those are and where the hell he learned them.

"Bullshit," Havok scoffs. He marches over and stomps Kash's sandcastle to smithereens. My jaw drops, eyes bugging out of my head.

"I'm gonna beat your ass," Kash yells, but his poorly contained smile lessens the effect of his threat.

They take off, chasing each other up and down the beach. I stay put and watch, laughing as they dodge and weave one another. Kash isn't wrong; they do feel like family. I'm growing more attached to them by the day. Havok finally catches him, tossing Kash over his shoulder before sprinting toward the water. I'm outright giggling as they crash into the waves, both dropping like dead weight. They're sputtering and laughing, every inch of them drenched. I don't think I've ever seen a more beautiful sight than Havok McKade grinning without a care in the world. He looks so genuinely happy it makes my chest ache.

They rise, trudging through the water as they playfully shove each other. Havok's white tee clings to his skin, the same colorful tattoos covering his arms now visible along his torso. I'm riveted, trying to make out the designs, when he peels the wet material up and over his head. It's not just my cheeks that heat this time, it's my entire body. His abdomen is lean but cut, and droplets of saltwater accentuate his defined muscles in a way I find far too appealing. I'm almost twenty; I understand my reaction. I just didn't expect to have this sort of response so soon, and certainly not to him.

"Got a little drool, pretty girl." Havok swipes his thumb across my bottom lip, a devilish grin on his face. *Oh God, if there was ever a good time for a sinkhole to randomly open up and suck me down, this would be it.* Kash laughs, shaking his body like a wet dog. Water goes flying, the cool droplets feeling glorious against my too-hot flesh. What a perfect time to dip my toes in. I say a quick *see-ya-later* and book it as fast as my achy ribs allow.

I spend a good twenty-minutes walking the shoreline, but never wander too far. The guys are within eyeshot at all times. They've got sandwiches pulled out when I make it back to my towel, and Kash hands one over as I take a seat. I smile at the turkey and mustard combo, a favorite of mine that Havok must've learned about from Mom. A bag of chips is placed between us, so I snag a few, popping them in my mouth while staring out at the endless expanse of ocean. It gives me chills, thinking of being out there. Tossed around by the waves with nothing but water in every direction, as far as the eye can see.

Once we've finished, I resume my earlier position. Both men follow a second later, their arms going behind their heads to act as a pillow. I'm sure I look stiff as a board, since I can't do that without wanting to cry. The sun feels good, leading me to close my eyes. I bet it's nearing a hundred degrees, but with the breeze coming off the ocean it's not as noticeable. This reminds me of summers spent with Mom and Grandaddy, fishing off the pier and helping him prep his boat. We'd refuse his offers to join him on his trips, likely residual trauma from my father's death, but it was nice to spend time together.

"Hey, Havok," I call out, breaking through the comfortable silence we'd fallen into. "Did you ever go to my grandad's grave?"

"Once. Why?" I feel him turn towards me, but keep my eyes closed.

"Just wondering how it looks. If anyone's taking care of it," I answer.

"I went with Liz a few weeks before she passed. She wanted a chance to say goodbye. We can always go visit, Say," he offers, his pinky finding mine again.

"That's okay. I have no plans to set foot in Pike's Bay ever again." My voice is steady and certain, brokering no room for debate.

"Then Krew and I will fly a drone in and you can see it from a screen in the office. I'll even pay the florist extra to deliver flowers as often as you want," Kash says matter of factly. My chest warms, his sweet sincerity making my eyes burn.

"We can hire someone to come out every six months to do routine maintenance. Make sure it's clean and whatnot," Havok adds with a dismissive wave of his hand, playing down the offer like it's no big deal. But it is. Everything they've done since the day Lochlan and Roan found me has been for the betterment of my wellbeing. They're selfless, and I know, without a doubt, they'd protect me by any means necessary. I have no idea how things would've gone had I chosen to go to the safe house, but I'm grateful that I'm here instead.

Kash twines his fingers with my other hand, giving it a squeeze. I'd do the same with Havok, but he's stuck with my injured side and the brace won't allow it. He keeps our pinkies connected, though. I'm so relaxed, it takes me no time at all to drift off. Content as can be, the three of us nap, paying no mind to the sun or anything else.

Chapter Twenty-One

Lochlan

Saylor, Kade, and Kash came in from the beach a few hours ago. They were sweaty and exhausted from the heat, her cheeks and nose tinged with pink, making it clear that she hadn't reapplied the sunblock I sent with them. I could've kicked both my brother's asses for not thinking to remind her. But damn she looked beautiful coming through the door, her face flushed and the setting sun framing her silhouette. Her eyes were bright and clear, despite how tired she was, and it soothed that thing inside of me that's desperate to bring Saylor back to life.

With everything else going on today, I didn't kick up a fuss about her wanting to turn in early. Of course, I want her to rest, but I've grown used to watching her eat. It helps to see with my own eyes that she's getting stronger every day, but Kash made sure to take some dinner and pain medicine to her room. We haven't seen him since. I've been anxious all afternoon, waiting for Denvers to call us back, but we haven't gotten so much as a text. The guys and I

—minus Kash, who's likely snuggled up to Saylor—are standing around the kitchen, eating our dinners in silence.

We're too lost inside our heads, thinking of every worst-case scenario imaginable to even enjoy the spaghetti Bolognese Krew made. Each bite goes in my mouth and down my throat without me really tasting it. I pull the fridge open to grab something to drink, pausing when I close the door back and notice a new list beside the others Kash made. This one's in his handwriting as well, so it must be something they worked on at the beach.

"What's this?" I nod to the list while looking at Kade. He swallows the food in his mouth, and then replies with, "Something the therapist suggested. Things she wants to do but didn't know if she'd ever get to." A burning sensation has me rubbing my chest as I read over each item. Simple shit like eat pizza and ice cream. And she thought, had likely accepted, that she wouldn't get to do those things again. Saylor didn't know if she'd ever leave that place, and even if she got to, she hadn't counted on being alive when it happened. It makes me want to rage and beat my fist into a fucking wall. She deserves everything written on this piece of paper, and I'm going to do whatever it takes to make every last one a reality. I whip my phone out and get to work.

"What are you doing?" Ro slides up next to me, watching over my shoulder as I scroll through laptops, looking for something that's user friendly but not a cheap piece of shit.

"If Saylor wants to get her GED, then she's

going to need a computer," I answer distractedly.

"That one," Krew points. I add it to the cart without question, knowing he'd be the best choice to pick out anything tech related. I start a new search for study materials, adding everything I come across that's highly rated.

"I'm not sure if Saylor thought about it or not, but she can also choose to get her high school diploma if she prefers to go that route. It can be done completely online. Maybe we should print some information out about both options, and then she can decide," Krew adds.

"Good idea," Kade mumbles around a mouth full of noodles. I nod in agreement, wanting to give her as many choices as possible.

"She needs a phone," Ro remarks, pulling his own from his pocket. "I'll add her to our plan and get her the same thing we've got. Grab a case too." I type in the make and model of the phone, but pause when the results pull up pages and pages of designs. Everything from plain to girly and glittery. Shit, I have no idea what to get.

"Go with that one." Kade points his fork at a light blue case that has a watercolor image of the beach on the back of it. *Perfect*. I hit the checkout button, double checking that no one can think of anything else to add, then swipe to pay. Two-day shipping has always been fine with me, but I'd rather have it delivered immediately. I need to do this for her, to fix the things I can because there's so much I have no control over. But this? *This* I can do. I'm just about to pocket my phone when it starts to ring, Denvers name flashing across the screen.

"Give me just a sec," I answer, nodding to the guys to head to the lower level. It's too quiet up here to talk freely. We descend the stairs as quietly as possible, gathering in the media room to hear whatever update he has for us. With the door closed, I place the phone on speaker. "Alright, we're good now."

"Jesus, Calloway. I'm not sure where to start." Denvers exhales, sounding like his day has been far more stressful than ours. I clench my jaw, knowing the next words from his mouth aren't going to be anything good. "Locals followed the coordinates and found a body. Young woman—estimated to be in her early twenties. Petite, blonde hair, blue eyes." I slump against the wall, feeling every ounce of blood drain from my extremities, leaving me lightheaded and sick to my stomach. There's no fucking way the victim's description is a coincidence.

"Time of death?" Ro croaks. My head jerks up, scrutinizing the way his hands are balled into fists at his sides and the sickly pallor of his skin. And then it hits me. He's wondering if she's been dead this entire time, or if she died because we didn't see the postcard sooner. What a fucked up game that would be, leaving someone's life in our hands, a looming countdown we're unaware of.

"Five to seven days. Hard to say for sure. Some...outside elements...have assisted with the decomposition." Ro deflates, but that anger of his still remains. "We might have a positive ID based on a missing person's report that matches the victim's description, but they aren't releasing anything until next of kin has been notified and confirms."

"What the fuck is this? Substitution killing, or a warning?" Kade tugs at his hair, pacing back and forth between the theater seating.

"It's hard to guess at the thoughts of a madman, but I think it's safe to say it's either him fantasizing about doing the same to Saylor, or it's a warning to get her to come out of hiding. That's a lot of guilt to carry, knowing someone's out there killing innocent women because they don't have what they really want. Sadly, it's rather effective," Denvers explains, but he really doesn't need to. We're well aware of what he's saying, but it's different being on this end. I drop my head as bile creeps up my throat.

"Have they determined cause of death?" Krew asks. I wince, not really sure I want to hear it.

"Nothing definitive, but upon first glance it appears she was raped and beaten. Her body was found bare, and they haven't come across a stitch of clothing within the search vicinity." *I'm going to be sick.* The guys swear, someone punches the wall, but it's all muffled from the panic fogging my brain. Everything Denvers just relayed hits me like a goddamn freight train.

I see *Saylor's* blue eyes in place of this woman's.

Saylor's long blonde hair.

Saylor's lifeless body, abused and violated, then discarded like a piece of trash.

There's no way in hell I'll let that happen. I'll

uproot everything and cart us off to the middle of fucking nowhere if I have to. This piece of shit will *not* take her. As much as it kills me, I know we have to lie. Because Saylor is the exact kind of good that would be devastated to know someone's died because of her. And my gut tells me this woman won't be the only casualty. If we want to protect her, she can't know about this.

"On a different note," Denvers says, bringing me back to the present. "The computer we found was work-issued. Not a thing on it."

Fuck.

"Well, we know he was recently in Fargo, North Dakota. So, that's a start," Krew chimes in. I hope like fuck that brilliant mind of his is already working a mile a minute, coming up with a plan to find this fucker before he can hurt anyone else. "And there's no reason to think he knows the physical location of the house."

"It's secure enough, so I see no reason to move Saylor just yet." We stiffen in unison, the thought of him even *trying* to take her making us defensive as fuck. Agent or not, that won't go over well. "I've gotta run. Keep this quiet, boys, and let me know if you find anything." Denvers ends the call without another word.

I drop my head back and close my eyes, giving myself a few minutes to silently rage against the self-control that's keeping me from tearing this room apart, piece by piece. I want to break something, let everything I'm feeling boil over until it floods out like poison. But I keep it contained, allowing it to fester and eat at my insides. I have to be the one who keeps his cool. It's my responsibility to maintain a level head and come up with a damn solution, not be a part of the problem.

"Okay." I stand, slipping back into the leadership role I both love and hate. "It goes without saying that Saylor won't hear a word of this. We keep her busy and happy. I don't want there to be any reason for her to think that something's off."

"We'll work through her list," Kade states. "I'll push her to keep adding to it so we don't run out of shit to do."

"This is fucked. I hate lying to her. We're trying to build trust, and when this comes out—which it fucking will—there's no way she won't feel betrayed." Ro shakes his head, glaring at the floor with his arms crossed, but his anger isn't pointed at any of us. It's the situation.

"We're backed into a corner, Ro. We've got a shit choice, or an even shittier one. And the latter will likely result in the woman we're all falling for being taken again. Or worse." I give him a hard look, rolling my eyes at the choking sound Krew makes. "Let's cut the crap and stop pretending like every damn one of us isn't feeling something we shouldn't be for Saylor. I won't act on it, and neither should any of you, but if the day ever comes that she initiates or gives me so much as an inkling that she feels the same way, all bets are off."

"Fuck you, Loch," Kade snarls. "I'm the one

she's known half her damn life. It was *me* that cared for her sick mother. *Me* that put Saylor on your fucking radar in the first place."

"That doesn't make her yours, dickhead," I growl.

"No, it doesn't. But I'm sure as fuck *hers*." Kade takes a step closer with every venomous word he spits, until we're toe-to-toe, glaring at each other in a way we never have before. "It won't matter who she's with, I will *always* belong to Saylor. At the end of the day, her happiness is what's most important. But I won't disappear from her life for you or anyone else. Got that, *brother*?" I roll my tongue over my teeth, loathing the truth and finality of his declaration.

"How about we stop the posturing, considering you're both peacocking over a woman who's emotionally unavailable. You sound disgusting." Krew throws the door open, clearly done with our bullshit.

Goddamnit.

I feel like a sick bastard. Saylor needs a support system and people she can rely on, not men salivating at the hope she might one day want more. Maybe Krew's had the right idea all along by keeping his distance. But as quick as the thought comes, it's banished. I could no sooner do that than go all day without at least three cups of coffee. I'm addicted to her just the same. Like I said, I won't act on it, but I need to do better about letting my thoughts get so carried away.

"Let's go. It's been a fucking day and I'm ready to call it quits." Ro stomps up the stairs, Kade and

I following a few steps behind. Neither one of us apologizes for the things we said. Maybe we both know that we're telling the God's honest truth about our feelings, or we just need some time to process. Either way, we each go our separate ways once we're back on the main level. I have the sudden urge to go to my office, just to be closer to Saylor. I keep waiting for the next nightmare, for her screams to rip me from sleep and clamp a vice around my heart. Every night that passes without that happening feels like a small victory.

Against my better judgement, I turn left at the end of the hallway. I'm feeding these thoughts I shouldn't be having, when I need to take a step back and remind myself that Saylor's fragile. The last thing I'd ever want is to hurt her in any way. Yet I still open her door, needing to see her. To know she's okay. I pull up short at the sight that greets me. Kash is in her bed, his back to the door as she lies on the opposite side facing him. Their hands are clasped together, the only point of contact between them, but it's somehow intimate. It reminds me of the way she held onto me in the hospital.

"Did you ever consider that she might need all of us?" Kade's voice is quiet behind me, but you'd think he screamed the words based on my reaction. On the outside, I'm still standing there, hand clenching the doorknob as I watch two broken people sleeping peacefully, finding comfort in one another. A feat they both struggle with, but currently isn't an issue based on the way Saylor's lips are slightly parted and Kash is borderline snoring.

On the inside, though? Something shifts. Maybe it's acceptance, settling in for the long haul. It sends a crack right through the possibilities I saw, creating a chasm between the '*one days*' and the '*maybes*'. I want to be selfish. For fucking once, I want to take something for myself instead of worrying about everyone else. I'll never regret what we've built, but I've always put the guys first. And looking at Kash, I know this won't be any different. I could never knowingly hurt him, and it's clear as day that he needs Saylor just as much, if not more, than she needs any of us.

The sad part, is that I know I'll take whatever scraps I can get. If it means Saylor's a part of my life, I'll play any role she needs me to. I'm no different than Kade. She sees us as the men entrusted to protect her. Friends, perhaps, but nothing more than that. So maybe I should focus on being what she needs right now and let the rest of it go. It was a farfetched idea to begin with, but now it feels downright ridiculous. I pull the door closed, taking a second to get my shit together so every sappy thing I've been thinking isn't written all over my fucking face.

"You're right." I turn to look at Kade. "She needs all of us to be what we promised her we'd be. Protectors. Friends. Family. Saylor trusts us, so let's not fuck that up." I walk straight to my room, not giving him a chance to say anything more on the matter. It wouldn't make a difference. A nagging little voice in the back of my head is taunting me, whispering that we're already screwing things up. That delicate thread of trust we're establishing is going to be tested when she finds out that Liam has escalated to outright killing. Made even worse by us keeping it from her.

But the thought of a guilt-ridden Saylor walking out of here, painting a giant ass target on her back to take his attention off of anyone else, makes me fucking rabid. We'll make her understand when the time comes. For now, my focus remains on keeping her safe, by any means necessary. With any luck, she won't pick up on the tension between us, or the extra worry we'll be carrying until this shit is resolved and Liam is dealt with.

I strip my clothes off and turn the shower on, hissing when I step inside and the icy water coats my skin. As much as I want to fist my cock and find release, I refuse to do that with Saylor so fresh on my mind. My feelings for her aren't innately sexual. Yes, she's a beautiful girl, but it's more than that. And right now, it feels dirty to look at her with lust and longing. Apparently, the line's drawn at even imagining it.

Let the cold showers commence.

Chapter Twenty-Two

Saylor

It's been two days since Kash and Havok took me to the beach. My skin is starting to flake from where I got a bit of sun, so I search the mounds of product in my bathroom drawers until I come across a moisturizing cream. Once I've lathered it on and no longer look like I'm molting, I head towards the kitchen. Something sweet fills the air, so I imagine Kash was in charge of breakfast this morning. That suspicion is confirmed when I find him pulling a casserole dish from the oven filled with fluffy cinnamon rolls.

"Those look *so* good." I stop beside him, practically salivating over the ooey-gooey goodness.

"Want to put the icing on?" He holds the melted sugar out with a raised eyebrow. "This is a big deal, though. Icing the cinis is akin to being chosen to put the topper on the Christmas tree."

"Oh, it is, is it?" I smile, trying to grab the mixture from his hand, but he's too tall and easily holds it of reach.

"You bet your cute ass it is! But.." he whispers, looking around conspiratorially, even though we're the only two in here. "Don't tell the others you're my favorite." Kash boops my nose, grinning brightly when my eyes cross. He hands me the icing and I quickly pour it on, drenching every inch while they're piping hot. Kash plates two, and then it's time for my favorite part: eating it. It's a religious experience, the way the first bite melts in your mouth. We both moan. It's a messy process, but we're too engrossed to wipe our faces.

"Jesus, what the hell's going on in here?" Havok saunters in, looking like he just rolled out of bed, despite it being ten-thirty in the morning. I blush, glancing at Kash sheepishly. He grins around the bite he just took, giving me an exaggerated wink, and I can't help but laugh. He joins in, and before long, we've both got tears in our eyes while Havok's looking at us like we might need to be evaluated. The noise must draw the others out, because one by one they filter in, curious about all the noise. They descend on the baking dish with hungry eyes, not that I can blame them.

"Here, do it again," Havok demands, shoving his cinnamon roll in my face.

"Do what?" I scrunch my nose in confusion.

"The food noise, Say. Come on, take a bite." He wiggles it again, so I take a small one to appease him.

"Mmmm," I hum sarcastically. Havok gives me a deadpan look, not the least bit impressed.

"You think you're funny, huh?" He grins

wickedly. "I'll take a partial refund since that was subpar." I have less than a second to try and decipher what he means. Havok swipes some leftover icing from the corner of my mouth, then proceeds to suck it off his thumb. Simply put, I catch fire. There's no other explanation for the heat flooding my body. Bending down, he whispers against my ear, "Delicious, pretty girl." And now I'm hot for an entirely different reason.

Krew takes pity on me, sliding me another roll before there aren't any left. I eat it without all the theatrics this time, consciously aware of all the men in the room. It's not been something I really focused on before, not until Havok decided to have a wet t-shirt striptease on the beach. Ever since then, I've become keenly aware that my roommates are all very attractive. Not just that, they're sweet and thoughtful. Funny and caring. They tick every box a woman could possibly have.

It's alarming, this new awareness. I get that these thoughts are natural, but it feels like I have no say so in the way my body responds. And I *never* again want to feel that loss of control that Liam exploited and feasted on. Just thinking his name makes me lose my appetite. I push the plate aside and drink half my water to wash away the sour taste in my mouth.

"You okay?" Roan looks me over, searching for something he won't be able to find. My issue isn't physical, it's mental.

"Just full," I lie, giving him a half-hearted smile. I doubt he buys it, but he doesn't call me out. The guys eat and chat about the things they need to do today, but I tune them out. Maybe I should bring this up with

Danielle? I don't want to be some broken woman who can never have an intimate thought without seeing the man who ruined it for me.

I should be in college right now, drinking and going to frat parties. I would've hidden in a corner, too shy to talk to anyone, or maybe these would have been the years that I shined. I might have come into my own and outgrew the need to people-please. Instead, my defining years are composed of a squat, two-room cellar below a psychopath's house. I threw up from a lack of food, not because I had one too many beers on a Friday night. My first orgasm was at the hands of a monster, not some bumbling man-boy who sweet-talked me into going to his room so we could '*talk*' someplace quiet.

He's taken so much from me, and it feels like he's *still* taking pieces. They're smaller, chips in comparison to the chunks from before, but parts of me, nonetheless. Every second spent thinking of him strengthens his hold over me. It's fresh, and there's plenty of time to grow and heal, but I don't want to waste my life shackled by Liam Price. My thoughts deserve to be occupied by good things, not stuck in the past, obsessing over something I can't change. It happened. And now I need to move on and learn to live with the memories. Too bad that's easier said than done.

"I need to run some errands, but why don't you guys show Saylor the other half of the house? She's been here a week and still hasn't seen it." Lochlan looks annoyed by that, but gathers his keys and stops beside me. "I'll be back soon. Keep these assholes in line." He smirks, kissing the top of my head before walking out the door.

"You're leaving *Saylor* in charge?" Kash yells, his face awash with mock disbelief. "That's the equivalent of a chihuahua leading a pack of wolves!" His rude comparison is met with silence. It's actually funny, because small or not, I feel certain I could make him do just about anything. All I'd have to do is ask.

"Are you making fun of my size?" I drop my voice, giving him the same sad eyes and poked-out bottom lip Havok received when he ate my biscuit.

"Oh, no." Kash points at me, slapping a hand over his face. "No, no, no, no. I know exactly what you're trying to do, my little Sour Patch Kid. Just like medusa, if I don't look, you can't get to me." I sniffle, smiling at the laugh Roan tries to cover up.

"Fuck," he swears. "Is she really upset? Guys?" No one answers him. Kash growls, peeking through his fingers at me. "Oh, shit. I'm sorry. It was a joke, Best Friend." He jolts forward, wrapping his arms around me. I roll my lips together, but when my gaze connects with Havok's, he bursts into laughter.

"Did I just get played?" Kash asks no one in particular. He pulls back, shaking his head at the sweet smile I give him.

"You can hack code like nobody's business, but somehow you're still so goddamn dumb," Krew jokes, pushing away from the counter. "I need to work on a few things, but I'll catch up as soon as I'm finished."

"Let's just agree that if push came to shove, you'd do anything I asked." I give Kash a pointed look.

"Now come on, I want to see this media room. I call dibs on movie choice." Sliding off my stool, I wait for them to lead the way.

"No pushing or shoving required. Those big blue eyes can get you just about anything." Kash winks, striding for the door that leads downstairs. I follow, surprised by how bright it is. Honestly, I hadn't asked for a tour because anything resembling underground feels a little too triggering at the moment. But after the mental pep-talk I gave myself this morning, the least I can do is try to move past one of my fears.

"This is actually the first floor of the house, but we treat it like a basement. We keep the few windows down here closed off with hurricane shutters, and the main door is secured inside that alcove." Kash points behind the staircase.

"Why build it this way?" I ask curiously.

"Basements aren't usually possible in Florida because of the water table," Roan explains. "And safety. With the firing lane, it wasn't possible to have windows on that side, and if anything were to ever happen, we've got this baby." He points to a slit in the wall, using his palm to activate the built-in keypad. A steel door slides out, looking like something from a bank vault. "If anyone ever set foot on our property with ill intent, this entire level would serve as a safe room. When we said you'd be protected here, we meant it." I swallow, pushing past the knot of emotions clogging my throat.

"And over here, well...it's pretty self-explanatory." I peek behind Roan, taking in the wall of glass that showcases a state-of-the-art gym.

"Wow," I remark, kinda lost for words. "That's impressive."

"And for your viewing pleasure, shows are twice daily. Early AM and late PM." Kash holds out his hands, acting like he's Vanna White. I snort and shake my head at his absurdity.

"At the very end is the firing lane. And to our right is the media room," Havok adds, strolling a few feet ahead. Overhead lights flicker on as soon we cross the threshold.

My eyes widen as I take in the six rows of reclining seats. They're on slightly different levels, giving each space a perfect view of the screen that stretches the entire length of the front wall. There's two on each row—one to the left, and one to the right—creating a makeshift aisle between them. The leather chairs are wide enough to fit two people, but I have a feeling these guys take up one each. There's a small jut-out at the back of the room with a glass drink display, popcorn maker, and bins of boxed candy —like you'd find at an actual movie theater.

"This is so cool." I spin around, wanting to see it all again in case I missed something.

"So, what movie are you going with, Say?" Havok tosses some kernels in the popcorn machine as he waits for me to answer.

"Um…there's one I came across the other day, but I can watch it by myself another time. We can pick something everyone likes." I tug at the hem of my sweater. I have no idea whose it is, but it's army green and extra comfy.

"Nope. You called dibs, it's your pick." Roan powers up the screen and hands me the remote. "It works just the same as the upstairs TV. The digital library is synced, so hit the genre and it'll take you where you need to go." Well, crap. I'd been joking, but I guess I'm stuck being the one to choose.

"You're gonna regret this," I mumble, scrolling through the lists as the scent of butter fills the air.

"Nah." Kash throws himself across a chair, his arms full of candy and soda. "You could make us watch paint dry and I doubt we'd complain." I click the movie I was looking for and hit pause.

"Okay, claim a seat, pretty girl." Havok has a bag of popcorn in one hand and a drink balanced in the other. I look at my options, deciding on the front left since I'm smaller than they are. I sit, pulling my feet up, only to have Havok follow me. He drops beside me, winking at the raised eyebrow I give him.

"Hold this for a sec." He passes me the tub of popcorn, then hops back up and grabs a blanket. He spreads it across us and gestures for me to hit play. I look to my right, finding Kash seated on the opposite side with a pout on his face. Roan is behind us, giving me a smile when I tilt my head back to check that he's good.

"Whatever we're watching is one hundred and forty-three minutes long." Kash points to the time displayed on the screen. "So, if we divide that by three, that's thirty-four point three minutes we each get with Saylor. I'm timing you, Kade." He shoots the man beside me a no-nonsense glare. Havok pays it no mind, telling me to go ahead and start the movie. I settle against the cool leather, watching the screen come to life. The moment the title appears, Kash cackles, laughing so hard he nearly chokes on a skittle.

"He loves Disney movies. Always chooses them to irritate Ro, but the big ogre won't say shit this time because you picked it," Havok whispers. I smile, wondering why they put up with so much just to make me happy. Am I not the same, though? I'd turn it off in a heartbeat if he asked me to. I focus on the movie, snacking on the popcorn Havok places between us. I laugh, watching the characters I remember from the first installment come to life.

"Thirsty?" Havok asks quietly, offering me some of his drink. I smile gratefully and take the cup. He fixates on my mouth, watching as I wrap my lips around the straw, placing them exactly where his had just been. The carbonation from the coke makes my throat burn, but it's heavenly. It's been five years since I've had soda. I've stuck with juice and water thus far, but damn it's good. I grin, trying to shake off the way my body tingles from the look Havok's giving me.

I hand his drink back, severing the intense staring we were engaged in. He clears his throat and leans toward the corner of the chair, lifting his arm for me to move closer. I snuggle against his side, trying to bring my attention back to the movie. I've missed the last few minutes entirely. Havok trails his finger up and down my arm, leaving goosebumps in its wake. I'm not sure he's even aware that he's doing it, but I certainly am, and I have no idea what to make of it.

"Time!" Kash yells, scaring the absolute shit out of me. "Pause it and get over here, Best Friend." I huff, peeling myself away from the warm cocoon we created. I head to the other side of the aisle, smiling at the way Kash looks downright giddy.

"Do you have a blanket? Because that's a requirement." I lift my foot, pointing at my frozen toes.

"On it." Kash sprints off to find one, then proceeds to wrap me like a burrito. He lifts me, placing my butt on the seat, his arms around my back, and situates my legs across his. I'm practically in his lap. He tells Havok to hit play, but a pang of uncertainty keeps me rigid. Kash must feel the way I tense because he pulls back to look at me, his eyes bouncing between mine.

"Shit, I wasn't thinking. I can unwrap you; I didn't mean to make you feel trapped." I sag, any bit of awkwardness I was feeling fades as his words wash over me. He's worried about something I wasn't even thinking about, and that's a miracle in itself. I should be freaked out by my immobility, but all I'm feeling is snug and safe.

"I'm good." I smile, dropping my head to his shoulder.

I get lost in the movie, laughing at the way Kash whispers the lines he's memorized. I don't think he can help himself, they just come right out. He plays with my hair, twirling the strands around his finger. I'm seconds from closing my eyes and succumbing to sleep when his phone vibrates.

"Do you have to go?" he whines, turning the alarm off and snapping his fingers at Havok, who somehow understands what that means and pauses the movie once again.

"Sharing is caring," I joke, climbing to my feet. Kash blinks at me, an odd look flashing in his eyes, but it's gone before I can think too much of it. I snatch the blanket before scurrying away. His low laugh follows me as I step around Roan's legs, taking the spot closest to the wall. The second my butt hits the chair the movie begins to play. I tuck the blanket around me and discreetly wedge my toes under Roan's thigh. He smirks, then plucks them right back out.

Before I can pout, his hand slips beneath the blanket and bands around my foot. He's like a freaking furnace with how much heat he puts off. I sigh, trying to catch up with the movie. A few minutes pass before his thumb starts stroking my ankle, which leads to him massaging the arch of my foot. Whatever's taking place on screen is background noise. I'm half asleep when he switches to the other one, making me groan at the first press of his fingers. *Loudly*. Havok jumps to his feet, the remote clattering to the floor as he scrambles to pause the movie.

"Sorry!" I squeak. Meanwhile, Roan's body shakes with silent laughter. "Foot rubs are nice! And I haven't had one in like…ever." I rush to explain, feeling childish and awkward.

"Cinnamon rolls and foot rubs," Kash whispers distractedly while tapping away on his phone, making me frown at his mumbled nonsense. "Oh, don't mind me. Just starting a list of things that cause you to make that noise, so we can refer back to it in the future." Havok snorts, running his hand through his silver hair, causing it to stick up in disarray. The lighting is too low for me to make out the expression on Kash's face, but I'm positive it's gleeful. I bury my face in my hands.

"Hey," Krew announces with a knock. "Loch's back. When you're finished, he needs you upstairs, Tink."

"Let's head up," Roan says, helping me to my feet. "I think you've missed important chunks of the movie anyway."

The guys start shutting everything down and gathering our food trash. When the room is back to the way we found it, we head for the main level. Lochlan is standing by the dining table, hands in his pockets as he rocks back on his heels. He looks nervous. My eyes are drawn to the table, noticing several packages spread across it. It's the most use I've seen it get since being here.

"Is everything okay?" I question. Lochlan readjusts his glasses, then clears his throat.

"Of course. These are for you." He nods to the packages.

"Me?" My head jerks back with the question.

"Yep. Go ahead."

I step closer, feeling five sets of eyes on me as I contemplate where to begin. It's disconcerting to have them all staring.

"Here," Lochlan says, stepping forward to hand me the biggest box. "Start with this one." Roan pulls out a pocketknife and slices the packing tape down the seam. From there, it's easy to pop the ends open. There's a Styrofoam block covering the item, so I wiggle it off. It promptly slips from my hand as I get a good look at the sleek, silver laptop nestled inside with an apple emblem etched in the center.

"What?" I whisper, running my fingers across the smooth surface. "Why?" I'm so confused, my thoughts are translating to simple, one-word questions.

"Kade explained the list you guys started down at the beach. So, we wanted to help you get started. If you're planning to get your GED, you'll need these things." Lochlan shrugs, as if it's no big deal when I know this laptop must have cost a fortune.

"Another one!" Kash claps excitedly, snatching a package up and handing it to me. I've barely wrapped my head around the first, but my fingers move without thought to tear open the poly-mailer. I slide the contents out, sorting through the various pens, pencils, and notebooks.

"Boring," Kash grumbles, shoving another package at me. Roan has already taken care of the tape, so I flip the box open. A study guide to getting your GED stares back at me. I flip through it, seeing multiple practice tests and informative material on every subject covered. Two other books are beneath it, much the same as the first, just made by different companies. I curl my fingers around the edge of the table, needing something to keep me steady.

They did all of this, *bought all of this,* so I can work towards something important to me. They not only listened, they *heard* me. I barely spoke about it, yet they understood how much this means to me. It was just another '*thing*' for Kash to write down, something I'd focus on a year or two down the road. But it's all here, at my literal fingertips, because they made it happen. I don't realize I'm crying until the first, fat tear splashes against the table. I hastily wipe my face and look up at the guys.

I can't believe they did this for me.

"Shit. We didn't mean to upset you, Say. If you aren't ready, that's okay. All of this will still be here whenever you are." Havok grimaces, rubbing at the back of his neck while keeping his eyes trained on the floor.

"No, that's not it. I'm just...overwhelmed, I guess. This is really sweet and thoughtful. Thank you. I'll pay you back for all of it. Krew can take it from the account Havok set up," I offer, wringing my hands together anxiously.

"You don't owe us anything, sweetheart. That's the point of it being a gift." Lochlan smiles, his honey-colored eyes warming as he watches me fidget.

"But.." I start to protest, so Roan presses his finger against my lips to hush me.

"No buts, Little Fighter. We did this because we wanted to, and because you deserve it. We'll help you as much and often as you need us to, but you're going to do great." He grins, the rare kind that makes his dimples pop.

"Krew can show you how to work the laptop," Lochlan states. "Oh, and this. It's identical to ours, but we tried to pick out a case that wasn't so bland and boring." He pulls a brand-new phone from his back pocket and hands it over. I blink at it, a high-pitched, hysterical sounding laugh tumbling out of me.

"This is too much." I try to give it back, but Lochlan holds his hands in the air like he's about to be arrested. So, unless I plan to shove it in his pocket like a sweaty dollar bill at a strip club, I have no choice but to hold on to it. "What the heck am I supposed to do with a phone? The only people I talk to are you guys, and if I need one of you, all I have to do is leave my room."

"Well, now you can save yourself the trip and text us instead." Havok winks.

"It's not about that, anyway. This, along with the computer, will give you access to the outside world. A sense of freedom. I know it's not much, but you deserve to be able to search for something on the internet, or online shop without asking one of us to help you do it. These are normal, everyday things you should have. I programmed our numbers in your phone already, so use them as much or little as you'd like." Lochlan gives me a stern look, but it's just a ruse to get me to stop arguing with him. I tug my bottom lip between my teeth, lacking the words to adequately express how grateful I am.

I step forward, pressing a kiss to Lochlan's

cheek, and decide to go with a simple, "Thank you." I walk to each man, doing the exact same thing, not once feeling any sort of discomfort from the intimate gesture. I genuinely trust them. And not the surface-level extension of good faith I'd given them when deciding to come here, but pure, blind trust that no matter what, they have my best interest at heart.

"Would you like me to help you set everything up now, or later?" Krew asks.

"Now's fine, unless you have something else you need to be doing."

"Nope. Let's go, Tink." He grabs the laptop and walks off. I toss a wave over my shoulder to the rest of the guys and follow after him.

I haven't been in the twins' office since the day I arrived. It seems like a sacred space for them. The lights are dimmed, so it takes a second for my eyes to adjust, but it looks the same as I remember. A few discarded energy drinks line their shared desk, but Krew slides them into the trash bin and motions for me to take a seat in Kash's chair. He powers up my computer, asking if I'd like to set a password to the home screen. I don't see a need for it, so I tell him as much.

"Privacy is important, Saylor. And it's something you haven't had in a really long time. I think you should add one," Krew implores. I nod, swiveling the laptop around while he looks in the opposite direction. It takes me a second to come up with something, but I bite back a smile when I type out: *LRKKH*. I use the guys' first initials, ordering them from oldest to youngest. Other than my birthday or Mom's, I don't really have anything else to use that I'd be able to remember. And I'm pretty sure there's some unwritten rule about using personal information like that for a passcode.

"Okay, all good," I tell him.

"Alright, the software has definitely seen an upgrade since you last used one of these, but the design is basically the same. I've connected the Wi-Fi and saved the password, so it's good to go from here on out. I'm also blocking your VPN so your location can't be traced."

"Is that a legitimate concern?" I turn my attention to Krew, a hint of alarm bleeding through.

"There's always room for concern when you're talking about the internet. Obviously, you need to stay away from social media for the time being, and anything you have delivered to the PO box should be addressed to SOTERIA. Regardless, there shouldn't be any reason to worry." He gives me a brief smile, then goes back to adjusting the user settings. It's clear he knows his way around computers. His long fingers move so quickly across the keyboard, I can barely track them. I watch him work, noticing how relaxed he looks in his element. The hardness I usually see has faded, his brown eyes a little lighter from the glow of the screen.

"You should be good to go. If you have any questions, my door's always open. Can I show you around the phone?" He shuts the laptop down, sliding it towards me so we can trade devices. Krew pulls my chair closer, giving me a better view.

"I know you didn't have a phone prior, but are you familiar with the basic operations?" he asks me politely.

I nod. "I used Mom's a good bit. I was supposed to get one of my own in a couple of months, when I started high school. But, you know…"

"Yeah, Tink. I know," Krew voices quietly. "This is the app store. Download or buy whatever you'd like. I've linked the business credit card to your wallet, just double-click this button to pay. Our Amazon account is signed into as well, so the delivery address is sorted."

"Can I not use my own card? I don't want to keep taking money from you guys. You've already done so much for me, and now you've spent even more on a laptop and phone, which is a whole bill in itself, not to mention all the food and the clothes and.." I ramble, my eyes widening as I list off everything given me to without a single complaint or expectation of repayment.

"Hey," Krew gripes, spinning my chair to face his. "Stop stressing over how we choose to spend our money. If I want to buy you a goddamn pony, I will." He narrows his eyes, begging me to argue.

"Will you put a sparkly cone on its head so I can call it a unicorn?" I ask him, my face a complete mask of seriousness. He snorts, shaking his head at me.

"You've been hanging around Kash too much. And the reason your card isn't attached is because A—we never ordered one, since we had zero intention of pulling anything from the account, and B—it would be counterproductive to link your name to anything that could potentially lead back to here. We aren't trying to hold your money hostage, Tink." Krew softens, wanting me to understand the reasoning behind their choice, and now that he's explained the how's and why's, it makes perfect sense.

"I get it. I just want to feel like I'm pulling my weight." I shrug, squirming in my seat as he watches me intently.

"I can understand that. Kash and I relied on Loch and Ro a lot when we first moved in with them. It took a while to get past feeling like we were indebted to them, but they didn't help us because they wanted something in return. Same goes for you. I promise, as soon as this is all over, you'll have full access to everything. And it will end, Saylor. We'll get you your life back. You'll have it all, Tink: a dream career, a doting husband, two-point-five kids, and a white picket fence. The whole works. One day, you'll look back and realize all of this," Krew waves his hand around. "Was just a steppingstone to the good part."

I swallow thickly, my heart thumping frantically as I try to maintain the appearance of being calm. What does he mean by all of '*this*'? As in him and the guys? I've wondered what will happen when Liam's no longer a threat to me, but I didn't imagine they'd disappear. I can't fathom not having them around. I've gotten stupidly attached, and now I'm questioning if they have any plans to remain permanent fixtures in my life once this is all said and done. I'll never see them as *steppingstones*.

Or is the *'this'* he's referring to the past five years as a whole?

I'm feeling confused and uncertain, so I thank Krew for his help and head straight to my room. Someone's placed the other items on my dresser. With new eyes, I can't help but wonder if they gave me these things so I'd sort my education out, giving me something to fall back on. Nothing they've said or done would make me think that, but Krew's words have me picking apart every interaction. Overanalyzing the details. There was nothing inherently rude about them. In fact, they were sweet, but the apathetic way he spoke makes me feel like an inconvenience. For all I know, he didn't mean it that way at all, but I don't have the guts to outright ask for clarification. That would be mortifying if his answer didn't lean in my favor.

Yes, Saylor. I did *mean, in a politer, round-about way, that your welcome here has an expiration date.*

I opt for a hot bath, hoping it'll help me clear my head. I don't want to fall back into the same pattern of questioning everything and wondering if I've done something wrong, eager to please everyone just to feel like I belong. I haven't felt that way here. And any time I've tried to cave and do what the guys want, they refuse to let me. I slip beneath the water, wishing I could scream, but knowing my luck, I'd accidently inhale and drown myself. Overthinking is torturous enough.

The guys stop by sporadically throughout the day, checking to make sure everything's okay. I tell them I'm fine. And I am. I just need to gain some perspective and lower my expectations. They don't owe me their undying loyalty or friendship. If we keep in touch once I'm no longer living here, that's great. But they have established lives, and I'm starting from scratch. I'd never hold it against them if we lost touch.

Later that night, I wake to Roan storming through my door, my own screams echoing off the walls and making my ears ring.

"I've got her," he pants roughly, shoving the others back out.

As he climbs in next to me and hugs me to his chest, I can't for the life of me remember what I was even dreaming about. But I have a sick feeling it had everything to do with my tumultuous thoughts before bed, and not the psycho who should be disrupting my sleep.

Chapter Twenty-Three

Saylor

I'm mid-way through my second session with Danielle when my phone dings. I glance at it, while trying to keep my attention on the topic at hand. For the most part, she's let me lead the discussion, asking what I'd like to talk about instead of hounding me with questions. I'm still feeling a bit raw over the whole Krew thing, and I'm pretty certain Danielle has picked up on the that fact my mind is elsewhere. I briefly considered bringing it up—to see if she could offer some insight and ease my worries—but squashed the idea rather quickly.

It's more likely than not that I'm making a mountain out of a molehill, but tell that to my brain. It's playing my insecurities against me, making me feel like a crazy person because I can't quit picking apart every word of my and Krew's conversation. I shake those thoughts away, tuning back in to the video call that I'm doing a horrible job of participating in. We've talked about Mom mostly. Everything Havok told me and the way he was there for her after I was taken, especially during the last few weeks of her life.

I've explained my complicated past with him and how his involvement in the aftermath of my disappearance makes me feel.

"And what about the list I asked you to start working on? Were you able to make any progress?" Danielle leans forward, her face filling more of the screen.

"I've got a few things written down. I'd like to get my GED. Without some sort of education, I doubt I'd make it very far. The guys gifted me a laptop and several different study guides so I could start working towards it," I answer, trying to let the excitement I'd initially felt worm its way back in.

"That was very thoughtful of them. I think that's an excellent goal to set for yourself, Saylor." I smile, looking at the clock for the millionth time. "This feels like a good stopping point for today. I'm guest speaking at a conference next week, but I'll be back in the office a day later than normal. Does that work for you?"

"That's fine."

"Perfect. If you need anything during the meantime, don't hesitate to reach out. Mr. Calloway has my contact information."

We say our goodbyes, and much like last week, I slump against Lochan's office chair and take a few minutes to decompress. Using my toes, I slowly spin myself. With my eyes closed, it feels like I'm on the world's smallest merry-go-round. Like one of those quarter machines that sits outside the old Grocery Mart back in Pike's Bay. My phone chimes again, making me stop and reach for it. Two unread messages from Kash stare back at me.

Kash: Pepperoni or pepperoni? Because there really is no other option.

Kash: Best Friend, I need an answer ASAP. We're about to get outvoted.

I smile, pushing myself up to go find the guys. They're exactly where they always are, scattered around the living room, looking positively bored.

"Finally!" Kash jumps to his feet. "You're the tiebreaker, Lemon Drop. What's it gonna be?"

I scrunch my nose. My default setting of wanting to put the responsibility on someone else's shoulders urges me to do just that. Like he knows exactly what I'm about to do, Roan raises an eyebrow, silently calling me out.

"Pepperoni?" It comes out like a question, but at least I give an answer.

"See, that wasn't so hard, was it?" Havok teases. "Besides, we're going to order whatever each of us wants. Who cares if we end up with six different pizzas. It's *pizza*. They'll get eaten." I gape at him, realizing I played right into their little scheme. It was effective, though.

"I just placed the order, so I'll head out now. It should be ready by the time I get there." Lochlan stands and drops a quick kiss to the top of my head.

"Are we too far out for delivery?" I ask.

"No, but we don't want anyone coming here. Even if we paid with cash, it's just not worth the risk. The house sits off the road a good bit, so most people have no idea we're even down here. With the beach being private as well, the likelihood of someone stumbling across us unintentionally is pretty slim. I'd like to keep it that way, especially now that we have you here." Lochlan tucks a piece of hair behind my ear, his eyes holding mine. Time slows as we gaze at one another, the rest of the room forgotten, but then he steps away, promising to be back soon before striding towards the door.

"Okay, Say. What piece would you like to play?" Havok points at the coffee table, where a game of Monopoly is being set up. In the thirty minutes it takes Lochlan to get back with the food, we've all made our choices—me being the doggy. We fill our plates and squeeze together, trying to give everyone a view of the board. The guys are big as it is, but six of us crowding around a four-sided table means we're shoulder to shoulder.

"Saylor goes first," Lochlan demands. I happily take the dice, knowing I'll need the head start. My goal is to snatch up properties as quickly as possible, because I royally suck at this game. I buy everything I land on, but somehow always miss out on the big ones that bring in the most money, and then I end up bankrupt. No one wins this game by having a hotel on *Baltic Avenue*. I roll a seven, landing on Chance. *Of course*. I might not have secured a property, but I am the proud new owner of a '*get out of jail free*' card.

I take a bite of my pizza when Havok, who's to my left, begins his turn. The noise that leaves me is... inappropriate. Even I understand that, but I have no shame when this may very well be the best thing I've ever tasted in my entire life.

"Pepperoni pizza," Kash mumbles to the heavens while tapping on his phone.

Good Lord, he's adding to that stupid list.

I toss a pepperoni at him, but he just eats it. The next hour passes with us laughing like hyenas and stuffing our faces. I've yet to make myself sick by overfilling my stomach, but there's a good chance tonight will be the night I break that streak. Kash and Krew are comically competitive with each other, and when the game is nearly over, I'm shocked to find myself still standing. Barely. It's down to me, Roan, and Lochlan, and it's my turn. I roll, squeezing my eyes shut as I wait to see how hard my quickly dwindling paper money is about to be hit.

Boardwalk. With a *hotel.*

"I'm out," I groan, shoving everything—properties included—toward Lochlan. It's probably still not enough.

"No, now you're my partner." Roan grins mischievously and tugs me closer.

The next few rounds are tit for tat. For every property we land on, Lochlan lands on one of ours. We're just exchanging money at this point, doing nothing to pull ahead, but not falling behind either. Until we get lucky, twice in a row, and Lochlan hits our most expensive ones back-to-back. Roan jumps up, grabbing me around the waist, and proceeds to twirl us in a circle as he gloats about finally beating Lochlan. I grunt. Even though he's gentle, it still adds pressure to my ribs.

"Shit, sorry. Got excited," Roan apologizes.

"It's okay. They're nowhere near as bad as they were. I haven't needed pain meds in days."

"You're going to if this giant fucker keeps grabbing you like that," Havok growls, shouldering between us so he can pull me away. He steers me to the couch, dropping beside me with a scowl on his face. He's like a protective older brother. The thought makes me giggle. It's such a stark contrast to how he used to be, it sets me off.

"Care to share with the class?" He cocks his head to the side, waiting for an explanation.

"I just find it funny that you're acting like a protective older brother." I press my finger between his eyebrows, trying to smooth out the line his scrunched expression is creating. "Especially since you did a lot worse when we were kids."

"A brother?" Havok repeats, his icy blue eyes flashing with...*something*. The guys cough, trying to cover their own laughs.

"Wait..." Roan interrupts. "What do you mean by he did worse?" Havok pales, shifting beside me uncomfortably. I look between him and the others, confused by their confusion.

"Um..." I lock eyes with Havok. He twines his fingers with mine, giving me a grim smile.

"They don't know," he whispers. My eyes widen, wondering how it's possible that he's kept such a huge part of our history a secret. It's obvious how close they are. If not the truth, then what reasoning did he give them for being so hellbent on finding me? It's clear as day that guilt was the driving force, but I press my lips together, unsure of what to say.

"Kade," Roan snaps. "What the fuck is she talking about?"

Havok lets go of my hand, a sigh of resignation falling from his lips as he moves to stand. He rocks his neck from side to side, as if he's gearing up for a fight. *Oh, God.* I push to my feet so fast it makes me dizzy. Havok shakes his head at me and draws closer to his highly pissed off friend.

"I bullied Saylor all throughout school. It started when she was in kindergarten and I was in second grade. She was the sweetest thing I'd ever seen, and I wanted to dirty her up. To make her life as messy as mine. I was jealous, but that doesn't excuse what I did. On the day she went missing, she approached me at the front of the school. We'd just been dismissed, so everyone was out front. Saylor asked me if I wanted some help studying for the science lab we had due at the end of the week.

"She was smarter than most kids her age, so she was taking the class a year in advance. Meanwhile, I was repeating it because I didn't give a shit about anyone or anything. I was embarrassed, and thought the other assholes standing near me overheard her. Feeling stupid, I lashed out. I'd convinced myself years prior that Saylor had it all, and I was severely lacking in comparison. I humiliated her, *loudly*, in front of half the school. I…I asked if that was her way of trying to get me to fuck her, if '*study*' was code, because she'd obviously been chasing my dick for years. I toyed with her, dragging it out as long as I could, and she missed the bus. *I'm* the reason Saylor was walking home on May 23rd, 2017."

Every monotone word Havok utters sucks a little more oxygen from the room. By the time he finishes, I can barely breathe. We never brought up the specifics of what he said that day. It was crass, and at fourteen I'd just been grasping sex as something more than a means to procreate. And now they all know.

"You're fucking dead." I watch, completely frozen, as Roan slams his fist into Havok's face. It happens so fast; I couldn't have stopped it if I tried. He staggers, then drops to his knees, not once trying to fight back or even get away. Roan lunges forward, grabbing him by the neck of his shirt, and yanks him to his feet. "Stay the hell away from her. Do you hear me?! You don't touch her, you piece of shit!" I jump to intervene, my feet finally unsticking themselves from the floor as my brain comes back to life.

"*Stop!* Stop..it." Tears are pouring down my face as I wedge myself between them. "You have no right! We've moved on. *He* apologized and *I* accepted. You don't get to *hit* him. Who gives you the *fucking right*?" I'm screaming, words flying from my mouth so forcefully it makes my voice crack. "No one deserves to be hurt out of anger. You weren't protecting yourself. You hit him to make *you* feel better. Just like Liam did to me." My bottom lip trembles, the last sentence coming out nothing more than a broken whisper. Roan pales, stumbling back a few steps from the blunt force of my accusation.

"Saylor..." He reaches out, trying to fix the damage he's caused, but I jerk away. His jaw clenches, hands balling into fists as his gaze drops to the floor. I sniffle, trying to get my tears under control as silence descends around us. Roan closes his eyes, as if the sound physically pains him, then spins and gives the room his back.

"*Goddamnit!*" he roars, tugging at his hair. His shoulders slump as he walks away, muttering curses as he opens the door to the lower level and slams it shut behind him.

I scan the other guys, noting the various emotions playing across their faces. A mixture of pity and anger. I wipe my nose, then drop to my knees in front of Havok. His mouth and nose are bleeding. You'd think I'd be used to the sight of blood by now, but all it makes me think of are the dozens of times I bled at the hands of an asshole who had serious anger management issues. I take a deep breath and push the memories away.

"Come on." I take Havok's hand, giving it a gentle tug. No matter how badly I want to help him, he won't be moving anywhere unless he puts in some effort. He climbs to his feet, a vacant, haunted look clouding his eyes. I lead him down the hallway, turning left toward our rooms. I stop outside his door, waiting for his okay. He nods, so I twist the knob and drag him with me. A lamp is on by his bed, so it's not completely dark. I head straight for the bathroom, flipping the light on before closing the lid to his toilet and making him sit.

My hands are shaking, but I find a washcloth

and run it beneath the faucet. Wringing the rag out, I step between Havok's legs and wipe his face as gently as possible. He doesn't complain or flinch, and I think my heart cracks a little more. My mind wonders to how many times he had his lip split as a kid, by a father who should have loved and protected him. And now, someone he sees as a brother—a brother he *chose*—has hurt him just the same. Because of me. No matter how wrong it was, Roan hit him out of some misguided idea that he was defending me. The last thing I want is to come between any of them, and it feels like I just did in the most horrific way.

"I'm sorry," I whisper, my eyes still wet with tears. Havok laughs, but it's disjointed and full of pain.

"Why the hell are you sorry, Say?" He tilts his head back, a bewildered look on his face.

"Because..." I hiccup around a sob. "You got hurt because of me. I didn't know you'd kept it a secret or I never would've said anything, I swear." I'm crying in earnest, the trembling that was isolated to my hands now spread throughout my entire body.

"Baby," Havok's pained voice pleads. His hands grip my hips as he rests his face against my stomach, his head shaking back and forth. Eventually, he pulls away to look me in the eye. "This was my fault and no one else's. I knew what would happen when I confessed everything. I've had years, pretty girl. *Years* to come clean, but I was ashamed. And now they *know* you, Say. Not just the shit in your file or stories I passed down from your mother. They know *you*. They care about *you*." His fingers flex against my side, begging me to understand. I bite my lip and look away.

Havok sighs and drops his hands. "Could you grab me a t-shirt and some sweats from the top right drawer of my dresser?" I nod. It feels odd to dig around his things, but it's the least I can do. I find what he asked for pretty easily and hand them over, closing the bathroom door behind me so he can change. I haven't been in any of the guys' rooms before. I glance around, seeing his walls are pretty bare. His bed is positioned like mine, but there's a shelf above his dresser.

That must be where he kept Mom, I think with a smile. That assumption's confirmed when I see a framed photo of the two of them. I'm too short to reach it, but it's definitely her. My eyes start to burn again. The door creaks open, revealing a sleepy-eyed Havok ready for bed. He glances in the direction of the photo, a tender smile touching his lips. Edging closer, he lifts it from the shelf and hands it to me. I gasp, my heart nearly bursting at the beautiful smile plastered across my mother's face. She's hugging Havok, her eyes focused on him instead of the camera.

"She loved you." It's a statement, not a question.

"Yeah." He shifts his body, his hand rubbing at the back of his neck. "Yeah, I think she did."

"I *know* she did." I hold his gaze, needing him to believe that without an ounce of uncertainty. He nods, but his eyes shine a little brighter. He walks to his bed and pulls the covers back. I sit the frame on his dresser, preparing to leave when he stops me.

"Will you stay?" The vulnerability in his voice

makes my stomach clench.

"Sure."

I move to climb in, wanting to give Havok the outside, but stop short at the pictures decorating his nightstand. I blink, wondering if I'm seeing things. Slowly, I reach out and lift the closest one. It's me. My front two teeth are missing and my hair is tied in pigtails. There's a half-melted popsicle dripping down my hand. I couldn't have been older than six or seven at the time. I put it back and pick up the next one. Me again. My palms are resting against my cheeks, eyes closed. There's a pink blush edged around my fingers. I remember this day. I'd been so embarrassed because Mom had just asked if I needed birth control.

No questions, Saylor. All I need is a yes or a no.

I can almost hear her voice. Boys hadn't grabbed my attention yet, but I was fourteen and she wanted to make sure I was prepared long before the day actually came. This had only been a few months before I was taken. I put the picture down and grab the last one. My heartrate kicks up a notch, seeing myself from just a few days back. I'm sitting at the island, Havok's black hoodie draped over my body and fuzzy socks pulled halfway up my legs. There's a slight smile on my face as I chat with someone. I carefully place it back on his nightstand.

"Why do you have these?" I ask curiously. I'm not angry that he does, just struggling to understand.

"I don't know if you're ready for that answer, Say." His eyes beg me not to push it. I nod, because I have a feeling I know it already, and he's right. I'm not ready.

"Come on. I'm exhausted, and all I want to do is hold you till we both fall asleep." I feel my cheeks flush as I slip between the cool sheets. I snuggle against him, laying my head on his chest. As soon as I'm situated, he wraps his arm around me.

"Sleep, pretty girl." Havok presses his lips to my forehead, breathing in deeply before pulling away. I sigh, letting everything from the night take a backseat for the time being.

Chapter Twenty-Four

Saylor

I've been awake for a while, but I'm trying to stay as still as possible. My cheek is pressed against Havok's chest, the steady rise and fall from his breathing the only movement between us. Just because my mind won't stop reeling doesn't mean his sleep should be disturbed too. I've been admiring the ink covering his arm while I have the chance to, without looking like a first-class creep. Most of his designs seem random, so I can't begin to guess at their meaning. Maybe they don't have one at all.

"You still lookin', or can I stretch?" Havok's sleep roughened voice pierces the quiet, making my face heat as he calls me out.

Not so asleep then.

"Sorry," I mumble, pulling back to give him some space. Despite being in one position all night, I don't feel sore or achy.

"Don't be." He smiles and turns to his side. I grimace at the purple bruising tinting his split lip.

"What's this one mean?" I point to a leaf on his

forearm, hoping to distract us from thinking about last night.

Havok smirks, a small chuckle escaping. "That would be a maple leaf. We did a marksmanship competition a little over a year ago, and I made a bet with the Canadian team that we'd out-shoot them. Winner got to pick the tattoo the other one would get. They kicked our asses, and since I'm the one who started shit-talking and couldn't back it up, the guys agreed it was my body that would be getting defaced. They chose a prominent symbol of Canada so I would always be reminded of the time our brothers to the north took home the win."

My grin grows as the story progresses, but I'm not really surprised that Havok would agree to—and follow through with—something so crazy. I think he enjoys the shock factor of doing and saying things that most people wouldn't. He's always been a very blunt person.

"I think Ro needs you right now," he whispers, his eyes finding mine. The abrupt change in subject throws me, but Havok barrels on before I can say anything. "I know he reacted poorly, but you deserve to have someone in your corner who'd got to bat for you the way he did."

"I didn't ask him to do that," I argue.

"I know." He nods, licking his lips. "And if the roles were reversed, and he was the one admitting to treating you the way I did, not to mention keeping it a secret from the rest of us, I probably would've punched him too. Or tried, at least. He's really fucking tall." He smirks, but I find it hard to make light of the situation.

"I hate that I feel so conflicted," I admit. "I regret screaming at him, but it was wrong for him to hit you. I don't want to be the reason for issues between you guys. It would make me feel like my being here is causing a rift."

"No, Say." He shakes his head sadly. "Ro and I fucked up, but it wasn't because of you. We're grown ass men who know better. He should've kept control of his emotions, and I should've owned up to my mistakes a long time ago. I'm not mad at him, though. You won't agree, but I needed him to hit me. Being able to apologize to you was everything, and it still doesn't feel like enough. I deserve to hurt the way I made you hurt."

I blink away the building tears, the underlying context too much for my heart to handle. Havok doesn't just mean the times he was mean to me at school. He blames himself for the years of hurt and torment I experienced as well, but that's not his burden to bear.

"I've already forgiven you; please let it go. These past five years…that blame lies on Liam. He chose to take and hurt me, not you, so stop feeling guilty for things you were never a part of." Havok wraps his pinky around mine, and even though he doesn't argue, I'm not sure he believes that he holds no responsibility. He's grown and changed so much, proved by the fact that he was the one who got punched in the face, yet he's worried about what his friend is going through. But he has to figure out a way to move past the anger he harbors for himself, or it's going to eat him alive.

"I'll go find Roan," I promise, slowly working my way free from the blankets piled across his bed.

"Thank you." Havok smiles, his eyes closing as he covers back up. "I'm gonna sleep off my ass whoopin' a little longer." I huff a laugh, closing his door behind me.

I shower quickly, pulling on Roan's sweater once I'm dried off. After laundry was done, the guys' clothes I've confiscated were placed back in my room, so I guess they don't mind me hanging on to it. With every minute that's passed since Roan stormed away, this disconnect between us has continued to grow. I'm worried that I screwed up by reacting so harshly. I just want to fix it and makes things right again. I creep down the hallway, not wanting to wake anyone who might be sleeping. When I step into the main room, Krew is the only person I see. I've been avoiding him after our conversation, trying to let the paranoia subside. He's leaned against the dining table, looking out of the slider while sipping on a mug of coffee.

I grab a couple of muffins, likely made by Kash. It's just after eight, so I wouldn't be surprised if Krew's sugar-loving counterpart is up and about somewhere. Placing two bottles of water in the crook of my free arm, I turn to face Krew, who I've yet to acknowledge.

"Good morning," I greet him softly. He dips his chin in my direction, forgoing a verbal response. "Do you know where Roan is?" That gets his attention. Krew's narrowed brown eyes flit over me, his guarded gaze quickly assessing my motives for seeking out his friend. I swallow thickly.

"He's downstairs." He looks away, taking another drink of his coffee. I attempt a hasty exit but struggle to get the door open. "For the record, he's probably not up for company." Too scared to open my mouth, I simply nod my understanding. Krew leans around me and twists the knob. I can feel the heat from his body against my back. His nearness, combined with the flat, unemotional tone he's speaking to me in has me scurrying down the steps so fast, it's a wonder I don't bust my ass. I'd rather face Roan.

A faint light filters through the glass walls of the gym, and since the rest of the area is completely dark, I decide to start there. Pushing through the door, I'm greeted by the low bass of a song thumping through the built-in speakers. My steps are hesitant as I navigate the maze of equipment, my eyes searching for any sign of movement. When I step past a weight machine and the back of the room comes into view, I stop short.

My heart stutters at the sight of Roan sitting on the floor, his back braced against wall with his elbows balanced on his bent knees. His head his hung, but it's obvious he's drenched in sweat, as if he's been working out all night and only recently stopped for a break. Looking closer, I notice there's a slight shake to his hands. My gut twists with guilt. I slept soundly through the night, but the same can't be said for him.

"Roan?" I move closer, worried he can't hear me over the soft music, but his eyes find mine immediately. I scan his face, noting how wrecked he looks. Taking a seat in front of him, I cross my legs and place a water and muffin between us. As far as peace offerings go, it's not the greatest, but he looks like he could use both. Roan pulls his phone out and taps the screen. A second later, the music stops, blanketing us in silence.

"I'm sorry I yelled at you," I tell him quietly, deciding to speak first since he's watching me like he's questioning if I'm really here or not.

"Don't be." He shakes his head, reaching for the water. "I'm so fucking proud of you." He grins sadly at the confused look I give him. "You put me in my place—called me on my bullshit without any worry of repercussion. Because you *trust* us. You know that you're free to speak your mind, and when you're finished, you'll still be safe." Huh. He might be right, or maybe it was the heat of the moment.

"I'm the one that's sorry. I feel like I keep fucking shit up with you. Making mistakes left and right." Roan drops his head back, his gaze pinned on the ceiling.

"You're not. It wasn't fair of me to compare what you did to Havok, to what Liam did to me. That was just…cruel." I bite my lip, frustrated that I ever spoke those words and gave them power.

"It triggered all those times that asshole took his anger out on you. Regardless, I should've known better than to get physical like that." Roan looks at me, his green eyes filled with remorse. "It feels like history's repeating itself."

"What do you mean?" I question, my brows drawn together.

"I had a sister. Elira. I told you that we came to the States when I was a kid, but we actually fled here. My father was involved with the Albanian mafia. Racked up a debt he couldn't pay, so he took us and ran. But they found us." His jaw tics. "They killed Elira as payment, and my father was the one who handed her over. We were forced to watch, and nothing about her death was quick or painless. I failed her, and it feels like I'm doing the same with you." My lips part, a shocked, heartbroken sound slipping out unbidden.

"I don't know what to say, Roan." I shake my head, discreetly wiping at the tears threatening to spill over. "I can't imagine going through something like that, and I'm so sorry you had to. Do I remind you of her?" I ask, trying to understand why he's comparing our situations. I'm here and alive, in huge part to him, so he clearly hasn't failed me.

"No." Roan snorts comedically. "I definitely do *not* see my sister when I look at you, Saylor." His eyes are focused on me with such intensity, my palms begin to sweat. "It fucked with my head when we found you. To see you bruised and bloody, not knowing if you were alive. But other than that, I don't see Elira when I look at you. I see a beautiful woman, who fought as best she could against an unbeatable enemy. Liam had the upper hand every step of the way, but you never gave up. And I know you could have. I'm worried that I'm failing you because it feels like I've done more harm than good."

I take a deep breath, trying to untangle my

thoughts and emotions, when all I really want to do is have a good, long cry. They see me so differently than I see myself, but it's clear Roan struggles with the same self-deprecation that I do.

"All these times you've built up in your head—the light getting turned off at the hospital, the parking garage, tying Kash up, punching Havok—you're giving them too much credit. There will always be a chance that something will trigger a bad memory. Some will be worse than others, but I'll get through it. I know I'm not as strong as I will be one day, but I'm not made of glass either."

"Shit, Little Fighter," Roan whispers hoarsely, sliding forward to erase the space between us. Hands framing my face, his thumbs stroke my cheeks. I'm surrounded by Roan and startled to find it so comforting. "I know you aren't weak. Hell, I think you're stronger than you realize. But I'll do my best to remember that the next time I fuck up, because it's bound to happen." He laughs lightly, making me smile.

"Now, can I please have a hug?" His voice is steady, masking the hint of worry clouding his eyes.

"Are you going to apologize to Havok?" I tease him.

"As soon as we're through."

"Okay, then." I grin, reaching forward to wrap my arms around him. Roan tugs me so I'm straddling his lap and buries his face in my hair. I tense, a tad uneasy with the change in position.

"Sorry," he mumbles, but doesn't let me go. "I

just needed you close for a second. I was scared as fuck you'd never talk to me again. You forgive me, right?" I relax, wanting to reassure him that I'm not going anywhere.

"Everyone makes mistakes. As long as you understand that it was wrong for you to hit him, we're good." I rest my chin on his shoulder, running my fingers through the loose strands of his hair.

"I know it was. But I still can't believe he said that shit to you." His arms flex, tightening around me as he thinks back to Havok's confession.

"Well, he *was* a dumb boy." I smile, even though Roan can't see it.

"I'd debate he still is," he grumbles, making me laugh.

"And just to be clear, *no one* wanted his dick. He was way too angry." Roan jerks back, his wide, disbelieving eyes boring into mine.

"Don't say that word." He sounds positively horrified.

"What word? D—." He slaps a hand over my mouth. I try to mumble around it, but all I really succeed in doing is licking his palm. Roan groans, his eyes closing as he searches for patience. I'm shaking from laughing so hard, but he grips my hips to halt the movement. His forehead drops to mine, my laughter dying a quick death. We're close enough to feel each other breathing. There are two very different urges warring inside of me right now.

On one hand, I'm aching to eliminate the

minuscule distance between our lips. I want to know what he tastes like. How it'd feel to finally share a kiss with someone. But on the other hand, I'm so scared I want nothing more than to bolt back up the stairs and pretend this never happened. Because it's not supposed to. Not this soon, at least. There's something wrong with me for even entertaining those sorts of thoughts this early on.

"We're good. You hear me?" His voice is gruff, but it's like he heard every thought going through my head. He's talking us both down from crossing a line. I nod, the motion bringing our lips so close they touch for the briefest second. I inhale sharply, making him swear. "*Fuck.*"

"What kind of muffin did you bring me?" Roan asks, determined to redirect us.

"Um...blueberry?"

"Good. That's good. Sounds awesome. Fucking brilliant, actually." I laugh, easing back to give us both some much needed space. When my butt is firmly on the ground, I grab the muffin that got pushed aside earlier and hand it to him. He smirks and takes a bite, the tightness in his body visibly dissipating.

"Fuck, that's good." Roan eats the rest in a matter of milliseconds. Meanwhile, I've barely had a proper taste of mine. He waits patiently for me to finish, then climbs to his feet. Extending his hand, he helps me up and tosses our trash. Our size difference still blows my mind. I have to crane my neck just to give him a grateful smile.

"Guess you've got some apologizing to do."

Glancing over my shoulder, I pin him a pointed look. "I'm going to go find Kash. I didn't see him this morning, and I want to make sure he hasn't gotten himself into any trouble."

"I'm sure he has," Roan remarks dryly. He trails me until the main hallway ends, then wraps his fingers around my good wrist. "Thank you." He leans down and presses a kiss to my cheek, brushing the corner of my mouth in the process. The faint contact sends my heart galloping all over again. He winks and leaves me standing there as he heads for Havok's room. I blink a few times, trying to clear the fog from my head. Turning right, I knock on the twins' door, hoping it won't be Krew that answers.

"It's open," Kash hollers. I peek my head in, hand covering my eyes just in case he isn't decent.

"It's me," I announce, cracking my fingers a bit when he doesn't yell for me to get out. Kash's amused grin greets me. I roll my eyes, closing the door behind me. "What's that?" I nod toward the book resting on the bed beside him. He looks over, his eyes flaring wide before he jerks a blanket over it.

"That? Oh, that was nothing. Just some light reading material," he rambles, his gaze landing on anything but me.

"Really? What's it about?" I cock my head, walking a little closer.

"Um...the lifecycle of honeybees. It's riveting. They play a vital role in our ecosystem." Kash nods rapidly, doing a splendid job of convincing himself, but certainly not me.

"Wow. Sounds interesting. Can I have a look?" I smile sweetly, batting my lashes to further seal the deal.

"Did I say riveting? I definitely meant boring. Total waste of time. So, what brings you by?" He fidgets, still refusing to look at me. I take my opening when his focus is on something across the room and launch myself over the foot of his bed. I scramble toward the book as Kash shrieks like a banshee.

"Best Friend!" he growls, attempting to cut me off, but I'm smaller and quicker. I snatch it away and shove it down my sweater. My body heats with embarrassment, because I have no freaking clue why I just did that. Kash raises his eyebrow at me. "Is that supposed to stop me?" He grins devilishly, not an ounce of remorse for his brazenness. I shuffle across the bed, nearly getting tangled in the mound of covers, and climb to my feet. I'm out of breath, slapping loose pieces of hair from my face as I go digging down my clothes for the big reveal. When I pull the book out and eye the cover, my jaw drops.

"Are you reading smut?" I ask in disbelief, my lips quirked in amusement.

"Hey! It's got plot, too, thank you very much," Kash retorts, trying his best to seem annoyed. Mom used to read every raunchy romance she could get her hands on, and the few times I accidently picked up her kindle instead of mine were pretty revealing. The covers alone told me everything I needed to know, so I never peeked inside of them. My brain wasn't curious the way it is now. I flip the book open, skimming through a few sentences, but nothing scandalous pops out at me.

"Sweetness," Kash warns, his bottom lip trapped between his teeth. I ignore him, skipping towards the back of the book. A few more pages of searching and I feel the blush I'd just gotten rid of come barreling back with a vengeance. *Jesus, that's graphic*. I shift from one foot to the other, scanning a few more passages. Kash chuckles, sauntering over to take his tome of filth from my hands.

"Any thoughts?" he asks, his voice pitched low. "Since you were so eager to read it and all."

"Uh...descriptive. Very descriptive." I laugh, the sound slightly manic. Kash smirks, his thumb brushing across my too-hot cheek.

"I think Kade was onto something. This shade of pink is definitely a new favorite of mine." I swat his hand away, fake glaring at the comment. "Come on." He pulls me back down, tucking me against his side as he pops a sucker in his mouth. We lie quietly for a while, my eyes scanning their room for more insight to both Kash and Krew. Their walls are dark gray, blending beautifully with the black furniture. Very dark and moody. There's only one bed, but it's king sized. I find that a little surprising, but to each their own.

"Are you okay? I sort of left the rest of you to deal with that bomb on your own last night." I toy with the leather bracelet on Kash's wrist as I wait for him to answer.

"That's because Kade is the one who needed you most, and you recognized that. Don't feel bad about being there for him. I think the real question is, are *you* okay?" Kash pinches my chin between his finger and thumb, tilting my face up so he can look me in the eye.

"I'm good. Havok and I have made peace with our past. I don't see a point in dwelling on it, and if I had known it was something he hadn't disclosed to the group, I never would have said anything. I know he has a lot of guilt and shame over the way he treated me, so I can understand why he didn't want to tell any of you." Kash hums in thought, but doesn't offer his personal feelings on the matter.

"As long you're good, then I'm good, Best Friend." I smile, enjoying the ease that always comes with being around him. "I bet I could take him, though. One good swipe at his knees and Kade would drop like a sack of shit." He snickers, the sound too adorable to match the badass vibe he's going for.

"Oh, my God!" I gasp, pointing directly beside him. "Is that a spider?!"

"What!" Kash screeches, flying up and over me as quickly as he can. I laugh—hard and loud—unable to hold it back a second longer.

"Yep. You could *totally* take him." I pluck the sucker from his mouth and stick it in my own, wiping the tears from my eyes. He fixates on where my lips are wrapped around his candy, his expression darkening to something I can't quite pinpoint.

"You find that funny, do you?" Kash grins, gripping me just above my knee. He squeezes it over and over again, making me twist and turn as I laugh like crazy. It feels like I beg for ages before he finally relents. He steals the sucker back, making a show of licking it before leaning down to speak.

"We just swapped spit, sweetness. Congrats, your best friend status has been upgraded." His breath is hot against my ear, but chills erupt in the wake of his words. At the promise in his voice. Kash pulls back, a slow, satisfied smirk stretched across his face.

And then he boops my nose.

Chapter Twenty-Five

Kash

It's rare for me to sleep in. Most nights I don't get more than five consecutive hours before my brain is up and running. Yet every time I find myself in Saylor's bed, I don't have nearly as much trouble. I could lie beside this girl forever. My arm is slung across her waist, my chest flush with her back. As casually as possible, I put some space between my very hard dick and her very soft ass. This is the most intimate position we've ever been in, and I sure as fuck don't want her to wake up in a panic because my cock is nestled against her like it's finally found its home.

Shit, this is the closest I've been to any *woman, not just Saylor.*

It's been two weeks since Ro popped Kade in the mouth, doing what the rest of us were too pussy to. He deserved what he got, not that I'd admit to feeling that way. It's clear Saylor wants to move on and keep the past in the past, and I respect that. But for three years, we were kept in the dark, and that betrayal still lingers. I'm trying to be understanding, put myself in his shoes and all that shit, but it's hard not to pass judgement. I, too, would be ashamed if I were him.

Kade's our brother; we've forgiven him. But there's a weird tension between us now that the truth is out and in the open. I can't help but notice how much we've been clinging to Saylor ever since. Aside from my idiotic twin, we've basically attached ourselves to the poor girl. It's a wonder she hasn't snapped and told us to give her some damn space. I press my nose to the back of her neck, soaking up the sweet scent of coconut lingering from her shampoo. I get a sick sense of satisfaction, knowing that I'm the one who picked it out.

"Did you just sniff me?" Saylor's sleepy voice makes me freeze. I'm bouncing around excuses in my head, searching for something slightly less creepy than the truth of *yes*, I did just inhale her like a man starved of oxygen, when she flips over to face me. She cracks an eye open, giving me a small smile before closing it right back.

"You weren't here when I went to bed," she mumbles, burying her face against my chest. "Did I have another nightmare?"

"No. Just couldn't sleep without you," I answer honestly, brushing a few strands of hair from her face. She hums in contentment, making me grin like a goddamn fool. I don't think Saylor even realizes how much she's allowed us to worm our way in. She takes comfort in us just as much as we do her. Loch's no touching suggestion flew straight out the damn window. If she had even once indicated she wasn't okay with us being this close, we would have backed off. But I think it's helped her, exactly like I thought it would. I don't want her to be like I was, afraid of my own fucking shadow. I've just now gotten to the point where I can go out alone without feeling the need to analyze every person I pass.

"Sleep, sweetness. I have to go into town for a bit, but I'll be back shortly." I drop a kiss to her forehead, but she's out cold. Extricating myself from the covers, I make sure she's tucked back in, then head to my and Krew's room to freshen up. My brother is lying in bed, arms folded behind his head as he stares blankly at the ceiling.

I should feel guilty, because I know it's fucking with him that I've been sleeping better with Saylor than I have with him. It's always been the two of us. Even when the guys came into the picture, I still needed Krew more than anyone else. He's had my back, protected me in ways that no one else ever has. It took me a long time to make it through a single night without waking up in a cold sweat, searching for a threat that no longer existed, but still plagued my mind, nonetheless.

"Little bro." I lift my chin in greeting and grab a fresh change of clothes from the closet. He grunts, never taking his focus from whatever he finds so fascinating above him. After I've washed my ass and dressed, I find the sad sack in the same position, looking more or less like someone kicked his puppy. Except Krew would never own a puppy. Too many warm and fuzzies attached to something so fluffy and cute.

"Okay, Grumpy Smurf. What's your deal?" I cross my arms and give him a glare that lacks any real intimidation, but whatever. I know what his problem is, but I'd rather he admits it. To voice his damn worries for once instead of internalizing everything like he always does. Sometimes it feels like I'm the reason for the way he is. For years, he had to be the strong one because I was so goddamn weak, and now that's all he knows.

"Fuck off, Kash." I laugh, but it's not a nice one.

"Get your shit. We need to run some errands." I snatch his hoodie off the dresser when he turns his back to me and head to Saylor's room. I lay it in her bathroom, hoping she'll see it when she wakes. It's barely after seven, so she's probably got another hour or so before one of the guys can't wait a second longer and coaxes her from bed with the promise of breakfast. I've definitely bribed her with food a time or two.

I grab a cereal bar on my way out, deciding to wait for Krew in the car. He stomps out ten minutes later, looking like Eeyore with all his doom and gloom. Stupid asshole. This is *not* my forte—being the serious one who puts shit into perspective. I like my lighter role and responsibility just fine. This sort of chat is best left to Loch, but seeing as it's *my* twin that needs the mental ass-kicking, I think it should be me who delivers it. He slams his door like a petulant child. I roll my eyes and wait till we're on the road to launch my assault, that way he can't flee the conversation so easily.

"Are you about done with this whole uninterested act?" I wave a hand in his general direction. He can deny it all he wants, but I know my brother. He's *definitely* interested. Right now, I'm more concerned with the wary looks he's been getting from Saylor. Any time they're in the same room she seems to shut down, like she's lost in her head.

"And do what exactly? Fall at her feet like the rest of you?" Krew scoffs, managing to piss me off even more. "The sad part, is that your dicks aren't even leading the charge, it's your goddamned hearts. How do you think this is going to play out, brother? *Honestly?* Loch's already made it known that he plans to pursue her. Kade's been gone for the girl since elementary school. And Ro? Good luck going against that giant fucker."

"She's not a fucking prize to be won," I spit. I hate hearing him lay it out like that, because every second I spend with Saylor, we grow closer. It's hard to imagine that they could have the same connection with her as I do, but I know it's true. I can see it.

"I'm aware." He glares at me, momentarily taking his eyes off the road. "I'm worried about what this is doing to *us*. This is our family, the first we've ever really had, and it's slowly being torn apart. Ro *hit* Kade. When have any of us ever laid hands on each other?"

I think on what he's saying for a few minutes, making sure my response isn't rushed or biased. My initial reaction is to defend Saylor, because it sounds a lot like he's blaming her. But I try to see things how Krew does, wondering if there's any merit to his observation. And...*nope*. I really tried, but I just don't view it that way, and I'm not convinced he does either.

"Wanna know what I think?" I pause for dramatic effect, just to annoy the stoic motherfucker. "I think you're full of shit. That in all actuality, you're just scared to feel something for her. To let another person in, because then they have the power to hurt you. I don't have all the answers. And yeah, there's a high probability that four of us are going to get kicked to the curb. But there's no fucking way I'm going to sit back and not even fight when there's a chance I could find happiness with that woman. The *slimmest* possibility is worth any heartache I might have to endure." Krew is silent, probably thrown off by my rare moment of seriousness. "All I'm trying to say, is that you can care about Saylor without it going beyond that. There's obvious tension between the two of you, and it's fucked up that you're feeding it. The least you could do is not make her feel like you want her gone."

"Did she say that?" Krew snaps his head in my direction, his brows lowered as he scrutinizes me.

"She didn't have to. Saylor tenses whenever you're in the room, like she's suddenly unsure if she's still welcome to occupy the same space."

"*Fuck,*" Krew swears, his fingers tightening around the steering wheel. "I don't know if it's even fixable at this point. I've thrown her so many mixed signals, she'd probably prefer it if I left her the hell alone."

"Nah. Just stop being an apathetic asshole." I grin, hoping this depressing fucking conversation can be over now. I pull a sucker from my pocket and pop it in my mouth, doing my best to wipe the image of Saylor in our bed from my brain, her plump lips wrapped around my...lollipop. That's the single hottest thing I've ever witnessed, and it was actually pretty innocent on her part. We're silent for the rest of the drive, stopping by the grocery store first to grab a few necessities. On our way back, we swing by the post office. I run in while Krew stays with the car.

I get some friendly smiles here and there, an overly flirtatious wink from the girl working behind the counter, but all I'm concerned with is getting in and out as quickly as possible. I might be better than I was at being around strangers, but I don't enjoy it. It makes my skin crawl when someone touches me like we're old friends. I don't flinch the way I used to because I'm not afraid of them, I just don't like it. I head straight for our box and shove the key in. As soon as I grab the stack of mail, I lock it and turn to leave.

I sigh at the blast of AC once I'm back in the car. *Fuck this Florida heat.* You'd think I'd be used to it by now, but after living in Washington for most of my life, I long for some cloud cover and rain. Krew reverses the SUV and heads for the house as I go through the mail. I'm holding my breath as I flip through the envelopes, tossing aside random junk flyers and coupons. Just when I think we're in the clear, my stomach drops at the second to last piece.

Another fucking postcard.

"Krew." I can hear the tremor in my voice as he glances my way, a harsh curse slipping out when he sees what I'm holding. He steps on the gas, trying to get us back as quickly as he can. I pull my phone out, shooting off a text to Loch. We've been gone about an hour. With any luck, Saylor will still be sleeping so we can address it immediately. This one is from Iowa, but there's no specific city listed. The back shows it's addressed to Saylor, just like the last one. Scribbled to the side are the words '*tick tock*' and another set of coordinates.

My hand starts to shake. He's teasing us, trying to draw her out. It makes me sick to think that there's a possibility he could get his hands on her again. *This* is what's going to send me spiraling into another manic episode, where I go days without sleeping. Before, it happened because I was too paranoid to close my eyes. Years of being dragged from my bed in the middle of the night fucked with my ability to sleep without fear of what I might wake to. But now? Now I'm going to be too terrified to take my eyes off of Saylor to even consider resting.

I throw my door open before Krew can properly park the SUV, sprinting up the stairs to the main level. Fuck the groceries; they can wait. I try to wipe my face of any worry as I open the door, just in case Saylor's up and about. Thankfully, it's just the guys waiting for us. Ro shakes his head and gestures for me to go back out to the garage. I hand the card over to Loch, who snaps a pic to send to Denvers. We're quiet as he studies it, but all I really want to do is throw my fist through the damn wall.

I'm scared shitless that Liam's one too many steps ahead of us. With today's technology, it shouldn't be taking this long to locate the fucker. He's disappeared completely. This man has no background in tech, yet he's flying under the radar like a goddamn pro. And I want to know how.

"When I get my hands on this bastard, I'm going to rip him apart. One limb at a time," Ro grits out, his voice drenched in hate. Can't say I disagree.

"Denvers just responded. Coordinates lead to Iowa City, right by another river." Loch stares at the phone like he wants to launch it across the room. "Said he'll be in touch as soon as he knows something." I'm pretty sure we all know what the local authorities are going to find.

"Tink's awake." Krew's looking at the security app, watching her walk down the hallway. He must have had it pulled up just in case. "Let's grab the food. At least it won't look so weird that we're all out here if we each carry some in." I take a few bags and head on up, eager to get my eyes on Saylor. It's been too damn long. I drop them on the floor and walk straight for my sweetness. Her eyes widen at the look on my face, but I just wrap my arms around her and bury my face against her neck.

Damn she smells good.

"Missed you," I whisper.

Saylor laughs, but thankfully doesn't push me away. "You just saw me."

"That was..." I pull back to look at the clock. "One hour and thirty-two minutes ago. Way too long in my opinion." She shakes her head at me as the other guys come through the door. I definitely left them with the bulk of the groceries, but fuck 'em. All's fair in claiming time with Saylor. Krew stops dead in his tracks as soon as he sees what she's wearing, his eyes cutting towards me accusingly, then fixating back on Saylor. His heated gaze rakes her body from head to toe, the blatant ogling going unnoticed by absolutely no one. Saylor shifts her feet anxiously, looking down at the sweater, then to Krew. The sweater. Krew. Her blue eyes flare with realization.

"I'm sorry," Saylor mumbles. "Is this yours? I thought Kash left it." She side-eyes me, and not in a good way. *Shit*. "I promise I didn't know. I'll go take it off." Krew walks toward her, causing her to stumble back a step. Fuck, it's more like he's stalking his damn prey. He stops inches in front of her, looking her up and down. His appreciation is obvious, and he clearly doesn't give a rat's ass that we're all watching him feast on Saylor like she's the best thing his code-hackin' heart has laid eyes on since he first discovered JavaScript.

"Keep it." I stare in shock as my twin drops his head lower, bringing his mouth to the shell of her ear. "It looks better on you, Tink." I'm close enough to hear the sharp intake of her breath, witness the goosebumps spread across her freshly tanned skin. I swallow and look away, not wanting my dick to spring to attention. Her reaction is hot as hell, even if I'm not the one that caused it. The guys start talking, steering the topic to safer territory as Saylor starts helping put away the food.

Clearly, the talk Krew and I had was effective. Though I'm kinda second-guessing my reasoning for finding it necessary to have him pull his head from his ass. I just added another competitor to the already overflowing pool of prospects. Loch says something to Saylor, making her laugh. I'm at a serious disadvantage experience-wise, but I won't let that get in the way. I'm going to woo the shit out of that girl. I smile at the thought, skipping my happy ass across the room so I can make her dance with me. Saylor giggles as I dip and spin her around the dining table, the tinkling sound claiming another piece of my heart.

We spend the rest of the day watching movies, doing our best to keep the mood up so Saylor doesn't notice anything's off. The sun has set by the time Denvers gets back to Loch. He excuses himself from the room to take the call, but Saylor pays him no mind, too engrossed with her popcorn and the teen drama unfolding on the television. It feels like he's gone for hours, but I keep my eyes on the movie when he walks back in and my phone buzzes in my pocket.

One by one, we discreetly read the text Loch sent to the group chat, not wanting to make it obvious that we're having a conversation Saylor's isn't privy to. When it's my turn, I pull my phone out and open the camera. Pointing it at Saylor, I tell her to smile. Her cheeks are filled with popcorn as she grins at me, looking like the cutest fucking chipmunk in existence. I snap the picture and set it as my background, then scroll to the unread message.

GC: Same description and initial COD.

Short and to the point; I expected nothing less. I've gone through a dozen suckers today from the stress of waiting on Denvers to relay what they found. And now I wish I didn't know. I can see that Saylor's safe, sitting just a few feet from me as she laughs at Ro—who's pretending to be enthralled by yet another chick-flick—but my mind is replacing Liam's latest victim with her. The thought of our blue-eyed girl being brutalized and murdered like those other women makes me homicidal. I jump up and shove my way between the two of them, pulling her as close as I can.

"You okay?" she asks me quietly, brows drawn together as she attempts to analyze my odd behavior.

"Just need you," I whisper, holding her gaze. Saylor watches me, or maybe she's waiting for me to elaborate, but eventually, she must decide that my reasoning doesn't matter. She turns and drops her feet between my legs, wiggling her tiny little toes beneath my thigh. With her head against my chest, I steal Kade's blanket and tuck it around us. Her soft sigh just about does me in.

All it took was me saying that I needed her, and here Saylor is, offering me more reassurance than she knows. I can feel each of her breaths and the steady pulse of her heart beneath my thumb. She has no idea what she means to me, and it fucking terrifies me that I could lose her. Not just to Liam, but to one of my brothers. I'm not sure I'd survive that.

Chapter Twenty-Six

Saylor

It's the Fourth of July, and today officially marks five weeks since I was rescued. Sometimes it feels like I was just there yesterday, alone and hungry. Cold. But then there are days I don't think about it at all. I'm not as consumed by what happened to me as I thought I'd be, and that alone confuses me to the point it makes my brain hurt if I think about it for too long. I brought it up to Danielle during our last session, worried that something's wrong with me, but she assured me that there is no right or wrong way to move forward with my life. The best thing I can do right now is show myself some grace and do what feels right.

I know a huge part of how easily I'm adjusting has a lot to do with the guys. If I were alone, with nothing but my thoughts to keep me busy, I'm certain things wouldn't be going so smoothly. Krew's words still linger sometimes, but I'm doing my best to put them out of my mind. I know it'd be smart of me to establish some boundaries, but I just can't seem to keep them at arm's length. I don't even sleep alone anymore. There's always someone next to me, keeping the nightmares at bay, even if they weren't there when I fell asleep.

Lochlan wants to barbeque and spend the day at the beach, so the guys have been prepping the food and grill while I get ready. I've been going through my swimsuit options, but I can't make up my mind. A big part of me wants to opt for the black one-piece again, but a tiny, devious voice in the back of my head wants me to try out the white bikini. My skin has a decent tan to it and my ribs no longer show. I was able to take my brace off yesterday after slowly working my way up to going without it for a few hours at a time. It was nice to shed another reminder of Liam and the damage he caused. For once, I look normal. There are no outward tells that hint at what I went through. Strangely, I even *like* the image reflected back at me, which I didn't think would happen for years to come.

Everyone seeks validation at some point in their life. I want to feel good about myself. My body appears healthy with the extra weight I've put on, and there's barely any trace of the bruising from five weeks ago. If I didn't know it was there, it wouldn't be obvious at all. It'd certainly boost my confidence to have someone look at me appreciatively, but it feels wrong to put the guys in that position just for my own benefit. Indecisive, I try them all on.

I choose a red two-piece with high-waisted bottoms. The wrap top crisscrosses my back and keeps everything snug. Plus, the color is festive and matches the holiday. I toss on a cover-up, swipe a bit of ChapStick over my lips, and pull my hair into a high ponytail. That's as good as it's going to get, but we're headed to the beach, not a dance club. Anything more would be a waste.

There's a drawer full of makeup in my bathroom that still sits untouched. I wouldn't know what to do with most of it anyway. Mom was supposed to walk me through that stage, but she'd been adamant that I didn't wear any in middle school. According to her, there was no point in rushing to grow up, because it wasn't all that great once you got there. She wanted me to actually have a childhood, but a big part of mine was taken from the both of us. I shake my head, dispelling the sad thoughts before they can plummet my mood and ruin the day.

I can hear the guys laughing as I make my way toward the main room. I smile, their voices alone lifting my spirit. I swear, it's like they're doses of happy and somehow fine-tuned to my emotions. Any time I'm headed to a negative place, one of them inevitably does or says something that draws me back. More and more, I find myself wondering what I'd do if I didn't have them. No answer I come up with is comforting, and it terrifies me that one day I might have to find out.

Kash is shoving snacks into a beach bag—all high in sugar—while Roan places the burger patties in the fridge to keep them cool. The dining table, which has yet to be used for eating purposes, is piled high with colorful beach towels. Lochlan walks in behind me, his hand grazing the small of my back as I turn to look at him. He's shorter than the other guys, around five-ten, I believe, but he still has a good eight inches on me. His honey-colored eyes are bright and unobstructed today. He must have put contacts in since we'll be dripping sweat within the hour, and he probably plans to swim.

"Hey, sweetheart." He kisses my temple. The brief contact, while likely innocent to him, makes my stomach swarm with butterflies. Lochlan's style leans more toward business attire and preppy, so I'm not surprised by his outfit. His mint green swim-trunks fall to mid-thigh, paired with a plain white V-neck and leather boat shoes. Aviator sunglasses hang from his shirt, and his brown hair is perfectly swept to the side. He looks like he just stepped off a shoot for *Abercrombie*, but he's so cute I can't bring myself to pick at him. Unfortunately, Havok doesn't have the same problem.

"Good God, dude. That might be your douchiest getup to-date. Quick, take a pic, Ro. This one needs to be framed." Roan brushes off the request with a roll of his eyes, but Kash comes to the rescue and snaps one. Lochlan flips them both off.

"I think you look handsome." I spear the two troublemakers with a mock glare, then bat my lashes at the man beside me. His smile is everything. It's slow and magnetic, making my pulse race. He looks at Havok, his eyes flashing with pure, male satisfaction.

"You hear that? *Saylor thinks I'm handsome*." Lochlan grins, slipping his arm around my waist so he can pull me in. My hands are fisted in the back of his shirt, which will likely leave wrinkles from how sweaty my palms are. We're chest to chest, my thudding heart hammering between us as he drops his head to speak against my ear. "You look beautiful." Three little words. That's all he says, but I'm floating on air.

I smile as I lean back, rising to my tiptoes to press a kiss to his cheek. His hands tighten for a split second, but then he drops them and steps away. As if we were in a world of our own, the rest of the room filters back in. My cheeks heat, but no one seems to be aware of my inner thoughts. Kash is back to packing and Havok is dumping ice in the cooler. Roan is the only one I lock eyes with, but he just winks at me.

"Okay, children." Lochlan claps his hands to get everyone's attention. "Since it's still early, we'll wait a few more hours before firing up the grill. Are we missing anything, or are we ready to go?" He glances at each of us, but I have nothing but myself to worry about since they've obviously handled the rest.

"Nope. We're good." Roan hefts the cooler up like it weighs nothing while Kash opens the slider. They all have something to carry, so I snatch a towel. I'd like to think I'm contributing, but we all know I'm not. I follow Havok out, making sure to watch where I step as I descend the deck. The moment my bare feet make contact with the hot sand, I wince, belatedly remembering that I left my flip-flops in my room.

"Shit," I swear, bouncing around like a cracked-out bunny. The ground is literal lava; there's no way I can make it down to the beach without losing a layer of skin. I scramble back to the last step, which is still hot as hell, and nearly topple Krew in the process. He grunts from the impact, his hands flying out to steady me.

"Anyone else love it when she cusses? So fucking hot." Kash mumbles the last sentence, but it's loud enough for everyone to hear. Lochlan smacks the back of his head, but I'm more focused on the way Krew still has his hands on my body.

"Hop on, Tink." He edges around me, but I just stand there, confused by what he's wanting me to do. "Come on." He points over his shoulder. "It's a piggyback ride, don't look so affronted." His smile lets me know that whatever expression I'm sporting isn't actually offending him, but that's not the problem.

"And you would like me to do that how? Should I climb you? Because there's no amount of hopping that's going to get me up there." I look at the distance from my current position to where my arms would need to wrap around his neck in order to avoid falling on my ass, and yeah...not going to happen without bruising another rib.

"So fucking sassy," Krew grumbles before dropping to a squat. "Is that better, princess?" I know he's mocking me, but the tone of his voice doesn't give that impression. I hesitantly wrap myself around him as he slides his hands beneath my thighs. Krew stands, taking my full weight like it's nothing. The breath I just took gets trapped inside my lungs. Every inch of my front is pressed against his back. We're at the end of the line, but I don't miss Havok mouth '*lucky fucker*' when we start to move. I smile and rest my chin on Krew's shoulder as he heads toward the water.

As much as the others have been more affectionate recently, the biggest change has come from Krew. I thought he was going to blow a gasket when he saw me in his sweatshirt, which I had no idea was his when I put it on, but it's like that moment shifted something. He still prefers his own company, I think, but there's been a noticeable uptick in the effort he's exuding to be more present. I didn't even realize he was coming to the beach with us until I bumped into him. He's quiet and keeps to his office more often than not, but the distance between us has definitely shrunk over the last week. Knowing he's been wishy-washy before makes me cautious, though. Krew's thumb strokes the outside of my thigh, bringing me back to the present. The ticklish feeling makes me wiggle.

"Tink," he growls, his steps drastically slowing. "Quit grinding your tight little body against me." I choke on my own spit, shocked by his blunt words. But this is Krew. When he's not being silent, he has no problem saying whatever comes to mind. He doesn't screen his thoughts in the slightest.

"I *wiggled*." He scoffs at my response, but picks up the pace to catch back up with the others. They've already dropped their stuff and started laying out towels by the time we get there. Krew stops a few feet away from the group, and in a move I couldn't possibly have predicted, he tugs me from his back to his front in one fluid motion. I blink at him, my face only inches from his.

In the slowest way possible, I slide down his body. I can make out every muscle he has as he controls the speed of my descent. My toes can't even reach the ground yet, so this is all him. When I feel his erection, a startled groan escapes me. His hands slip over my butt then disappear, causing me to drop the rest of way. I take a deep breath and try to put some space between us, but he grabs the back of my head and pulls me in so he can speak without being overheard.

"I won't play this push and pull game like the others, Tink. And I certainly don't make a habit of depriving myself. You aren't fragile, and I refuse to treat you that way. You need to be sure of what you want because I'm not a fan of teasing. Doling it out maybe, but receiving? Not so much." He kisses my forehead and saunters off, like he didn't just short-circuit my brain. I stand there, my back facing the guys as I try to work through the shock of Krew's unexpected declaration.

I don't understand my lack of reaction. I'm caught off guard by how straight forward he was, sure, but there's no panic or urge to flee. The idea of a man hard and turned-on because of me should be repulsive. There might not be a timeline for every aspect of healing, but surely there is when it comes to sexual trauma. One word of his in particular sticks out like a glaring neon sign. *Teasing?* Is that what I've been doing to them? I *was* just contemplating a particular bikini with them in mind. God, how does this man have the ability to constantly make me question everything he says?

"Say! Get your fine ass over here," Havok yells, making me jump. I whirl around, deciding to put a pin in my overthinking. I head to where they've set everything up, trying to appear cool and unaffected, but my body is still humming in response to Krew's.

I drop my towel, laying it out next to Lochlan's. Roan quickly vacates the spot he'd already claimed to take my other side, shoving Havok out of the way so he can beat him to it. I laugh, happy that the two of them are back on track. It would've killed me if their relationship was permanently damaged because of me. Directly or indirectly, I'd been the cause of that fight.

"Dad! Ro pushed me," Havok whines, brushing sand from his face and body after climbing to his feet.

"I need a goddamn vacation." Lochlan slides his sunglasses on, then reaches behind him to pull his shirt off. One-handed. *Why is that so hot?* It's not even sexual. His build is lean, with a hint of definition along his abdomen. He has no tattoos that I can see, just a small trail of hair that leads to the waistband of his shorts. I look away, pretending the bird flying above the water is the most fascinating thing I've ever seen, instead of Lochlan.

But it doesn't end there. One by one, they each strip down. I'm sure my jaw is on the ground by the time they're finished, but Jesus Christ. There is a *lot* of skin on display. I can't even look at Roan without wanting to run my fingers across his stomach. There's no way his abs are real. And Havok...I want a personal tour of all those tattoos that are typically hidden. When the twins stand side by side, I give up completely and close my eyes.

"You okay?" Roan asks, a note of laughter in his voice.

"Yep." My answer comes out at a higher pitch

than normal, but he doesn't comment on it, being the smart man that he is.

"Sunblock, sweetheart. I don't want you getting burned again."

"Right." I stand and pull my cover-up off, turning to Lochlan for the bottle he was waving. Five sets of eyes follow my every move, but I pretend not notice or feel the heat of their stares. I'm able to get most of my body, but I can't reach my back.

"Let me." Lochlan takes over before I can decline. His hands work the sunscreen in, from my shoulders to the base of my spine. It ends too quickly, but I do a decent job of concealing my disappointment.

"I'm gonna go...cool off," Roan rushes out, power walking towards the water. The twins and Havok mumble something along the same line, then take off after him. I flop back, ridding my mind of handsome men and the unnerving way my heart is racing. I soak up the sun, wiggling my toes as I hum along to music streaming through Kash's portable speaker. Lochlan is quiet beside me, like he somehow knows that my thoughts are trying to spiral and I need a minute to get my crap together. I can hear them laughing and splashing around, their banter making me smile. Just as I start to settle, someone flings water all over me. I shriek, bolting up to find Roan shaking his body like wet a dog.

"Thought you could use a cool down too." He smiles wide, revealing those dimples, and drops to his towel.

"Hey, Best Friend. Look what I brought you." Kash digs through his snack bag until he finds what he's looking for. He whips out an e-reader and passes it down. "It's logged into my Kindle account, so borrow or buy whatever you'd like."

"Really?" I squeal in excitement. Kash laughs, telling me it's no big deal and to have at it. So that's exactly what I do. I browse his library first, wanting to see what he's been reading recently, especially after catching him in his room with alien smut. There are a few he hasn't started yet, one of them being the first in a series. The cover catches my eye, so I click the description. It sounds good, so I decide to give it a go.

I get lost in the digital pages, swiping my finger every few seconds as the story sucks me in. In no time at all, I've made it halfway through. I wish I could slow my progress, not ready for it to end, but I've always been a fast reader. In second grade, my teacher actually gave me an A- on my report card because of it. In the comments section, she'd written that I failed to follow instructions when she told me to slow down. Mom pitched a fit and had it corrected, making sure I was moved to an accelerated program after that.

"Whatcha readin'?" Kash stands over me, his wet shorts dripping water along the backs of my heated thighs. At some point, I flipped to my stomach, using my body to shield the screen from the glare of the sun. As soon as he catches the title, he straightens, stepping to the side as he rubs the back of his neck. "Oh."

Oh? What the heck does that mean, and why say it like that?

“Sorry. Did you not want me to read from your library?” I sit up, placing the e-reader aside so I can face Kash fully.

“No, no. That’s fine. I’m just not sure that’s the right book for you.”

“Huh?” My nose scrunches in confusion. That doesn’t even make sense. “It’s about a witch.”

“Right. And her new group of guy friends.” He stares at me, like he’s expecting me to figure out his hang-up from a simple look.

“Yeaaahh…” I drawl, wondering what that has to do with anything. It’s a big part of why I like the book so much. It reminds me of how easily I connected with these five. Mostly. Krew’s iffy some days.

“Shit,” Kash swears, looking at the ground as he works his jaw in contemplation. “Um…well, they’re friends *now*, but they’ll eventually be more.”

“Who?” I sit up a little straighter, excited for a spoiler.

“All of them.”

“Come again?” I ask at the same time Lochlan’s drink of water goes down the wrong way and he starts hacking up a lung.

“It’s called a reverse harem.” Kash grins at the blank look on my face. “One girl, three or more guys.” Lochlan continues to cough.

“Oh. *Ohhhh*.” My eyes widen slightly. “Like, they’re *all* together?” I do this weird thing, where I shove my fingers between each other, which makes zero sense, but I'm trying to approach this like I'm not some naïve little girl who's completely clueless about relationships.

"No. At least not in this story." Kash holds my gaze as he answers. "They're devoted to the girl. Basically, four separate relationships."

"Well, that seems selfish," I scoff. That's not real life. Even with my limited experience and knowledge, I know that jealously and the set number of hours in a day would never allow that sort of situation to thrive. Sounds like a disaster waiting to happen. Kash drops his head back as he laughs.

"Maybe some people deserve to be selfish, sweetness." He smirks at me, and I get the sudden feeling that he isn't really talking about the girl in the book anymore. I swallow, wondering if I should continue reading. He turns without another word and heads back up the path that leads to the house. "Ro's getting the food off the grill, be back in a sec!"

I glance at the time on the screen, shocked to see it's late afternoon already. I forgot how easily the hours slip away when you're lost in another world. I hop up, gently stretching my stiff body. I'm sure my ribs will be a little more sensitive after lying on the ground for so long. I meet Roan halfway so I can help him carry the food down. He tries to fight me on it, but I get my way in the end.

Krew and Havok are throwing a football, their game quickly forgotten once the burgers come into view. Lochlan refuses to let anyone eat until he finishes making my plate, so I try to hurry him along.

It's clear the guys have worked up an appetite. No one says much as we stuff our faces. I manage to eat half of what was prepared for me before I'm too full to take another bite. I gawk as Roan finishes his plate *and* mine. It's insane how fit he his, but I suppose muscles like that require a shit ton of calories. He'll burn it off in no time.

"Drink." Lochlan hands me a bottle of water. I raise an eyebrow at his bossiness, but honestly, I doubt he can help it. It's engrained in him to call the shots. "Don't look at me like that. You haven't had anything since we've been out here and you need to stay hydrated." I press it to my lips to hide my smile. It's ridiculous, but it makes me happy that I have someone—*multiple someone's*—to care about the small stuff.

When everyone's finished, we go back to doing our own thing. We're together, but not. Lochlan resumes watching the rest of us, and I decide to walk the beach for a bit to collect some shells. Just like before, I stay within eyesight of our group. Anytime their voices start to sound too far away, I turn and walk the other direction. As I'm heading back, I spot Kash jumping around, waving a chip in the air.

"Here, birdy-birdy," he calls to it, like it's a cat instead of a long lost relative of the pterodactyl. I don't care that it's not factually true. It is to me and my brain. Those beaks are way too pointy to be coincidental. Out of nowhere, Kash screams bloody murder. The noise that leaves him sounds like it should've come from a small child, not a grown man.

"Oh my God, get it off. Get it the fuck off!" He

starts flapping his arms, doing a great impersonation of the bird that's now fleeing the scene. Roan is frantically searching for the problem, but I saw it happen. In fact, I knew it would, because those flying blobs of feathers are evil.

"It shit on me, Loch. *Shit!*" The pause that follows feels like it lasts a lifetime, and then the guys are doubled over, laughing their asses off. I press a hand to my mouth, biting back my own as Kash runs for the water. He shivers in disgust, letting the waves wash the poop from his arm. I'm wiping tears from my eyes as he traipses back toward us. As soon as he catches sight of me partaking in his misery, a wicked smile spreads across his face.

"Oh, sweetness." Kash shakes his head. "You better run." I roll my eyes, but then he takes off at a dead sprint. I squeak and head for Roan, knowing he'll protect me. Sadly, I'm cut off by Havok, who steps directly in my path to safety. I spin around, but Kash is already on me. I throw my hand out, as if that will keep him away, when he prowls forward with determination. As gently as possible, he bends and scoops me up.

"Kash!" I flail, thinking he wants to get me wet, or maybe wipe off any remaining bird crap, but then he starts for the water. With purpose. Havok's hot on our heels as he brings us closer and closer to that liquid graveyard. "No, no, no, no." I'm cursing up a storm, clawing at his back as he strides through the incoming waves. Without a second thought, I wrap my arms and legs around him like a monkey, scooting as far up his chest as I can get. Kash groans, his teeth nipping at my shoulder.

"Get me out of here. Right now, Kash Davenport!" If I knew his middle name, I'd use it too. Mom always meant business when she dropped all three. He drags his hand up my side until it rests against my face, his thumb stroking my cheek as he uses the other arm to hold me up. I don't even care that he's touching my butt, I just want to get the hell away from this water.

"Hey, look at me." Kash presses our foreheads together. "You think I'd let something happen to you?"

"There are sharks out here. You're not the apex predator," I whimper, looking all around us for any sign of a threat.

"I'd fight a fucking shark, sweetness." I snort at Kash's growly voice. "What? You think I can't take a measly Great White?"

"Great White?!" I screech, my breaths growing harsher by the second. Kash just laughs.

I'm going to kill him.

"Whatever the threat, Best Friend, it wouldn't stand a goddamn chance." He tugs my hair, forcing me to focus on him. "Face your fears, sweetness. We've got you."

"We?" I go to look, but something brushes against my back and I freeze.

"*We*," Havok whispers, pressing in closer so I'm sandwiched between the two of them. "You're covered on all sides, baby. Nothing is going to get to you. It'd have to go through us first." I want to argue that a shark, Great White or not, could easily do that—and then I'd be down two of my favorite people—but I think it would ruin what they're trying to accomplish. They want me to face the thing that scares me and trust that no matter what, they'll take care of me.

The ocean.

Liam.

Regardless of the *thing*, they have me.

I exhale slowly, allowing my muscles to relax, then slide back down a few inches until I'm nice and snug. That creates a whole new problem. Kash is staring at me with so much heat in his eyes, I feel lightheaded from the attention. I shift, but Havok bands his arm around my middle at the same time Kash digs his fingers into the backs of my thighs. The simultaneous pressure makes me gasp. Havok drops his head, pressing a faint kiss to my spine. My eyes flutter as I bite my lip. I'm not dumb enough to mistake what's happening. I'm turned on, and even though we're surrounded by water, I'm absolutely certain my bikini bottoms are wet from something else entirely.

"Sweetness," Kash whispers, his lips lightly brushing mine. *He's going to kiss me*. I know it, and have no intention of stopping him, even though Havok is right here with us, his fingers stroking my stomach. And then something touches my leg, ripping a scream from my lungs. Havok laughs, pulling a glob of seaweed from the water lapping around us.

"Okay, enough bravery for one day." I'm pulled

away from Kash, who looks like he needs a second or two to get his hormones back in check. Havok carries me to dry land, handing me over to Lochlan, who's waiting with a clean towel to dry me off. I let him wrap me up and hug me to his chest, refusing to let my mind wander. There's too much to process, and if I give it any space it's going to consume the rest of my evening. So instead, I go with Lochlan, fitting myself between his legs as the last rays of sunlight fade from the sky. With my head resting against his shoulder, I grin happily as the first firework bursts through the darkness.

They told me earlier that the rich guy next door, the one who sold them this piece of land, throws a big party every year. Even with the distance between us, the view is unobstructed. Vibrant colors paint the night, one after another, and I can't help but marvel at how something so pretty is only achieved by setting it on fire. But then it's over. A bang, followed by an explosion of light, and all that's left are ashes.

"Looky what I got." I turn my head to find Kash waving around a sparkler, his hips swiveling as he attempts to dance and belt out *The Star-Spangled Banner*. Horrendously off key. "Oh, say does that..." Lochlan flinches at the crack in Kash's voice, trying to cover his ears.

"America is *not* proud, dude. That's...horrific." Havok ducks at the hurled sparkler Kash launches at him, setting off a fight that involves the twins going against Roan and Havok. Their weapons of choice are more sparking fire sticks, which seems about right for these men. They hop around the beach, cussing every time one of them gets burned, but I just close my eyes and listen to the chaos surrounding me.

It's perfect.

Chapter Twenty-Seven

Saylor

"Saylor? Are you with me?" My wandering thoughts are interrupted by Danielle's voice, drawing me back to the here and now. "You seem a little distracted today. Is everything okay?"

That's because I *am* distracted. I woke this morning to Lochlan's arm banded around my waist, and the second I moved, he moved with me. As if his body was aware of mine, even in his sleep. He'd tightened his hold, which did nothing for my overinflated bladder, and tugged me closer. I'd felt his arousal, hard and pressed against my ass. It made my head fuzzy and my stomach twist, but in a way I liked. My brain has been working overtime since my eyes opened, analyzing every interaction I've had with the guys over the past month. All the little things I've put off thinking about because I knew the moment I did, worry and indecision would swamp me.

"Sorry. I'm good, just have a lot on my mind." I smile, but Danielle isn't buying it. She's made a career out of reading people and studying how the mind works. I'm not fooling anyone, least of all her.

"Is there something you'd like to talk about?" I weigh my options. I could switch gears and avoid the topic, hoping she picks up on my hesitancy and drops the inquisition. But Danielle is the only other person I speak with, and there's a good chance she can help me work through the riot of emotions I'm experiencing.

"In cases like mine, do the women eventually want intimacy? Do they find normalcy with a partner at some point?" I bite my lip nervously as I wait for her to answer.

"I wish I could give you a straightforward yes or no, Saylor, but that simply isn't possible." Her placating smile is mildly frustrating. "Like I've said before, there is no right or wrong way to move forward after experiencing something like you, and sadly many others, have. I can say that, based on the information I have, there are cases far worse than yours and those women are thriving. They've gone on to marry and have children, but that doesn't mean it was an easy journey to get to that point.

"But there are also cases that aren't nearly as traumatizing as yours and they struggle every day just to get out of bed. Everyone responds differently. The only guidance I can offer is that no matter what it is —school, job, relationships—make sure you're doing it because *you* want to. Not because you think it will help you move on. Constantly check in with yourself and ensure that you're doing said things for the right reasons."

"Okay." I nod, mulling over what she's said,

though it's hard to take her advice into consideration when I honestly don't know what I want.

"Is there someone in particular that's brought on this line of questioning?" Danielle asks, her eyes kind and free of judgement.

"No." I shake my head because it's *not* someone. It's *multiple* someone's, and despite being sexually delayed, even I know it isn't normal to have feelings for five men at the same time. It's not just attraction, there's more between us than that, but it's undeniably prominent. "I'm just not sure what's normal and what isn't. If there's a certain amount of time that needs to pass before I can entertain the idea of something… more."

Danielle smiles knowingly. "Remember when I said that you should do what feels right? Well, that applies to this as well, Saylor. No one but you will know when you're ready for something more. Trust yourself. Although, I do recommend that whoever you take this step with, whenever that may be, the two of you should talk about what happened beforehand. It could greatly reduce your chances of having triggers or flashbacks."

"I'll keep that in mind." My face heats from discussing such an intimate topic, but I'm glad I brought it up.

"Our time is up, but as always, I'm only a phone call away should you need me. Day or night, Saylor." Danielle smiles sweetly, helping to settle my frazzled nerves.

"See you next week." I wave, clicking the *end*

call button. Like every time before, a surge of relief floods over me that I made it through another session without being forced to talk about things I'd rather forget. I'm not sure if it's my perception of therapy that's skewed or if I just have an exceptional psychologist. Either way, I'm grateful that it's Danielle I spend an hour chatting with every week.

My throat is dry, so I pop open the drawer Lochlan pulled a water from the first time he set me up in his office. Realizing I chose the wrong one, I go to close it. Just before it shuts, something catches my eye. Slowly, I tug the handle to reveal the contents once again. My brain can't make sense of what I'm seeing, but dread washes over me, making my coordination stiff and clumsy. Mindful of what I'm handling, I carefully pull out the stack of papers and lay them on the desk.

A picture of a girl, her face eerily similar to mine, stares back at me. The image is printed on plain computer paper, so the definition isn't the greatest, but I'm able to make out her features pretty easily. Her name and birth date are listed as well.

Anna Beth Parker – March 11, 2002

I place it to the side and turn to the next one. My hand goes straight to my mouth at the gruesome sight I'm met with. It's the same girl—Anna Beth—but her body is lifeless, lying stiff on a steel autopsy table. She has visible bruises and lacerations on her face and neck, so I can only imagine what's hidden beneath the cloth that's covering the rest of her. At the bottom of the page, it states her cause of death: *asphyxia due to strangulation*. Beyond that, a torrent of other injuries are cited. Ones that make my own pale in comparison.

I shove it away, flipping to the next piece of paper, but it's identical to the first, the only difference being the name. Looking closely, I can see a few distinctions between her and the first girl, but they both hold a scary resemblance to me. Her name is Kenzie Rivers, born August 2, 1999. I turn it over, knowing what I'll find but unable to stop myself.

Her body is covered like Anna Beth's, with similar striations and coloring. Same cause of death, but it's the other injuries I fixate on. Bile creeps up my throat as I scan the list rapidly. Blunt force trauma to the head, resulting in a skull fracture. A stab wound to the lower abdomen. *Rape*. Oh God, was she strangled before or after these things were done to her? I push the image away and close my eyes. I never should've gone through Lochlan's desk. These must be cases the guys are currently working. They've spent so much time hovering and worrying over me, it's been easy to forget what they do.

After a few deep breaths, I pry my eyes back open. My nose scrunches as I catch sight of a postcard from North Dakota. I find it odd that it'd be mixed in with the papers I just stumbled across, knowing how organized and precise Lochlan is. I pick it up, finding another beneath it with *'Iowa'* stamped across the front. Weird. I flip the one in my hand, then drop it instantly. I jump from the chair, nearly making it flip in my haste. I can hardly draw in a breath as I read and reread the words written. The card's addressed to me, my name scrawled in blood-red ink.

This isn't what I think it is; it can't be. They

would've told me. But the proof is right in front of me. I check the one from Iowa, finding it just as creepy and confusing. Tears blur my eyes, making it difficult to find the trash can before I lose my lunch. I tug on the bottom drawer, blindly searching for a water. Twisting it open, I rinse my mouth, using the ruined bin to spit it back out in. I pull myself up on shaky legs, a hollow pit forming in my stomach. Gathering the papers, I glance at the time. My sessions with Danielle are only an hour long. It's a miracle someone hasn't come to check on me.

There are so many things that I'm feeling right now, but I harness the anger and hurt fighting for dominance and fling the door open. Their low voices echo down the hallway. Normally, I'd find that sound comforting, but all I feel is trepidation as my feet carry me closer and closer to a truth I'm not prepared for. My free hand is shaking as I come to a stop at the edge of the main room, the other clutching the papers. They're lost in their own world, talking and smiling, but I watch them. Searching for any clue that something's amiss.

Havok's relaxed on the couch, looking completely at ease. His legs are spread wide, his favorite pair of boots on his feet. Lochlan is scrolling through his phone, likely checking his emails since I've had his computer, somehow juggling a conversation with Roan at the same time. Krew is lying on one side of the sectional, an arm thrown across his face as Kash sprawls on the floor below him, mumbling around a sucker. There's nothing obvious, no one thing in particular that hints at the possibility of them keeping secrets, but I *feel* it. As usual, Kash is the first to spot me.

"Best Friend!" He jumps up, grinning around the strawberry lollipop he's so fond of. I throw my hand out when he's within a few feet of me. I can't think straight when they're touching me, and I'll need all my faculties for this conversation. "Saylor?" Kash implores, his feet coming to a dead stop. Like background noise, I hear the others stand and shuffle closer, but my eyes stay trained on Kash, knowing he's the easiest to read.

"Am I?" The question comes out so choked it's barely more than a whisper. Kash cocks his head, that gorgeous face of his twisting with confusion. "Am I your best friend? Because best friends don't keep secrets. Is there anything you want to tell me?" I helpfully fill in the blanks, watching him closely as my words begin to register. He stiffens, his posture growing rigid, jaw clenched tightly. The epitome of guilt. My bottom lip starts tremble, so I tuck it between my teeth. I don't want them to see how hurt I am.

"What's in your hand, Saylor?" Lochlan steps forward, looking as put together as ever in a pair of gray chinos, a plain V-neck hugging his top half perfectly. His pants rolled at the ankles, his bare feet giving the illusion that he's relaxed. But I note the flex of his fisted hands, despite them being shoved inside his pockets. I hold the papers up, giving the guys an unobstructed view of what I'm holding. Roan swears, his hands going to the top of his head as he paces at the back of the group. Any doubt I'd been clinging to is thoroughly erased with his reaction.

"I was looking for a water. Found these instead." I toss them to my right, watching as they scatter across the dining table. "What the hell is that?" I direct my question to Lochlan, knowing whatever decision was made to keep me in the dark ultimately came from him.

"We received a postcard a while back. It was mailed to the P.O. box. We didn't know about it for several days, but immediately informed Denvers as soon as we discovered it. We relayed the coordinates written on the back, and the local department was dispatched to investigate. They found the body of Anna Beth Parker." Lochlan's voice is strong and unwavering, like he's not the least bit ashamed.

"How long ago is '*a while back*'?" I grit out, my anger rising by the second.

"Technically, it came the Monday after you got here. But we didn't notice it until Wednesday." My eyes widen as I stumble back a step. Kash jerks forward, like he wants to reach out and steady me, but the glare I give him suggests he should back the hell up. His gaze falls to the floor immediately. I left the hospital on a Saturday. How would Liam have known where I was going before *I* did? It'd take at least three days for mail to get to Florida from North Dakota. The timeline doesn't make sense.

"Who are those girls?" Deep down, I know. But I'm hoping, by some miracle, that I'm completely off track and there's another answer that won't leave me wracked with guilt.

"We think they're substitutions. Women Liam chose that look like you, since he no longer has access to what he really wants." *Oh, God.* I suck in a sharp breath, but it feels like needles are pricking my chest. "He wants to lure you out, Saylor. He's obviously aware that you're staying with us, but the address to the actual house remains a mystery. You're still safe here."

"But he knows the city," I state, the realization nearly knocking me on my ass. "If he has me pinpointed to a roundabout location, why not come here?"

"Because he's toying with you. He's escalated —dramatically." I snort derisively. *Understatement of the century*. "He doesn't know for sure that you're in Florida. We have the house in Washington as well, and a post office box for when we're there. Denvers had a contact check it. They found the same postcard from North Dakota. I think he sent them to both locations because he isn't sure where we are."

"And the other one from Iowa? It was there, too?" I ask, a hint of relief leaking through. Lochlan shakes his head, stealing it back just as quickly.

"It could've gotten lost in the mail," he replies, but his reasoning convinces neither of us.

Or...he's somehow figured out that we're in Florida.

"Why?" My eyes fill with tears, but I square my shoulders and raise my chin defiantly. "Why not tell me?" His gaze hardens as he yanks his hands from his pockets, erasing the cool demeanor he'd been intent on keeping. Lochlan steps closer, leaving a scarce few inches between us. I hold my ground, even though I'm trembling from the hurt and anxiety coursing through me.

"That psycho fuck is taunting you. He wants to guilt you into doing something stupid." My hackles rise at the implication that I'd be so reckless. "He'll keep taking girls who look like you, doing despicable things to them, just to try and draw you out. I told you that I'd do everything in my power to keep you safe. Well, sweetheart, this is me doing that. I couldn't risk you offering yourself up to him." I flinch.

"And you all agreed?" I look to each of the guys, wanting—*needing*—to know if they were all on board with this. Their guilty nods feel like a knife to the heart.

"Wow," I whisper, crossing my arms over my chest. The need to protect myself is bearing down on me. "Did it ever occur to you that I'm not that stupid? I spent five years with Liam Price. I have firsthand knowledge of how evil that man is, and now you're telling me that he's escalated? I'm one person. If I walked out of here, determined to make my location known, what would that accomplish? No one knows where he is; there's no foolproof way to bait him. Honestly, it's insulting that you think I'd risk not only me, but all of you as well, in what would no doubt amount to nothing more than a suicide mission.

"I'm heartbroken that he's taken the lives of two innocent women, but I refuse to make his actions my fault. *He* did those things, not me. If we could figure out a way to stop him that ensured our safety too, I'd be all for it. But I won't willingly go to him after just escaping the hell I'd resigned myself to. Except none of you thought to discuss this with me, the one person this affects the most and has every right to be kept in the loop."

"Saylor," Lochlan croaks, thick emotion clogging his throat. He extends his hand, but I step back.

"You asked me to trust you." I hold his honey-colored eyes hostage. "I did. Blindly. Yet you keep giving me reasons why I shouldn't. It works both ways, Lochlan. How am I supposed to trust you, when you obviously have none in me?" My words trail off as the first tear, of what will likely be many, finally breaks free and slides down my cheek. I tried, but it was impossible to keep them at bay.

"You're killing me, pretty girl." Havok looks wrecked, but I can't cater to him when I'm feeling just as defeated.

"I need to be alone right now," I mumble, walking backwards until I'm certain they're going to stay where they are. I glance at Krew, his usually unreadable face revealing far more than I'm used to.

Guilt.

Regret.

Remorse.

I close my eyes, severing the connection, then spin around and sprint for my room. My heart is racing, my mind trying to absorb everything that's been thrown at me. I knew that Liam was still a prominent player on this twisted chessboard he's concocted, but I naively assumed his time was being spent running for his life, not actively pursuing me. And to this extent...so publicly and without a single care that his face is plastered all over the country as a wanted fugitive. Images of those girl's flash behind my closed eyelids, the morbid scene making my stomach cramp. I rush to the bathroom and slide to the floor, just in case I need the toilet. My head thumps against the wall as I release an exhausted sigh.

They were young. Too young. So much life left to live. Mistakes to make. And that asshole took it all away. I've known for five years how cruel and heartless Liam truly is, but I can't believe he's taken things this far. Cornered dogs bite, and that's exactly what he is. His anonymity is gone, the hold and power he wielded over Laiken County—all of it. There's nothing more dangerous than a person who has nothing left to lose. Why now, though? Liam had me for years, giving him plenty of time to act out the things he did to those women.

Every time the lock turned and that heavy steel door slid open, I braced for the inevitable. The day he'd finally take things beyond the invasion of his fingers, or when his hits would cause irreparable damage. But it never came. It's clear that Liam is capable of far worse violence than he showed me, and I'm not sure I want to think too long on why it is that he never hurt me the way he did Anna Beth and Kenzie. The idea that he might see me as '*special*' makes me sick.

And the guys...

My heart physically aches at how betrayed I

feel. I was beginning to think of myself as a part of the group, not just some job they took on. It hurts to know they think so little of me, or that I'd ever risk them by putting myself in danger. Just my being here paints a target on their backs. It terrifies me that Liam knows who they are now, that he might see them as an obstacle. The thing that's keeping us apart. And they are. I'm confident they'd put themselves directly in the line of fire if it meant protecting me. It's scary, that initial realization of how deeply you care for another person. Caring for *five* someone's? Downright petrifying.

We should've talked about this, discussed the situation like grown adults so I didn't have to be blindsided by those pictures. If they would've had a little faith in my ability to think rationally, this could have been avoided. I have no idea where my place is or how I fit with them. I've never felt like a burden. Thus far, the playing field has been equal. But instances like this serve as a reminder that I'm *not* a member of their team. I'm the interloper, peering in from the edge of their circle, desperate to be included. Maybe I wouldn't be so upset if things hadn't progressed between the six of us. There's an undeniable connection tethering me to each of them, but none of us have been brave enough to broach the subject.

We've been tiptoeing around the subtle changes that have happened over the last few weeks. The purposeful touches that linger a little more with every passing day. I'm not sure there *is* a way to explain the shift. It doesn't feel plausible to have feelings for more than one person, but I do. I think I'm broken. Defective. Maybe this is the resulting damage of Liam's abuse—my inability to choose. I may never be normal, so that white picket fence and boring husband Krew was so adamant about might never come to fruition. There's a good chance I won't have that. Definitely not with any of these men. I can't imagine settling down with one of them and having to see the others on a regular basis. It'd break my heart and rip their group apart.

The thought of being the thing that drives a wedge between the guys makes me wonder if we should put an end to this—whatever *this* is—before things escalate any further. It'd hurt a lot less than months from now, or whenever I'm sent on my way. I can't speak for them, but more time together will only complicate my feelings. That doesn't mean I have to act on them, though. I lie across the floor, my cheek pressed against the cool marble, and try to clear my mind. It's pinging from one thing to the next and draining me dry.

I want to forget the last hour, but I'm also glad that I know. Not quite sure where this leaves us, but they have some groveling to do. My eyes flutter, the crappy day weighing them down. I try to fight it, but eventually succumb to sleep. I should've known it'd be anything but peaceful.

Chapter Twenty-Eight

Krew

When Saylor's ear-splitting scream echoes throughout the house, I'm not taken aback. I've been expecting it. That's why I've had my ass parked outside of her room, waiting for the moment a nightmare managed to claw its way in. I knew there was a good chance she'd have one. The instant you become vulnerable, just about any setback or shitty day can bring one on. I should know. Tonight, I had to crush up a sleeping pill and put it into Kash's drink. If I hadn't, he wouldn't have slept at all, or he'd be exactly where Saylor is right now—lost to an invisible enemy wreaking havoc on his mind.

I slip the key from my pocket and quickly unlock her door. My eyes scan the room, immediately noting her empty bed. Kade is the first to appear, but Loch and Ro are right behind him. I shake my head and slam the door in their faces. Harsh, but I fucking knew this was where we'd end up. I find Saylor on the bathroom floor, her tiny body trembling uncontrollably. I scoop her up and tuck her against my chest.

"Krew?" her sleepy voice questions. There's relief in the way she says my name, but then she tenses, like she forgot for a second about everything that went down and how pissed she is.

"Don't fight me, Tink. You can go back to being mad tomorrow, but there's not a chance in hell I'm going to leave you in here to suffer when I know you sleep better with one of us next to you."

I can't make out much of her facial expression, but the tautness of her body tells me she'd like nothing more than to kick me out. Reluctantly, she relaxes and I slide us beneath the cool sheets of her bed. If anyone else had beaten me in here, she wouldn't be giving in so easily. My relationship with Saylor isn't as solid as what she has with the rest of the guys. That's a result of my own issues, but I doubt she feels as betrayed by me as she does by them. Especially Kash.

Fuck, the look she gave my twin made me hurt for him. He paced our room for hours, mumbling apologies to the dead air. When he smacked his head against the wall, his eyes glistening with agony, I knew I had to step in and do something. He's going to wake up pissed, but he'll get over it. I'm mad as fuck myself. At this entire situation. The guys. Even Saylor. It took restraint not to shake her earlier, to make her see reason and force her to understand the impossible position we're in. Loch has probably downed an entire bottle of Jack, and that uptight asshole never drinks. It won't matter that we all agreed this was the right course of action, he's going to take full blame and responsibility. Denvers himself said Saylor was to be kept out of this for the time being, and he's the real shot caller.

Saylor finally settles, her stilted breaths evening back out, but sleep evades me. It might be normal for the other guys to take turns sleeping in here, but I never have. I definitely get the fucking appeal. Just being next to her eases my worry. I can't even claim to be impartial anymore. I'm just as gone as they are. We're on thin ice, but it's starting to crack. Someone's going to cross a line we can't come back from, and I wouldn't be surprised if it's me. I'm not the one she needs though, despite my heated confession on the beach.

She tests my will every goddamn day, but Saylor isn't ready for the shit I'd do to her delectable little body. I question if she's ready for anything—vanilla or otherwise. I'm not sure how much more I can take of her prancing around the house in those tiny ass shorts and our sweatshirts. She could tempt a monk. It feels like I stare at the ceiling for hours, my thoughts scattered all over the place, before I eventually exhaust myself and find some sleep.

I swear I've just closed my eyes when I'm drawn back awake by that prickling sensation of being watched. I peel an eye open to find Saylor sitting cross-legged on the bed, her gaze intent on me. The sun is pouring in through the window behind her, making her look like a fucking angel. *Yeah, I've definitely drank the damn Kool-Aid.* We stare at one another, neither of us saying a word for several awkward minutes. I pry my sleep-deprived body up so we're level with each other and wait her out. I can see her wheels start to turn behind those bright blue eyes, and when she's good and damn ready she'll let me have it.

"I'm surprised that you're the one who came to the rescue last night," she speaks quietly. Her posture's relaxed, but I sense she's trying her best to put on a brave face.

"I think we've both underestimated how much I care, Tink, and I had a feeling you'd need one of us. Figured I was the least likely option to be kicked out on my ass." I cross my arms in a sad attempt to protect myself after admitting that my feelings aren't strictly platonic. Those other four assholes have been head-over-heels since day one, but I'm the straggler, arriving late to a party that's already started—and that's no one's fault but my own. I don't particularly enjoy putting myself out there. Women have been nothing more than a good time for me, no emotions involved. But that's the thing about Saylor, she's hooked me without an ounce of physical exchange.

"I don't want to be angry at any of you, but my feelings are hurt." She looks away, mimicking my crossed-arm stance.

"As you should be," I tell her, giving her knee-jerk response validation. "But I'd like you to put yourself in our shoes for a minute. I won't sugarcoat shit, so bluntly put, I think it's safe to say that we care for you in a way that goes beyond a business relationship. Truthfully, beyond friendship." Saylor's cheeks pinken, her poor bottom lip getting abused as she bites it nervously. Fuck, what I'd give to make her blush for an entirely different reason. "That being said, we wouldn't have jeopardized a client we have no emotional attachment to, much less you. We should have trusted that you'd look at this sensibly but at the end of the day, keeping you safe is what's most important. I'm sorry if our method of achieving that hurt you, but we did what we thought was best."

Saylor nods, neither agreeing nor disagreeing with anything I've said. I sigh, forcefully removing myself from her bed. I could use about eight more hours of sleep, but there's a fat chance of that happening.

"We aren't the enemy, Tink." I press a kiss to her cheek, relishing the shocked inhale it earns me. I leave her to her thoughts, knowing she'll come out and face us when she's ready. It sounds conceited, but I have a theory that being here with us has helped her speak up and voice her feelings. We keep Saylor accountable, ensuring she doesn't clamber back inside of that people-pleasing mold she's been steadily shedding. Loch and Ro are standing in the kitchen, looking like they've slept even less than me. Kade's sprawled across the couch, knocked out so heavily he's mouth breathing.

"How is she?" Loch asks, sipping on a cup of coffee. If I had to hazard a guess, I'd say it's not his first —or even third—of the day.

"Sad and hurt, but she'll come around," I answer. Ro scoffs disbelievingly, not that I can blame him. He's already fucked up and had to make nice with her, likely feeling the fragile hold he has slipping through his meaty ass paws.

"I'm going to kill that bloody wanker." I smile,

saying nothing about his British euphemism popping out. “I hate this hold that Liam still has on Saylor’s life. We need to put an end to it, and stat." A-fucking-men to that, but I'm lost on how to. For someone like me, who thrives on solving complex shit, this is torture. He’s outsmarted us at every turn, and I have no starting point to even begin a search.

“You donkey-dicked weasel,” Kash snarls roughly as he stumbles from the hallway. He still looks half asleep, making me wonder if I was a little heavy-handed on the dosage. “Where is she? Where’s my girl?” We freeze at my brother's outright claiming of Saylor. Even Kade seems to rise from the dead. Before any of us can comment, he slumps against the wall. I snort, walking over to help him to the couch. He’s back asleep before I can get him properly situated.

“Christ, how much did you give him?” Ro asks, pulling the pill bottle from the medicine cabinet to doublecheck I haven’t overdosed him.

“They’re prescription for a reason, asshole. I only give them to him when he’s bordering on manic. They usually knock him on his ass for a good while.”

“I need to talk to her,” Kade grouses, scrubbing a hand across his face. “I’ve made too many mistakes with Saylor as it is, and I swore I wouldn’t hurt her again.” The poor fuck looks miserable, much like the rest of us.

“Leave her be. She needs time to process.” I pop a k-cup in the Keurig, desperate for caffeine. “The best thing we can do right now is give her some space. Let the shock wear off. She’ll see that our intentions weren't malicious, but we don't need to rush her. Saylor needs to come to that conclusion on her own."

"Easy for you to say, you got to sleep next to her." Ro scowls at me, like he hasn't been in her bed plenty.

"Right. Let's keep busy, then. Krew, there's a new inquiry I'd like you to take a look at. I skimmed through it, but from what I've gathered there's a boy missing outside of Nashville. His parents reached out after being referred by a previous client. Age seventeen. He was visiting the city with a group of friends to scope out the music scene since he has plans to move there after graduation. Friends lost sight of him at the bar, and he never resurfaced after last call. They haven't seen him since." Loch switches to business mode seamlessly. I nod along, eager to give my focus to something else for the time being. I said all I could think to say, it's up to Saylor now.

"On it." I snag a breakfast bar from the pantry and head for my office. In here, I don't feel the harmful lies my stepfather force-fed me. I'm not a failure or a piece of shit. This is where I thrive and come to life. I crack open a Red Bull and settle in, preparing for a long day of digging. No complaints, though. Anything to take my mind off of last night and the way it felt to lie beside Saylor. Too fucking good. The circumstances were less than optimal, but it forced me to man the fuck up and show my hand. Silver-linings, I suppose. I shake the thought away and refocus my attention on what I needs to be done.

As much as I'd love to daydream about that long blonde hair wrapped around my fist, those hypnotic blue eyes peering up at me from where Saylor's knelt between my thighs...*fuck*. Great job of *not* going there, asshole. I've never let a woman affect me like this. Damn sure not to the point of distraction. I like sex. Love it, actually. But emotional attachments aren't my forte. Until she walked in, this girl I hadn't thought of as anything more than someone I was drawn to and protective of because she meant something to Kade.

I tried—I really did. To keep my distance and maintain that barrier between us. But she dismantled my walls in no time. I'd laugh if it weren't so fucking pathetic. I gave my brothers hell for falling at Saylor's feet like sad little saps, desperate for anything she'd give them. And despite knowing that this is going to go to shit one way or another, I can't stop myself.

As soon as I let the idea take root and allowed myself to think of her in a way I damn sure know I shouldn't, all bets were off. I hate the imbalance of power, because it's entirely in her favor at this point. I don't do well with change. When Kade came into the picture, it took me a lot longer to warm up to him than it did the others. And Saylor? She's changing every-fucking-thing. Sighing roughly, I toss my breakfast trash and try to ignore the way her scent still clings to my goddamn clothes.

Relaxing against the familiar feel of my office chair, I power up the monitor screens and quickly locate the email that Loch was referring to. I get lost in my work, researching the bar the kid was last seen at. There's no surveillance inside the establishment, but I check the surrounding businesses to see if they might have caught anything. Proper protocol would dictate that I submit a request for any footage they have, but where's the fun in that if I can just hack my way in? When Kash and I studied coding, it was to fuck up the perfect little life our stepfather loved to flaunt. It was never my intention to make a living from it, but damn if things didn't work out beautifully.

That asshole's rotting in a six-by-eight cell, hopefully getting the shit beat out of him on the daily, and I've got more money than he ever thought of having. In fact, I *know* ole Archie is miserable and rethinking his life choices, but I make a mental note to check in with my contact. Just to be sure and all.

When I finally come up for air, it's nearing dinnertime. The stiffness in my back tells me I've been at it for hours, but it's easy to slip away when I'm focused and in my element. My stomach growls, reminding me that I've barely eaten anything. Thankfully, I can smell a faint whiff of garlic coming from the kitchen. With any luck, Ro's making his famous lasagna, because I could eat a whole fucking cow right about now. I've just pushed back from my desk, stretching my body out, when I hear the tell-tale crash of someone stumbling down the hallway.

Fuck.

I'd bet my entire stash of energy drinks that Kash is up and aware, pissed as hell at me, and well on his way to Saylor's room. I throw the office door open, catching a glimpse of him as he turns the corner. I take off after him, knowing my twin has the patience of a gnat and won't give Saylor any more time to stew unless someone intervenes. Unfortunately, I'm a few seconds too late when I go to grab him. Kash snarls at me, arms loaded down with snacks, as if he's planning to hole up in her room for the foreseeable future.

And then he slams the goddamn door in my face.

Chapter Twenty-Nine

Saylor

I've spent the entire day in a weird fog. After waking up next to Krew, my emotions have been all over the place. He was the last person I expected to comfort me from a nightmare. Maybe it was his own history with shitty dreams that led him in here, but I never anticipated that he'd stay. It was strange, yet fascinating, to watch Krew sleeping, taking in the small things I hadn't noticed before. Like the freckle below his left eye. It's not very obvious because of his darker skin, but I was drawn to the slight physical difference distinguishing him from Kash.

Once he'd caught me staring, I felt a bit embarrassed, but not as much as I used to when stealing glimpses of him. There's a high chance it was leftover anger that kept my bravery intact as I listened to him explain their reasoning for why they'd essentially lied to me. By omission, but hurtful, nonetheless. Danielle has always left our communication open-ended, so I took advantage of that and dialed her number for the first time outside of one of our scheduled sessions. I hated to bother her, but I needed someone who isn't directly involved to shed some light on the situation.

Her input was helpful, but also grounding. Danielle reminded me that even though I've formed friendships with the guys, my safety is paramount above all else. Likely even more so now that we've blurred the boundaries by involving our feelings. Ultimately, she told me that if I'm entrusting my life to them—to which I have been—then I need to have faith that whatever choices they make are in my best interest. I know them well enough to confidently say that their decision wasn't made with the intent to hurt me.

Danielle also reminded me that communication is key in all aspects of life—business and personal—and if I want to be more involved going forward, I need to speak up and voice that. In theory, it sounds rather simple, but it isn't for me. Especially when it feels as if a key factor for their secrecy was a lack of faith that I wouldn't fly off the handle and do something stupid. I comprehend the logic, but it does nothing for my confidence. I've always questioned my ability to make the right choice, which is why I typically go with the flow and leave the decision-making up to everyone else, but the guys have been trying to break me of that.

So why shove me back in my shell when I finally start to feel comfortable? I spoke up for myself last night, but that was mostly my hurt and anger talking. We need to have a conversation once the shock has fully worn off, but I'm nervous as hell to be the one who initiates it. I'll have to grow a backbone eventually, because my hunger isn't going to allow me to cower in my room forever.

I'm pacing back and forth at the foot of my bed, working up the nerve to face them, when my door bangs open. Kash stumbles in, growling behind him before he kicks it shut. His shaky fingers struggle with the lock, but he gets it after a few tries. His arms are loaded with junk food, to which he promptly deposits onto my bed. I'm still as a statue as I watch him, my brows pinched in concern. He turns, causing me to gasp as I take in the state of him. *'Sick'* doesn't really cut it; he looks seconds from throwing up or passing out. Kash's skin is clammy, and sweat dots his forehead.

"Are you okay?" I question, stepping a bit closer. His breaths are labored, like the effort of walking back here took too much out of him.

"Sugar withdrawal. I'll be right as rain in a second," he huffs, tearing open a bag of Twizzlers. I stare in amusement as he scarfs down a good dozen in record time.

"Better?"

"Nuh uh." Kash shakes his head, tossing the bag aside. He stalks toward me, the heated look in his eyes causing me to retreat until my back meets the closet door with a thud. He crowds me, bracing the palms of his hands on each side of my face. He's so close, I can feel every puff of air that leaves his lips as he speaks. "I think it's a Saylor withdrawal that's got me all messed up. Need my sweetness, but not the candy type."

I'm certain the thump of my heart can be heard outside of my body. There's a whooshing in my ears, the space between us charged enough to make me dizzy. I grip the hem of my shirt, belatedly realizing that it's Kash's and the only thing I'm wearing besides some boy shorts beneath it. I gulp, feeling eons past my comfort zone, but desperate to live in the moment.

"Can I kiss you, Saylor? Please say I can kiss you," Kash pleads, the need in his voice rendering me speechless. Like my body has a mind of its own, I nod. It's slight and barely discernable, but he homes in on the action like it's the answer to all he'll ever need to know from this point forward. Kash licks his lips, drawing my eyes to his mouth. He exhales, a relieved smile making a quick appearance, then slowly, his hands cup my cheeks, the warmth of his skin serving as a balm to the anxiety threatening to overwhelm me. I forget how to breathe the second our lips brush.

Kash groans, the small bit of contact snapping his restraint. His mouth presses into mine, the kiss tender and sweet. The tension I've been carrying slips away, and next thing I know, my hands are fisted in the front of his shirt. He shifts closer, the hardness of his body making me gasp. Kash takes the opportunity without a second thought, his tongue pushing its way in and tangling with mine. I have no idea if what I'm doing is even right, but based on the sounds he's making, I don't think it's wrong. I'm breathless when he pulls away, dropping his forehead to my shoulder. He's been half bent over just to reach me, so I doubt he's very comfortable, but he doesn't appear to be in any hurry to move.

"Damn, sweetness," Kash groans, his voice dripping with desire. He edges back, refusing to push the moment beyond a kiss. I think he knows that alone was enough to send my mind into a tailspin for days.

Holy shit, I just had my first kiss.

Kash pecks my lips once more, then puts several feet of space between us. I'm appreciative and disappointed at the same time. His cocky, satisfied smile makes me laugh, breaking up the tension. He snags my hand, wrapping his arms around me as he buries his face against my neck.

"God, I missed you," Kash mumbles, the words tickling my skin and making my shoulders scrunch. I can practically feel him grinning.

"I saw you last night!" I laugh, trying to shove him away, but his hold only tightens.

"Too long." Kash spins me around and drops me on the bed, carefully avoiding his precious snack pile as he takes the other side. "I would've been here sooner had my asshole brother not drugged me," he gripes, looking thoroughly put out.

"Wait. *What?*" I gape at him in horror, my traitorous mind conjuring up the moment Liam stuck me with a needle. It latches on, recalling how quickly the sedative spread and the instant loss of control. I swallow thickly, pushing past the lump in my throat. There's no way Krew would do that to his brother.

"Hey." Kash interrupts my mental freakout, pressing his hand to my cheek to get my attention. "Not like you're thinking, sweetness. He gave me a sleeping pill. I had them prescribed years ago, but I seldom need them anymore. I hate taking it because they're strong and knock me on my ass, but Krew was right to give it to me. I was panicked, desperate to get back here and fix everything. I'm not healthy when I get to that state, and I damn sure didn't need to be around you." His sad smile has my heart in a stranglehold.

"I'm sorry," I whisper, feeling guilty that shutting him out caused such a reaction.

Kash's head is shaking before I'm even finished speaking. "You have nothing to be sorry for. We fucked up. But for the record, it killed me to keep it from you. I should have told you, but I didn't because a part of me agreed and worried that you'd want to bait Liam. I can't think about you being in danger like that, Saylor. It's not a reality I'm willing to entertain." Kash flexes his hand, his jaw clenched tightly. It's rare to see him so worked up and serious. It instantly makes me miss that easygoing smile and his playful demeanor. I lean over, pressing my lips to his cheek, but he turns at the last second and I connect with his mouth. We both smile, laughing as we pull away.

"So much better than candy," he groans, licking his lips with exaggeration. I roll my eyes, grabbing a bag of chips to snack on as Kash gets my laptop from the dresser. He logs into Netflix, picking a random comedy before settling back against a stack of pillows. Holding his arm out, he waits for me to snuggle closer. With my head rested on his chest, I get lost in the movie. Every time Kash shakes with laughter it brings a smile to my face. He makes it impossible to stay mad at him, but if I'm being honest, they all do. I have no say in my response. All it takes is being near them and I'm completely disarmed.

We binge on junk, watching movie after movie. When I suggest something in the horror genre just to get a rise out of him, he tickles me until I can't breathe. It's the perfect way to end the day, like Kash somehow knew I wasn't ready to face them all just yet, so he barricaded us inside my room to give me some more time. It's after midnight when he powers off the laptop. My eyes are heavy with sleep as I bundle beneath the covers. Kash's arm snakes around my waist, pulling me in so we're pressed together. Brushing my hair aside, he drops a kiss to my neck. I sigh, refusing to fixate and overthink. Instead, I take Danielle's advice and simply do what feels right. And being here, wrapped in him, that feels inexplicably *right*.

"Do you forgive me?" Kash whispers, his words barely penetrating through the fog of exhaustion blanketing me. I roll so I'm facing him, tucking my face in the crook of his neck.

"Yes," I answer, pressing my lips to his throat. Kash squeezes me, his audible exhale giving away his relief. We fall asleep just the way we are, twined together, and not once do I wake from a nightmare.

When my eyes do open, it's from something far more pleasant. It takes me a minute to come around, but when I do, I realize Kash is drawing lazy circles on my stomach. Which means my shirt is pushed up. My entire body flushes with heat as I press my lips together. It's obvious he's awake, but what's the right way to go about letting him know that I am, too? Would he still be doing that if he knew? I'm torn between feigning sleep for a while longer and desperately needing the bathroom. After a few more seconds pass, I can't help but wiggle.

Kash groans, his hand sliding up until he's cupping my breast. My eyes widen, but it seems he's just as shocked by the action because he springs up, nearly falling off the bed in his haste. I slowly turn over, noting how flustered he looks. He rakes his fingers though his disheveled curls, his eyes flitting around the room, focusing on anything but me. I bite my tongue and fight back a smile.

"Morning," he croaks, attempting to clear his throat. Several times.

"You touched my boob," I tease him, jumping right to the chase and addressing the awkwardness hanging between us. His face goes slack as he blinks at me, a choked sound falling past his parted lips.

"On accident!" Kash holds his hands up innocently, looking absolutely petrified that he might have offended me. And that right there is how I know he's intrinsically *good*. He'd never do anything I didn't want or wasn't ready for. Needing to set his mind at ease, I climb from the bed, adjusting my shirt as I go. Stopping in front of him, I smile sweetly, secretly loving the way his rapt attention is all for me.

Rising to the tips of my toes, I give him a quick kiss, not wanting to deepen it without having brushed my teeth. "Well, that's too bad." I bite my lip, wondering who the hell took control of my body and said those words. I can feel the heat of my blush ignite across my cheeks, embarrassment surging to the forefront. Kash's eyes widen, but then a smirk lifts the corner of his mouth. I drop my head, shocked by my own forwardness, but he just chuckles. That low sound, filled with assuredness once again, is quickly becoming one my favorites. It makes me flushed and antsy, for reasons I refuse to think about right now.

"I'll go make breakfast. See you soon, sweetness." Kash winks, leaving me alone with my thoughts. As soon as the door shuts behind him, I exhale loudly. Same as last night, I push away the worry that tries to take over and head for the bathroom. I quickly shower, clipping my hair back since it doesn't need to be washed. After brushing my teeth, I search my closet for something to wear. I've gotten so used to donning the guys' stuff around the house, but I'd like to look a little more put together today. A cute outfit might serve as a bit of armor, but at minimum, it'll make me feel good. I choose some cut-off denim shorts, paired with a plain white crop top. I can finally wear a bra again, but like most women, I'd rather go without.

When I've procrastinated for far too long, I take a deep breath and pull my door open. As luck would have it, Havok is coming out at the same time. He stops abruptly, his icy blue gaze taking me in from head to toe. I watch his throat bob as he assesses me. I've always felt like I didn't measure up to his standards when he'd look at me, but not anymore. Now, I think I might exceed them. It's heady and confusing, trying to blend the two versions of him.

"Hey, pretty girl." Havok smiles, but it doesn't reach his eyes. He runs his tongue over his teeth, giving his attention to the floor. We stand there quietly, neither of us moving or talking, until he finally looks back at me and squares his shoulders. He steps forward, barely leaving an inch of space between us, and takes my hand in his. He laces our fingers together and brings them to his mouth, pressing a sweet kiss to our joined knuckles. "I'm so fucking sorry, Say."

"I know," I tell him, because it's obvious how torn up he is.

"I promised I'd never hurt you again, but I did." Shame washes over him, but he's being way too hard on himself. It wasn't Havok alone that got us to this point, and I'm just as at fault for reacting as shittily as I did. I could've handled it better.

"We'll talk things out, but for now, can we go get some breakfast? All I had to eat yesterday was junk, and I'm pretty sure Kash made pancakes." I smile, giving his hand a squeeze.

"We can do whatever you want, pretty girl." Havok winks, oblivious to how it affects me when he does that. It should be outlawed. He leads us to the kitchen, the sweet scent of powdered sugar and maple syrup growing stronger the closer we get. The guys are all present, as expected, and their eyes follow me as I take a seat at the island. Roan sits next me, his blank gaze staring straight ahead. Lochlan and Krew are shockingly seated at the dining table, sipping on cups of coffee, watching me like a ticking time bomb.

Kash slides a plate in front of me, filled with pancakes and three slices of extra crispy bacon. I smile appreciatively, ignoring the butterflies taking flight in my stomach. Going with my gut, I pick my food up and make my way over to take the empty seat by Lochlan. He sets his mug down carefully, suspiciously eyeing the weak smile I give him. Looking at Krew, who's seated across from me, I do the same. It doesn't take long for Roan and Havok to join us, their plates overflowing in comparison to mine.

Kash is last to grab some food, but instead of taking the free chair next to me, he picks me up and claims mine, placing me on his lap once he's seated. I squeak, my eyes flaring wide as I glance around the table. I try to move away but he just holds me tighter. Other than Havok's narrowed eyes scrutinizing the intimate position, no one says anything.

"Sweetness," Kash grunts. "I need you to quit moving your ass like that." His words are whispered against my ear, but there's no mistaking he said something to make me blush.

"Favorite fucking color," Havok grumbles around a mouth full of pancake.

When it's clear I won't be going anywhere, I sigh and settle in. To my annoyance and gleeful little heart, Kash proceeds to cut my food up and feed it to me. I moan around the first bite, causing him to bang his head against my shoulder. Faintly, I hear him counting to ten, murmuring something about restraint. I catch Krew's eye, smirking at the look he gives me. It's obvious I'm messing with his brother, but he's the one who insisted on being used as a chair and treating me like a toddler who doesn't know how to use eating utensils.

"Saylor, I think I speak for all of us when I say how sorry I am for keeping you in the dark. The blame lies more with me than it does them." The others huff soundly, and someone—Roan, I think—mutters '*bullshit*' under their breath. "From this point forward, you'll be included in everything." I gaze at Lochlan, weighing his words. The only hesitation I find, and it could just be me picking apart the details, is the '*this point forward*' portion. What else don't I know?

"Apology accepted. But..." I stare at those honey-colored orbs, searching for any hint of a lie as I ask the question I really need the answer to. "Is there anything else I need to know about?" His head tilts to the side, in confusion or contemplation, I'm not sure.

"Loch said we couldn't touch you unless you touched us first," Kash pipes in, holding up a piece of bacon for me to take a bite of. "We didn't listen, though," he whisper-yells, making me sputter out a laugh.

"Specifically, I said we shouldn't initiate touch until you were okay with it. As in a hug or a pat on the back," Lochlan deadpans, looking uncomfortable as he tries to clarify Kash's statement. I bite my lip when my mind wanders to how '*friendly*' Kash and I have become. As if he's thinking the same thing, his hand slides over my thigh and squeezes. "But no, there isn't anything else you aren't up to speed on."

"Okay," I say with a nod, accepting another forkful of food from Kash. "I just want to be a part of the decision-making process, especially when it's me who'll be most affected by the outcome. I know you guys were scared of how I'd respond, but I need you to have a little more faith in me than that. So, with that being said, what do you know so far?" I aim the question at Lochlan, knowing he likes to lead the conversation when relaying information.

"Honestly, not a whole lot." He pushes his glasses up his nose, a nervous tic of his I find adorable. "From the timeline Denvers and I have put together, it seems Liam fled the Friday before you were found, which adds up, based on when he was last seen in Pike's Bay. It would have taken him a couple of days to make it to North Dakota, and based on the decomposition of the first body, it's safe to say he got right to work."

I flinch, thinking of the picture and long list of injuries she sustained. "Anna Beth. Her name was Anna Beth." I give Lochlan a pointed look. I know they have to maintain a certain level of detachment in these situations, but this is personal for me. I refuse to let those women be forgotten.

"*Anna Beth.*" He nods apologetically. "Liam likely sent the postcard right after placing her at the coordinates, and then hit the road. The second one from Iowa was received June 28th. Kenzie's body was recovered in the same state, leading us to believe he followed a similar timeline. As of right now, we haven't gotten anything else, but if and when we do, you'll be the first to know," Lochlan promises, and maybe it's foolish, but I believe him.

"Thank you," I tell him, though it doesn't

sufficiently convey how important is to me to be included. I gather my and Kash's plate and take them to the sink to rinse. Roan joins me, placing them in the dishwasher as I hand them over. The others continue eating while the two of us work silently, cleaning up the mess from Kash's cooking. I swear he gets more food on the counters than he does anywhere else. Once everything's wiped down, I turn to find Roan right behind me. I startle, my back meeting the edge of the island. He smirks, shocking me silent when he grabs me by the waist and sets me on top of it. He braces an arm on each side of me and leans down, erasing some of our height difference.

"I don't give a shit that Loch already gave you some group apology; I want you to hear it from me. I'm sorry, Little Fighter. No more secrets, I swear." Roan's green eyes shine bright with guilt, bouncing back and forth between my blue ones as he waits for my response. His hair is tied up today, much like my own, but I wish I could run my fingers through it. Maybe one day, he'll even let me braid it. I grip the edge of the counter to keep from reaching out, a sly smile working its way across my face.

"We're good, Roan."

"Yeah?" He leans in closer, resting his head on my shoulder. He turns just enough so his face is aimed at my neck and inhales deeply, making me shiver. "I intend for us to be *great*, Saylor." He backs away, smiling as he goes. I shake my head, attempting to clear the long list of questions hammering at my brain.

Hopping down, I open the fridge and pull out

the milk, having to push aside a few bottles of beer to get to it. Next, I get the Hershey's syrup from the pantry and a glass from the cabinet. Mom always made me chocolate milk when I was feeling out of sorts. I noticed the guys had everything she used a few days ago, and I've been craving some ever since.

Once I've mixed it and put everything back, I lean against the island, my gaze falling to the two lists tacked to the fridge. I smile at the one scribbled with my likes and dislikes, noting a few new additions. Under '*likes*' there's: the beach, building sandcastles, and reading. I snag a pen and add chocolate milk. Under '*dislikes*' there's: the ocean, fist fighting—to which someone has written '*duh*' next to—and secrets. I snort. That was quick, but I appreciate the effort.

I glance at the other list, realizing nothing's been added since Kash started it that day at the beach. Makes sense, seeing as I'm the only one who can really decide the things I want to do now that I have the freedom and means to. Remembering the beer I just had to rearrange, I smile and grab the pen again. Standing back to admire my work, I can't help but wonder what the guys will think.

Get drunk.

Chapter Thirty

Saylor

It's been four days since we sat around the dining table for the first time, unknowingly starting a new breakfast tradition. It's nice to sit together, instead of having them hover around me like I'm a spectacle to be watched while eating. Everyone's been busy lately, Lochlan and Krew the most, as they're working on a new case. I haven't seen much of either of them, both holing up in their respective offices. It's weird, but I miss them. They're right here, easily accessible, but I don't want to intrude and mess with their workflow.

Deciding I've kept my head in the sand long enough, I finally put my new laptop to use and Googled current events. I worked my way through the past five years, realizing I missed an entire pandemic while being held in captivity. But I'm happy to report the Kardashian's still corner the market in reality TV. There was so much to catch up on, so that was a good way to pass the time.

I finally cracked open my GED material. I've been too nervous to read through any of it, afraid of how little I might recognize. But to my surprise, there's a good bit I understand. It's mostly math that I'll have to work on. Even though Krew presented the option of getting my high school diploma, I didn't give it much thought. I'm sure it sounds weird, but it feels like that opportunity has come and gone, and I'm not interested in going back in time.

It always felt worth it—the long hours of studying and lack of a social life—because when it was all said and done, Mom would get to see me walk across the stage and receive that rolled up piece of paper. She's no longer here, and there won't be a graduation—no matter which route I take. I want the quickest option, preferring to get it over and done with. There's no telling what career path I might take, but I'm certain a GED will suffice.

After reading for several hours, the words begin to blur. I close everything up and push it aside, wondering what the others have been up to all day. Deciding to find out, I climb to my feet, stretching as I go. Once I'm in the hallway, I make a split-second decision to knock on Lochlan's office door. I can hear him clicking away at his keyboard, so I know he's in there, I just hope I'm not bothering him. I wait for him to answer, but he never does. Swallowing past my nerves, I step inside cautiously.

"Lochlan?" I call out quietly. His head snaps up, a smile lighting his face as soon as he sees me. "I knocked, but I don't think you heard me."

"Sorry. I've been hyper-focused on this backlog of paperwork." He winces, looking guilty when he has no reason to be. This is his job.

“No worries. I can come back later. Just wanted to say hi,” I tell him, wishing I hadn’t interrupted.

“Absolutely not,” Lochlan states vehemently while pushing back his chair. “Come here.” The fervent demand has my feet moving instantly. I stop in front of him, but apparently that’s not good enough. He tugs me down, draping me over his lap.

“There. That’s better.” He drops a kiss to the top of my head. “Missed you, sweetheart.” I relax completely, amazed at the reaction a few simple words can evoke. It’s nice to know he's felt the distance between us as much as I have. I’ve gotten used to having them close by at all times, and after the argument we had last week, there’s been a disconnect with Lochlan. It’s a miserable feeling.

“Same.” I tilt my head back and peck his jaw, making his hand flex against the back of my thigh. After resituating me, he lifts his fingers and tucks some hair behind my ear.

“Hi,” Lochlan whispers, nudging the tip of my nose with his.

“Hi.” I respond just as quietly, enjoying the bubble we’ve found ourselves in. He’s so handsome it’s painful. I can't wrap my head around the fact that not one of these men has a girlfriend. Or maybe I’m just unaware if they do have women they’re talking to. It’s not exactly something we’ve discussed.

“Are you seeing anyone?” I blurt, my mouth working against my brain in the worst way possible. Lochlan arches an eyebrow, his honey eyes filled with amusement. I groan, pressing my forehead to his chest. I'd take the question back if I could, but once it popped into my head, it refused to go unanswered. I feel his body shake with silent laughter, but he places his hand beneath my chin and tilts my face upward.

"Tell me, sweetheart. Do you honestly believe that I'd have you sitting across my lap like this if I were?" Lochlan's responding question stuns me, his words alone holding me hostage. I bite my lip, unsure of what to say to that. His gaze drops to my mouth, making goosebumps prickle my flesh. "There's only you, Saylor," he whispers, bringing forth an entirely new set of questions. I look away, too anxiety-ridden to continue down the path we're headed. Too confused.

Lochlan seems to sense that, and simply goes back to working. He doesn't ask me to move or leave, content to have me close any way he can. I understand that a little too well. So much so, my eyes begin to close, and before I know it, I've fallen asleep. I'm not sure how long I'm out for, but enough time has passed for my neck to twinge painfully from the way my head was positioned. I stretch my arms, causing my back to arch. Looking up, I find Lochlan smiling down at me, an emotion I can't quite name shining in his eyes.

"Good nap?" he asks, his fingers toying with the hem of my shorts.

I nod, knowing I need to get up, but not especially wanting to. "How long was I asleep?"

"Forty minutes or so."

"Sorry. Didn't mean to use you as a bed," I joke, trying to push myself up by using the arm of his chair, but his response causes me to stumble, putting me right back where I started.

"Me. My bed. Your bed. All are acceptable, love." He grunts when I drop back down, his hands steadying me as I scramble to my feet. I'm flushed all over, an obvious tell that can't be missed.

"I'm going to go see what the others are up to." I hike a thumb over my shoulder, hopefully in the direction of the door. Lochlan smirks at my flustered state, but like the gentleman he is, he doesn't comment on it.

"Thank you for coming to see me." He smiles, his eyes twinkling behind his glasses. When did those become so attractive? Kids in school were always picked on, but Lochlan pulls them off like they were specifically designed for the sole purpose of enhancing his appeal. Before I can embarrass myself any further, I tell him it was my pleasure—*literally*—and flee from his office. There's no one in the living room or kitchen, and I have zero desire to knock on Krew's door after the hour I just spent with Lochlan. Deciding to search the lower half, I head down the stairs.

I spot Roan lifting weights at the back of the gym, but leave him to it. He seems focused, and I'm a little nervous he might try to bench press me if I wander in there. Just for the fun of it. The media room is void of life, and since I'm unsure of what the firing lane entails, I leave it unexplored. As I turn to head back up, my face collides with a hard chest. I squeal, jumping back from the sudden and unexpected contact. Havok laughs, scooping me up and over his shoulder. He's gentle, but the air still rushes out of me.

"Put me down, you nutjob!" I pant, slapping my hand against his back.

"Never, pretty girl." I can vividly picture the smug smile he's sporting. I growl, doubling down on my efforts. Using both hands, I grab the edge of his Calvin Klein briefs peeking from the top of his jeans, and yank as hard as I can. His steps falter, causing us to stumble through door.

"Did you just give me a wedgie, Say?" Havok sounds appalled, but the amusement in his voice is unmissable. I grunt, too much blood rushing to my head to form a proper response. "Naughty girl," he groans, slapping my butt before continuing on his trek to who knows where. I gasp, my hands going to his ass to leverage myself up.

"Oh, *baby*. Give it a good squeeze while you're down there." Havok laughs, jostling us down another set of stairs. A second later, the polished concrete floors of the garage come into view. When he flips me back upright, I have to grip his forearms to keep from falling over. I'm not sure if my face is red from embarrassment, or the blood trying to work its way to the rest of my body. I glare, hoping it conveys how unimpressed I am with his manhandling.

"Turn that frown upside down, pretty girl." Havok presses his fingers to the corners of my mouth and pushes upward. I snap my teeth at him, wondering if this is the moment I resort to physical violence.

And I gave Roan so much crap for bruising his

pretty face.

“Careful.” He crowds me against the SUV I was brought here in. “Biting is a kink I’m completely on board with.” His smile is predatory, and not for the first time today, I feel like an inexperienced little girl. As quickly as Havok descended, he retreats, a bright smile taking over his face. His outfit today is no different than any other I’ve seen him in—black ripped jeans, an old rock band tee, and his signature Doc Martens. Yet somehow his tattoos seem brighter, his silver hair more fascinating. His clothes might look thrifted, but they likely cost more than I could fathom spending on a single outfit. It's the complete opposite of the hand-me-downs he wore back in Pike’s Bay.

“Are you ready?” Havok grins, rubbing his hands together excitedly.

“Uh…for what?” I look around, wondering if I missed something obvious, but nothing jumps out at me.

“To learn how to drive, silly.” My stomach drops as I glance at each of their vehicles. Not one of them looks like something I should be testing my ability to maintain a lane in. They’re way too expensive for that sort of experimentation.

“And what will I be using to learn?” I give him pleading look, hoping with all the hope I can muster that he’s going to lift the garage door at any second and reveal a beater I can ding to hell and back without consequence.

“Take your pick.” Havok waves his hand out

like a salesperson, making me groan. I turn to look at my options, but none of them are promising.

"Havok..." I start, but he cuts me off.

"We're just going up and down the driveway, Say, so don't give me any shit." He folds his arms and spreads his feet apart, readying himself to fight me on it. "You're not going to fuck anything up on a half-mile stretch of gravel."

Don't start counting those chickens, buddy.

"Which one is yours?" I ask, thinking I should pick his just to spite him for making me do this.

"Which one do you think?" Havok cocks his head, eyeing me as I turn to inspect each of the vehicles. I know the SUV is Lochlan's, or maybe it's SOTERIA's as a whole. Next to that is a white BMW with glossy black wheels. The windows are tinted so dark, you can't see a thing inside of it. Next in line is a lifted Ford Raptor, black from one end to the other, top to bottom. Last, there's a gunmetal Audi. No idea what the model is, but I recognize the emblem of overlapping rings.

Bingo.

"That one." I confidently point to the Audi.

Havok's eyes narrow at my quick assessment. "What makes you so sure?" I shrug, debating if I should elaborate. I'd hate to offend him. When he doesn't seem to take that as an answer, I sigh and hope my words come across the way I intend them to.

"You grew up with nothing. It's natural you'd want a flashy car. It's common, really. Most people who come from very little want to own nicer things. A way to say *'hey, I made it'*." I wait for him to laugh or brush me off, maybe turn things around like he used to. His easy nod of agreement only serves as further proof of how far he's come. "Besides, you were always a cocky little show-off." I grin, trying to bring some levity back to the conversation. His loud laugh echoes around us, so it must've worked.

"I'll show you cocky," he grumbles, pulling his keys from his pocket. I catch them just before they smack me in the face. "Let's go, pretty girl." My lips part, shocked that he's offering up his own car, but somehow not at the same time. Havok takes the passenger seat, leaving me no choice but to get behind the wheel. The second I close the door, my worry ratchets up another hundred levels.

His leather seats are softer than a baby's butt, and the display screen looks like something from a UFO. In other words, this car is going to put a dent in that bank account he amassed for me when I inevitably have to replace or repair it. Havok taps a button built into the visor above me and the garage door begins to lift. My palms are sweating so profusely, I'm not sure I can even grip the steering wheel.

"Is it automatic?" I look down, feeling stupid for asking when the answer is obvious.

Havok chuckles, clearly amused by my nervous babbling. "It's dual, but you won't be using the paddles to shift. I'd like to keep my transmission in one piece." I scowl but nod my head in agreement. Smart call on his end.

"Alright, let's get this show on the road. Press and hold the brake, Say." I do as he says, then tap the button he points at. The engine roars to life, the hum of power making me smile giddily. "Good girl. Now drop the shifter into reverse and back us out." Following his instructions, I watch the camera that pops up, allowing it to guide me. I ease off the brake, barely touching the gas, yet we still fly out way faster than I expected. I squeak and slam my foot back down.

Havok grunts, bracing his hand on the dash to keep from jolting forward. "Shit, Say. You just squashed the fuck out of that bug." We both laugh, the saying reminding me of all the times Mom would use it when she'd stop too quickly. "Take a deep breath and go again. You've got this." I shake off the nerves and let my foot up, allowing the slight slope of the driveway to pull us backwards. It's a slow crawl, but better than me gunning it.

"Now, put it in drive and turn the wheel. There's plenty of room to spin us around." Havok grins, watching me closely as I grip the gear shifter. As soon as we're facing the straightaway that leads to the main road, I press the gas with a little more force. My brain completely malfunctions when I try to slow us down some, and I wind up using both feet. Havok laughs, not the least bit worried about the damage his precious car stands to sustain with me in control.

"Lighten up, pretty girl. You're doing great."

"Easy for you to say. You've always had a reckless streak." I grimace, realizing too late how insensitive that sounded.

“Never with you, Say.” I glance at him, the sincerity in his voice tugging at my chest. “I’d dive headfirst between your feet and hit the brake with my damn hand before I let anything happen to you. I've told you before, but I’ll say it a million more times if I have to—I got you.” I let my stress fade away and relax against the soft leather seat. For the next half hour, Havok patiently guides me up and down the driveway. By the time we make our last trip back and head for the garage, my confidence has grown exponentially.

Parking makes me more nervous than the actual driving, but I thankfully manage to steer clear of hitting anything. As soon as the engine cuts off, I throw my door open and jump out. I take a much-needed drag of air, then turn my grin on Havok as he rounds the front of the car.

“I did it!” I launch myself into his waiting arms, my laughter joining his as he catches me.

“You sure as fuck did.” He gently sets me on the hood, his hands holding my hips as he looks at me with pride. “So proud of you, baby.” The air shifts, the space between us evaporating before my very eyes. *Baby*. He’s used that endearment before, but there’s something about it that drives me crazy. We stare at one another, me lost for what to do and him searching for...something. Whatever it is, he must find it.

“Say.” Havok brushes his nose against mine, then trails it down the line of my jaw. I feel like I'm on fire, debating if I should push him away or draw him closer. “Goddamn, this is my favorite color.” He presses sweet kisses to the apples of my cheeks, groaning as he moves in closer and forces my thighs to spread so they'll accommodate his frame. The anticipation is killing me, waiting to feel his mouth on mine. He does the exact opposite though, instead stepping back and putting an end to whatever he'd been gearing up to start. Like a bucket of ice water, the abrupt change in course douses my libido, adding more confusion to the mix.

"Come on." Havok holds his hand out. After a moment of contemplation, I reluctantly take it. My mind is working extra hard, churning out one theory after another as to why he pulled away. He must sense the question I'm not brave enough to ask because he stops us at the base of the stairs and cups my face with his hands. "When we go there, Say...I need us to be on the same page. I want you just as desperate for me as I am for you. Want your hands fisted in my shirt, urging me closer. Your fingers tugging on my hair as you beg me not to stop. But you aren't there yet, and that's okay. I'm not going anywhere." He drops a lingering kiss to my forehead, but I'm too stunned to speak.

I'm restless, the need thrumming through my veins making me want to act on impulse and do all the things he just described, but I bite my tongue and keep those thoughts to myself. He's right. My mind and body were at war, alternating between it being too much and not enough. Until I know for sure that this is what I want—to explore intimacy with any of them—it isn't fair of me to start something I can't or won't finish. Not to mention, I've kissed Kash, and just earlier I was curled up on Lochlan's lap like a contented freaking housecat. Shame tries to rear its ugly head, but I force it away. I blindly follow Havok inside, deciding not to fixate on the impending problem. This connection between the six of us will need to be addressed at some point, but not today.

"There you are!" Kash hops down from the island, pulling a sucker from his mouth right before smacking his sticky lips next to mine. I glance at Havok, but he's already in the kitchen, snagging a coke from the fridge and not paying us any mind. I make a dramatic show of wiping the kiss away, groaning about the sugar trail it leaves behind. Kash expels a sharp breath in feigned offence. "Oh, no you didn't," he growls, grabbing me before I can make a run for it.

Kash tosses me on the couch, his hard body coming down on top of mine as he rains kisses all over my face, making sure to wipe his mouth against my neck as well. I'm laughing so hard tears fill my eyes. I beg him to stop, but he just doubles down. I'm vaguely aware that Lochlan is watching us from the opening of the hallway, his eyes lighting up every time another giggle breaks free.

"Did you learn your lesson?" Kash pulls back to look at me, his breaths coming in quick pants from all the work it's taking him to keep me from wiggling away.

"And what would that be?" I goad him, enjoying the playfulness that comes so easily between us.

"That my kisses are here to stay," Kash whispers, bringing the lollipop to my mouth. I have no idea how he held onto it this entire time, but

I'm not surprised. He'd never let sugar go to waste. Slowly, he runs the candy over my closed lips. Quicker than I can process, he darts his tongue out and licks it away. "Mmm. So good, sweetness." And then he's gone, sauntering off to join Havok while I lie here, flustered and dumbfounded. I take a quick peek to see if Lochlan's still watching, relieved to find he's made his way to the kitchen too.

I shake off the moment and walk over, gazing at Kash as I purposely lick the remaining strawberry flavor from my mouth. He stops speaking mid-sentence, his attention completely derailed. I grin, happy I could return the favor and scramble his brain a bit too. Grabbing a barstool, I bite back a laugh as Havok repeatedly snaps his fingers in front of Kash's face. He grunts and tunes back in to the conversation. A few minutes later, Roan and Krew amble in, the latter looking dead on his feet.

"What's that smell?" I ask.

"Shit." Kash whips around and pulls a tray from the oven. "*That* would be pizza tots." I lean over, admiring the individual pans of tater-tots, pizza sauce, cheese, and varying meats for toppings. They look delicious.

"Yum." I grin, excited to try another one of Kash's creations. He hands me a plain pepperoni, but I opt to give it some time to cool off before digging in.

Havok opens the fridge and takes a few beers out. "All for you, pretty girl. Your wish is our command." My eyes widen when he winks and places one in front of me.

"To the point of drunk and not an ounce more. Got it?" Lochlan pins me with that authoritative gaze of his. I'm sure he's balking at the idea of me consuming alcohol while still being underage, but I appreciate that he's setting aside his Boss Man hat for the night. Doesn't stop me from teasing him, though.

I flutter my lashes, giving him the sweetest smile I can manage without laughing. "Yes, sir." Roan chokes on his drink, but Krew pats his back, a smirk finding its way to his tired face.

"Real cute, sweetheart," Lochlan whispers against the shell of my ear, nearly making me drop the bite of food I was about to shovel in my mouth. He moves along, grabbing his own tots before making his way to the couch. Havok pops the top on my beer and nods at me to give it a try. Like all sane people when trying something new, I sniff it first, my nose scrunching at the foul scent. With very low expectations, I take a tentative sip.

"Blech." I shiver in disgust as the guys all laugh. "How in the world do people drink this?"

"It's an acquired taste," Havok teases. "Or you just get used to cheap shit and learn to like it."

"Nope. There's no chance I'll ever like that." I shake my head, eating more of my food in hopes of overpowering the aftertaste, giving Kash a thumbs up in the process.

"Figured you'd say that." Havok dips down momentarily and pulls out a clear bottle of vodka. "Whipped cream flavor." Before I can question how smart it is to start with something so strong, Krew passes him a shot glass. It's filled and placed in front of me a second later.

"Uh..." I hesitate, glancing at Lochlan. I feel certain he's going to veto the hard stuff if he was already hesitant about a beer. He smiles, dipping his chin for me to give it a go. Alrighty then.

"Just toss it back," Roan encourages. "That's the only way to do it."

Not wanting to chicken out, seeing as this was my idea in the first place, I pinch my nose and pour it down the hatch. The burn makes me cough, but overall, it's not too bad. The sweet vanilla flavoring is far better than the piss they tried to make me drink.

"Hell yeah!" Kash fist pumps the air.

We eat, Havok refilling my shot glass every so often, and at some point, music gets turned on. Miley Cyrus' *Party in the USA* blares through the speakers, making me squeal in delight. I hop on the coffee table, the alcohol I've ingested warming me from the inside out. My body feels light and limber as I sway my hips to the beat. Kash, who's just as tipsy, sings the lyrics into the handle of the broom he's straddling. He thrusts against it, looking ridiculous but somehow sexy at the same time. I laugh and close my eyes, content to bask in the happiness I'm feeling.

I'm yanked from my reverie, strong hands pulling me off my makeshift dancefloor just as the song changes. I blink, finding myself face to face with Kash. He gives me a lopsided grin as hums along to the Backstreet Boys. We spin in circles until I'm passed off to Lochlan. He watches me tenderly as Havok hands me another shot. I swallow it quickly and give back the empty glass. My fingers itch to muss up his perfectly styled hair, so that's exactly what I do. My inhibitions are lowered, allowing me to initiate contact I normally wouldn't. Lochlan indulges me, not once complaining as I play with the soft brown strands. When my eyes start to close against my will, he places me on the couch and tucks a blanket around me. I smile as he presses a kiss to my forehead, my hand latching around his wrist as he goes to pull away.

"You're the best watcher-over," I slur, wanting Lochlan to know how much I appreciate the way he takes care of me. Of all of us. Amused chuckles fill the room as I snuggle deeper into the plush cushions and let sleep claim me.

I shift, my eyes blinking open sometime later. It hasn't been long since I drifted off, but the music is gone and the only visible light comes from a faint glow in the kitchen. Everything starts to spin. Flopping to the ground, I use someone's leg to help me stand. *Havok.* He's sprawled across the floor, his lips barely parted as he draws in a deep breath. I turn to walk away, letting my hand guide me as I blindly stumble to my room. I'm hoping a shower will help sober me up, because I'm clearly still drunk.

I strip, leaving a trail of discarded clothes from my door to the bathroom. But once I'm beneath the hot spray, all I can think about are the encounters I've had with the guys since being here. The ones that make me question everything. Why them? Why so soon? *Why so many?* I press my thighs together, recognizing the ache between my legs, but too terrified to do anything about it. I huff in frustration.

How the hell am I entertaining the thought of *more*, when I can't stand my own hand? Wanting to prove myself capable, I trail my fingers down my stomach. With a steadying breath, I drop one lower, brushing it over the bundle of nerves begging to be touched. I whimper at how good it feels, but the moment the pleasure registers, Liam's face flashes through my mind. I jerk my hand away as tears build behind my eyes. *I hate him*. I don't want to be broken anymore. Angry with all of it, I turn the water off and shove the door open.

I dry myself as quickly as my inebriated state allows me to, eager to be back with one of the guys. They make it better. The negative thoughts. The memories that linger right below the surface. Just... *everything*. I throw some clothes on and make my way to the living room. I only have to hold the wall twice, so I think the alcohol is fading. I could really go for some chocolate milk, though. I tug the fridge open, glaring at the harsh light, and immediately decide it will take way too much effort to mix everything.

My eyes snag on the list as I close it, an easy smile forming. I grab a pen and crookedly scratch out '*get drunk*'. They wasted no time making that one happen. In some far, dark corner of my mind, I start to wonder what else they might be up for helping me with. I blame what I do next on the vodka still lingering in my system. In fact, the whole ordeal feels like an out of body experience. I grin like a loon once I'm finished, tossing the pen back in the junk drawer.

I shuffle toward the couch, finding Havok in

the same spot as before and Kash bent halfway over the arm. As much as I'd like to snuggle the both of them, they aren't in prime snuggle positions. I have a feeling tomorrow morning will be rough enough without the added ache of sleeping on the floor. With that thought, I go in search of another cuddle buddy. There's a faint glow coming from Krew's office, but if he's awake it's because he's working, so I keep it moving. I turn to the right, knowing the other side is empty, and push through the first door I come to.

"*Sonofa...*" I swear, wincing at the pain flaring through my poor stubbed toe. I glare at the boot, giving it a wide berth as I continue banging my way around the foreign space. When my fingers graze the edge of a bed, I hoist myself up, grunting from the coordination it takes to not topple back off. I feel my way up a thick thigh, making a pit stop at the toned abdomen I find so I can give it a few appreciative pats. *Roan*. No one in the history of ever is built like him.

"You good now, or do you need another feel?" There's a smile in his voice, and I'm not the least bit surprised to find him awake, watching me make a fool of myself. My knee digs against his leg as I try to make my limbs work. *But at least it wasn't the family jewels.* Roan snorts, placing his hands under my arms so he can pull me up. I drape across him, sighing at the vast amount of surface area I have to rest my body on.

"Sweet dreams, Little Fighter," he whispers, playing with my hair and making it all too easy to welcome sleep.

Chapter Thirty-One

Havok

I wake with a groan, every inch of my body achy and stiff. I blink through the harsh morning light, rotating my head just enough to see behind me. Kash is still passed out across the couch, but Saylor is noticeably missing. I feel well beyond my years, having to use the damn coffee table to get myself upright. My muscles protest every step of the way, stomach churning from the mix of beer and liquor I stupidly tossed back last night. Shit, I haven't gotten that drunk since my blackout phase shortly after Say went missing.

My mouth is so fucking dry I can't get my tongue to work properly. Hand to God, I'm never drinking that much ever again. Squinting, I eye the kitchen and aim my body in that direction. Jerking open the medicine cabinet, I pay no mind to how loud I'm being. Kash has woken everyone in this house at least a hundred times at the ass crack of dawn. It'd serve him right to suffer alongside me. I fumble with the stupid child lock on the Tylenol, close to banging it on the counter when it finally gives way.

I pour four of those blessed little pills into the palm of my hand, not bothering to put anything back where it goes, and grab a cold water from the fridge. Leaning against the island, I close my eyes and will the nausea to fade a fuck-ton quicker. Mixing alcohol is such an amateur move, but I didn't stand a chance at resisting Saylor when she begged me to join in and take shots with her. I smile, remembering the way she let loose last night. Twirling around the living room like a goddamn vision of everything good and right in the world. She's the embodiment of hope. A second chance I never saw coming, and I'll do everything I can to keep her happy and smiling. Which apparently includes putting my liver through the wringer.

Now that the edge is gone and I don't feel so close to hurling, I peel my eyes back open. Bringing the bottle to my lips, I take another sip. Like a comic spit-take, water goes flying everywhere. My focus is pinned to the list on the fridge, the one that Saylor is supposed to add to, suggested by her therapist. I slap my hand over it, like that will somehow erase the scribbled words from my brain, then spread my fingers apart, needing another peek to ensure my mind isn't playing tricks on me. Yep. Still there.

Holy fucking shit.

"You look like ass," Krew jabs, sauntering over to the coffee maker. That's saying something coming from him, considering he's slept a total of eighteen hours over the past four days. As soon as his back is turned and he's focused on brewing himself some caffeine, I yank the paper from the magnet holding it in place and quickly tuck it in my pocket. And not a second too soon. Lochlan walks in, looking just as tired as Krew, but there's no coaxing those two from their offices until they're good and ready. Kash groans, sounding absolutely miserable. His body thumps against the floor, making me wince, and a pained whine follows. The three of us share a secret smile, knowing how much of a lightweight he is. Hell, I think Saylor drank more than he did.

Speaking of the blue-eyed beauty…

Ro enters the main room, immediately drawing our attention. Not so much him, but who he's holding. Saylor's slumped against his chest, her arms tucked beneath her, and that sweet face I love is buried in the fucker's neck. Meanwhile, his meaty arm is braced beneath her ass as his free hand strokes her spine. Her tiny little feet swing with every step he takes, making me wonder if she's even awake. Ro snags a barstool, keeping Saylor in his lap, and that's when my brain catches up to what she's wearing.

A t-shirt. *My* t-shirt. It's ridden so far up her thigh I can make out the edge of something red and lacy. My cock perks up instantly. Ro scowls, noticing what my attention is on, and repositions her so that nothing is showing. I roll my eyes. The bastard had her in his bed all night, and now she's in his arms; I think it's time to share.

"Hey, pretty girl." I step closer, adding my own hand to the mix. She doesn't budge, even as my finger traces her perfectly shaped eyebrow. "Can you open your eyes, Say? Let me see those gorgeous blues, baby." I tune out the rest of the room, my gaze riveted to the slight pucker of her mouth.

"Hurts," she whimpers, pressing herself further into Ro. Lucky asshole.

"What does, sweetheart?" Loch shoulders me out of the way, his dad mode kicking in and demanding he fix whatever ails her.

"Head." Her one-word answers make me smile.

"Let's see if this'll help." Loch carefully unties her hair from the knot she has it in. He takes his time, making sure not to tug it any more than necessary. Once the long blonde strands fall around her shoulders, Loch runs his fingers through it, massaging her scalp in hopes of easing her headache. Saylor moans, the noise so goddamn illicit it sends a rush of blood straight to my groin. Ro clears his throat and surges to his feet.

"Your turn." He passes me Saylor, and I happily take his seat. The sight of someone so big getting all worked up makes me grin, but he just flips me off. I run my hands up her back, working in unison with Loch to make her feel as good as possible. Her body goes limp, a sweet sigh falling from her lips. Unbidden, an image of us teaming up to make her feel good in a completely different manner pops into my head. I bite my lip, somewhat ashamed of the half-hard state of my dick. Krew passes some Tylenol over, along with a bottle of water, and I hold Saylor's head back to help her wash it down.

She snuggles closer, content to lie where she's at until the pain meds take effect. The guys get busy with breakfast, but I stay seated and soak up the moment. I drag my nose along her neck, inhaling that familiar scent of coconut and something uniquely Saylor. Brushing her hair aside, I press a few light kisses to her shoulder. She hums, the sound making my lips curve. Taking a liberty I probably shouldn't, I lick my tongue across her flesh, wishing like hell I could taste every inch of her perfect little body. Saylor's gasp syncs with my groan, causing her to pull back. Our gazes clash, her breaths slightly sharper, but she smiles, making me feel ten feet tall from the look she gives me.

"Good morning, sleepyhead." I run my thumb across her bottom lip, my need to constantly be touching her growing more and more by the damn day. She grunts in response but accepts the cup of coffee Ro brings over. I've noticed she doesn't drink it very often, but today seems like a good exception.

She smiles in appreciation, bringing the hot liquid to her mouth to blow on it. I barely repress my shudder. I'd be surprised if Saylor doesn't feel how hard I am beneath her with the way our bodies are lined up. One day, she's going to ride my cock just like this. *Fuck*. I drop my head to her shoulder, forcing myself to think of something else. I meant what I said yesterday. Until she's positive of what she wants, we're at a stalemate. Although, the words burning a hole in my pocket make me wonder if she's a lot closer to figuring that out than I thought.

Once the food's ready, we move to the dining table. Much to my dismay, Saylor sits alone, looking more awake with every bite she takes. Her bacon is cooked just the way she likes it, making her hum and wiggle as she goes to town. We'd spend hours watching her eat and be happy about it. Knowing how underfed she was still fucks with my head sometimes.

Out of nowhere, Kash pops up from the living room floor like a damn whack-a-mole, making Saylor choke on a scream. "I'm here!" His wild eyes ping around the room as he raises his hand, like he's waiting to be called on by a teacher. He flops over the couch, the walk around it apparently too much for the princess, and trudges to the table.

"You look a little green, brother." Krew pokes him in the forehead, causing Kash to go cross-eyed. I'm sure that didn't help with his queasiness. I grin, watching closely as he grips the table to right himself. He doesn't respond, just shoves a biscuit in his mouth and eats with his eyes closed.

"What the hell was in that Devil juice?" Kash whines, gently laying his head on the table.

"It was whipped cream flavored, you little bitch." Roan laughs, head thrown back as he revels in his misery.

"Says the guy with a man-bun," Kash snipes, his hangover making him a helluva lot bolder than he'd normally be. There are certain things you just don't do. Like cuss in church or question a man's masculinity when he can bench press your body weight with one arm.

"I'm shocked there's something sweet you can't stomach. It's a goddamn Christmas miracle." Ro smirks, patiently waiting for Kash to give him another glare, then puffs up, jumping toward him just the slightest. Kash shrieks, shoving away so fast both him and the chair topple over. He lies there, sprawled across the tile, a comical wheeze escaping from having the air knocked out of him. Ro drops down beside him, giving his cheek a pat. "I could be bald, little bro, and it still wouldn't make my dick any smaller."

Saylor snorts but covers it up with a cough. She's come so far since she walked through our door. This woman seated across from me is funny and smart and she doesn't shy away from shit the way she first did. That alone gives me the go ahead do to what I'm about to. Saylor grabs our empty plates and takes them to the kitchen, but I wait until she's finished to strike. I want her complete attention for this.

"Hey, Say. I got your request." I cross my arms, searching for any sort of reaction. Her nose scrunches in confusion, so I expand upon my vagueness. "With the addition to your list." I nod at the fridge. Her eyes follow to the blank spot where it used to be. Nothing. She looks at me curiously, trying to figure out what the hell I'm talking about. I doubt she's still feeling buzzed, so more than likely, she has no recollection of what she wrote.

Oh, this is going to be fun.

"I'm guessing you added it at some point last night. Maybe after the rest of us passed out." I arch an eyebrow, waiting for the moment that clarity sparks. I'm playing with fire, but Saylor can burn me anytime she wants. I'll probably get off on it.

"Well, what's the request?" Krew asks, completely unaware of the game I'm playing.

"It's specific to me. Something Saylor needs my help with." I smirk, wondering how deranged I look as my gaze eats her up. "I guess I could read it, though." I shift to pull the paper from my pocket, but pause when her eyes widen. Ah, there's that realization I've been waiting for. Her lips part, that sexy pink flush spreading up her neck and cheeks. I wink, pretending to still reach for the list as she finally springs into action.

"Havok Rhett McKade!" Saylor screeches, hands planted on her hips as she thumps that little foot on the floor for emphasis. "Don't you even *think* about it."

Fucking adorable.

That probably hurt her more than it intimidated me, but hearing her call my ass out—middle name and all—only makes my grin grow. I love pushing her, a part of me always has. I need her to know that there's no ill intent behind my teasing though, so I right myself and keep her drunken request between the two of us. The guys wait for an explanation, but they won't be getting one from me. I'm just grateful to have found it first. Any one of them would've jumped at the opportunity the same way I did. Besides, I *want* to help her. Not for my own selfish reasons or what it could lead to, but because I'm worried there's more to her scribbled confession than meets the eye.

I go about my business, cleaning up the kitchen and righting the living room, pretending like our little showdown never even happened. It takes her some time, but Saylor eventually relaxes. She hangs around for a bit, but retreats to her room shortly after lunch.

I let her go, knowing she needs the space. I could've handled things differently, but I figured if I made light of the situation it wouldn't be so awkward for her. I'll give her some time, but not very much. I can't keep myself away from her on a normal day, much less when I have questions I'm dying to know the answers to.

I want all of Saylor's truths, and I hope like fuck she'll give them to me.

Chapter Thirty-Two

Saylor

I've become very interested in studying for my GED. In fact, it took up most of my time yesterday, and so far, the majority of today as well. It has nothing to do with avoiding Havok. Just a coincidence. An added benefit, if you will. When he started teasing me at breakfast, I'd been clueless at first. I couldn't even remember how I ended up in Roan's room, much less anything else. But the more Havok pushed, the more my mind spun through the events of our drunken night. The only explanation for my temporary lapse in sanity is the alcohol. There's no way in hell I would've written that down otherwise. Just thinking about it makes me cringe.

Make myself orgasm.

Even alone, my cheeks heat with embarrassment. It's mortifying that Havok knows, and worse, the rest of the guys might also if he's been running his big fat mouth. Since he didn't earlier, I'm inclined to think he hasn't. It would've been the perfect time to out me, but he was oddly mum on the subject after I was brought up to speed. Sighing, I close the notebook I've been working through for the past hour. History is my weakest link, but today even more so because I can't focus long enough to retain anything I read.

I keep wondering what Havok is thinking. The assumptions he's formed over the last twenty-four hours. Honestly, I'm shocked he hasn't snuck in to confront me yet. I've had my door locked, but I'm under no illusion that such simple mechanics would stop any of them. If they really wanted to, they'd have no problem getting in. At least out of everyone it was Havok who found the list. Kash would've been okay as well. There's a comfortability with those two that makes awkward situations easier to face.

The unexpected knock on my door sounds like a death knell in the otherwise quiet. I debate feigning sleep, but it's unlikely to serve as a deterrent. With slow, dread-filled steps, I make my way over and twist the knob. I've fully accepted that it's time to face Havok, but shockingly, it's not him I find on the other side. Instead, Roan stands in front of me, arms crossed and a smirk tilting the corner of his mouth. I have to crane my neck to look him in the eye, but on the way up I notice the black tactical pants and fitted t-shirt he's sporting. It's strained across his chest, putting every dip and divot on display.

"You busy right now?" he asks, giving me the same once over I deliberately gave him.

"No, not especially," I tell him. "Do you need me for something?"

"For something…" he mutters, shifting the

weight of his body. "I want to teach you how to shoot. You up for it?" My eyes widen, his surprising answer leaving me a bit speechless and stumbling for an answer.

"Like...with a real gun?" Brilliant, Saylor. You're an eloquent wordsmith, with whom no one can compete. Roan quirks an eyebrow, amusement dancing in his bright green eyes.

"As opposed to what, a water gun?" His lips flatten, attempting to bite back a laugh at my expense.

I roll my eyes with a huff. "It's a valid question, Big Guy. Why would a beginner start with actual bullets instead of pellets or paintballs?" My answer makes perfect sense to me, so I have no idea why he's looking at me like that.

"Because if the time ever comes when you need to pull the trigger in a real-life situation, it won't be some bullshit BB or ball of paint that hits your target." Roan speaks softly but with an edge of firmness, politely stressing the importance of his explanation.

"Okay." I drop the teasing, sincerely interested in what he's trying to teach me.

"Let's go, Little Fighter." Roan nods, gesturing toward the hallway.

"Am I dressed okay for this?" I close the door behind me, hurrying to keep up with his longer strides. He glances back, giving my black leggings and oversized sweatshirt a quick dip of his chin.

"All good." Roan stops beside the entrance that leads to the lower level, allowing me to go first. I scurry down the steps and wait for him to join me. Despite how nervous I am, a flicker of excitement begins to take root. “Beautiful, too.” Roan bends to whisper, the compliment rolling off his tongue effortlessly. I’ve never seen the firing lane before. Never really thought it was something I *needed* to see. When Roan opens the door, bright overhead lights coming to life and illuminating the entire space, I'm a bit taken aback by how big it is.

“This is where we keep the bulk of our weapons,” Roan says, placing his hand on the biometric scanner built into the wall. It’s an exact replica of the one by the staircase. After analyzing Roan’s fingerprints, a second door to the right swings open. I take a cautious step inside, my jaw dropping at the vast amount of firepower that greets me. Various types of guns cover every inch of wall space, and to my left, I find bins of ammunition, meticulously labeled and organized. “We’ll start with a small handgun today. Something with minimal kickback.” I nod, pretending to understand.

Roan gathers what we need, including safety gear, and leads me back to the main area. The door closes behind us, the lock reengaging automatically. Now that my eyesight has adjusted, I have a better view of what the room entails. I note the long, concrete corridor, several targets staggered at different distances towards the end. A waist-high worktable is positioned at the head of the firing lane, which Roan uses to spread everything out so he can give me a breakdown of what’s what.

“First things first—this is a 9mm, and that’s the

magazine." He points to a slim black rectangle. "This stores the bullets and slides into the handle of the gun, like so. Always—*always*—keep the safety on until you're ready to fire." He tilts the gun, showing me the small switch, and flicks it back and forth. I nod, rubbing my sweaty palms against my thighs as Roan fits me with a pair of safety goggles, followed by some bulky earmuffs. He grins, standing back to observe how ridiculous I look.

"No teasing," I mutter, poking his corded chest with my finger. He doesn't even flinch.

"You look adorable." His dimples pop out, gracing me with their presence. I like to think of them as an indicator for how happy he is. I guess my current get-up really tickles his fancy. Roan spins me around, then tugs my hair into a ponytail. When I turn to face him, seeing his own still knotted back, I'm confused as to where the elastic came from. Sensing my question, he gestures to his wrist. "Started wearing an extra, just in case." I've always thought the concept of '*swooning*' was fictional, but apparently not. I swoon *so* hard. Roan shows me every day how thoughtful and sweet he is, yet the small stuff still floors me. Nuances most wouldn't think twice about, but they're everything to me.

"Now for the fun part." Roan slips behind me, bracing his palms on my hips, and shifts me forward so we're facing the targets. Not sure I'd call this fun, but to each their own. I blink and the gun is placed in front of me, Roan's arm outstretched as he spouts off more instructions. "Make sure the weapon is pointed down range, then pull the slide to the rear," he explains, demonstrating each step as he goes. "Now there's a bullet in the chamber. From here, all that's left to do is flick the safety off, aim, and squeeze." Roan passes me the gun, placing his steady hand over mine.

"Breathe, baby girl." His lips brush my ear, making me shiver. "It's just practice. There's no threat you need to neutralize, so take your time and wait until you're ready. There won't be much recoil, so don't be afraid of that. You've got this." Roan nudges the inside of my foot, so I widen my stance. "Good. What's next, Saylor?" I think back on everything we've gone over and tap the safety with my finger. "That's it. Now, point and aim for center mass. When you're ready, pull the trigger, Little Fighter."

Dredging up every ounce of bravery I can find, I take a fortifying breath and zero in on the piece of paper that's closest. I'll be happy just to clip it. Flicking the safety, I press my finger to the trigger and squeeze. I squeak in surprise, nearly dropping the gun, but thankfully Roan's there and quickly takes control. The noise of it going off barely penetrated the thick foam protecting my ears, but the act of actually firing a weapon has me trembling. Roan immediately flips the safety on and tugs my headgear off. His hands frame my cheeks, those green eyes probing mine as he talks me down.

"Hey," he voices quietly. "It's okay. You don't have to do this, Saylor."

"I'm okay," I insist, flexing my fingers to stimulate some blood flow.

"You're shaking." Roan frowns, rubbing his

hands up and down my arms.

"It was just…scary," I admit.

"It is," Roan agrees. "Firearms are dangerous, especially when they aren't given the respect they deserve. Your reaction is good. You understand the power you're wielding, the damage that can be done, and that's important. You should never be flippant or cocky, but you need to be comfortable and sure of yourself if you plan to fire a gun. That's why we're here. It'll take time, but with enough practice you'll start to gain confidence."

"Is…is there a reason you want me to learn? Do I need to be worried about something?" I question, curious why he brought me down here. I pray they aren't about to be sent out on a case, leaving me here to fend for myself. A wave of panic washes over me. "Are you guys leaving?!"

"What? Of course not. We've limited our workload for the time being, and even if we were needed in the field, at least three of us would stay behind." I exhale, guilt niggling at me for taking up so much of their time. "We'd never leave you here alone, baby girl. Never." I lean in, dropping my head to his chest.

"There's always a chance something could go wrong, and if that ever happens, you'll at least have a way to defend yourself. That's my only motivation, Saylor. The thought of you cornered and helpless…" Roan trails off, a pained grimace twisting his face. "I can't imagine anything worse." As his reasoning resonates, I think of how weak I felt for five years, reliant on the mercy of a madman. I never want to feel that way again. Brute force won't get me anywhere, but a bullet might.

"Can we go again?" I step back and straighten my shoulders.

Roan chuckles, a proud grin stretched across his face. "That's my girl."

I blush, clearing my throat as he turns us back around and hands me the gun. For the next thirty minutes, I aim and shoot, barely making contact with the target. Eventually, my arms get tired and we decide to call it quits for the day. Roan holds out the tattered practice sheet like a proud parent admiring their kindergartner's barely decipherable finger painting. His eyes light up, eyebrows wagging playfully.

"I'm so proud of you." Roan wraps me in his arms, plucking me off my feet as he spins us. I laugh, closing my eyes to ward off the dizziness.

"It looks like I was aiming for the wall, but accidentally got the paper a few times." I snort, scanning my work and finding it *severely* lacking. One corner in particular took a beating.

"Better than Kash when he was first learning." Roan jokes, handing me the paper. We work in tandem to get everything back in its proper place, but the gun is left lying on a table inside the arms room.

"It needs to be cleaned," Roan explains. "I'll get to it later. Gives me something to do when I can't sleep." Hand in hand, we head out. At the base of the steps, Roan turns and squats. "Hop on." Not one to pass up a free piggyback ride, I grin and twine my arms and legs around him. He shoulders the door open, nearly running into Kash as we stumble from the stairwell.

"Best Friend thief!" Kash growls, reaching out to pull me away. Roan spins, darting to the opposite side of the dining table so it's situated between them. I laugh, swinging my legs as we turn towards the kitchen. Roan snags one and playfully bites my toe. I squeal and squirm, giggling uncontrollably at the ticklish feeling.

"Love these little toes." He gently kisses the inside of my ankle, turning me to goo as I melt against him. If the slight shake of his shoulders is any indication, my reaction doesn't go unnoticed.

"Look!" I wave my practice target at Kash. "If you ever need me as backup...you're totally screwed." I grin, handing him the sheet so he can get a closer look.

Kash nods, trying to play up my utter lack of skill because he's nice like that. "It's...something, sweetness." A snort sounds behind me, so I tug Roan's ear like a blinker. He shakes his head in exasperation, but obliges my request.

"Don't fill that pretty head of hers with fake compliments. That," Havok points to my paper, "was an absolute pointless massacre of a good tree. Say Baby, I think you're directionally challenged." He smirks, that infuriating look of smugness shining in his icy blue eyes.

Butthole.

"Is that right?" I ask him sweetly, snagging a

half-empty bottle of water from the counter. Without warning, I send it flying, clapping my hands when it hits him square in the forehead.

"Ow, you little shit," Havok growls, his smile growing devilish as he starts for us. I claw my way up Roan's back, yelling for him to run, but we're backed into the kitchen with nowhere to go. My butt meets the island as an idea begins to form, but I refuse to take my eyes off of Havok. Without giving myself a chance to second guess my choice, I shove away from Roan and slide across the marble, spinning so I can hop off on the other side. I land and bolt, cackling as I round the couch and scan the room.

Havok prowls closer, his steps sure and precise. No matter which way I attempt to go, he cuts me off. Again. A tiny opening is all I need to make a run for it. I huff, brushing loose pieces of hair from my face. My ponytail is barely hanging on at this point. The sound of the door opening steals our attention. Lochlan walks in with a stack of pizzas, his steps slowing as he takes in the stand-off happening in the living room. My stomach growls loudly, making everyone laugh. With Havok distracted, I test my luck and try to skirt by him.

Just when I think I'm in the clear, his arm snakes out and bands around my waist, tossing me over his shoulder. I grunt, my hands landing on his back as I push myself up. This position is becoming way too commonplace for my liking. Havok heads toward Lochlan and snags a box of pizza. I poke my lip out, hoping their designated leader will take pity on me and put the menace carting me around like a sack of potatoes in time-out.

"Sorry, love. He caught you fair and square." Lochlan winks, leaving me sputtering as Havok strides away.

"This isn't Win-A-Saylor! I'm not a carnival prize!" I screech as we turn the corner, the guys' laughter following us until Havok kicks my door closed. I swallow, realizing this is the moment I've been dreading. He has me right where he wants me, and I doubt I'll be leaving anytime soon.

Certainly not with my dignity intact.

Chapter Thirty-Three

Havok

Saylor stiffens the second I have her to myself. She's been avoiding me since breakfast yesterday, and it's high time we rectify that. I'm not so much of an asshole that I can't understand her embarrassment. The thing is, she has no reason to feel that way around me. We've been through too much for petty shit like insecurities to stand between us. That said, it doesn't mean I won't broach the subject delicately. For her. Can't say I've ever cared about a woman's feelings before, but Say's not just anyone. She never has been.

I toss her on the bed and drop the pizza between us. The anxiety wafting off of her is palpable, but I stay silent. I know she's waiting for me to address the giant ass elephant prancing around in a neon string bikini, but it can wait. Right now, I want back that easiness we've grown into. I need Saylor to know that she's safe with me, that I'll never hurt or betray her the way I did when we were kids.

And maybe that's why she's so on guard right now. Because she, of all people, knows how cruel I can be. The possibility of her thinking I'm still capable of doing something like that stings like a bitch. It's warranted, though. I put Saylor through some god-awful shit back in the day. The fact she can even look me in the eye is a miracle. I pull her laptop over and scroll through a few movies, deciding to go with something light and funny. Hopefully, it'll bring the mood up and she'll relax.

We tuck in and start eating, but Saylor never loses that rigidness stringing her tight. When she's made it clear she's full, I toss the box to the floor and resituate my pillows. By the time the movie ends, I think she's even more worked up. I sigh, running my hands though my hair. My frustration isn't aimed at her, but myself. I've clearly gone about this all wrong, and now I'm wondering if I've taken us several steps backward from all the progress we've made. I know she's attracted to me. I had her pressed against my fucking car, for Christ's sake. Felt the uptick in her pulse.

Was that response to me, or stimulation in general? I felt pretty confident at the time, but now I'm not so sure. Is she feeling pressured or rushed? I need to know. I can't sit here in silence in hopes she'll finally come around. Knowing Saylor, she never will.

"We have to talk about this, Say. My head is taking me to some pretty dark places, and I need to know if I've pushed you for too much." I turn, watching her for any sign of regret, but she just stares at me in confusion. "Unless I've seriously misjudged the signs, there's something here. Attraction, at the least. So, what is this? What's this mean?" I pull her list from my pocket, the crumpled piece of paper looking ragged. I can't count how many times I've read those three words since yesterday morning.

"That's…that's not what this is about." She waves a shaky hand at the scribbled confession. "I'm humiliated I even wrote it. You finding it was just the cherry on top. It's not exactly something I want to talk about with you, or anyone really." I lick my lips, searching for the right thing to say. I tend to bulldoze, but I refuse to take that approach with this. She needs to let me in on her terms.

"Saylor Elise Radley, there's not a goddamn thing you could say or do that would change how I feel about you. I want you secure enough in what we have that nothing's off limits between us. If you're not there yet, then…that's okay. I won't stop trying, though."

Her gorgeous blue eyes shimmer. "It's not about you and me. Honestly, my feelings are probably making it worse. You aren't some stranger I can confess my secrets to and never have to see again. We live together, Havok. Share a house and friends. I don't want to make things awkward for you or me." I grind my jaw to keep from saying something I shouldn't.

We share a lot more than that, baby.

"Are you talking to your therapist at least?" I ask, trying to be supportive. Saylor scrunches her nose, making me groan in frustration.

"Damn it, Say." I stand, needing to put some space between us before I do something stupid. *Like fix her little problem my damn self.* "You can't just let shit fester. She's being paid to help you, so what the fuck are the two of you chatting about for an hour every week, if not this?" I'm unraveling, heated words flying from my mouth before I can filter them. I don't understand, and it makes me the worst piece of shit, because all I can think about is that Saylor's nowhere close to being ready for anything with me—*with anyone*—if she hasn't even addressed what happened to her.

All this time, I thought she was healing, working past her trauma, but apparently not. I close my eyes, searching for a thread of patience. She's still my girl. Always will be. No matter the label—friend, lover, former bully—I'm not going anywhere. I'm hers for as long as she'll have me.

"You think I don't know that?!" Saylor slides off the bed, stomping over to glare at me as she delivers her own verbal lashing. "At first, I didn't want to think about it. I liked that Danielle didn't force me to dredge up the past or what that man put me through. I was finally free of him, and all I wanted was to pretend he never existed. That those five years didn't happen. Is it so wrong to want to live in the now? For the woman I am *today*? I can't change what happened to me, so what's the point in talking about it?" When her tirade trails off, Saylor's flushed and out of breath, but I'm just getting started.

"You're giving me whiplash, Say," I growl. "You want to live in the present? Fine. Fucking *live* then. You aren't, though. You're still holding on to the past, clinging to pieces that Liam took like the two of you are playing some twisted game of tug-of-war. But guess what, baby? That spineless bastard will never know what it's like to be on the receiving end of your consent. This power you're giving him is a fucking illusion."

"It's not that simple!" she snaps, her body trembling with rage. At me. At Liam. The goddamn injustice of it all. "Don't you think I'd put him to rest if I could? He's like a damn cockroach that just won't die. Whether it's my dreams or everyday life, he haunts me."

"Because you haven't dealt with it!" I roar, chest heaving as I purge my anger. It seeps from my pores like thick, sticky tar. This hold he has on her needs to fucking go.

"I don't know how!" Tears stream down her face, her shoulders slumping in defeat. *Fuck*. I press forward, backing Saylor's small body against the wall. I cup her heated cheeks, stroking away the salty trail of pain she can't contain any longer.

"Then let me help, baby. *Please*." My plea is strained, but seeing her like this hurts beyond comprehension. I'd rather take a knife to the gut than watch Saylor compartmentalize to the point it's beginning to harm her, whether she realizes it or not. "Talk to me. Tell me everything. You'll find no judgment here. I can't keep watching from the sidelines, Say." Her breath stutters, but she wraps her hands around my wrists, gripping me for support. God, I want to be that for her. All she has to do is open up.

"I…I don't even know where to start." She bites

her lip, but I erase another inch of space, putting us chest to torso. Her height deficit is really hindering our heart-to-heart. I grab her, walking us to the bathroom and place her pert little ass on the counter. She blinks, but doesn't protest my manhandling.

"Wherever you want, baby," I tell her, sliding my hand beneath her curtain of blonde hair so I can rub the tension from her neck. Her eyes fall closed, searching for courage to voice the things she's never told me or anyone else.

"He hurt me, but only with his f-fingers," she whispers hoarsely, the bitter confession tearing at her fragile resolve. *Only*. As if that makes it any better. "It was painful. He wasn't gentle or sweet like a boyfriend would be. I think he wanted it to hurt so I knew what he was capable of. After a while, my b-body just responded. I s-s-swear I didn't l-like it," Saylor sobs, pressing her face to my chest. I squeeze my eyelids together, warding off the image her words try to conjure.

"It's okay. Breathe, baby." I brush my lips against her temple.

"The first time it happened, I got sick after. Liam was thrilled to know he made me orgasm. From then on, he was softer, coaxing pleasure from my body like it was a game to him. The stakes had been raised. He knew what he was doing to me was far more painful than the rough way he used to touch me. Now, I'm broken. I tried to erase his touch and replace it with my own, but I can't. My mind associates that feeling with Liam. So, yes, he did take something from me I might never get back. That's my big, dirty secret."

Saylor keeps her gaze aimed on the floor, refusing to look at me as she rips my fucking heart out.

That shrimp-dick motherfucker is going to die. I don't give a shit what Loch or Denvers has to say. I don't care that it's wrong—illegal and immoral— to take another person's life. Mark my words, that piece of shit will pay. His atonement will not take place in a guarded prison cell. I'm sending his ass straight to Hell.

"I'm so sorry, Say." I pinch her chin between my fingers and tilt her face up. "There's those pretty blue eyes I love." They're swimming with tears, but I don't regret making her talk to me. "You can't help that your body responded, baby. It doesn't mean that you wanted it. Liam never had the right to touch you. One day, I'm going to cut his fucking hands off for it." She snorts, thinking I'm joking, but if the opportunity ever presents itself, I plan to make good on my threat. We stay like that for a while, holding each other in the quiet as we sort through our thoughts. It isn't until the room starts to darken that I realize how much time has passed.

"Come on. Let's go snuggle." Say doesn't protest, letting me lead her to the closet so she can change into something to sleep in. She's barely going through the motions, her strength zapped after revealing something so personal. I help pick out a sweatshirt—mine, of course—and turn my back so she can put it on. The last thing she needs right now is some horny asshole ogling her. Once Saylor's decent, I pull the covers back and help her into bed. I shed my shirt, but keep my joggers on. No point in torturing myself unnecessarily.

I settle Say against me, sighing at the way her head finds the crook of my neck. I feel every breath she takes, the light puffs sending shivers down my damn spine. Christ, I'm fucking putty when it comes to her. I trace my fingers up and down her arm, content to just hold her. I don't care how long it takes—if it's months or years—I'm determined to make Saylor see herself the way I do. Strong and resilient. *Not* broken. Far from it.

"I'd never done that before Liam. Touched myself, I mean. So that experience is singular to him now." I freeze at hearing her whispered revelation. I can't say I'm not shocked, because I certainly am. She was fourteen; I'd been twiddling my dick since I was in single digits. *Jesus*. "I tried again the other night, when we got drunk. I got in the shower, ran my hand down my body, but the second I felt anything his face appeared. Mom used to tell me that hate is a strong word, but where Liam's concerned, I don't think it's strong enough." *Goddamnit*. She sounds so fucking defeated and it's killing me. Screw it, here goes nothing. I swing my body over hers, bracing my upper half on my forearms. She sucks in a startled breath, but doesn't knee me in the balls. I'll take that as a good sign.

"Do you trust me?" I hold her gaze, needing to see the answer more than hear it. She nods, but that's not good enough right now. "Words, Say. I need words."

"I trust you."

I exhale in relief. "I want to try something. Are you okay with that?"

"Yes," she responds with another nod.

"If you need a second, tell me to pause. If you want me to stop altogether, say stop, baby." I lace our fingers together and raise them above her head. Slowly, I lean in, showing her my intentions and giving her plenty of time to pull away. Hovering just out of reach, a part of me wants Say to make the first move and take what she wants. But that's not going to happen tonight. I press my mouth to hers, groaning at the long-awaited contact. I've thought of this moment a thousand times, but nothing could've prepared me for the actual reality of how good she'd feel. I snag her bottom lip between my teeth, and when a pleased gasp causes them to part, I take the opening and ease my tongue in. A faint moan escapes her, the sound going straight to my cock. I kiss Say like I'll never get to again, reveling in the way she meets my every stroke.

"Havok," she whispers, panting as I pull away.

"You good?" She nods eagerly. "Thank fuck." I run my nose along her jaw, nipping at her ear before peppering kisses against her neck. The sweetest sighs fill the air, making my dick throb painfully. *Not tonight, buddy*. I carefully unwind our fingers, but lead her hand with mine. I watch her for any sign of alarm, but Say's eyes are wide with excitement, her pupils blown with need. I guide her, teasing her pebbled flesh until we reach the top of her panties.

My sweater has ridden up, exposing the baby pink boy shorts she's wearing. I look back to Saylor for guidance, waiting for the okay before taking this any further. She nods, making my cock rejoice, despite the fact he won't be getting any relief. Touching her like this is a fucking gift. I trace her slit through the fabric, groaning at the wetness I find. Even in the dim closet light, I can still make out the blush that spreads across her face. Desperately needing more, I dip our hands beneath her underwear. Regardless of her touch being the prominent one, I nearly combust at the feel of her clit.

"Pause," Saylor chokes out, her eyes wide with fear. I stop instantly, my free hand going to the side of her face. I don't take our fingers off her sex, but I make sure to keep them still.

"Look at me, baby." Say's blues clash with mine. "It's just me. No one's here but the two of us." She nods, her body softening with each second that passes.

"Keep talking. It helps to hear your voice," she tells me. "He…he was always quiet."

"Okay. I can do that." I lightly shift her finger, noting every twitch she makes. "Eyes on me, baby." I move us again, testing her limit, but she doesn't stop me. Her breathing shifts, the slow, controlled inhales and exhales coming quicker with each stroke. "Move your fingers, Say." I ease mine away. Drifting lower, exploring every inch or her slickness.

"Hav..ok," Saylor stutters, but it's time she captain the damn ship.

"You're okay. I'm right here." I stop, calling on every ounce of strength I possess to keep myself from doing anything she hasn't agreed to. "What do you want? You need my fingers in your pussy, Say?" A strangled noise falls from her lips. "Nuh uh. Don't get shy on me now. Yes or no? I need consent, baby." I watch her throat work, swallowing past the trepidation and fear trying to keep her prisoner. Her nod is small, but there's determination in her eyes. That tells me all I need to know.

She wants this. Wants me.

Slowly, I press the tip of my finger against her entrance, dipping in and out with soft, shallow strokes. Each time, I work myself in a little farther. I'm keenly aware of her, making certain she's here and not lost in her head. When I've pushed myself in as far as I can, Say's eyes flutter, her lips parting on a pleased sigh. I drop my head, holding still as I wait for her to adjust. *Fuck, she's tight.* After a few deep breaths, I pull myself together and ease my finger back out. She moans, but the stillness of her own hand makes me falter.

"Keep moving, Say. You stop, I stop." She obeys, picking back up where she left off as I finger fuck her nice and easy. The combination of pleasure has her wiggling, searching for something she can't quite find. I keep a steady pace, not wanting to do anything to hurt her, but it's damn near killing me. Fisting the sheet, I admire my girl. The flush tinting her creamy skin, the sweat gathering at her hairline. I want to lick it. Every pant and moan she makes edges me closer and closer.

"That's it. Keep going, Say." I lean back, resting on my heels. I want to see her. All of her. I tug her panties down, my brain derailing and forgetting to ask if she's okay with it. She helps kick them off, so I guess that's my answer. *Fuck me*. Her bare pussy comes into view and I lick my lips at the sight. "You're fucking perfect." I speed up, matching my tempo with hers.

"Feel good, baby?" I ask, fixated on the way my finger slips in and out of her. I glance up, smirking at the rapid nod of her head. Her hips flex, seeking more, and I'm all too happy to provide it. I add another, stretching her gently. Say growls, the cutest fucking sound I've ever heard, making her frustration known.

"I…I can't." Her hand falls limp. She's close, I can tell by the way she's fluttering around my fingers. But her touch isn't getting her there. She needs more. Needs *me*. I drop between her thighs, using my shoulders to keep her legs spread. Say gasps in surprise, but makes no move to stop me. With one last look, I lap her pussy from one end to the other, lightly biting on her clit before soothing it with my tongue. Saylor bucks against me, moaning so loudly it'll be a miracle if every one of the guys isn't sitting out in the hallway, desperate to hear more. I twist my fingers, stroking her to the point of delirium as my tongue works that bundle of nerves.

"Let go, Say. Come for me." She writhes beneath me, her muscles tensing as she slaps a hand over her mouth. Her pussy squeezes my fingers and I close my eyes, committing the feel of her orgasm to memory. Precum leaks from my cock, but I pay it no mind. I'm too mesmerized with watching Say fight to catch her breath. As she floats back down, I ease my fingers out and bring them to my mouth, savoring the taste of her release. Her eyes track my every move, but she doesn't look put off by the action. Quite the opposite, actually.

"God, you taste good," I groan, grinning at the way her cheeks turn pink. Dropping beside her, I pull her limp and sated body across mine. We're both sweaty, but neither of us seems to care. I don't try to fill the silence, knowing Saylor well enough that talking through what we just did so soon won't go over well. She's relaxed, though, and that's enough for now. I run my fingers down her spine, my eyes heavy with sleep.

"Havok?" Say whispers.

"Yeah, baby?"

"I need to tell you something." She twines our fingers together, squeezing them nervously. Those words, along with '*we need to talk*', are historically terrifying where relationships are concerned. I keep quiet, waiting to see what she has to say. "I kissed Kash." I still, giving my brain a second to catch up.

"You're mad," Saylor states, not questions.

"No, not mad," I tell her honestly. "I'm…not really sure what I'm feeling. Jealousy, maybe? Not that he kissed you, I expected the rat bastard to try at some point. I think I'm annoyed he has that first with you." I tug my lip between my teeth, wishing I could junk punch the little fucker. I'm not oblivious to the way my brothers feel about Say, but it's an odd situation, no matter how you look at it.

Saylor scoffs. "I hardly think you should be upset that you missed out on a kiss when you just claimed several of my firsts yourself." Her deadpan tone makes me grin.

"You're damn right, I did." I roll so we're facing one another and place my hand on the back of her head. My hold is possessive, because that's exactly how I feel about this girl. Crazed with the need to claim her. "Your orgasms? Those belong to me now, baby. Maybe my brothers as well, but definitely not to *him*. When you think of pleasure, that pig-headed fucker won't even be an afterthought. You'll see me in your dirty dreams, Say. Me when you close your eyes and play with yourself. *He. Owns. Nothing*. All mine, pretty girl. It's all mine." I slam my mouth to hers, cementing every declaration I made, needing her to understand just how fucking serious I am.

"As for Kash, that's between you and him. Same for Loch, Ro, and Krew. You call the shots, Say. Always. If you want it, take it, baby. As long as I can have you too, I'll learn to live with sharing. Might not be any good at it, but for you? I'll try to be." Her stunned blue eyes look back at me like I've lost my ever-loving mind, and maybe I have. Watching her fall apart still has me in a dopey state of masculine satisfaction, but I doubt I'll feel any different come tomorrow. There's not much I wouldn't be willing to do to make Saylor happy.

"Get some sleep, pretty girl. It's a problem for another day." I kiss her forehead, drawing her closer so I can bury my face in her coconut scent.

Truthfully, I hope it's not a problem at all.

Chapter Thirty-Four

Lochlan

My phone rang just after 4am, the local authorities in Nashville calling to inform me that they've found personal effects belonging to the missing teenager we've been searching for. As much as I was hoping to do this remotely, it's just not possible. I tossed a few days' worth of clothes in a bag and went to find Kade, knowing he'd be pissed to leave Saylor. Imagine my surprise when I eased her door open and found the two of them wrapped around each other, her bare ass on display with his hand clamped on her hip possessively.

I stood in the doorway like a fucking statue, my eyes roving over every inch of her flesh like a voyeuristic asshole. But then the guilt crept in, and I quickly left them to it. I'm not sure what happened, but it was obvious something had gone down. I'm on my third cup of coffee in the span of two hours, waiting for the rest of the house to wake. I run through a mental checklist after booking our flight, making sure everything's good on the home front before we have to leave. Anything to take my mind off of Kade and Saylor. If I were a lesser man, I'd send the prick across the country on another job.

Fucking wanker.

Kash is the first to join me. No surprise there. He's bright eyed and bushy tailed, the exact opposite of what I'm feeling at the moment. I leave breakfast up to him, knowing he needs something to keep him busy or he'll wander back to Saylor's room and get the same eyeful I was gifted. Krew and Ro appear a few minutes later, eyeing my bag by the door. Neither asks for details, aware that I'll fill them in once we're all accounted for. *Speak of the devil and he shall appear.* Kade walks in, a cocky swagger to his step. Or maybe it's just my imagination. My fingers flex around my coffee cup, eyes narrowed suspiciously. The little shit is whistling. Our gazes clash, causing his steps to waver. He knows. He might not know *how* exactly, but he knows that I know.

Kade recovers seamlessly, carrying on like it's a normal goddamn morning when it's anything but. Meanwhile, my blood pressure is through the damn roof. They all find a seat, leaving the food untouched until Saylor wakes. Just as I open my mouth to explain that we're needed in Tennessee, Kade cuts me off.

"I think of everyone at this table as a brother, so remember that five minutes from now," he begins, the serious tone of his voice grabbing our attention. "Last night, my relationship with Say became...more. I'm not giving details, that's not anyone's business but ours. All I'm going to say is that Liam really did a number on her mentally. If she wants to expand on that she can, but I won't be. I refuse to break her trust." One by one, we stiffen in our chairs. I'm sure their thoughts mirror my own. I push my glasses up anxiously, anticipating Kade's demand for us stay away from her.

"So, that brings the count to two. Kash stole her first kiss, like the snake he is, but I'm fully aware that all of you are interested." My eyes fly to Kash, waiting for him to deny it, but the sappy grin on his face tells me all I need to know. *Bloody hell.* "Say's worried, even if she didn't voice it in so many words. After we were…together…she felt the need to confess about kissing Kash, like she'd done something wrong. But she hasn't. We'd have to be blind to miss that Saylor's attracted to each of us. If she needs to explore that, then so be it. I know none of us would hurt her, so if she wants a relationship with the four of you also, I don't see an issue."

I'm speechless. Truly. I take another sip of my lukewarm coffee, trying to imagine the logistics of the picture he's painting. It's not as off-putting as I thought it'd be.

"Let me get this straight. You're suggesting we *share* her?" Ro grits outs, to which Kade responds with a shrug. "She's not a fucking toy to be passed around!" He leans across the table, pointing a threatening finger at Kade.

"Watch your goddamn mouth." Kade surges to his feet, meeting Ro's anger with a heavy dose of his own. "Saylor deserves the world, and if being with you assholes is what makes her happy, who the hell am I to judge? I'm not even positive that's what she wants, but if it is, I made sure she knows there's nothing wrong with her for feeling that way. For caring about five men instead of one. If you want any chance of being with her, you better get on board, *brother*. Because I'm not going anywhere."

"Actually, you're going to Nashville." I cut their bickering off, knowing we won't be coming to any sort of agreement in the next few minutes. "Kade makes a valid point. We all have feelings for Saylor, but I think we should table this. Going forward with what he's suggesting requires more consideration than we have the time for right now. It's not something we need to rush into without everyone being certain they're okay with it. In the meantime, the case in Tennessee requires some groundwork and the two of us have a flight to catch." I stand, effectively ending the conversation. Like I knew he would, Kade follows me to the kitchen, storm clouds gathering in his eyes as he grinds his teeth together.

"Is this you punishing me?" he snaps accusingly. I arch an eyebrow and lean against the island, my feet and arms crossed casually.

"Why would I be punishing you?" I question.

"Don't play games, you twat." That *almost* makes me smile. "Are you seriously so fucking insecure in your own relationship with her—that I'm giving you the go ahead on, by the way—you have to send me to bumfuck nowhere?" I drop my arms and square my shoulders.

"First of all, the last thing I need is your approval to do anything," I grind out. "Second, you were already coming *before* I walked in to find you and Saylor half naked."

"Fuck," Kade swears, tugging on the ends of his hair in frustration. "Can you not see how this is going to look to her? That I'm leaving right after we crossed into new territory?" He drops his head back and stares at the ceiling.

"Give her some credit, Kade. Saylor knows we have other jobs that need tending to. She's not the type of woman who'd want you to push your responsibilities to the wayside. It's a few days, at most. And if you're serious about wanting to explore this group thing you're suggesting, then maybe it's best we give the other three some time to come around. I'm not going to be the one who needs convincing."

"Of course not, you dirty fucker." He grins, poking me in the nipple before I can stop him. I glare and slap his hand away.

"Go pack. We have to leave soon." His mopey face is the last thing I see before spinning on my heel to seek out Saylor. I need to speak with her and explain the sudden trip. As much as I'd love to leave her sleeping, we can't wait around much longer. I knock, but there's no response. Thinking she's still dead to the world, I turn the handle and push the door open.

"Saylor?" I call out just as she exits the bathroom, wrapped in nothing but a towel and fresh from the shower. Her shoulders glisten, the damp strands of her hair hanging loosely. *Christ almighty, she's a literal fucking wet dream*. I close the door slowly, making sure my steps are purposeful as I draw closer.

I can see the uncertainty in her pretty blue eyes, that glimpse of what Kade was talking about making an appearance. I run my thumb down the bridge of her nose, over those pouty lips, tugging at the bottom one just the slightest. Her breath hitches, and like the fool I am, I fixate on her mouth. Imagining all the things I'd love to do with it.

"Lochlan?" Saylor's voice breaks through the haze and I drop my hand. Clearing my throat, I step back and take a seat on the edge of her bed.

"I wanted to let you know that Kade and I will be leaving for a few days. The case in Nashville needs some hands-on attention. We shouldn't be long, though." Her nose scrunches.

"He's still missing?" she asks.

"Yes, but we have a trail to follow, so there's hope." I grab her hand and pull her close. If I'm not going to be seeing Saylor for several days, I want to get my fill while I can.

"But the two of you will be safe, right? You're not at risk?" Her concern is cute.

"We'll be perfectly fine, love." I wrap my arms around her waist, praying she doesn't bite my head off for being so forward. To my surprise, she starts to run her fingers through my hair. I lay my chin against her abdomen and peer up at that sweet face I can't shake. It's been with me for three years now, but my response to her has shifted to something far beyond the need for justice and answers. Saylor smiles, straining to hold back her girlish giggle. I fucking love that sound. The innocent, carefree lilt she was deprived of for five long years.

"What's so funny?" I question with a grin of my own.

"I've wanted to mess this perfect hair up for quite some time," she replies teasingly.

"Is that so?" I skate my fingers down her body. She shivers, but something tells me it has little to do with her being cold.

"Mmhmm." Saylor nods, her eyes closing as I draw circles on her thighs. Her ass is so close, all it'd take is a slip of my hand and I'd be clenching it. Instead, I do us both a favor and dig my fingers along her sides, until she's screaming for mercy, tears pouring down her cheeks from laughing so hard. I flip us, dropping her on the bed as I brace myself above her. Beneath this flimsy piece of terrycloth, her body is bare. If I fixate on that for too long, I'm afraid of what I might do.

"You can play with my hair anytime you want, love." My voice is low, laced with need and sexual frustration. I cradle Saylor's head, the weight of what I'm holding not lost on me in the slightest. She's everything I've ever wanted. It just so happens that my brothers feel the same way I do. "I'm going to miss you, sweetheart."

"I'll miss you too." Saylor runs her fingers over the backs of my arms. I'm not sure she's even aware that she's doing it, but who fucking knew that could be an erogenous zone. I lightly press my lips to hers, completely forgoing my initial plan to let her lead. There's no way I could have walked out of here without knowing what it felt like. Saylor blinks a few times, but then leans up and kisses me back, her fingers threading through my hair once again. *Fuck me*. Maybe we won't leave after all. I pull back and drop my head to her shoulder, shamelessly breathing her in.

"I don't want to go, but I have to," I mumble, brushing my lips over her neck just to get a reaction. I love the way she squirms.

"I know." She nods, but it's apparent she's as reluctant as I am to put a few states between us.

"Keep your men in line while I'm gone." I kiss the tip of her nose and stand, pulling Saylor with me.

"My men?" she squeaks, her eyes widening at my choice of words.

"They listen to you better than they do me. I'll see you soon, love." I wink and pull the door open, knowing damn well I could find a million reasons to keep prolonging our departure. Kade is standing just outside, waiting like a good boy for his turn to steal a few minutes of her time. He eyes my hair with a grunt of annoyance.

"Fucker." He shoulders past me and slams the door closed. This whole idea of exploring individual relationships with Saylor might have been his idea, but even he's going to struggle with the learning curve. I smirk and let them say their goodbyes in peace. We need to be on the road within the hour, so I stop by Krew's office to get hard copies of anything I might need while we're away. His desk is littered with empty drink cans, the mess making my eye twitch. It's his chaos though, and if it works for him, so be it.

"Here's his file. Missing person's flyer, point of contact—it's all there. For anything else, shoot me an email." Krew passes me the accordion folder. He might not appreciate organization, but he knows I do and never fails to have everything put together just the way I like.

"You need to sleep and eat something with substance. Take some time off. If I need you, I'll let you know." I give him a pointed look, knowing the man will work himself stupid if he isn't made to rest.

"Stop projecting. I'm fine—as always—but what about you?" Krew cocks his head, leaning back like he doesn't have a care in the world.

"What's that supposed to mean?"

"It means, Boss Man, that you're stressed about leaving Saylor, so you've gone into daddy mode. We'll be fine, including Tink, so go do what you need to and wrap this shit up. Don't let your focus be back here when it's needed elsewhere." Krew has never been one to mince words, which is probably why he and Kade butted heads so much in the beginning. They're a lot more alike than they think.

"I hear ya, loud and clear." I push off the wall to leave, but stop short. "Whatever way you're leaning, make sure you're all in, Krew. Don't hurt her. You've been hot and cold since day one, and I know it doesn't have anything to do with Saylor exactly, but she deserves all of you. If you can't give her that, then don't offer anything at all." We stare at one another, my words hanging between us like a threat. I suppose in a way it is. If he toys with her, brother or not, I'll beat him fucking bloody.

"I won't hurt Kash, but if he's on the same page, I have no reservations. I want Tink more than I've wanted just about anything, but that doesn't mean I deserve her. None of us do. But ultimately, that's her decision." I lift my chin in understanding, then head for the main room. Kade saunters in as I'm filling a to-go mug with coffee, grinning like a damn loon.

"And you bitch about my sugar intake. The amount of caffeine you consume is going to make your heart explode," Kash scoffs, fake gagging at the bitter liquid.

"We all have our vices, baby brother." I ruffle his hair and shoulder my bag, laughing off his snarl of irritation. "I'm sure after I've spent days on end with Kade I'll be ready to exchange my drink of choice for hard liquor."

"'Tis true," Kash agrees. Kade rolls his eyes at the two of us, pocketing the keys to the Tahoe. "Be good boys and catch all the bad guys." Kash smacks a sticky kiss to both of our cheeks, cackling like a crazy person as he takes off down the hallway before either of us can put him on his ass. I bet the little shit is going straight to Saylor's room too. Lucky bastard. I shake my head and jog down the stairs, ready to get this over and done with. I can't remember there ever being a time when I've dreaded a job, but here I am, wishing we never agreed to take the case to begin with.

And that makes me feel like the scum of the earth. There's a boy missing—who's hurt at best, dead at worst—and his family is desperate for answers. This is why we started SOTERIA, which is the only justification I have for driving away. We aren't leaving Saylor to go play bodyguard to some high-maintenance princess. This person genuinely needs our help. It pacifies my frustration, but not entirely. Every mile we put between us and her feels inherently wrong. Like forcing something that isn't meant to be.

"I know, brother," Kade sighs, feeling just as conflicted as I do.

"We'll make it quick," I promise, praying I'm not jinxing us before we've even gotten started.

I close my eyes, letting the sway of the vehicle lull me half to sleep. I could've used those extra hours this morning, but the odds of resting after seeing what I did were slim. Even if we have to work twenty hours a day, I'm determined to be back in Florida by Wednesday. That gives us five full days to gather what we can and track down every lead we have. If nothing comes of it by then, I'm going home. My phone vibrates against my thigh, the notification making me smile. Saylor barely uses hers, so to see a text from her is a pleasant surprise.

Saylor: I lied. I actually missed you before you even left. Stay safe and come back to me.

Sweet Lord above.

It takes herculean effort to keep myself from telling Kade turn around. I drag in a deep breath and type out my response, grateful I have this connection to her and won't have to go through the guys just to speak with her.

I promise, love. Nothing's going to keep me away from you longer than I have to be. Tsunami, catastrophic earthquake, zombie apocalypse. They wouldn't stand a chance, sweetheart.

I grin and lick my lips, hoping to find a faint taste of her still lingering. Shit, I can't remember the last time I've felt this happy. Probably never.

Saylor: You're ridiculous, but I appreciate the dedication.

Ridiculously crazy about you, love.

I'm coming on strong, but fuck if I'm going to lose out on precious time with her while those other three assholes get to weasel their way in. I want Saylor to know where I stand, without question, and if texts and phone calls are my only means of relaying my feelings for the time being, then I'll use them to my advantage. I have no intention of fighting fair where she's concerned. Somewhat mollified, I blank my thoughts of what's awaiting me at home and give my attention to the file in front of me. Krew's done most of the leg work on this, so I'm not as versed as I should be on all the details.

I settle in and familiarize myself with Jasper Dixon. With a name like that, the kid sounds famous already. Let's hope we find him so he can give that dream of his a chance to come true.

Chapter Thirty-Five

Saylor

I've done a pretty decent job of keeping busy since Lochlan and Havok left for Tennessee. Kash is a great distraction, always finding something for us to do to help the hours pass. I spent the first day being lazy, trying to wrap my mind around everything that transpired with Havok the night before. I still have no answer for the way I feel. The way he touched me—tasted me—has been playing on repeat every moment since. He's caused a ripple in my thoughts, and these new ones springing up are far needier. I wasn't prepared for the way my body responded, the release I felt when succumbing to my wants.

At one point, when my emotions were all over the place, I resorted to talking to my mom. Or her urn, I should say. If she were still here and we were our happy little family of two in Pike's Bay, I highly doubt I would've been forward enough to discuss sexual partners with my mother. But at present, she's all I've got. I could always call Danielle, but this is personal, and if I'm being truthful, I'm scared she's going to tell me something I don't want to hear. It doesn't matter that she's never leaned that way, or that she's constantly telling me I'm the only one who knows what's best for me. Even the slimmest possibility of her putting doubt in my mind is what keeps me from picking up the phone.

Every part of my being revolts at that the idea of what we did being wrong. I haven't felt this right since waking up in the hospital, disoriented and orphaned. Our progression to this new stage was natural, and no matter what, he will *always* be the one who helped me move past something I never thought I'd get over. Havok has played many roles in my life —asshole, caretaker, protector—but this feels like the most important. Eventually, Kash pried me from my bed and insisted we spend Friday at the beach. We searched for seashells and gorged ourselves on so much junk food, it's a miracle we didn't need our stomach's pumped. Roan even came down and chased Kash with a sand crab.

When I finally climbed my exhausted butt into bed that night, the two of them had drained me so thoroughly, my mind couldn't possibly think of anything else but sleep. It's now Saturday, and even though I've talked to both Lochlan and Havok every day, I'm missing them like crazy. Breakfast just isn't the same without them. Their empty seats are too distracting, so the rest of us have come to some sort of silent agreement to sit at the island like we used to.

I'm munching on a bowl of semi-soggy Froot Loops when someone wraps their arms around my middle and tugs me off the barstool. I sputter around the bite of cereal I'd just taken, tilting my head back to glare at the rude offender. Kash's amused brown eyes twinkle, but there's not a hint of apology to be found on his handsome face. He takes my seat and plops me on his lap, so I go back to eating my breakfast.

"Sweetness, I've just discovered something quite interesting." Kash rests his chin on my shoulder, his thumb tracing the hem of my shorts.

"And what would that be?" I entertain him, but knowing Kash, it's something off the wall.

"Well, you see, I was doing the laundry, and like the good little houseboy that I am, I made sure to check all the pockets before adding anything to the washer. Does this look familiar, Best Friend?" I twist to see what he's talking about, finding a folded piece of paper in his hand. He waves it, a devious grin taking shape. *My list.* As soon as it registers, I choke for the second time in a five-minute span. I reach to yank it from him, but he laughs, springing off the stool and dropping me on my feet.

"Kash." I harden my eyes, cock a hip out, and hold my hand between us. I'm channeling every mom stance I've ever been on the receiving end of, but it does me no good.

"I love it when you get all angry like that, sweetness. So fucking cute." He backs away, but keeps his eyes on me. *Oh, I'm going to show him angry.* With a sad attempt at a war cry, I lunge for the big meanie. It's obvious he wasn't expecting me to get this bent out of shape, but I've had enough humiliation where that damn thing is concerned. The few seconds it takes him to get over his shock work in my favor. I slam against his chest, jumping to reach the list before he can raise it any higher.

"Oh, no you don't." Kash spins, but I'm not letting him get away that easily. Hopping on his back, I wrap my arms and legs around him and hold on for dear life. He chuckles, like he finds my efforts to subdue him downright adorable. Wanting—*needing*—to get that piece of paper before he can read it, I wedge my forearm beneath his chin and squeeze. I'm sure he could fling me off without ever breaking a sweat, but he lets me believe I've bested him. Kash drops to his knees in front of the couch, and fast as a whip, I slip around him and confiscate the evidence.

I unfold the paper, relieved to find that Havok crossed out the last line. My chicken scratch is completely unreadable. I shake my head, a shy smile gracing my lips. I bet he was pleased as pie to know that he was the one responsible for seeing to that accomplishment. I can vividly picture his smug face as he marked it off. I turn to tease Kash and let him know that he can place it back on the fridge if he'd like, only to find him still kneeling on the floor, head resting on his crossed arms as he rocks back and forth.

"Kash?" I call his name, thinking he's just out of breath or playing up my lack of strength, but then I notice the way he's shaking, his hands balled into fists. Something's not right. I drop beside him, lightly touching his shoulder, but he flinches at the contact. I pull back immediately, a jolt of worry going through me. "Kash, it's Saylor. What's wrong?" The longer he goes without responding, the more I start to panic. I eye the hallway, wondering if I should go find Krew.

"I'll get your brother, okay? Give me just a second." I move to stand, but Kash lays his hand over my thigh and shakes his head. "Kash, please. I don't know what's wrong. If you won't talk to me, then at least talk to Krew." Another shake of his head. What in the hell is happening right now? I watch his back rise and fall as he takes slow, measured breaths. I'll give him another minute, then, regardless of whether he wants me to or not, I'm going to wake Krew. He's been resting these past few days after working so much, but I'm sure he'd want to know what's going on. It feels like an eternity passes before Kash finally looks at me. Gutted and broke—it's the only way I can describe the state he's in. The sight steals my breath and makes my eyes water.

Kash pulls me closer, hugging me so tightly it borders on painful. I take control and climb onto his lap, wanting to fix whatever's wrong. He shudders against me, his fingers running through my hair. I don't ask him to talk. Right now, I just want him to be okay, despite not knowing what has him so torn up in the first place. Suddenly, Kash climbs to his feet, keeping me in his arms, and makes a beeline for my bedroom. Once we're inside, he carries me to the bed and lays me down gently. His body is wedged between my legs, his cheek resting on my stomach. I thread my fingers through his curls and wait for him to speak.

"My stepfather was abusive." His words halt my movement, but I shake away the sick feeling and continue stroking through his hair. There's a good chance he needs the distraction to say what he needs to. "He was powerful—rich and influential—and to a man like that, nothing is off limits." *Oh, God.* Please, *please* don't let this be headed where I think it is. "He was angry or aloof, nothing in-between. I'm not sure he knew how to be anything else. He beat the shit out of me, sweetness. Krew did his best to intervene, but the asshole loved picking on me the most because I was the weaker one.

"He played head games with Krew, but when it came to physical violence, I was his preferred choice. A bad day at the office for him could equate to a broken arm for me. Most of his hits were intended to do maximum damage, with minimal evidence of his brutality. Hospitals were avoided at all costs, but even when I did have to be taken in, my injuries were always downplayed as a result of me being a hyperactive kid. He..he liked to wrap his hand around my throat and restrict my airway when I least expected it."

I can feel the blood drain from my face. I'm horrified, sick to my fucking stomach at hearing what the twins endured as kids, but I'm also disgusted with myself for bringing back such disturbing memories for him. A choked noise escapes me as I bite back a sob. The sound has Kash flying up, his eyes raking over every inch of my body. I sit up, an apology on the tip of my tongue, but he cuts me off.

"Don't," he growls, pressing his thumb to my lips. "Don't you dare apologize. How many times have we screwed up, sweetness? Triggers are finicky little fuckers, but it's not your fault. You didn't know, and that's more than I can say for any of us." I shake my head as a tear escapes. Kash groans and swipes it away, replacing it with a kiss.

"I didn't tell you that to make you feel guilty. We know so much about you, so it doesn't feel right to keep my past—the parts that made me the man I am today—a secret. I've worked through what happened to me, but every once in a while, something will drag me back. I know how to cope with flashbacks, so please don't feel bad."

"Is that the reason you were prescribed sleeping pills?" I question, my voice gritty with emotion. I've wondered about them, but never felt it was my place to pry.

"Yes. In the beginning, I couldn't sleep. It's still a struggle, if I'm being honest. Krew was next to me for years, keeping watch, and it's not something I've been able to let go of. It's fucking pathetic that I still share a room with my brother, but it's what I've needed to function. The first time I was able to fall asleep without him, was because of you." I gape at the revelation. I just assumed it was a twin thing. They have a deep bond, so it's never seemed weird to me that the two of them stay together.

"Did your mom never step in?" I can't fathom watching my hypothetical children, much less real ones, being abused by the man I married and doing nothing to stop it. Kash scoffs, telling me everything I need to know about the woman who birthed him without uttering a single word.

"I think she always looked at us as a burden. Our father was mixed, came from lesser means than her, and that wasn't acceptable to her family. She threw away love for wealth, and we were a constant reminder of that." I hope she regrets her choices for the rest of her life. She doesn't deserve them, or the right to call herself a mother.

"And your stepfather? Where's he at now?" *Please say he's dead.*

"If only, sweetness." Kash's knowing laugh makes me blush. His ability to read my thoughts like they're being broadcasted on a jumbotron is disturbing. "Archie Sellers is currently incarcerated at FDC SeaTac. Krew and I hacked his servers, gathered every bit of dirt we could find, and sent it to the district attorney. We watched in glee as his empire fell. Our mother fled when the house was seized, and we haven't seen her since. We timed the whole thing to align with our eighteenth birthday, so that's when we moved in with Loch and Ro."

"Wow..." I mutter, in awe of these two men who've come so far after being dealt such a crappy hand. I might've had an unfortunate intermission, but for the majority of my life, I knew the love of a parent. I had a happy home. "I hate that you guys had to go through that, but I'm glad it led you here."

"Me too, Best Friend." Kash gives me a sweet smile. "Let's watch a movie now. I've met my quota of seriousness for the next five to seven business days." I laugh, but the man behind that happy-go-lucky exterior makes a lot more sense now. I see him clearly. His need to make light of the tough moments is understandable, and I vow to help add to as many of those as I can. It's the least he deserves.

Kash drops a kiss to my nose and tells me he'll be back in just a minute. I flop against my pillows, tapping my phone to check for any missed messages. I've been glued to it more these past two days than I have since Roan gave it to me. I grin when I see the notifications displayed on the screen.

Havok: Earlier today, I locked the bathroom door in our hotel room and hid the key. Loch had to piss outside and almost got his ass beat by an elderly woman with a cane. I had to bribe her with a jar of moonshine so she wouldn't call the cops.

I burst into laughter. The image of always-put-together Lochlan Calloway getting caught with his willy out by some little old lady is just too much.

And you just so happen to have a stash of 'shine for such an occasion, right?

His response comes through a few seconds later.

Havok: Nah. Found some at the corner store. Better than money around these parts.

I shake my head and click on Lochlan's message.

Lochlan: Exactly *how* attached are you to Kade? Scale of one to ten.

Meh. Solid six.

I smile, biting my lip. This back-and-forth teasing is fun. I should've texted with the guys sooner.

Lochlan: Good to know. I'm thinking I'll tie him to a tree and leave him for the bears.

Not a fan of indecent exposure, huh?

Lochlan: That old bat was crazy. She nearly whacked my balls off.

Giggling, I send him a laughing emoji.

Lochlan: Miss you, sweetheart. Can't wait to be home.

Miss you too. So much.

God, I *really* freaking do.

Havok: A *six*?! You wound me, baby.

Didn't think your ego needed the truth.

Havok: And what's the truth?

Too attached. The scale isn't big enough to give an actual number.

Havok: *Fuck*. Just a few more days, Say. I can't wait to get my hands on you.

My blood heats, remembering all the things he did to me.

Can't wait.

I have no idea who I am right now, but I kinda like her. This wild, excited girl who's pushing back the timid, shy outer shell I haven't quite shed. I want to *feel*. And if there's one thing these guys do, it's that. Whether it be happiness or anger or lust, I've had no shortage of emotions since meeting them.

"Surprise!" Kash shoulders my door open, his arms full of blankets and sheets. He's out of breath, but sporting the biggest grin. "We're gonna build a fort."

"Is that so?" I raise an eyebrow, locking my

phone and placing it on the nightstand.

"Yep. Now move your cute ass so I can start the building process."

Alrighty then.

Chapter Thirty-Six

Saylor

Approximately one hour later, Kash has assembled the fort to rival all forts. He explained—in painstaking detail—the proper way to tie your corners and the best fabric to use if you want to achieve optimal inside space with minimal droop in the middle. Several times, I thought about stabbing my eardrums with a pencil, but one look at his excited face made the whole lecture worth it. The little details—his hyperactivity, love of sugar, and fear of creepy crawlies—those are the things I love most about him. He wouldn't be Kash without them.

Jesus, I think I really do love him.

He's tied one corner of the sheet to my door, the other end to the closet, and the back piece is connected to my headboard. Two more are draped across it to hang around us, giving the illusion that we're in a little hut atop my bed. We've got a mound of blankets, my laptop streaming a comedy, and enough snacks to last us through the night. Kash gets teary-eyed at the end of *Moana*, so of course I tease him about it. He tickles me relentlessly, not stopping until

I threaten him with turning on *Eight Legged Freaks*. He visibly shudders at the mention of the movie.

We've just started the first *Hunger Games*, but I'm more focused on Kash than I am the movie. He's really something special. Without fail, he took me right under his wing and helped me through my first few days here. He shopped for me, made sure I had all the necessities, and not just basic drugstore brands either.

"Make myself orgasm," I blurt. Kash chokes on a piece of candy, his shocked gaze snapping to me. Honestly, I'm just as surprised by my rushed words as he is. He keeps coughing, so I pat his back a few times to help him through the fit he seems to be having.

"The fuck?!" Kash sits up, wiping his watery eyes as he pins me with a look of alarm. "What does that even mean?"

"The list. That's what I wrote. The thing that Havok was teasing me about the morning after we got drunk." I felt this need to tell him, especially after he shared so much with me, but now I'm wondering if that was a dumb idea. I don't want Kash to feel like he's being kept on the outside of a secret, and that's the vibe I got when he waved that piece of paper at me.

"You wanted to...make yourself orgasm?" he questions slowly.

I nod. "Long story short, Liam made me... *arrive*...and it's messed with my head. I couldn't touch myself without thinking about him."

"And Kade obviously helped with that because it was crossed off the list," Kash states, like he knows the answer already.

"Yes," I whisper, suddenly nervous he's going to be angry with me.

"Huh." He stares at the wall, not saying anything for the longest time. We're edging toward awkward when he drops a truth of his own.

"I'm a virgin." I blink, certain I heard him wrong.

"How?" If I sound incredulous, it's because I am.

"Well, my P has never entered a V…" Kash spells it out for me. I smack his arm with the back of my hand, trying not to laugh at his sarcastic response.

"You know what I mean. You're…" I wave my hand at him.

"I'm…*what*?" His eyebrows scrunch together, completely unaware of why I find that so shocking.

"Hot," I deadpan, making a sinful grin spread across his face.

"Oooh, do tell, sweetness. What other words would you use to describe me?" Kash props his chin on his fist, those brown eyes twinkling with mischief.

"Let's see…" I start counting off everything I can think of on my fingers. "Sweet, funny, pre-diabetic, chicken-shit—at least when it comes to bugs—what else?" I tap my chin, but Kash tackles me, cutting off my train of thought.

"You little brat," he growls, burying his face against my neck, his stubble making me squirm.

"Wanna know how I'd describe you?" I nod, biting my lip as I stare at him above me, the glow of the laptop making his jawline even sharper. "Beautiful," he whispers, kissing my cheek. "Innocent." A kiss to my nose. "Kind." My other cheek. "Smart." My forehead. "*Perfect*." Finally, his lips land on mine, his sweet words resonating somewhere deep inside of me. A place only these men seem to penetrate, and without even trying. They're stealing parts of me too, but I'm not mad about it.

I pull Kash closer, groaning when he slips his tongue in my mouth. Our first kiss—*my very first*—pales in comparison to the way he's making me feel right now. Like I'm on fire. His hand settles on the base of my throat as I arch against his hold. I need...*more*. Sliding my hands under the back of his shirt, I sigh when my fingers find his heated skin. Kash pulls back suddenly, his chest heaving as he glances down at me. Whatever he sees makes him smirk, and in a move too hot for words, he reaches back and whips his shirt off.

"Sweetness," Kash groans, fisting the hem of my sweatshirt. I nod my permission, and he wastes no time ridding me of it. "Fucking hell." He presses a kiss to the hollow of my throat, then works his way down. When his teeth graze my nipple, I nearly come off the bed. Kash just chuckles, the sound undeniably sexual.

"Kash," I pant, grappling for a single brain cell to spit out what I need to say. "I'm a virgin too." He freezes, easing back to look me in the eye.

"You and Kade didn't..." He trails off, his face giving no hint of how that makes him feel.

I shake my head. "We did...other stuff."

"I'm not trying to get into your pants, sweetness. Okay, that's not entirely true. But sex wasn't where I thought this was headed. We can stop right now."

"That's not necessary." I prop myself up on my elbows, knowing the conversation requires more attention than I'm giving it. "I want to. With you." Kash says nothing, making me wonder if I totally misread the situation.

"Fuck." He drops his head back, lacing his hands together behind his neck. "Fuck. Fuck. *Fuck.*" I shift, feeling embarrassed and desperate to go lock myself in the bathroom for the next few years. Kash grabs me before I can escape, his grip firm but gentle. "No. You don't get to run away after saying that. What's that mean, Saylor? Do you only want this with me because I'm a virgin, too?" He looks angry, but I don't understand why.

"What? No, of course not. I mean, yes, I do think being with you takes the pressure off. But in the sense that I feel safe taking this step with you. Neither of us has done this before, but even if you had, I'd still want it to be you." Kash's smile grows with every word, but now I'm thinking I'd rather knee him in the balls.

"Don't get mad, sweetness. I had to know it's me you want, not my inexperience. I'm a virgin by choice. I don't particularly enjoy the touch of strangers, and no woman has ever intrigued me enough to change that. Not until *you*. And for the record, just because I haven't had sex, that doesn't mean I'm some fucking boy scout and don't know what I'm doing." Kash slides his hands beneath my shorts and grips my butt, making me gasp.

"You called me Saylor." He rarely uses my actual name anymore.

"I'm sorry," he says, his lips brushing over mine. "I'll never do it again." I sigh, feeling foolish that we're bickering about something so trivial, especially when he just had his tongue in my mouth.

"You really want this?" he asks. I nod, putting myself out there yet again. "If we do this, does that mean it's just you and me?" I still, shame washing over me as I realize what he's asking. Even more so that I can't give him the answer he wants. He groans, but it's the miserable kind. "That was unfair. Can't blame me for trying, though." Kash winks, easing some of my panic. "I'm not asking you to choose. Just don't leave me behind, okay?"

"Never," I promise.

"I want this, sweetness. So fucking bad. But I don't want to hurt you." Kash swallows, his face pinched with worry. I understand that first times aren't supposed to be mind-blowing. I have no doubt pain will be involved. But it didn't hurt when Havok had his fingers inside me, so I'm hopeful it will at least be bearable.

"You'd never hurt me," I tell him honestly. "No matter what, I'll enjoy it because it's you, Kash." I run my thumb between his eyebrows, smoothing out his bunched expression.

"Okay," Kash agrees. "As long as you're sure."

"Positive."

"You hear that, big fella? Time to soldier up!" Kash drops his gaze, speaking directly to his crotch. I laugh, the last of my apprehension fading away. This is why being with him was an easy choice. Kash pops the clasp of my bra with expert precision, tossing it over his shoulder in the next breath. It happens so fast I don't even have time to feel shy. He swears, eating up the sight of my bare breasts. As he teases one nipple with his tongue, his fingers tug at the other. I grab his hair, holding him against me, just in case he gets any bright ideas about stopping.

Kash chuckles, the vibration going straight to my sex. "You like that?" I grunt in response, too focused on the wet feel of his mouth. "Spread your legs, babe." I do, eager for more and struggling to keep myself from screaming at him to hurry the hell up already. Kash leans back, making me hiss at the loss. He smirks, freeing me of my shorts and underwear all at once. I'm completely naked, not an inch of me hidden from his penetrating gaze.

"Goddamn, sweetness." Kash licks his lips.

"Your turn." I lift my chin and wait for him to strip. Kash slips his pants and briefs off so fast, I can't help but laugh at his eagerness. But then my eyes take him in, from head to toe, and I feel just as awestruck. He grips himself, stroking his length as he watches my reaction to him.

"Wow," I croak, enthralled with the way he's touching himself, completely unashamed of his nudity.

"Is that a good wow or a bad wow?" Kash asks, his head tilted to the side slightly.

"Good. Definitely good," I respond, but my attention is more on him and what he's doing. Kash snorts, climbing back over me with a pleased smile.

"You're so fucking beautiful." The way he stares at me takes my breath away. His fingers stroke between my thighs, making my eyes close, but I pry them back open, scared to get too carried away and forget where I am and who I'm with. I refuse to let Liam ruin this. Kash is the only person I want to see right now, so I keep my focus on him. "So wet. Because of *me*." I nod, not that he was asking. His finger slides in easily, quickly followed by a second.

"You with me, sweetness?" Kash glances up, checking that I'm okay. I grind against his hand in response. He curses and adds another. I moan, fisting the blanket beneath me as he picks up the pace. His thumb brushes my clit and I lose it, my orgasm hitting so hard and fast all I can do is gasp for breath and ride it out. Kash stares at me in wonder, but I'm the one who should be amazed right now.

"Shit," he swears.

"What's wrong?" I lie there like a limp noodle, trying to gather the energy to sit up.

"No condom," Kash answers. I look at him, biting my lip as I contemplate the repercussions of what I'm about to suggest.

"Neither of us has been with anyone, and I had

bloodwork done at the hospital." Kash snaps his head up.

"You're not on birth control, babe." His words say one thing, but the way he's looking at me screams he'd like nothing more than to have nothing between us. "I won't risk you like that." I deflate, hating to end our night like this, but he's right. It'd be stupid to go any further without protection.

"I'm going to hell for this," Kash snarks, sliding off the bed. My door opens a second later, causing our fort to dip. I blink at the swaying fabric, wondering if he just left me here—*naked*—and bailed. My door clicks shut a second later, and then Kash is back. He's waving a condom, a guilty smile on his face.

"Where'd that come from?" I ask, curious about its sudden appearance when he made it seem like he didn't have any.

"Kade's nightstand." He winces, rubbing at the back of his neck. My eyes widen. "I swear, he doesn't go out and hook up with random women. Not all the time. They're random, I mean, but seldom. I'm gonna shut the fuck up now." I press my lips together, fighting back the laugh begging to be released. So, *that's* why he looks so uncomfortable. Not because he stole the condom, but because he doesn't want me to think that Havok's a manwhore. It's sweet, in a weird way.

"I'm not worried about what Havok did before me. If there's one thing I'm certain of, it's his feelings for me," I tell him softly, holding my hand out. Kash nods and gives me the condom. As he situates himself in front of me, I tear the wrapper open.

"Over the tip, sweetness. Then roll it down." Kash guides my hand, helping me cover his cock. His breath hitches as I work it on.

"You okay?" I grin, enjoying the strong reaction my touch elicits.

"Yep. Just trying not to embarrass myself." I snort, easing back once he's fully covered. "If at any point I need to stop, you have to tell me." I nod, knowing I won't but wanting to put his mind at ease. He slides himself over me, spreading my wetness on the condom. Every time he nudges my clit, it makes me see stars. After a few strokes, he presses against my entrance. I stiffen automatically, wrapping my hands around Kash's forearms to help keep me grounded.

"Relax. We'll take this as slow as we need to." I exhale, matching my breathing with his as he kisses me sweetly. He pushes in a little more, but there's no pain. More pressure than anything. He's taking '*slow*' to the extreme and it makes my impatience bubble over.

"Put your dang P in my V, Kash," I growl, trying to use my heels to urge him forward. The anticipation has to be worse than the actual act. He laughs, sliding his hands behind my head to cradle it. Kash looks at me like he's got the whole world in the palms of his hands. I smile, holding his gaze as he pushes all the way in. My lips part on a whimper. My natural response is to move away from the sting, but I stay still, letting my body adjust to the feel of him. Tears still spring to my eyes, though.

“I’m so sorry, sweetness.” Kash brushes them away and kisses me softly. “I need you to know something. The day you got here, when we were at the beach, that’s when I fell for you. The moment you decided to fight my fears for me. It was innocent and pure, but it’s grown into so much more. I love you. I’m *in* love with you. I need you to know that, to know that what we’re doing means something to me. I knew the moment I laid eyes on you that one day, you’d be the most important person in my life. And you are. You’re everything to me, sweetness.”

My tears fall freely at his confession. I knew Kash cared about me, but I had no idea his feelings were this strong. I never imagined I’d have this. And now I have it five times over. If I think on it too much, it makes me panicky. Words feel too difficult at the moment, so I swivel my hips instead, coaxing Kash to move. His low groan makes me even more desperate.

“Fuck,” Kash swears, drawing his hips back before easing back in. His thrusts are slow and sweet and it’s killing me.

“Please,” I huff, trying to sync my movements with his.

“You want more?” I nod, a string of *‘yeses’* escaping me. Kash chuckles, pinching my nipples as he grinds himself against my clit.

“Oh, God,” I moan. He moves his hands from the back of my head and grips my ass, tilting my hips up. The new angle short-circuits my brain.

“That’s it, babe.” Kash speeds up even more, dropping a hand between us. His fingers work to make me come, but I doubt the added stimulation was even necessary. I bite his shoulder as my orgasm hits, terrified we're making enough noise to have Roan and Krew aware of what we're doing. I groan, rocking my body, dragging out every ounce of pleasure he's so graciously giving me. Kash thrusts a few more times, then comes with a curse. His arms shake from holding himself up, but I tug him down, needing to feel his weight against me.

We lie there, his fingers lightly brushing the hair from my sweaty face as I trace his spine, content to stay where we are until our breathing returns to normal. I can't believe we just did that, but I have no regrets whatsoever. Kash shifts, accidently kicking the laptop. The movie starts playing again, the first line echoing through the silence being, "*Happy Hunger Games, and may the odds be ever in your favor!*" We cackle, the timing too funny to put into words. He pulls out of me, causing us both to groan, and heads to the bathroom to take care of the condom.

I close my eyes, seconds from falling asleep, but then Kash is back, pressing a warm cloth between my legs. I jolt, tilting my head so I can see him. He's completely focused on cleaning me, his tongue poking out just the slightest in concentration. I smile, a rush of emotion clogging my throat.

"Up." Kash grabs my hand and pulls. "I read that women need to pee after intercourse, so off you go. It's tinkle time." I gape at him, wondering what the hell he's been reading, but then I remember his wall of smut and rethink the question. Who knows what the man has learned. I cover my boobs. Ridiculous as it may be, it feels weird to walk around naked. "Nuh uh. No hiding." Kash slaps my arm away, making me scowl.

"So cute, sweetness, but we'll have angry sex another time." I scoff and lock the door behind me. A shy smile lifts my lips when I catch sight of my reflection. My cheeks are flushed, eyes bright and full of love. Kash lifts the covers when I walk back out, our fort lying in a pile on the floor. I climb in beside him, a quick peek revealing he's still sporting his birthday suit as well. I snuggle closer, laying my hand across his abdomen.

"Goodnight, sweetness." Kash kisses the top of my head.

"Goodnight," I whisper, leaning up so I can press my mouth to his. "And I love you too, Kash."

"Yeah?" He grins, our lips still brushing from how close we are.

"Yeah. I really do."

Chapter Thirty-Seven

Saylor

I've yet to open my eyes, but I can feel the weight of Kash's stare. It's heavy and potent, making me restless under the sheer intensity of it. I know it's him because I can smell the sweet scent of his sucker. I doubt the sun has fully risen, and the man is already pounding back sugar.

"Stop staring," I grumble, desperate for a few more hours of sleep.

"Can't," Kash responds, stroking the pad of his thumb over my exposed nipple. I gasp in surprise, cracking an eye open to watch him. "Your tits are out, and I just wanna…" he trails off, making grabby hands at my chest. I try to cover my smile by pressing my face into my pillow, but Kash flips me to my back and straddles my hips. He rotates his lollipop to the other side of his mouth, using nothing but his tongue, looking downright edible with his sleep rumpled hair and boyish grin.

"Are you sore?" Kash whispers, his brown eyes scrutinizing my naked body from head to toe. My cheeks heat under the appraisal, but I do my best to embrace the way his heated gaze makes me feel. Powerful. Adored. *Whole.* I rub my thighs together, wincing at the slight twinge of discomfort it causes. I shrug; the ache isn't too bad. Kash narrows his eyes. "That's a yes, sweetness. Maybe I should kiss it better?" My mouth opens, but no sound comes out.

"I'm thinking I'd like to have you for breakfast," Kash drawls, pulling the sucker from his mouth. Slowly, he traces the sticky candy over my nipple, then licks the same path with his tongue. I hiss when his teeth tug at it, biting just enough to make me whimper. "*Delicious.*" He continues his assault on my other breast, teasing me to the point I'm bucking my hips beneath him, eager for any sort of friction. His thigh or cock, either will do.

"Ah, ah, ah." Kash stops me by bracing a hand on my hip, his fingers digging into my flesh as he fights for restraint. "I'm exploring. Mapping out every inch of your body and committing it to memory." He punctuates his words by dragging the sucker down my stomach and swirling it around my bellybutton. My heartrate kicks up a notch as he continues to follow the same course with his tongue. "I need to know every spot that makes your breath hitch and causes goosebumps to pebble your skin."

"Kash," I call out in warning, my fingers tugging on his hair as he slides the candy between my legs, over my clit, and down to my opening. This is a couple hundred steps past what we did last night, and even though my body is responding to everything he's doing, it feels dirty and well outside my comfort zone.

"You trust me, sweetness?" Kash presses

against that bundle of nerves, the hardness of the sucker eliciting a long, unbidden moan from me. I nod, his question requiring very little thought. *Of course, I do.* "Spread your legs and let me taste you. I need to fuck you with my mouth." Who the hell is this? I know sweet, playful Kash, but that man has taken a backseat to the dirty-talking alpha controlling my body. I drop my knees, doing as requested without an ounce of fight. He teases me, creating a trail of stickiness from top to bottom, followed by the flick of his tongue licking me clean.

I'm sweating, on the verge of begging him to make the ache go away, when he prods my entrance. Kash inserts the sucker just enough to edge me closer without adding to the tenderness of losing my virginity. I squeeze his head with my thighs, wanting to keep him where he is so he'll finish what he started. Kash chuckles at my impatience, but finally pulls the candy away. He shoves his tongue inside of me, groaning as I arch my back and grind against his face. I'm seconds away from the orgasm he's been dangling in front of me like a damn carrot when the door flies open.

I scream, yanking my hands over my chest so quickly, I'm pretty certain I rip some of Kash's hair out in the process. He covers me instantly, cursing at the wall of muscle standing wide-eyed and slack-jawed in my doorway. Roan takes in the state of our tangled bodies, the discarded clothes and empty condom wrapper scattered across my floor. Whatever he might be feeling, he hides it well, not a single emotion cracking the through blank look he fixes on his face.

The evidence is damning; anyone with a brain can deduce what happened between Kash and I. It's only seconds, but it feels like the whole, embarrassing ordeal lasts a freaking lifetime.

"Dude. Ever heard of knocking? This isn't the swamp, *Shrek*. We have doors for a fucking reason," Kash growls, his eyes hard and unflinching as he berates the veritable giant. Roan blinks, like he's coming out of a trance, and drops his gaze to the floor. He shuffles from side to side, the nervous act so off-key for a man his size.

"Uh. Sorry." Roan scrubs a hand down his face, his movements jerky and uncoordinated. "I'll just..." he points behind him and flees. He's there one second and gone the next. I blink, wondering if I hallucinated the entire thing, but when my eyes meet Kash's, his brown orbs alight with mirth, I know that no such luck exists. I groan, pulling the blanket over my face to hide my flaming cheeks. Kash just laughs and tugs it down.

"Now, where were we?" he questions, attempting slide between my legs and pick back up where he left off. I sputter in protest, planting my hand against his chest so I can shove him away, quickly slipping from the bed as I do.

"Absolutely not." I point my finger at him, grabbing one of the sheets we used for the fort and wrapping it around myself. His bottom lip pops out, but he can't beat me at my own trick. I know exactly what he's trying to do, and I won't be falling for it.

"But...I'm still hungry." Kash smirks, fluttering

his lashes at me, but I shake my head. The man is a damn menace.

"Then go eat a breakfast bar," I whisper-yell. "That was humiliating. I feel like…like—" My shoulders drop as tears sting my eyes. I tilt my head back, blinking rapidly to keep them at bay.

"Hey." Kash scrambles to the end of the bed, cursing the blanket his leg gets tangled in, and sandwiches my face between his hands. "What? You feel like what, sweetness?"

"A selfish brat," I mutter, wishing he wasn't holding me hostage with his gaze. "This feels wrong, to have feelings for five men. Even worse to act on them. This isn't normal, Kash, and it's certainly not fair to any of you. Roan is the easy one to read, yet he just shut down completely from catching the two us together. God only knows what he thinks of me now." I shudder, closing my eyes to hide the hurt that possibility brings me.

"Fuck, babe." Kash presses his forehead to mine. "Listen to me—this isn't one-sided. Our feelings play just as much a part in this as yours do. We fell for you so easily, Best Friend. It didn't take long for us to surmise that we'd end up here. How you'd come to feel about any of us was a mystery, but we damn well knew where *we* stood. Our attachment was formed three years ago, and it's only grown and evolved since then. It was harmless at first, when we were only acquainted with the young girl we were desperate to bring home. But then we got to know you, sweetness. Beyond the case file and media frenzy.

"You don't get to feel guilt or shame over this. Fuck everyone else because their opinions don't matter. The six people who live here are the only ones who get any goddamn say in what happens between us. You've had enough taken from you, babe. Don't let fear take anything else. Whatever you want, it's yours. Do what, or *who*, makes you happy." Kash grins, lifting my chin so I can physically see how sincere he is. "Kade brought the situation to our attention before he and Loch left, and while I can't speak for anyone else, I want you to know that I'm okay with you being with them. If that's what you want, you'll get no pushback from me."

I scrunch my nose, confused and slightly overwhelmed. "What do you mean he '*brought it up*'?" I question.

"Uh," Kash hesitates, clearly wondering if he screwed up by saying something. *To be determined.* "He just mentioned that you guys were exploring more of an intimate relationship." He rushes to explain at the widening of my eyes. "No details, I swear! He was very clear about keeping whatever happened between the two of you to himself." Kash scratches his head, looking flustered and uncomfortable. Too bad. I'm not exactly thrilled they had a family meeting concerning something that very much involves me, yet chose to leave me out of it. *Again.*

"Kade knows how we feel about you. He made it known he wouldn't stand in our way if we tried to pursue something with you too, but he wouldn't be backing off either. The ball's in your court, sweetness. Well, more like five sets of balls, totaling ten altogether." Kash winks as I roll my eyes. It's like he can't go a solid five minutes without cracking a joke. Too much seriousness makes him twitchy, I think.

"Good to know, I guess." I shrug, needing time to regroup before I can check in with myself and determine how I'm really feeling.

"Really?" Kash seems shocked by my easy acquiescence. "Shit, I'm getting better at these pep talks." He wags his eyebrows. "Come on, sweetness. Let's go run you a bath."

We're almost to the bathroom when he stops and backtracks to the bed, tossing the covers off as he searches for something. My jaw hits the floor when he pulls the stuck sucker from my sheets and pops it in his mouth, not a single care that it's covered in lint and *me*. He makes a pleased sound, strutting past me as I stand there, stupefied by the things he does, even though I shouldn't be at this point. I shake my head and follow behind him, leaning against the counter as Kash turns the water on and drops a scoop of lavender bath salt in.

"Relax and soak for a while." He tucks a piece of hair behind my ear. "I need to run to town, but I'll be back in a bit. If you think of anything you need, shoot me a text." I nod as he boops my nose, swooping in to peck me on the lips hard and quick. Kash leaves me smiling, grabbing the condom wrapper on his way out. I close my eyes, waiting for the tub to fill, and think about how quickly things have changed. I'm fighting with logic, who's urging me to slow down, to wait and grieve the loss of five years. The loss of my mom.

But in a way, I already have. I lived those years—day in, day out—I was there for every second, minute, and hour that passed. Why should I keep dwelling on the time I lost when I could be living, doing all the things I prayed I'd get the chance to, but never expected to happen? I'm no longer being held against my will, but sometimes, it feels like mind is still there, stuck below the ground in that godforsaken room. As for Mom, I lost her the day Liam took me. I grieved her long before she was actually dead.

I turn the tap off and let the sheet fall to the floor. Stepping in, I ease myself beneath the hot water, groaning at how good it feels. I'm sore, but not as much as I thought I'd be. It's disturbing to think about, but I'm sure the way Liam treated me made my first time easier. I've known pain in that part of my body, and there's a massive difference between intentional hurt and the kind I experienced with Kash. He'd never cause me harm; not purposefully. None of them would. I slink below the surface and wet my hair. After shampooing and scrubbing myself clean, I towel off and drain the tub. I wish I were bold enough to own the shame of Roan walking in on us, but I'm not wired that way. I dress in leggings and an oversized sweatshirt, dreading having to face the man but knowing I need to.

It's quiet as I make my way through the house, my eyes searching every nook and cranny, certain I'll be cornered and subjected to a round of twenty-one, highly invasive questions at any second. I breathe a sigh of relief when I find the kitchen and living room empty. Deciding to make myself something to eat, I head to the pantry and pull the things I'll need for cheese quesadillas. They're simple enough I don't have to worry about burning the house down.

I've just tossed some butter in the skillet when I notice that Krew's office door is cracked. A sliver of his face is visible from the illumination of his computer screen. Honestly, I'm surprised he took as much time as he did to catch up on some sleep. And I'd be willing to bet the only thing he's put on his stomach since he went back to work are far too many energy drinks. I bite my lip, debating if I should interrupt, but surely he won't turn down food. I toss another quesadilla on after I plate mine, and once they're both done, I take a fortifying breath and head towards the inner sanctum of Krew Davenport.

I tap my knuckles against the door, causing it to open a bit more. At first, he doesn't even register the interruption, too focused on whatever he's looking at to notice me. I clear my throat, standing there awkwardly as I try to balance two plates and the bottles of water I shoved beneath my arm. Krew's head snaps up, his brown eyes blinking several times to clear the fog from his brain. It's obvious he's hyper-focused on something and I've just severed his train of thought.

"Sorry." I scrunch my nose. "Thought you might be hungry, but I can set this in the microwave for later if you want?" Krew pushes back from his desk, his legs spread wide as he shakes his head.

"You're good, Tink. What'd you make?" He lifts his chin at the food, so I close the gap between us, letting him take the waters so I can hand him a plate.

"Nothing special." I shrug in response, knowing my culinary skills are lackluster in comparison to the guys'.

"Looks good to me." A shocked squeak escapes me when Krew snags my hand and pulls me down, situating me on his lap. "Might as well eat together." I sit there for a second, too stunned to do much of anything but gape at the desk in front of me. We've shared a few moments, and I'm not so dense that I don't recognize the attraction between us, but Krew has always been more reserved with his affection. I take a hesitant bite, willing my mind and body to relax. After several minutes pass without either of us speaking, I study the screen he has pulled up. It's a video, paused on a dark alley, the picture black and gray and kind of grainy.

"What are you working on?" I question, curious about the footage, but also anxious to end the silence.

"The case in Tennessee. We couldn't find any surveillance of the front of the building, but we got lucky and someone's dashcam caught the kid as he stumbled out the door. I know he hooked a right, but it's a guessing game after that. The car turned at the next intersection, so they've got nothing else either. Right now, it's a process of elimination. I'm checking each possible route, combing through any security footage we've obtained so I can rule out the directions he *didn't* go." I nod, licking salsa from my finger as Krew starts the video and resumes working.

He doesn't seem bothered by my presence, so I settle in and watch. It's obvious he enjoys what he does. He taps away at the keys and switches between screens so quickly, it's hard to keep up. But it's fascinating, seeing this side of him. I'm not sure he even realizes it, but his hand has worked its way beneath my sweater. It's resting against my stomach, his thumb stroking back and forth lazily. I bite my lip, shifting just the slightest. Krew tightens his hold, tugging me until my back is flush with his front. He brushes my damp hair aside and places a kiss over my pulse.

"You aren't ready for me, Tink." Krew punctuates his claim with a nip to my ear, making me jump from the slight sting. "I'm not soft or sweet like my brother. I *fuck*. I'll push you, test your limits until you're crying, begging me to make you come. I won't treat you like you're fragile, because you fucking aren't. Until you're absolutely positive you want what I'm offering, I need you to stop moving your tight little ass over my cock." His hips thrust upward on a grunt, the hard outline of him unmistakable against the thin fabric of my leggings.

I'm speechless. Intelligent thought completely leaves the building, and all that's left are images of what he's describing. I don't have much to go off of, but my graphic imagination has no issue conjuring the carnal way he'd take me. And it would *definitely* be a taking. Krew would never cede control, and right now, that's something I need.

"Go find Ro. I can practically feel the big fucker pacing. Not sure what had him running scared this morning, but I have an idea." Krew pushes me to my feet and blatantly readjusts himself. A pang of disappointment spears my chest at being dismissed so easily. Is this how it's always going to be between us? Him pushing me away if things get too heated, just because I'm not ready for the type of sex he described. I grab our plates, preparing to hightail it out of there, but his fingers grip my wrist, bringing my hand to his mouth.

"Don't mistake this for something it's not, Tink. I want you. And maybe I haven't made that abundantly clear in the past, but I'm telling you now. *I. Want. You.* There's no reason to rush when I'm not going anywhere." I exhale audibly, his words soothing me in a way I can't quite pinpoint. Krew kisses my knuckles and turns back to the monitor, his focus on his work once again.

I smile and take our dishes to the kitchen. After cleaning up my mess from cooking, I start the dishwasher and wipe down the counters. Anything to stall and avoid the inevitable confrontation with Roan. Giving myself a mental shake, I square my shoulders and pull on my big girl panties. I doubt he's in his room, so I head for the lower level. As the door clicks shut behind me, I can feel the bass of his music thumping through the glass walls of the gym. It's a wonder they haven't shattered. The moment I step inside, I flinch from how loud it is.

Rock music blares through the speakers, but by some miracle, the clang of weights still penetrates the screamo-band. I follow the gym-bro call of grunts and groans until I spot Roan. My steps falter at the sight of him. He hulks a bar full of plates above his head, the veins in his arms standing out starkly from the strain it causes him. He's shirtless, every ripped abdominal muscle on proud display as he curls the weights in and drops them to the floor. I can actually feel the thud it makes. Roan plants his hands on hips and tilts his head back. He's fighting to catch his breath, but Lord help me, I'm all too pleased with the effort he's exerting.

You're a single-minded hussy, Saylor Radley.

His phone is lying a few feet between us, so I scoop it up and turn the volume down. Roan glances in my direction, that blank look still etched on his face as he takes me in. I'm quickly dismissed as he goes back to his workout. It hurts just as much as I expected it to, maybe even more. I never thought Roan would disregard me so easily. He lies back on the bench, furiously lifting the bar up and down. I clench my hands to ward off the tremble and step closer to the angry bear. I know how the saying goes, but I'm going to poke. It might not be my finest idea, but I hate that he's upset with me.

"Roan?" I call his name, knowing he can hear me, but he pretends he can't. He hops up like his ass is on fire and starts a brisk walk on the treadmill. I sigh and follow, determined to fix this. "Roan?" I try again, standing right beside him, so I know my voice isn't lost over the noise of the machine. A muscle in his jaw tics, but other than that, I get no response. Fed up with being iced out, I yank the emergency stop cord and let the cards fall where they may.

"Fuck," Roan swears, stumbling to catch his

footing as the belt comes to a halt. He steps on the sides and narrows his eyes at me. “Really?”

“I’ve always heard the bigger they are, the harder they fall. Thought I’d test the theory.” His lip twitches, like he’s fighting a smirk, but he wipes it away in the next breath.

“I could’ve been hurt, Saylor.” Roan climbs off, crossing his arms as he stares me down.

“You were going like two miles per hour. Do you really think I would’ve done that if I thought it might hurt you?” Roan cuts his gaze to the side, refusing to answer my question. And then I realize why.

“Wow,” I whisper hoarsely. Walking in on Kash and me this morning really messed him up. So much so, he's questioning if I’d intentionally cause him pain. There’s no way this is going to work. Five guys and one girl doesn’t make sense outside of a porno. The last thing I want is to feel cheap and used, but the look on Roan’s face tells me everything I need to know. He sees me differently now. Tears spring to my eyes so quickly, I don’t have time to fight them off. They fall in heavy rivulets, further scorching my heated cheeks.

“Goddamnit,” Roan curses, smacking the padded wall with his hand. “Please don’t cry. I didn’t mean it like that.”

“Really?” I hiccup around a sob. “Then how’d you mean it, Roan, because your silence was pretty fucking loud.” I cross my arms, subconsciously protecting myself from any more hurt he might cause. He looks wrecked by the action, his green eyes going glassy as he falls back a step.

"Fuck, baby girl." He doesn't give me a chance to pull away. Roan lifts me, bracing one arm beneath my butt while the other cups the back of my head. He's walking, but I don't look to see where we're going. I press my face against the base of his throat and close my eyes. Sweat coats his skin, but I couldn't care less. I cling to him, my fingers digging into his back as I murmur nonsensical apologies over and over again. He jogs up the stairs, taking the steps two at a time, but I still keep my eyes shut. A few seconds later, a door shuts behind us, quickly followed by another. Roan sets me on the counter, but I hold him tighter the second he tries to pull away.

"Saylor, look at me. Please fucking look at me," he begs, wrapping my hair in his fist. He gives it a gentle tug, forcing me to meet his gaze. "I'm so sorry. You did nothing wrong. I promise you; I didn't mean for my silence to be construed that way. I'm not upset about you and Kash." I give him a disbelieving look.

"Upset isn't the right word. Or maybe it is, but what I feel isn't aimed at *you*, Little Fighter. I don't think it's right to pass you around like this. You're too special, too…everything, Saylor, to be treated like you're not." Roan pulls a tissue from the box behind me and wipes the snot from my nose. I'll agonize over that later.

"Why would you think I'm being treated badly?" I ask, sincerely wondering if he's seen something that's made him question if I am or not.

"I don't think you are, but you might see it that

way one day. If we do this, it's basically agreeing to shared custody. How would you feel if you left Loch's bed, only to crawl into mine? Would you feel used, like you're being shuffled from one man to the next?" His words end on a frustrated growl.

"*Roan*," I softly say his name, placing my hand over his heart. "I don't have a clue what I'm doing. I've questioned the way I feel at least a couple hundred times. Want to know the conclusion I've come to? There is no right answer. For anything. Not the way I heal from Liam's abuse, or if and how we choose to explore our feelings. Whatever we decide, it's up to us. You've known these men a lot longer than I have, so you should know that they'd never treat me like I'm nothing but a warm body to pass the time with."

"I know." Roan sighs, resting his forehead on my shoulder. "I'd fucking kill them if they did."

"And it would always be my choice if I decided to share a bed with any of you. You can rest assured that if I'm in yours or theirs, it's because I want to be."

"You're right; I know that. I'm just terrified that this will end horribly and I'm gonna lose you. I'd rather have you the way we are now, than nothing at all." Roan rocks his head back and forth, like he's trying to banish the idea before it can fully form.

"You'd never lose me, Big Guy. Even if we crash and burn, I could never feel anything but love and gratitude towards you." He pulls back, searching for any hint of deception.

"You really mean that?" His hands grip my thighs, squeezing them gently as he waits for me to answer.

"I mean, you did sneak me a french-fry after busting me out of Hotel Hell. I think that links us for life, but what do I know?" I shrug, biting back a grin as his green eyes brighten.

"For life, huh? I like the sound of that."

"Good. But Roan?" I trace my finger along a thin scar beneath his chin. "If you decide you want more, then you need to be the one to take the risk on us. I'm already sure, but that doesn't mean you have to be. Our pages will align at some point, and the story will make a lot more sense, but until then, read at your own pace." I press a kiss to his chest, right over the rapid beat of his too pure heart. His eyes close as I slip off the vanity and edge around him. Just before I shut the door, I glance back, noting the white-knuckle grip he has on the counter.

"And take a shower, stinky-butt." Roan pushes away from the sink and turns the water on. His deep laugh follows me, and I smile, knowing we'll be okay. No matter what.

Chapter Thirty-Eight

Saylor

I stop short at finding Kash and Krew in a hushed conversation in the kitchen. I'm not sure what I should do—back away and leave them to it, or clear my throat and make myself known—but my choice is made for me when Kash jerks his head up and finds me creeping.

"Hi." I wave. *Wave.* "I didn't realize you were back." I take a few steps, watching the two of them as they attempt to school their expressions into something opposite of what they're actually feeling. It's not difficult for Krew. He's perfected that emotionless look he's so fond of. Kash, on the other hand, isn't quite as adept in the art of deception. Or maybe it's *me* he struggles to hide himself from.

"Just walked in. Want to raid Kade's bedroom and hide all of his underwear? I'm itching for some tomfoolery, Best Friend." Kash rubs his hands together like an evil cartoon villain. I raise an eyebrow, convinced they're hiding something. Kash always leans toward distraction, and his spur of the moment plan reeks of it.

"Oh, no. He's going to be so disappointed that he has to go commando," Krew deadpans, looking pointedly at me. "What a blow that'll be, brother." I snort, even though the sexual innuendo makes my skin flush.

"Alright, out with it." I cross my arms and tap my foot impatiently.

"We're not keeping secrets, Tink. Just trying to get the facts straight first." Krew laces our fingers together and spins me. I'm on his lap a second later, just like earlier in his office. Kash watches the two of us with an oddly pleased smile. "We haven't been able to get Loch on the phone, and he's the only one with a direct line to Denvers." I stiffen, knowing the only reason they'd need to contact the FBI agent is because of Liam.

"I'm sorry, sweetness." Kash kisses my forehead and slides a postcard from his back pocket. I take it, willing my hands to remain steady as I read it. '*Oklahoma*' is written in bold white letters across the front, proclaiming it '*The Sooner State*'. I close my eyes and flip it over, knowing the hard part has yet to come.

In blood red ink, Liam states '*I'm so close, I can almost taste you*'—followed by a string of coordinates. Bile rises up my throat, but I press my lips together, refusing to let the words of a psychopath hold so much weight. Maybe I should take them more seriously, considering the rapid deterioration of Liam's mental state, but I have something I didn't before. Five, to be exact, and they'll never let him have me.

"I sent an email to Denvers, letting him know that Loch was away on business but I needed to speak with him urgently," Krew tells me, placing his hand on my stomach once again. The contact is grounding, but I still jolt when Roan walks in. He picks up on my tense expression instantly.

"What's wrong?" He erases the distance between us, his eyes falling to the postcard in my hand. "*Fuck.*" I slide it over so he can read it for himself. "This motherfucker is testing my sanity," Roan spits, slamming it on the counter. I hate what that tiny rectangle represents. It's a death note, signed and delivered to taunt and punish me for hiding. It's the grave of an innocent woman who had the unfortunate luck of sharing features similar to mine, and being in the wrong place at the wrong time. Krew's phone rings, jarring me from my thoughts. I go to move, but he tilts us and slips it from his pocket.

"This is Krew," he answers, putting it on speaker and placing it between us.

"It's Denvers. What's going on?" It sounds like he's in a tunnel.

"We got another one. Can I send a picture to the number you're calling from?"

Denvers swears, his voice echoing just the slightest. "Yeah, send it on through. It might take me longer to get back with you, but I'll fill you in as soon as I can." Krew snaps a photo and attaches it to the message, watching the screen until it reads '*delivered*'.

"Understood."

"How's Saylor?" Denvers questions.

“Raisin’ Hell. Straight trouble, that one,” Roan chimes in with a smirk on his face. I glare and kick him in the shin. He hisses, rubbing at the battered spot, but we both know he barely felt it. His reaction is for my ego, not his.

“I’m fine. Thank you for asking,” I respond with a proper answer.

“Good. Don’t take any shit, sweetheart. Those boys could do with being dropped down a peg or two.” It's evident he's smiling.

“Men. We’re *men*, old man,” Kash snaps petulantly. “I took my vitamin gummies. I ate the nasty broccoli. These are man muscles, damnit.” I shake with silent laughter. This is not the time to be joking.

“Alright, big fella. You’re the manliest man there ever was.” Roan pats him on the back placatingly.

“Jesus, you guys are twisted,” Denvers comments. “Listen, keep your head up, Saylor. I know this isn’t easy. If you need anything, like a new place to live, send out the SOS and I’ll be there.” Their faces are perfect mirror images of displeasure. They obviously don’t appreciate his suggestion.

“Thank you for the time and work you’re putting into this. I’m sure it’s not easy for you either.” I can’t imagine chasing down one psycho, only for a new one to pop up right after. In Denvers' profession, it’s never really over. There’s always a new case, ready and waiting to be solved. “As for the roommate situation, all’s good on that front. If anything changes, my code word is Peter Parker." He laughs, but Kash looks bewildered.

"Take care. I'll be in touch soon." Denvers ends the call, starting the clock on our waiting game. I note the time on the stove is just past 2pm. It's going to be a long day.

"Peter Parker?" Kash mutters, more to himself than me.

"Yeah, he's the one they shine a bat signal in the sky for when someone needs saving, right?" I confuse the two superheroes on purpose, watching with glee as their brains implode. They've made me watch enough of those movies I couldn't possibly mix the two up, but it's fun to make them think that.

"I'm telling Loch," Kash gasps in horror. "He's going to be so disappointed in you." I snort, turning to look at Krew.

"Do you have a map of the U.S.?"

"I have a few, actually." He slides us off the stool and heads for his office. We follow, patiently waiting as he searches through a few cabinets. He unrolls the biggest one he has and spreads it across his desk.

"Got any tacks?" I ask. Krew hands me a new package, and I gesture to the wall to make sure it's okay for me to hang it. He nods, so I place a pin in each corner to secure it, then add three more—one to each of the states Liam murdered an innocent woman in. Stepping back, I scrutinize the zigzag his killing spree creates. It's not a straight path, or the easiest route to Florida, but why would he choose that when there's a chance the FBI might figure out his next move.

"I'm guessing there wasn't a postcard from Oklahoma in the Washington P.O. box?" I question absently, still staring at the map like the answer to Liam's whereabouts might miraculously pop out at me.

"No. I had it checked yesterday and nothing was there," Krew answers, confirming what I already knew.

He knows.

"Well, it's obvious he's on his way here. In a roundabout, path of most resistance sort of way," I mumble, a sad dose of acceptance washing over me. There's no point in pretending that isn't the case. Hoping it's just a coincidence will do nothing but leave us unprepared.

I study the states between Oklahoma and Florida. Considering we're in the panhandle, practically in Alabama, he could breach the state line easily. It wouldn't even take him a full day of driving. Liam had to have mailed the postcard a few days ago, which means he could very well be here by now. I doubt he stuck around the scene of his crime any longer than he had to. Getting caught this late in the game would enrage him, and it's not a risk he would take. I swallow thickly, my skin growing clammy at the thought of him being so close.

He could've seen Kash while he was out. It wouldn't be difficult for him to tail one of the guys home. Liam has proved repeatedly that he knows how to avoid detection. Does he know what they look like? Are their pictures listed on the SOTERIA website? *Oh*

God, I can't breathe. I spin around so quickly, I make myself dizzy, but I need to make sure the doors are locked. The back slider is always open.

"Baby girl." Roan appears in front of me, holding my chin between his finger and thumb. "Take a deep breath for me." I close my eyes until I have a better grip on my emotions. "That's good. Talk to us, Little Fighter. What's going on in that pretty head of yours?"

"Do we have enough food to last us through the week?" It's the first thing that leaves my mouth, the filter sorting my thoughts obviously going on a temporary hiatus.

"I panic over running out of snacks too. No need to be embarrassed, sweetness. It's a legitimate concern." Kash nods at me in solidarity. "Don't fret, though. I stocked up while I was out."

"Christ, that was dumbest shit you've ever said." Roan glares at him. "What's the real problem, Saylor?"

I take a deep breath, terrified to voice my worries, like that might give them life somehow. "There's a good chance Liam is already here. If we go off the previous timelines, his latest victim has been dead for three to five days. That's more than enough time for him to travel here. He might not know the exact location of the house, but he has us pinpointed to the general area."

"Technically, we're outside the city limits. Our physical address isn't in the same zip code as the post office," Krew explains, but it's still too close for comfort.

"Is there a chance he knows what any of you look like?" I glance at each of them. "Because all it'd take is him recognizing one of you while you're out and about. For all we know, he could've followed Kash home today. I'll never again underestimate that man's abilities. If he's aware that Lochlan and Havok are away…" Roan steadies me, lifting me up and setting me on Krew's desk.

"It'd be the perfect time for him to strike. He'd think that we're weaker, more exposed with less manpower." Krew nods in understanding. "He'd be wrong, Tink. Really fucking wrong." He speaks with conviction, not a trace of worry coming through.

"Remember what we told you; no one steps foot on this property without us knowing. We've got you." Roan cups my cheek, giving me a reassuring smile.

"And I'd never let a tail follow me home, sweetness. That's insulting." Kash sniffs haughtily. "Definitely something Kade would do, though." I huff a laugh, trying to let some of their confidence bleed into me.

"I know I'm safe with you guys, I just hate that we're separated right now. Every time that happens in a scary movie, someone always dies." I confess my ridiculous thoughts, because they're real to me.

"It won't be this way for much longer, Tink. As soon as they wrap things up in Nashville, they'll be on the next flight out." I nod at Krew, struggling to push back the sudden sting behind my eyes.

"Come on, let's turn in early. How's a movie in bed sound?" Roan picks me up like I weigh nothing, cradling me against his chest.

"Sounds good, actually." Krew squeezes my hand, and Kash kisses the tip of my nose on our way out. Instead of going to my room, Roan takes us to his.

"My sheets don't smell like you anymore. I don't like it," he huffs, tossing back the covers so we can slide beneath them. He keeps me close, my head on his chest with a leg curled over his. Roan powers on the TV mounted to his wall and starts an episode of *Friends*. It serves as background noise more than anything. My eyes grow heavy in no time, the stroke of his fingers through my hair lulling to me sleep far quicker than melatonin ever could.

"You don't stink anymore," I comment, slipping away to the sound of his throaty laugh.

I'm sleeping so soundly, it takes me a while to realize that my phone is ringing. It's on silent, but the continuous vibrating eventually wakes me. I blindly run my hand over the bed, but come up empty. Roan is no longer beside me, the place he was lying now cool to the touch. Cracking an eye open, I follow the glow of the screen lighting up. It cuts off just as I detach it from the charger, but starts right back up a second later. I don't bother looking to see who it is, knowing there's only two possible options.

"Hello?" My voice cracks as I answer.

"Love," Lochlan greets me on an exhale. Hearing him on the other end of the line helps clear the lingering drowsiness from my mind. "How are you, sweetheart?"

"I'm okay." It's not completely true, but his attention is needed elsewhere. I don't want to bother him, especially when he's several hours away and there's nothing he can do.

"Now give me the honest answer," he demands, his tone sweet but firm. I sigh, using my free hand to apply pressure to my eyes. *I will not cry*. "What is it, love?"

"I just miss you," I answer honestly, hoping he doesn't hear the hitch in my voice.

"God, Saylor," Lochlan groans, followed by a series of thuds. Like he's knocking his head against the wall in frustration. "I miss you too. So much, sweetheart. I'm sorry we're not there; we shouldn't have taken this case."

"It was the right thing to do," I sniffle. "Your lives can't stop because of me."

"Oh, I beg to differ. They ground to a halt." I laugh, but it's watery, a tell Lochlan picks up on immediately. "Are you crying?" I shake my head, even though he can't see me.

"The fuck?!" Havok snaps in the distance. "Give me the damn phone, Loch." A scuffle ensues, the two of them cursing each other to hell and back before Havok comes out the victor. He's out of breath, his quick footsteps sounding through the phone before a door slams. I smile, picturing the two of them fighting over who gets to talk to me. "What's wrong, baby?"

"Nothing," I promise. "Just missing you guys."

"We'll be home soon, Say." Havok grunts, his words coming out choppy as Lochlan bangs his fist against the door. "Fuck me, he's feisty. Don't let his size fool you." I snort, feeling lighter by the second as I listen in on their bickering.

"Open up, you cheeky fucker," Lochlan growls.

"Okay, okay. Calm your tits, *mate*." Havok unlocks the door to wherever he's barricaded himself, laughing as Lochlan stumbles in on a curse.

"Swear to Christ, Kade, I'll put you on princess duty for the next five years if you don't hand me the damn phone." Havok gasps dramatically.

"Well, I never," he sputters. "Did you hear that, Say?"

"What's that even mean?" I giggle.

"It's cruel and unusual punishment, baby. No one should have to babysit spoiled trust fund brats who fold after half a Smirnoff, vomit all over their thousand-dollar heels—which somehow becomes my fault—and end up needing an escort from the club because they turn into tantrum throwing toddlers."

"Sounds awful," I retort. "Guess you better be a good boy, then." That earns me an indignant scoff.

"I'll show you fucking good," Havok grumbles.

"Listen, love," Lochlan cuts in. "We need to head out soon. A few of Jasper's friends are supposed to be at the bar he went missing from. I want to watch them for a bit, see if we can pick up on any discord between them."

“Are they suspects?” I question, assuming they’d have been ruled out by now.

“Not sure yet, but we’re leaning that way,” Havok answers.

“I’m sorry we weren’t there today. I know it wasn't easy." Lochlan’s apology isn’t necessary, but there’s no point in telling him that. “It doesn’t change the damage he’s already done, but he *will* mess up, sweetheart. Liam may be keen and observant, but he’s not invincible.” I have no doubt that will happen. It’s the length of time it’s going to take that I have a problem with. Every day that passes puts another woman at risk.

“Get some sleep, Say. We’ll be in touch tomorrow,” Havok tacks on after several seconds of silence on my end.

“Be safe,” I tell them, wishing we didn’t have so many miles between us.

“Always, love.”

I reluctantly end the call, stretching across the bed to plug my phone back in. The time on the screen shows it’s just past eleven. I stare at the ceiling, the dim glow of the bathroom light providing just enough visibility to keep me from freaking out. My thoughts drift to the woman the Oklahoma authorities will undoubtedly find after following the GPS coordinates Liam left for us. Did she have a family? A husband or kids? So far, his victims have all been single. It’s a small mercy that he hasn’t widowed or orphaned anyone, but I wouldn’t put it past him.

After tossing and turning for a while, unable

to fall back asleep, I consider going in search of Roan. I interrupted his workout earlier, so there's a good chance he's in the gym. Eventually, my body gives in and I drift off. Sometime later, the bed dips, a thick arm snaking around my middle. I sigh at the contact, wedging my cold toes beneath the tree trunk he calls a leg. Roan hisses, but makes no move to push me away. With a satisfied smile on my face, I sink against him and pass back out.

Chapter Thirty-Nine

Saylor

"Little Fighter," Roan whispers, brushing my hair back so his breath tickles my ear. I groan and roll over, not ready to face another new day. "I've held Kash off for hours. I guarantee you, his wake-up call won't be nearly as pleasant."

"You call this pleasant?" I gripe. Roan chuckles, gathering my foot in his hand. He massages my arch, turning me into liquid. "You were saying?" I can picture the cocky smirk he's wearing without opening my eyes, but I do anyway, just to catch a glimpse of his dimples.

"What time is it?" I stretch, palming the nightstand for my phone.

"Almost lunch time," Roan answers, grinning at my surprise. "Did you know that you spread out like a starfish when you sleep?" He cocks his head to the side playfully.

"Are you implying that I hog the bed?"

"Hey, those are your words, baby girl, not

mine." Roan holds his hands up innocently.

"Guess I'll sleep somewhere else then." I shrug, scooting back so I can get up. I've barely made any progress when Roan's fingers wrap around my ankle and tug me back. I laugh, attempting to wiggle away, but it's no use. He climbs over me, gathering both of my hands in one of his as he grins down at me. "If anyone's a bed hog, it's you. You take up way more space than me. Look at how big you are!" My eyes roam his body, gesturing to the stark difference in our sizes.

"You think I'm huge?" Roan smirks, bringing his face closer to mine. I scrunch my nose, realizing the double meaning behind my words. Without conscious thought, my gaze drops between us. "Don't look at me like that, Saylor." Roan's rough voice cracks through the tension.

"Like what?" I glance back up, noting the hard set of his jaw.

"Like you're hungry." I don't respond. I told him yesterday that whatever we become, it'll be on his terms. But I won't hide the way he affects me. Since the night Havok touched me, my body has come to life. I'm done overthinking the way I feel. There's always been a thread of intimacy between us—even from the start, when Lochlan comforted me by simply holding my hand. We have too much bad on our plates to not embrace the good.

Roan trails a finger down my arm, watching my face the entire time for any miniscule reaction. My lips part when he veers off course and drags it between my breasts. His body weight grows heavier on top of me as he wedges himself between my thighs. It's almost too much, the width they have to stretch to accommodate him. Roan presses his thumb to my mouth, applying the slightest bit of pressure.

"Open," he demands hoarsely. I comply, wrapping my lips around him as he rocks against me. I can feel every hard inch, and it's a *lot* of inches. Our clothes leave very little to the imagination. Satisfied, he slips from my mouth and shoves my sweatshirt up. Tugging my bra aside, he circles my nipple with the wet pad of his thumb. My groan is met with another perfectly timed thrust. Slow and hard, the pressure hits my clit precisely, and I know it won't take much for me to finish. "One day, it's gonna be my cock in your mouth. I'll coat these gorgeous tits with my cum." He grinds down again, drawing a whimper from me as my eyes roll to the back of my head.

"Need you so bad I can't think straight," Roan confesses, our lips close enough to touch.

"Please," I beg. For what exactly, I'm not sure. He licks a path from my throat to my mouth. It's hot and dirty, making me even wetter. I chase the feeling, meeting him thrust for thrust, the rough pinch of my nipples doing me in as a cry rips free.

"Fuck, yes. Let me hear you, Little Fighter." I'm completely at his mercy when I come, trying to keep quiet but failing miserably. I moan his name, arching my back as I writhe beneath him. He doesn't stop, and I'm past the point of sensitive when he finally pulls away. I pant, struggling to peel my eyes open. Roan stares back at me, transfixed on my mouth. Not giving myself a chance to chicken out, I lean up and press my lips to his. I don't try to deepen the kiss, keenly aware that he just made me orgasm without ever initiating one. Maybe it's a different layer of intimacy for him.

I've barely pulled back when he dives in, parting my lips with his tongue as he forces his way in. Roan's kiss is different. It's invasive. Claiming. He steals my oxygen, making me scramble to gain the upper hand so I can break the hold he has on me. And even then, I'm yearning for more. We're both breathing heavy when the door bangs open, quickly followed by Kash flopping down beside us.

He bounces off the mattress, turning to his side so he can prop himself up on his elbow and rest his face on his palm. I lie there like a statue, thinking there's no way this is happening two days in a row. I doubt I can play it off, considering Kash knows exactly how I look when I'm flushed and sexually satisfied. And judging by the shit eating grin he's sporting, he's well aware of what we were up to.

"Cockblocker," Roan curses, dropping his face to my neck.

"Turnabout's fair play," Kash chides. "And I need some Saylor snuggles. You hogged her all night and half the day. God, you singletons are greedy. I mean, look at you, sweetness. Your only-child syndrome snagged you *five* boyfriends. A literal handful!" Kash cackles, all too pleased with himself for his ill-timed joke.

"Seems like we're sharing just fine to me," Roan comments.

"Yeah, but you're stingy. Now move, ogre."

Kash jabs him in the side, making Roan grunt and roll to his feet. He pulls me up just as Kash reaches out, ignoring the curses he slings. I'm led to the bathroom and handed a towel. Roan turns the shower on, then crowds me against the sink.

"Up," he whispers, sliding his hands beneath my top. I lift them, letting him undress me. Next to go are my leggings, until all I'm left in are my bra and panties. His eyes heat, taking in every detail of my mostly naked body. He's still hard, the outline of his cock vivid and unmistakable. I reach out, clueless as to what I'm doing, but wanting to make him feel good too. Roan stops me and takes a step back.

"Not today." He kisses the inside of my wrist. "If you touched me right now, we wouldn't be leaving this room anytime soon," he admits, dipping his hand between my legs. I choke on nothing but air as he traces the soaked center of my lacy boy-shorts. "That's mine, baby girl. I did that." I grip the counter as he brings his fingers to his mouth and licks away the evidence of my release. *Jesus, what have I gotten myself into?* I've gone from zero to sixty in the blink of an eye.

"Take your time. We'll be in the main room when you're done." Roan kisses the top of my head on his way out. I stand there, feeling shaken from the inside out—in a good way—as steam starts to build and fog the mirror. I strip down the rest of the way and step beneath the hot stream. I don't have any of my stuff in here, so I use Roan's soap, making sure to keep my hair to the side since I just washed it yesterday. I wrap myself in a towel, belatedly remembering that I have no clothes either.

Thankfully, someone left me a matching lounge set on the bed—complete with under garments.

My stomach growls as I head to the kitchen. I missed dinner, along with breakfast and lunch today, so it's no surprise that I'm starving. Kash snags me as I exit the hallway, twirling us in circles until he drops us both on a barstool. I slap my hands on the counter to make the room stop spinning, swearing retribution one day soon. Maybe I'll find his stash of suckers and hide them.

"Here, Tink." Krew slides a bowl of pasta in front of me. "Leftovers from dinner. Eat up." I shove a forkful in my mouth, groaning at the perfectly seasoned alfredo sauce. It's undignified how quickly I consume the entire helping. I contemplate licking the bowl clean, but I'm currently being watched like a zoo animal.

"Why was that so hot?" Kash mutters. I snort, shaking my head at him. A gust of wind would likely have the same effect. Roan elbows Krew, who's staring at me pensively.

"Right." Krew clears his throat and leans on the opposite counter. "We heard back from Denvers. Are you good to talk about this now?"

Meaning: A*m I going to lose the food I just ate?* My stomach has been in knots since reading that damn postcard. Digesting my lunch isn't going to change the sick feeling I get every time Liam delivers another taunt.

"Go ahead. I'll be fine," I answer, leaning on Kash for support. His fingers twine with mine, giving my hand a squeeze.

"Her name was Rina Movey. Twenty-three years old. She was in her last year of nursing school. The ME estimates she's been deceased for six days. The coordinates led to another green space by a river in Tulsa." I knew what they would find, but stupidly, a part of me hoped that Liam had deviated once again. He's never going to stop. Not until he has what he wants. I have little faith that the FBI will find him before he slaughters another woman.

"Don't take this on, Saylor. There's nothing we can do at this point. If there was a way to draw him out without risking you, we'd do it in a heartbeat. But Liam's crimes aren't yours to bear. He chose to kill those women, and I promise you he'll pay for it." Roan holds my gaze, delivering every word with confidence.

"I know. I just want this to be over. For the women who could unknowingly cross his path, but for me too. I won't be truly free until he's no longer a threat. I can't leave the house or run errands with you guys. I'm still a prisoner." Kash flinches, but my words aren't a representation of them. "I love being here. Love being with the five of you, but I want to go to a movie or out to dinner. It's not fair that he's still dictating my life. He's claimed enough of it."

"I swear, Best Friend…when Liam is taken care of, we'll go on a month-long vacation. Pick a place. Pick several, actually. Whatever you want, we'll make it happen." He places a kiss on my spine.

"Try not to dwell, Tink. I know it's a big ask, but I'm combing CCTV footage every chance I get. If he's within a hundred-mile radius, I'll find him." I smile at Krew, deciding it's best not to inquire about how he has that sort of access.

"Let's go watch the new Spider-Man movie downstairs. Ya know, the one with Peter Parker. Aka *Spider-Man*." Kash nudges me, but I feign indifference, pretending I have no idea what he's implying.

We shuffle down the steps and head towards the media room. While Roan pulls the movie up, the rest of us fix ourselves a snack. Or in Kash's case, *several* snacks. I claim a seat, pleasantly surprised when Krew snags the spot beside me. I smile and take a bite of the jerky stick he holds out for me. The movie sucks us in, making me laugh one minute and cry the next. I swear I hear a sniffle from Kash's side of the aisle. When the credits finally roll, I stand and stretch, stealing the last bit of Krew's drink. We clean up our mess, putting everything back the way we found it, and head upstairs.

"Batman's so cool," I sigh wistfully. "Peter's really lucky. Not all superheroes have such neat powers." The sound of the guys' footsteps fade behind me. I turn at the base of the stairs, pressing my lips together as I glance back at them. They're staring at me strangely, concern flooding their faces. Likely wondering what my IQ is.

"Maybe she needs to be powered off, then turned back on," Kash comments absently. "Or we could put her in some rice. I dropped my phone in the toilet once, and a bowl of rice fixed it right up." I can't help the laugh that tumbles out of me.

"Surely you guys don't think I'm that dense?" I narrow my eyes playfully.

"*Brat*," Kash swears as he lunges for me. I squeal and take off running up the steps. I trip, laughing as I catch myself on my hands before springing back up.

"Goddamnit, Kash. If she has one fucking bruise, I'm going to kick your ass!" Roan's shout follows me as I fling the door open and run for my life. I slide at the end of the hallway and hang a left. Instead of going to my room, like he'd expect me to, I head for Lochlan's office. I have just enough time to wedge myself beneath his desk when I hear Kash searching next door. I slap a hand over my mouth, knowing I'm liable to give myself away by laughing before he actually finds me.

"Come out, come out, wherever you are," Kash singsongs, striding into the room with purpose. "I'm going to spank that cute little ass of yours when I find you." I roll my eyes. "I can do this all day, sweetness. Didn't you know? Men love to hunt. Makes us all growly and shit." I snort, the faint noise escaping before I can rein it in. My heart thuds faster in the seconds that follow, waiting for the moment he discovers me.

"Gotcha!" Kash yanks me out and tosses me over his shoulder, swatting my butt as he carries me back to the living room, going on and on about reaping the fruits of his labor. "Caught myself a woman, brother." I'm dropped on the couch unceremoniously. Batting the hair from my face, I look up to see Kash grinning at me.

“Always figured you’d have to trick one. Run while you can, Tink.” Krew winks at me.

“My turn. You get to count this time,” Kash declares, sprinting off to find a place to hide. “Out loud, Best Friend!” Roan shakes his head, lifting me up and placing me on the island. He inspects my leg, turning it from side to side in search of an injury that doesn’t exist.

“I’m fine,” I huff, secretly loving his overprotective nature. Roan’s gaze clashes with mine, something dark and delicious simmering in those green depths.

“The only bruises I’ll ever be okay with are the ones you’ll get from kneeling at my feet while I feed you my cock.” He speaks so quietly, the dirty words are barely more than a whisper. I gape like a fish, struggling to come up with an appropriate response.

“Uh…what am I supposed to be counting to?” I croak, choosing avoidance for the time being.

“Eternity, for all I care. Leave the fucker waiting.” Roan kisses my forehead and joins Krew, who's focused on his phone, his eyebrows dipping together as he studies the screen. A sly smile tilts the corner of his mouth as he hands it off to Roan, who barks a laugh at whatever he sees. Deciding enough time has passed, I get to my feet so I can start my hunt for Kash. I’m sure he’ll take a normal game of hide-n-seek to the extreme. He’ll stay hid for hours just to spite me. I’m nearing the hallway when the door to the garage flies open. I feel my heart sink to my feet as I whirl around, expecting the absolute worst. My eyes widen at the unexpected sight, my brain refusing to believe it's real.

"I won rock-paper-scissors fair and square, you fucking wankstain," Lochlan snarls at Havok, gripping the hood of his jacket as he tries to run ahead of him. He's clotheslined by his own clothing, a comical gag escaping him as he stumbles back.

"What kind of fool believes a street kid who's been hustling hoity-toity assholes like you since he was in diapers?" Havok loosens the fabric from his neck, working it from side to side. "Men play fair when the stakes aren't that high. You must not find them enticing enough, brother." Havok shoves Lochlan as he goes to move around him, making him flip over one of the barstools. He lands on his back with a grunt. I cover my mouth with the edge of my top, trying to decide if this is all in good fun, or if someone's going to wind up with a broken nose.

"Take another step and I'll fire your ass," Lochlan spits, rolling to his side so he can peel himself off the floor. Havok just laughs, continuing his path to...me. They're fighting each other to get to *me*. I drop my shirt, smiling at the crazy idiot. In the next blink, his feet are swiped out from under him and he's lying face first on the ground. I gasp at the sound his head makes when it cracks against the tile.

"Always so cocky, Kade. Better luck next time, mate." Lochlan squats beside Havok and pats his cheek condescendingly. When he stands, his focus is lasered on me. He charges forward, donning the hottest smirk I've ever seen. His button up is only half tucked in after their altercation, his tie hanging limply, but the disheveled look is really working in his favor. I laugh when we collide, jumping up to wrap my arms and legs around him. He doesn't stop until we're closed behind the twins' office door and I'm pressed against it. Lochlan cups my cheeks and kisses me, both of us sighing at the taste of each other. He slips his tongue in, expertly stroking it with mine.

"Missed you, love," he pants roughly, keeping us as close as possible.

"I can't believe you're here." I smile, running my fingers through his hair. "How'd you guys pull that off?"

Lochlan shakes his head, peppering my neck with kisses. "We'll talk about it tomorrow. Tonight, I need to hold you." I nod, getting a sense that things didn't go that great in Tennessee.

"I need to check on Havok. Poor guy might have a concussion." I give Lochlan a pointed look.

"Please," he scoffs. "His head is way too hard." I stand firm, giving him that narrow-eyed glare Mom was so good at it. "Fine," Lochlan caves. "Stay with me tonight, though?" I agree and press my lips to his for another quick kiss. Dropping to my feet, I walk out to find Havok in the same spot we left him. He's on his back now, arms and legs spread, like he's been making snow angels. I kneel at the top of his head, leaning over so he can see me. When I meet his icy blue gaze, a sweet smile spreads across his handsome face.

"I tried to fight for you, Say." Havok winces, rubbing at the tender knot on his eyebrow. "Like I said, he's a feisty bastard." I bite back a laugh, remembering the way he went down like a sack of bricks.

"Spoiler—it's not a race," I whisper, giggling at the indignant face he makes.

"Say Baby, men turn everything into a race. We can be standing next to a stranger at the urinal and decide to see who can piss the quickest."

"Sounds like a bunch of macho idiocy to me. And now you're gonna have a nasty bruise on this pretty face." I run my thumb between his eyes, down his nose and over his lips. His blue orbs cross comically as he tries to follow the movement.

"You think I'm pretty?" Havok asks, a dopey grin curving his mouth.

"The prettiest." I lean down and kiss him, lost in our own little bubble on the floor. "Mmm, just like Batman," I joke, knowing the others are close by, and likely listening in. Havok jerks back, but he doesn't have anywhere to go since the tile is pretty immoveable. Roan doubles over laughing, his green eyes sparkling as I wink at him.

"MJ and Peter Parker share the upside-down kiss, love. That's Spider-Man, not Batman," Lochlan explains sweetly. His earnest expression is too much, and I lose it. I'm wiping tears from my eyes as Havok sits up and searches the room.

"Where's Kash?"

Shit.

Chapter Forty

Saylor

It took us the better part of an hour to find Kash last night. He was wedged beneath my bed with ear buds in, an explicit audiobook blaring through them—loud enough to be heard from several feet away—passed out with a sucker hanging from his mouth. Krew had to drag him out by his feet since we couldn't reach the headphones to turn the volume down. It startled him so much, he jolted awake and smacked his head on the metal frame of my bed. Now he and Havok have matching bruises.

I'm certain when Lochlan and I finally crashed it was just the two of us. I'd fallen asleep with my face buried in the base of his throat, breathing in the faint scent of his expensive cologne while he held me closely. But there's a distinct weight behind me now, even though I haven't moved once throughout the night and Lochlan and I are still chest to chest. I feel like I'm being baked alive from the amount of body heat being produced beneath the thin duvet covering us.

"Tell me, Kade," Lochlan grumbles sleepily.

"Does that feel like Saylor's leg to you?" Havok jerks his hand away, shaking it off like he can rid the appendage of cooties.

"Ew, fuck," he swears, disgust dripping from his scratchy voice. "Let's not make this a thing. I was unconscious, asshole."

"You shouldn't even be here," Lochlan huffs as he tugs me closer. "Never mind the fact that you so easily mistook my much bigger and hairier thigh for Saylor's. Pretty offensive, if you ask me." I keep quiet, too entertained by their back and forth to butt in.

"You know what I find offensive?" Havok whisper-yells, lifting his head up to punctuate his annoyance with a glare. "Your stupid fucking face." I barely suppress a snort. They've definitely been cooped up with one another for too long.

"*Get. Out.*"

"Make me," Havok taunts, connecting his foot with Lochlan's shin.

"Bloody hell," he grunts. I squeak when Lochlan tightens his hold and rolls me over his body, putting him beside Havok and me safely tucked on the other side, clear of the crossfire. Lochlan wraps his fingers around the metal slats of his headboard and starts shoving Havok from the bed with his feet. Popping my head up, I watch the two of them battle it out. Despite his best efforts, Havok still ends up in a heap on the floor. He lands with a curse. If they don't take a timeout from each other, he's going to be black and blue.

"Fine." Havok climbs to his feet, firing eye

daggers at the back of Lochlan's head. "One hour, Say. That's all you get before I break back in and steal you." He leans over, using the side of Lochlan's face as support, and pecks me on the mouth. He adds a little more oomph to closing the door than he needs to, but I just roll my eyes. I have no idea who decided that women should be labeled the '*dramatic*' gender, but they've clearly never been in the presence of these five men. Lochlan turns, his honey-colored gaze going soft at the sight of me.

"Good morning, love." He smiles, tucking a strand of hair behind my ear.

"Hi." I stare unabashedly, taking in the relaxed state he's in. It's scarce for Lochlan to let the weight of responsibility fall to the wayside, even for a little while. But he's fully present at the moment, looking adorably rumpled from sleep. A crease dents his cheek from where he had it pressed against his pillow all night. I trace it lightly, loving the way his eyes close from the contact. Lochlan grabs my hand and brings it to his mouth. Placing a kiss on the tip of each finger, he trails his lips over my wrist, down to the bend of my arm, then back again.

I twine my hand with his and hug it to my chest, allowing my eyes to wander around the room. I'd been too tired to take notice of much last night, but with the sun shining through his window, I'm able to make out a lot more of the space. His style matches the rest of the house—sleek and modern. Aside from his bed, the only other furniture in the room is a dresser and single nightstand. There's not an ounce of clutter. I'd be willing to bet his clothes are folded perfectly, each piece in its respective spot, and the drawer of his nightstand is organized to a T. If I didn't know Lochlan, I'd think his personal space was cold and sterile. But that's not it at all. He just likes for things to be nice and neat.

"Tell me something I don't know." I grin playfully.

"Like what, sweetheart?"

"Well, I know you were born and raised in Upstate New York. Mostly. You spent your summers in London with your Nan. I've heard how you met the guys. That the reason you got into the business of private investigation and security is because of your savior complex. So, what don't I know?"

"Honestly, love, that about covers it." Lochlan toys with the strap of my tank top. "I have no tragic backstory that shaped me into the man I am today. No disadvantaged upbringing that I had to overcome. I grew up with wealth, but lacked attention and affection. My parents were indifferent, too busy climbing the corporate ladder to be bothered with raising a child. Despite that, I hold no resentment towards them. They did the best they could with their lack of emotionally availability. I never wanted for anything, received the best education, and I got to visit my Nan for a couple of months every year. If anything, I learned exactly what not to do as a parent one day."

I want to argue that his childhood *was* kind of tragic. I can vividly picture a small version of the man before me, playing all alone in some stuffy old mansion with no one to talk to or pass the time with. It's a testament to his Nan that he's as well adjusted as he is. I'm grateful that he had someone to love him, even though their time together was short. Lochlan's right—he'd never be that kind of father. Any future kid of his wouldn't have to go a single day without knowing how loved they are.

"Do you still talk to them?" I ask, curious if they have a better relationship now that Lochlan's an adult.

"Once or twice a year. Usually on my birthday or Christmas." He shakes his head at my tight expression. "They have their lives, and I have mine, love. Don't pity me for something I have no remorse over. My family is right here—those four assholes and you." I melt, dropping my head to his chest with a sigh.

"I've been wondering," I mumble, pulling back slightly so that my words aren't muffled. "Why SOTERIA? Is it something you came up with, or was it a joint effort?"

"SOTERIA is the goddess of protection," Lochlan reluctantly answers, a hint of pink tinting his cheeks. "My younger self was a nerd." He shrugs, playing off his embarrassment.

"Was?" I cock an eyebrow at him. Glaring playfully, he rolls us, lifting me easily so I straddle his thighs.

"Am I too tame for you, sweetheart?" Lochlan holds me in place, his fingers flexing against my hips as he bites his lip.

"Not at all," I answer truthfully, reaching over

to grab his glasses off the nightstand. I slide them on him, in awe of how handsome he is. "I happen to like the nerdy look." Lochlan makes a pleased sound, using his hold on me to his advantage. He drags me closer, right over his erection, slipping a hand to the back of my neck as his mouth takes mine in a sweet kiss. It's a complete juxtaposition to the arousal pulsing between us. When he pulls away, I lean in for more, subconsciously chasing the taste of him.

Lochlan chuckles, gripping my butt in both of his hands as he stands and walks us to the bathroom. He places me on the vanity between his two sinks and hands me a new toothbrush. I smile gratefully, sneaking glances at his shirtless torso every few seconds. He has no tattoos or scars, his skin smooth and flawless. He spits, turning to face me with an amused glint in his eyes as he props his hip against the counter. I scrunch my nose and go back to brushing. After rinsing my side out, I drop my toothbrush in the holder, claiming the spot beside his, and turn my attention to Lochlan.

"What happened in Nashville?" I ask, watching as he pulls a fresh towel from the linen closet and starts the shower.

"A mess that I wish I'd caught onto sooner," Lochlan sighs heavily. "The night Jasper went missing, he'd taken laced drugs without realizing it. A friend of his—another guy in their group—was the one that provided them. Along with their supplier, two others were aware that something wasn't right. They caught up with Jasper before he made it too far from the bar, but he started seizing. They panicked, forgoing 911 and basic human decency, and let the kid die. They dropped him in the closest trash can and went back to partying. Later that night, the three of them retrieved his body and dumped it a few hours away, closer to the mountains."

"Jesus." I shake my head, disgusted by the cruelty. "How could they do that to someone, much less a friend?"

"They're cowards. The moment Jasper stopped breathing, they had a choice to make. They chose self-preservation over doing the right thing. You'd be surprised by how many people would respond the same way when backed into a corner. Morality goes flying out the window, and that '*every man for himself*' mentality clicks into place. Thankfully, at least one of them felt remorse and caved after being questioned. Jasper's parents have a modicum of closure for the time being, but they'll get their day in court."

"I'm sorry." I step forward and wrap my arms around him. "I know it's not the ending any of you hoped for, but I'm sure his family appreciates everything you did to get to the bottom of it."

"It's okay, love. Not every case pans out the way we'd like." Lochlan squeezes me, rocking us from side to side as the room grows muggy. He kisses my forehead, pushing back to slide his sweats off. I blink furiously, shocked that he stripped down so casually, and without an ounce of warning. Lochlan smirks, erasing the space between us until our chests are flush.

"For the record, you can stare at me anytime

you'd like." Lochlan traces my mouth with his thumb. "I'm yours, sweetheart. Any time, any place." He pulls away without another word, closing himself behind the glass door of his shower. I have no idea how much time passes as I fixate on the distorted image of his naked body, but his teasing voice cuts through the spell he put me under.

"Your hour's almost up, love. If Kade barges in and joins us, we'll be broaching an entirely different type of sharing." My mind derails at the image of what he's insinuating. Try as I might, words refuse to form. I turn and flee from the room, deciding my lack of response is better than anything that could have left my mouth. I'm ashamed for even *thinking* what was on the tip of my tongue. I make it to the safety of my own room without interruption, breathing a sigh of relief as I lean against the door.

I'm being ridiculous. Shame and insecurity have no place here if we want this to work. Eventually, we'll need to sit down and establish some boundaries. Determine what we're comfortable with and what's a no-go. It makes me anxious just thinking about the conversations we need to have, but it can't be avoided forever. What I'd really like right now is a hot bath. I peel my pajamas off and turn the water to the highest temperature I can tolerate. After going through the bath bombs Kash bought me, I choose a floral scent and drop it in. My limbs turn to jelly as I sink inside the tub. With my eyes closed, I tilt my head back and hum along to the song playing on my phone.

"Hey, pretty girl." I startle so badly, it's a wonder I don't drown. My hand flies out to the grip the side of the bathtub, but lands on a firm chest instead. I cough, attempting to clear my lungs of water. I glare at Havok, but the innocent smile he gives me all but erases my annoyance. "Slide up, baby. I'm comin' in." I avert my gaze as he strips his clothes off, edging forward so he'll have some space to slip in behind me. I doubt he cares about privacy, but I give it to him anyway. For some reason, my stomach dips with nerves.

"Shit, that's hot," Havok hisses, ripping his foot back from the water. "What the hell, Say?"

"Don't be a baby," I tease. "It feels nice once you're in."

"Yeah, because you've burnt all your nerve endings to a crisp, and can't feel yourself being boiled alive." His sarcasm makes me smile. It takes at least five more tries before Havok fully submerges himself. "Oh, fuck. *My dick*. My dick burns, Say. It's on fire." I toss my head back on a laugh.

"Not funny," Havok growls, wrapping his arm around my waist to jerk me back. Water sloshes over the edge, soaking my bathmat and the floor. I settle against him, letting my head rest on his shoulder. Havok runs his hand up my stomach, between the valley of my breasts, before stopping at the base of throat. He cups my neck, applying the slightest bit of pressure. I tilt my face up, our blue gazes clashing with a potent mixture of want and love. "I missed you, baby."

"I missed you too." I exhale, closing my eyes as he trails kisses along my jaw. Havok slides his legs over mine, using their weight to push my thighs apart. His free hand tweaks my nipple as he grazes my ear with his teeth. I groan, rocking my hips against him. When he slips his fingers inside of me, I jolt from the sudden invasion.

"You're okay," Havok whispers, licking the pulse point on my neck. "It's just me." I relax, sighing at the first stroke of my clit. He takes me right to the edge before ever moving his fingers. He's being gentle, going nice and slow, but it's too drawn out.

"More," I plead.

"How, baby?" Havok groans. "You want it faster?" He speeds up, teasing me with short, quick strokes. "Or maybe harder?" His fingers slam inside of me, his palm grinding against my clit. I shatter, burying my face in his neck as I sob his name. "Jesus." Havok rips me from the water and spins me around. I straddle his lap, dropping my head back on a moan as he wraps his mouth around my nipple. His fingers grip my ass as I rock forward, sliding myself over the hard length of his cock. Havok clenches his eyes shut, muttering curses as I speed up. But all I can think of is *more*. I want him. All of him. I tilt my hips, aligning us just right, then drop back down. I whimper at the sting, but my eyes never stray from Havok's.

"Fuck," he swears, gripping me tightly to keep me from moving. His icy gaze is filled with worry. "You okay?" He takes a shaky breath, staring at me intently. I nod, biting my lip as I wait for him to realize that this isn't my first time. It doesn't take long. A million emotions flit across his face.

"Kash?" he questions, giving no clue if he's pissed or hurt.

"I'm sorry," I whisper, wishing we had this talk earlier. I should've been honest before taking it this far.

"I'm not upset, baby." Havok kisses me tenderly. "A little envious, but not upset." He frames my face with his hands and rests our foreheads together. "Right now, I'm trying to keep myself from fucking you on the floor like a savage. Your tight little pussy is choking my cock. Feels so good, Say." He sounds tortured, but I'm not sure what the problem is.

"Yes." I nod like a bobblehead. "*That.* Let's do that, please." Havok snaps his head up, his eyes wide and crazed.

"You want me to fuck you, baby?" Another nod from me. "Hold on." I've barely had a chance to tighten my arms and legs around him before he pushes to his feet. Water drips from our bodies as he sets me on the counter, making me gasp from the coolness. Or maybe it's the way his cock jumps, hitting nerves I never even knew I had. "If it's too much, tell me." I dig my heels into the backs of his thighs instead of responding. He slides out, leaving just the tip in, then thrusts forward. He groans, his gaze transfixed on the way I'm stretched around him.

"Look how pretty, Say." Havok trails a finger through the wetness coating his cock, groaning as he pops it in his mouth. He pulls out and yanks me from the counter, then turns me so I'm facing the mirror and he's standing behind me. "Put your hands here."

He lays them by the sink. "Now bend over and tilt your ass back. Good. Just like that." My legs tremble as he lines himself up and eases in. The angle makes it seem like he'll never fit. Reflexively, I rise to my tiptoes to escape the bite of pain.

"Relax. I've got you." Havok surges in deeper, banding his arm across my front to keep me still. It steals the air from my lungs. I swear he's touching organs he shouldn't be. "Hang on, baby. I promise to make it better." He pulls out, and pushes back in. Over and over. Until the slight discomfort mixes with pleasure and makes me go limp. "That's it." He gathers my hair and wraps it around his fist. With a tug, he pulls me till I'm upright. "Watch. I want you to see who's fucking you." My eyes meet Havok's in the mirror. The image of us, sweaty and lost in one another, will star in every fantasy I have going forward.

"It's my cock your pussy is clenching." He slams back in. "My finger that's teasing your clit." He pinches it, making me whimper. "And it'll be my name you scream when you come." I moan, pushing back to meet his thrusts. With one hand between my thighs and the other wrapped around my throat, I cry his name as wave after wave of pleasure rocks through me. My legs give out, but Havok takes my weight, bending me at the waist so he can fuck me in earnest. "God, baby. Fuck. Fuck. *Fuck.*" At the last second, he pulls out and finishes on my back.

Shit.

"We didn't use a condom," I blurt, stumbling to the side as I spin to face him. He steadies me, looking just as wrung out as me.

"I know, Say. That's why I pulled out." He drops his head back as he works to catch his breath. "I've never went without one. I got carried away, but I swear it won't happen again. I'm sorry, baby." I'm shaking my head before he's even finished speaking.

"I'm the one who practically accosted you without even asking if you wanted to have sex." Havok looks at me like I've lost my mind.

"The answer is always yes. I'll never *not* want to have sex with you, pretty girl." He takes my hand and walks us to the shower. "And I specifically remember telling you that if you want something, you should take it." Havok pulls us beneath the water before it's had time to heat up. I screech, scrambling back to avoid the spray, but he holds me tighter. "That's payback for making me sit in lava." He smiles down at me, pushing wet strands of hair from my face. God, he's gorgeous. I love the way our bodies look pressed together, the contrast of his tattoos against my unmarked flesh. It's still surreal, to have the attention of Havok McKade in a good way. I can't imagine not knowing him now.

"I love you," I voice softly, resting my chin on his chest. The grin that splits his face leaves me a little breathless.

"I love you so much, Say. The thoughts I have..." he trails off and shakes his head. "They'd scare you, baby. If you knew how gone I truly was, you'd run for the hills." I roll my eyes, knowing there's not a thing he could say that'd make me want to leave him. He turns me, pours my shampoo in his hand, and starts working it through my hair. I press my lips together, sending up a silent thank you to whoever granted me a second chance with this man. After he's washed my entire body, I take over and treat him to the same exquisite torture.

My eyes are heavy by the time Havok shuts the water off and wraps me in a towel. He doesn't bother dressing us. Once we're dry, he carries me to bed and burrows against me, cocooning us beneath my heavy comforter. His lips touch mine, barely making contact as he whispers, "Sleep, pretty girl."

And I do.

Chapter Forty-One

Krew

I can't take stop staring at Saylor. She's perched on Ro's lap, slurping down a bowl of cereal as he twirls a strand of her long blonde hair around his finger. She spent yesterday with Kade, and if either of them thinks they were discreet, they need to have their hearing checked. Like a true fucking creep, I stood outside her door, listening as he railed her into next week. I know she fucked my brother too. I'm happy for him. I'm sure he made it sweet and memorable.

They both deserved to have their first times be with someone they care about. Unlike me, Kash recoiled at the idea of sharing his body with anyone after having gone through what we did. He needs a connection that goes past physical attraction. It's no wonder Saylor was the one to evoke that sort of response from him. I've never seen my twin more enraptured by anyone than he is by that blue-eyed girl.

Me, on the other hand? I fucked the first woman who let me. I was still a kid when I lost my virginity. Hell, my nuts had barely dropped, but that didn't stop me. She was the first in a long line of many. I'd fuck them and walk, never going back for seconds. I dealt with my trauma the way I saw fit. Sex became an escape I craved. Archie Sellers didn't exist during the space of time I'd get lost in a warm body. His barbed words evaporated. I was in control, choosing if and when anything happened, on my own goddamn terms. But at the end of the day, those women meant nothing.

I'd still have to go home and face the Devil. Spend night after night, barely getting four hours of sleep so I could keep watch over Kash. It stopped working after a while, and all I was left with was a shit ton of self-loathing, and the ability to fuck. *Well.* I dipped my toes into every sexual fantasy I could, trying to chase the high I felt in the beginning, but it never came back. My past has been the sole reason I've kept my hands off of Tink. The appetite I've built isn't bland by a long shot. I'd never dream of hurting her, but a part of me craves the day she'll cry for me.

I've yet to even kiss her, knowing damn well the moment I do, it's going to be a free for all. If I tasted her, I wouldn't be able to stop at just her mouth. I'd convinced myself to give Saylor some time, but the sounds she made yesterday have me rethinking her need for an adjustment period. Kade didn't go easy, and watching her wince as she sat down earlier made my cock twitch. One day soon, my restraint's going to snap, and I'll break her in the best way possible.

"Why was this in my nightstand?" Loch enters the kitchen, holding up a value-sized pack of condoms. "I swear they aren't mine, love." He shoots a faint look of panic in Saylor's direction.

"I stocked up when I went to town on Sunday. You're welcome." Kash smirks. "Figured I should replace the one I stole from Kade." My twin shrugs, tilting his head back to drop some Skittles in his mouth.

Saylor chokes on a bite of Cocoa Puffs, coughing so hard her eyes begin to water. I pat her on the back, fighting to keep my expression neutral. She looks to Kade, the two of them sharing a silent conversation that's easily deciphered. *The silver-haired fuck is about to rage.* He takes a deep breath, and cracks his neck from side to side.

"You took her virginity with *my* condom?!" Kade tosses his fork at Kash, pegging him square in the face.

"Fucking *ow*." My brother glares, rubbing at the red mark on his forehead. "It's not like you were using it. The only action you've gotten lately is from your own hand. And like the gentleman I am, I made sure to let our girl know that you're a *reformed* manwhore, and the rubber was from your fuckboy days."

"Actually, my dick was nice and sated as of yesterday," Kade retorts, leaning back with his arms crossed, a proud grin quirking his mouth.

What a fucking idiot.

"How about now?" Saylor dumps her glass of ice water in Kade's lap, drenching the crotch of his gym shorts. "Is your dick still good?" Her eyes are filled with fire as she hands him his ass. It's the hottest thing I've ever seen. Kade jolts back so quickly, he loses his balance, landing roughly on the hard floor. The wind gets knocked out of him, making me grin at the stupid noise he makes.

"Shiiiiiiiit," Kade groans. "I deserved that."

"Yes, you did," Tink growls adorably, standing to help the asshole to his feet. If I were her, I'd let him struggle. "Now you'll have another bruise, you big butthole." She grunts, tugging on his outstretched hand. Saylor's come so fucking far, especially when it comes to prioritizing her own wants and needs, but she'll always have a softness to her. Her heart's too big to act maliciously, and even when she's slightly aggressive, she can't help but soothe the sting of her words or actions.

"That was Eighth-Grade-Havok. And in case you're wondering, he's still an asshole." Saylor speaks quietly, but the conviction in her words makes my chest fill with pride. Kade does a decent job of masking his flinch, but the hit lands hard. The way it was intended to.

"I'm sorry, Say. That was too far." Her eyes close as she nods. "If it's any consolation, I've got some major shrinkage going on. I could whip it out, like a tit for tat situation. I'd definitely be embarrassed." Saylor slaps a hand over Kade's mouth, wisely trapping any remaining stupidity he was preparing to spew. She goes easily when he wraps his arms around her. Tink's on his lap, making no move to go anywhere, but Kade holds her tightly, like he's terrified she might run away.

"Since we're all here, I think we should go

ahead and get this out of the way," Loch starts, pulling out a chair so he can take a seat. "Things have obviously progressed, so I'm going to assume that we're all on board with giving this a go. First and foremost, we need to hash out limits and define what this is."

"Explain," Ro demands, in that gruff, no-nonsense tone of his.

"Sharing, for one. We need to figure out who is and isn't okay with what." Kash's eyebrows dip as he listens to Loch.

"Uh, I thought that part was settled?" *Oh, big brother.*

"So fucking innocent." I ruffle Kash's hair, grinning as he swats my hand away. "What Loch is trying to say, is are we comfortable with more than one partner at a time? And before any of us comment, that question is pointless until Saylor has given her answer." I look at Tink, my eyes tracking the blush that spreads from her neck to her cheeks. She looks to the floor, like it might open up and save her. But there's no rescue on the way. If she's grown enough to fuck, she can damn well talk about it.

"There's no room for shyness, Tink. You have to communicate." I hold her gaze, watching closely for the moment she lets go and squares her shoulders. I've witnessed the switch a time or two, and it never disappoints. I lift my chin in approval, eager for the day she submits so easily while tied to my bed.

"I'm not opposed to it, but I'm not saying yes either. I think something like that needs to develop naturally. If the moment arises and we're all okay with exploring it, I don't see the problem. We'll only go as far as everyone's comfortable with." Saylor exhales loudly, twisting her fingers together as she boldly gives us her opinion on the matter. Fuck I want to kiss her.

"It's gonna be a no for me." Ro shakes his head profusely. "I don't have a problem with seeing you guys kiss or hug her, but that's my limit. My dick won't be going anywhere near one of yours, and I damn sure don't want to watch my girlfriend have sex with someone else. As far as I'm concerned, Saylor has five, individual relationships. What she decides to do with each of you is your business. I don't need specifics." He shifts uncomfortably, darting his gaze to Tink before focusing elsewhere.

"That's understandable," I respond with a nod. "The best thing we can do is keep an open mind, but I agree. For now, we should respect each other's time and space with Saylor. Keep the PDA to a minimum."

"I'm down for exploration," Kade comments, placing a kiss on her shoulder.

"Same," I agree, looking at my twin expectantly. I can see the wheels turning, the image of Saylor splayed out between us flashing through his mind. It wars with the part of him that wants her all to himself, but he's most definitely intrigued.

"Maybe," Kash shrugs. I give my attention to Loch, waiting to see where he stands on the subject.

"I'm with Saylor. It'd have to be a right time, right place sort of thing."

"I think everything else can be discussed with Tink, one on one." My phone vibrates, so I pull it out, squinting at the alert that just came through.

"Thank fuck," Ro sighs in relief. Poor bastard's gonna have a rough time adjusting. "Let me be perfectly clear, though. If any of you embarrass her again by discussing personal shit, acting like this is a fucking game to see who can score first or how often, I'll rip your dicks off and shove them down your throats." His tone is deadly, leaving no doubts about his follow-through.

"That goes without saying." Loch stands, effectively ending the conversation. As everyone scatters to go about their day, I watch Tink as she heads for the kitchen. Her steps are measured, like she's in a daze. When it's just the two of us, I join her, leaning back to observe her stilted movements as she mixes up a glass of chocolate milk. When she turns to face me, I grab her and drop her on the counter. Her legs part, allowing me space to stand between them.

"You're freaking out," I state, knowing for a fact that her pretty little head is overrun with anxiety.

"What makes you say that?" Even her voice has shifted, sounding meek and uncertain. That'd be a dead giveaway if it wasn't so obvious by simply looking at her.

"For one, you're acting like a zombie. And this." I point to her cup. "You drink chocolate milk for comfort." Saylor sighs, not bothering to argue with my assessment.

"Did we really just have a family meeting to lay

out the ground rules for sex?” She winces, staring at a spot behind me. I place a finger beneath her chin, and lift her gaze to mine.

“Yes,” I answer bluntly. “This is serious. You aren’t a fleeting interest, or a way to pass the time. Relationships are hard enough with just two people involved, but we have six sets of feelings on the line. A lot can go wrong here. The least we can do is brave the tough conversations, regardless of how uncomfortable they are, if it will help avoid unnecessary strain in the long run.”

“You’re right,” Tink agrees, her posture loosening as we openly speak about the matter. “I want this to work. It’s weird to talk about, though. I’ve never been a very outspoken person, and it’s strange to have sex discussed so flippantly." Even now, when it’s just the two of us, she can't help but squirm under the attention.

“Oh, Tink.” I stroke the bend of her thighs, toying with the crease of her panties. “You’re far more vocal than you think. Are you aware of how loud you get when you come?” Her breath hitches. “I listened. Heard every sound you made. He must have fucked you good, princess. But when I take you, I plan to make you beg. First, for me to give your body what it needs after being kept on edge for so long. Then, you’ll beg me to stop. Because one orgasm won’t be enough for me, Tink. I won’t even let you come down before I’m right back at it. You’ll give me one after another, until I’ve wrung your body out so thoroughly, your legs shake and tears stain your cheeks.

"After that, I’ll lick your cunt clean, lapping up

every drop. I earned it, after all. I'll take my time, knowing you're too exhausted to stop me. I'm going to own you, Saylor. Make you crave me the way I crave you. And the best part?" I slip my thumbs beneath her shorts, gliding one over the soaked fabric covering her pussy. "You want it. You're weeping for my cock, aren't you?" Her eyes flutter as she sways unsteadily. "Answer me, Tink."

"Yes," she whispers, darting her gaze around the room to make sure no one else is witnessing the moment her downfall begins. She can deny it all day long, but Saylor's kinky as fuck. You don't entertain a relationship with five different men if you want plain and boring. That brazen, take-what-I-want side of her might be repressed by a heavy coat of trauma, but she's climbing free of it.

"You certainly fucking do. Now, *own it*." I pull my hands free and crudely rub her wetness on that pouty mouth of hers. Saylor jerks back, wearing a stunned expression, but I don't give her the opportunity to overthink. I lick my tongue across her lips, groaning when she responds and does the same. The slight brush makes my balls tighten, desperate for release. "Every day, Tink. A touch here...a touch there. I'm going to edge you to the point of pain. Let's see how long you last." I wink, watching the hunger I created catch fire and simmer in those pretty blue eyes.

I take off towards the garage, leaving Saylor wet and needy without a backward glance. I plan to stoke that flame, feed it till it's blazing and she's burning up with need. To do that, I have to get the hell away from her. I can taste her pussy on my lips and it's making me crazy. The door slams behind me as I jog down the steps. Placing my hand on the scanner, I wait for the lift to open. I'm staring at the alert I got earlier when someone comes in behind me. Looking back, I'm slightly disappointed to find Loch approaching. A part of me hoped it was Tink chasing me down, begging me to finish what I started.

"What's going on?" he questions, gesturing to the phone in my hand.

"Cam 2 went offline. I need to check it out." I start walking, not the least bit surprised when Loch follows beside me. We have surveillance on the front and back side of our property, as well as inside and outside of the house. Cams 1 and 2 are positioned at the front two corners, on each side of the gate, while 3 and 4 capture the back two corners near the beach. 5 and 6 record the garage and deck area, with 7 and 8 posted inside—one on the main room, and the other downstairs. It's not often we have a glitch, but it does happen from time to time.

"Don't push her too far, Krew." I whip my head to the side, an angry glare at the ready. "Wipe that pissy look off your face. You know damn well I have every right to be concerned." I clench my jaw, wishing I had a leg to stand on, but he makes a valid point. At my lowest, Loch had to pull me from a three-day fuck fest with a woman whose name I never bothered asking. She was willing and ready—my only two requirements. Anything past that was inconsequential. When Loch kicked in our dingy hotel door, he saw a lot more than just my over-sexed dick.

He might've even blushed.

The worst part of that whole experience was going home to Kash, who'd lost his ever-loving shit while I was out plundering random pussy. I'll never forget the state he was in, or the fact he regressed tremendously from my carelessness. It was years ago, not long after we sent Archie to prison. My manic spiral came in the form of regret, wishing we had handled our stepfather differently. Him being behind bars had done little to satisfy my need for vengeance. That didn't come until later. I've often wondered if Loch or the others know about the lengths I've gone to, to make sure that piece of shit suffers.

"I'd never hurt her. And despite what the rest of you might think, she isn't made of glass." I shove my hands in my pockets and quicken my steps.

"I know that. She's tough as fucking nails. But I wouldn't be bringing this up if I didn't have a reason to. I won't say any more about it because I trust you, just remember that she does too." It takes a lot of fucking effort to keep my fist from rearranging his pretty boy face. Loch might mean well, but he doesn't have the slightest clue about the shit I like, or how that trust he's trying to weaponize and use against me translates to the bedroom. When Tink gives me free reign of her sweet little body, she's going to *want* what I'll do to her. Because she trusts me implicitly.

I'm saved from responding when we come to a stop at the concrete post where Cam 2 is anchored. I frown, tilting my head to the side so I can assess the damage from all angles. The lens is cracked and hanging by a thread. I look around, trying to figure out what the hell happened.

"Goddamnit," Loch swears, leaning over the barrier as he stares at something on the ground. I heft myself up, taking in the partially shredded frisbee. Piecing shit together, I glance across the street to see the grass is freshly mowed.

"Since when does the county mow this far out?" I question, dropping back to my feet.

"Never," Loch answers. "I'll make a few calls. Maybe someone bought the lot without us realizing." I snort. *Not fucking likely*. I make it my business to know who does what, and when they do it. If we had new neighbors, I would have known about it by now. I remove the damaged camera, grateful we keep a few extras on hand, just in case. By the time we go retrieve a new one, get it set up and resecured, half the damn day is gone.

Saylor's sequestered in Loch's office, having her weekly meeting with Danielle, so we head to mine and Kash's. I'm shocked to find him there, spinning himself in circles. He's taken full advantage of the downtime we've had lately, but he deserves it.

"Little brother," Kash coos, chomping on a sucker. I kick his chair aside and drop down, choosing to ignore his petty endearment. Wiggling my mouse to wake the monitor back up, I run the new camera to make sure everything's working properly. The angle looked fine from my phone, but it never hurts to double check. Once I've cleared it, I rewind the feed from earlier, stopping a few minutes before it went out. After explaining to Kash what happened, the three of us sit back and play the recording.

It doesn't take long for the culprit to make an appearance. Someone clearly went for a drunken joyride. I watch in amusement as a heavyset man tears through the brush across the street on a rusted lawnmower. It's going way faster than it should, likely from being altered. He has a bandana wrapped around his bald head, wearing cut-off blue jeans that are far too short for someone with a nut-sack, and nary a shirt in sight. There's a beer balanced precariously in one hand, while he uses the other to steer. However, the pièce de résistance has to be the massive American flag he's attached to the ass-end of his pimped-out Snapper.

"Aw, look at the patriotic bastard." Kash grins, propping his chin on his fist as he stares longingly at the screen. "You go, big boy. Wave it loud and proud. In Bud Light we trust!" I blink at my brother, curious as to what the official diagnosis is. There has to be a medical term or politically correct phrase I can use to call him a dumb motherfucker.

"Can we get one of those?" Kash ponders.

"Absolutely not," Loch answers immediately. "You'd somehow manage to run your own fucking foot over and chop it off." Kash grumbles in protest, but eventually comes to the same conclusion.

The feed goes black shortly after the man disappears from the frame. We watch it several times, but the frisbee never makes an appearance. My only guess is that it came from an angle that was out of view. At least we know what happened. Sadly, the twelve-hundred-dollar piece of equipment fell victim to a goddamn Florida-Man out spreading his daily dose of patriotism.

"I love this bloody country," Loch laughs. "The entertainment is top tier."

"I wonder if he drove around on the 4th with a Roman Candle, yeeting out fireworks like a badass." Kash makes finger guns, complete with a sad, "*pew, pew pew*."

And I'm done.

My brain could use a rest. Or maybe I'll go jerk my cock in the shower while I relive the feel of Saylor's cunt beneath my thumb, nothing but a thin pair of panties separating her flesh from mine. I beeline for the bathroom, needing to come a time or ten before I'll be able to focus on anything else.

I knew she'd fucking ruin us. Yet here I am, eager and ready for the devastation. I can only hope that it's a beautiful descent into madness, because there's no way any of us will be able to move forward after this. It's Saylor or bust, so I pray like hell she's planning to keep us.

Chapter Forty-Two

Saylor

It's been a week since our cringe-worthy group sex discussion. I've yet to bring up our new dynamic with Danielle, and I'm not sure I plan to. But we did delve into Liam, specifically the day I went missing. It's the first time we've ventured there. I gave her a play-by-play, breaking down the timeline of events that led to my abduction. She's helped me realize how badly I distrust my own judgement now. I knew something was wrong; my gut was spot on, but I chose to ignore it. I overthink everything, which is likely the cause for my obsessive googling.

I've read through every article and blog post I could find on multi-partner relationships. It's been… *enlightening*. But the main conclusion I've come to, is that there's no one-size fits all. What works for some people, doesn't for others. However, I was surprised to find it's not as uncommon or taboo as I imagined. For now, I'm trying to trust the way I feel. It's dangerous to let my heart lead, but we'd never make it off the ground if my brain were in the driver's seat.

I've been a little distant this week while trying

to work through everything, but the guys have been great. They haven't pushed for anything beyond a few kisses or hugs. I also had a three-day period, which was brutal. Kash brought me every chocolate concoction he could think of, along with a heating pad and his e-reader. Lochlan promised as soon as we were able to, he'd get me an appointment so we could discuss birth control options. I don't have a lot to go off of, but I'm pretty confident it isn't normal for a regular cycle to be so sporadic and painful.

Krew's kept his word, taking every opportunity presented to tease me relentlessly. The first time, he cornered me in the media room. We'd been the last two to leave. I felt his breath against my neck, then his tongue and teeth. His whispered words were just as dirty as before, but the ache I left with had me pressing my thighs together for the rest of the night. Worst of all, he *knows* how affected I am. Every time he catches me staring, a wicked smirk carves across his handsome face.

Our most recent encounter happened in his and Kash's room. I went to return the borrowed stuff Kash lent me, when out waltzed Krew, fresh from the shower, wearing nothing but a towel tied around his waist. I still haven't decided if my timing was spectacular, or a product of the worst luck ever. I turned to leave, but his hand slapped the door closed, his hard body trapping me against it. He made me stand there, refusing to let me turn around, while he pleasured himself.

Truthfully, I doubt I would have left if he'd given me the option to. I didn't even watch him, but somehow, I was more turned on than I've ever been. The sounds he made, the way my name was spoken —low and guttural—as he came. *God, help me.* It's refused to leave my mind. Krew kissed my shoulder, wiped himself clean with the back of my shirt, and sent me on my way. Needless to say, his plan to drive me crazy is working flawlessly.

I've just wrapped up with Danielle when the door opens. Lochlan saunters in, a wide smile curving his mouth. He pulls me up and sets me on his desk, taking the empty office chair for himself. I place my feet on his spread thighs, grinning as I wiggle my toes up and across his abdomen. Lochlan grunts, twisting to the side when I hit a sensitive spot. With narrowed eyes, he clamps a hand around my ankle and starts tickling me.

"Mercy!" I squeal, laughing hysterically as I twist and turn to get away, but he refuses to let up.

"Oh no, sweetheart. You're the one who started this," Lochlan taunts, gripping my knee with his other hand. He digs his fingers in repeatedly, making me scream for help.

"I'm going to pee!" I shout as a last-ditch effort.

"Go ahead, love. I won't think any less of you." His smirk is flat-out devious. When Lochlan finally relents, I flop back, panting like I've just run a marathon. He strokes the arch of my foot, using the perfect amount of pressure. I have my eyes closed, enjoying the impromptu massage, when I feel his lips ghost across my ankle. He kisses his way up my calf, stopping at the inside of my thigh to bite down lightly, then soothes the sting with his tongue. I gasp, arching my hips in invitation.

"You beckoned, princess?" Roan barges in, completely severing the moment. Lochlan eases back, appearing nonplussed at the interruption. I tilt my head, meeting vibrant green eyes and my favorite dimpled grin. Roan hovers above me, sparing my and Lochlan's position a brief glance before focusing on my face. I've tried my best to avoid situations like this, to respect his boundaries. "Need some help, Little Fighter?" A rush of air leaves me at his teasing tone.

"Ro, did you know that our girl squeals like a stuck pig when you poke and prod her just right?" My eyes widen at Lochlan's innuendo-filled question. Does he have any idea how out of context that could be taken? The twinkle in his honeyed gaze says *yes*, he certainly does, and he's enjoying the hell out of making me sweat. Roan chuckles, using the spare hair tie on his wrist to wrap my hair in a knot. He has a serious fascination with rearranging my long blonde strands.

"I wonder what she'd do if I got ahold of these piggies?" Lochlan steadies my foot, and grips my little toe between his fingers. "Which one goes to the market?" He cocks his head to the side, like he's trying to remember the way the saying goes. Nope. No thank you. My mother subjected me to that particular torture quite enough for one lifetime.

"How 'bout that evac?" I make grabby hands at Roan, eager to get away. "You like my toes. Remember? Those are *your* toes, Big Guy. Now get me out of here." He chuckles, shaking his head at my theatrics.

It's safe to say they're rubbing off on me. This level of desperation and bargaining has Kash written all over it.

"At your service, baby girl." Faster than I can track, Roan slides me away from Lochlan. As soon as my feet are free, he grips my butt with one hand and braces the other on the back of my head. And then I'm airborne. His fingers find purchase between my thighs as he bends down and flips me over his shoulder. I land on Roan's back with a grunt, instinctively wrapping my arms and legs around him. Slowly—*purposefully*—he strokes my sex before repositioning his arm to help hold me up. I exhale unsteadily, confused if I'm dizzy from the tilt-a-whirl toss or his teasing. Both, most likely.

As Roan starts to walk, I look back at Lochlan with a victorious smile plastered on my face. He quirks an eyebrow at me, so I blow him a kiss as we turn the corner in the hallway. Feet swinging, I hum the melody to *All I Do Is Win* by DJ Khaled. Roan snorts, mumbling beneath his breath about me being trouble with a capital T. I lay my cheek on his back, enjoying the free piggyback ride. As we enter the main room, Krew comes through the slider, his brows pinched together as he stares at his phone.

"Everything okay?" I ask, bouncing my eyes between his.

"Yeah," he answers distractedly, but it's not very convincing. "Cam 4 is glitching. Looks like a seagull ate shit and took it out."

"Seriously?" I scrunch my nose, trying to

picture how it happened, but failing to come up with anything plausible.

"Would you like to see the crash site for yourself?" Krew grins, spinning on his heel to make the trek back to the camera.

"Hey," Kash calls, jogging down the steps to catch up with us. Havok and Lochlan follow a few paces behind. "Is this a field trip? If so, who's in charge of snacks?"

"Watch out for that crab." Roan points to the left of Kash. "Looks angry. Prone to pinching."

"*What?*" Kash screeches, shuffling back so quickly he trips over his own feet and lands on his ass. "I don't see it. Where the fuck is it at, Ro?!" He whips his head back and forth, searching for a crab that I'm fairly positive doesn't exist.

"Get the hell up," Havok huffs, gripping Kash's shirt in his fist as he yanks him to his feet. "How many times are you gonna fall for that shit?" Kash blinks, seeming to finally clue in that Roan was only messing with him.

"One of these days, I'm going to catch your big ass off guard." Kash glares hotly at the man still lugging me around, my added weight clearly insignificant as we easily trudge through the sand. "And you." Kash turns his attention to me. His eye twitches from the effort he's exuding to feign annoyance. "Aren't you supposed to be my secret threat, ready and willing to go against any creature of the yuck variety to protect my honor? We shook on it and everything. Your lack of action wounds me, sweetness." He presses a hand over his heart, forcing tears to his chocolate brown eyes.

"And in return, you were supposed to make me cupcakes. But have you? No. Not a single one. I think it's safe to say that our agreement is null and void due to lack of follow-through on your part." Kash gapes at me, sputtering nonsensical excuses and renegotiation terms. I press my lips together to keep from laughing.

"So it's settled, then." He boops me on the nose. "I'm going to rectify my oversight, posthaste, and you'll continue being my first line of defense in regard to all the vile things that should've been excluded from Noah's Ark. Horrible miscalculation on Sky Daddy's part. This entire predicament could have been avoided if the unsavory types were vetoed. Seriously, who saves cockroaches?" Kash trails off, momentarily lost to a philosophical deep dive. He's adorable when he rants.

"Deal." I reach out and tug him closer, bringing his mouth to mine for a quick kiss. "Even sealed this time." I grin, my lips still skating over his as I quietly say, "I love you." Roan stiffens, but shakes off the tension a second later. I didn't mean to make things weird for him. Kash mouths back *'I love you more'*—obviously picking up on the same displeased vibe Roan is radiating.

"Here lies the mangled body of one dumb as fuck bird," Krew states, stopping at a tall wooden post on the back end of the property. Lochlan squats to examine the poor seagull, looking from it to the camera in confusion.

"I don't think the crash killed it. More like it was already dying, and that's *why* it crashed," Lochlan speculates, using a nearby stick to shift its body. I tuck my face into Roan's shoulder, feeling queasy from the gruesome cut he exposes under its wing. I might have a strong dislike for birds, but I take no glee in its mutilation. "Foot is damn near severed too."

Do not gag, Saylor.

"Looks like a shark got the poor bastard," Roan comments absently. Like the image of a Great White springing up from the ocean to grab a mid-day snack topside is no big deal. *Hello, nightmares.*

"I'm sorry. A *what*?!" My voice reaches a decibel I wasn't aware existed. If Roan's flinch is anything to go by, he agrees. "You two made me go out there!" I point an accusing finger at Havok and Kash. "I could've been a goner. Mosquitos love me! It's not that big of a leap to assume a shark would too." I've gone full crazy, clinging tighter to Roan, as if I'm at risk of being eaten at this very moment. On land. A good thirty feet from the water.

"Oooh, I like Flustered Saylor a whole lot, but Overdramatic Saylor might be my new fav." Kash nods profusely, sending me an exaggerated wink.

"Is that so?" I snap mockingly. "Well, I really like Playful Kash, but I think *my* new favorite will be Blue-Balls Kash." His smirk evaporates with a quickness. Havok doubles over, laughing his ass off at Kash's expense.

"Atta girl," Roan comments proudly, giving my thigh a firm squeeze.

“Back to the seagull,” Krew cuts in. He’s pretending like I don't amuse him, but I know him better than that now. He thinks I’m funny. “I don’t care if a shark did the damn thing in, or if the bird simply forgot how to bird. It’s dead as shit, and so is our camera.” Krew glares at the poor thing, as if death wasn’t punishment enough. “At this rate, we’ll need to purchase backups by the dozen.”

“I’ll place an order today.” Lochlan stands and brushes a hand over his leg, swiping nonexistent sand from his cute, pleated shorts.

“So…” Kash gives the battered glob of feathers a pointed look. “Do we forgo niceties and simply bury Mr. Shit for Luck? Or are we thinking a small wake, some finger foods…” He pauses, giving us a chance to chime in. We don’t. “I mean, a proper Viking send-off sounds badass, but that seems a bit insensitive, considering he could wind up shark bait. Again. His name ain’t Shit for Luck for no reason.” Lochlan lifts his glasses and pinches the bridge of his nose, mimicking our own thoughts exactly.

“I have a headache now. Thanks for that,” Lochlan deadpans. “I don’t care how you get rid of it, just get rid of it. Build the damn thing a mausoleum if you’d like, so long as I never have to hear you talk about it ever again.” Kash claps excitedly.

“Thanks, Dad!” He smacks a wet kiss on Lochlan’s cheek and grabs Havok’s hand, skipping off in the direction we came from, presumably to gather the tools needed to bury a seagull. He drags Havok along, not the least bit perturbed by the man’s displeasure.

"That should keep him busy for a while," Krew states, shaking his head at the fading outline of his twin. "Let's go before they get back. I refuse to listen to the eulogy of a goddamn bird." Krew starts speed walking, determined to put some distance between himself and the future burial site of Shit for Luck.

May he rest in peace.

As we follow behind Krew, I decide to put my lack of core strength to the test. I slip my leg around Roan, starting a slow scoot against his side. Like a baby bear trying to climb a tree, if it were weak and lacking basic bear skills. When I finally align with his front, I'm a sweaty mess. My noodle arms shake from the strain, and my hair has mostly fallen from the knot it was in. I brush a few strands from my face, finding Roan's bright green eyes watching me with interest.

"You good now?" His lip quirks to the side, making his dimples pop out.

"Yep." I sigh when he takes my weight. "Needed a change of scenery. I like this view better."

"That so?" Roan questions softly, trailing his hand up my spine before gripping the back of neck. I groan as he works the kinks out, dropping my head back to stare at the darkening sky. His steps slow, my tense muscles stealing his attention.

"You're fucking exquisite. You know that?" He presses his face to my throat and inhales deeply. "I love the way you smell. Like coconut and honey." He licks me, tasting the salt of my sweat above any lingering bodywash. I pull back, letting our breaths mix as we gaze at one another. His hair is down today, so I take the opportunity to run my fingers through the soft, ash-colored strands. Roan sighs, sweetly nudging my nose with his. Refusing to wait another second, I lift my chin and kiss him. His tongue strokes mine, tangling us together in a heady mix of bliss and agony.

Thunder cracks through the quiet, causing us both to jump. We laugh it off, but note the ominous looking clouds rolling in over the ocean. The waves have picked up, churning the calm water into choppy swells. It's summertime in Florida—also known as the rainy season. Showers tend to be sporadic, sometimes lasting only a few minutes, and then the sun will reappear and scorch everything in its path. This, however, looks more like a storm.

"Let's get inside, baby girl." Roan tucks me close and quickens his pace. Poor Mr. Shit for Luck. I'm thinking he's going to be waterlogged by the time Kash is able to proceed with his funeral. We slip inside just as the rain hits, coming down in sheets so thick it's hard to make out anything past the deck area. Roan sets me on my feet, holding me by the elbow until my stiff legs decide to cooperate. I head to the kitchen to help Lochlan, who's busy plating a stack of BLT's while trying to toe open the pantry door at the same time. I brush him aside and grab the bag of chips he was going for.

"I'll never be able to look at a fucking seagull without hate," Havok growls, stomping through the garage door. He's soaked from head to toe, looking seconds from committing a mass murdering of innocent birds. Kash saunters in behind him, shaking his body like a wet dog. A pleased grin splits his face, which only enrages Havok even more. "You're love drunk, and it's turned you into a sentimental pain in the ass. *My ass*, to be specific."

"Sorry, bro." Kash pats his cheeks lovingly. "I'm not into guys. The only ass I plan to bring any pain to is our girl's." I snort and choke at the same time —at a loss for words—but shock fails to make an appearance. Kash's lack of filter no longer fazes me. Havok's icy blue eyes connect with mine, glinting with devilry. A sinful grin quirks his mouth as he takes deliberate steps in my direction. He's barely a foot away when I realize his plan.

"Havok." I throw my hand out in a poor attempt of stopping him.

"Say Baby," he calls out seductively. "Come here and let me hold you." Havok swoops in before I can map out an escape, wrapping his tattooed arms around my body. My scream breaks into a laugh as he spins us around, nuzzling his wet hair all over me. He croons a love song against my ear—*horribly*—as we sway to a beat only he can hear. "I love you, pretty girl."

"I love you too." I press my lips to his, keeping it short and sweet, conscious of the audience we have.

Since we're supposed to have some sketchy weather for the next day or two, we decide to puppy pile in the living room for the night. While the guys pull out extra blankets and pillows, Havok and I head to change. I'm in the closet, searching for a pair of panties when he walks in like he owns the place. His heated eyes devour my naked flesh, staring at me hungrily.

Before I can protest, he drops to his knees and throws my leg over his shoulder. Havok doesn't tease me or work his way up to hot and heavy. He buries his face between my thighs, licking and sucking my clit with such intensity, I think I might black out from the onslaught. I come so quickly it catches me off guard. Slapping my hand out, I grip the doorframe and bite the inside of my arm. My muffled scream still punctures the silence. As he eases my leg back down and I slump against the dresser, I absently wonder if Roan will be pissed if he heard me. Sight and sound are two very different things.

"Fucking delicious," Havok groans, slamming his mouth over mine. I taste myself, but it doesn't bother me. "Dinner's waiting, Say." He walks out, leaving me to sort myself before joining the others. My legs are jello, but I finish dressing and head back to the living room, looking somewhat put together. I breathe a sigh of relief when no one comments on our disappearing act, plopping down next to Krew on the massive pallet they made. The remainder of our night goes by without a hitch as we eat and binge *MasterChef*.

"Anyone want cookies?" Kash hops up, planning to make some either way. It's a resounding yes, so I pause the show while he starts the oven. No one passes up an offer like that. Well, no one but Havok it seems.

"Nah," he comments lazily. "I've already had

dessert." He winks at me, sending a furious blush over my entire body.

They damn sure know what we were doing now.

Chapter Forty-Three

Saylor

I woke to being bookended by two eerily identical men. Snug between Kash and Krew, I decided to ignore the obvious erection poking me in the ass. I was too comfortable to move, and the rain battering against the slider lulled me right back to sleep. There was a moment, while we stretched and groaned, when our positions became a bit more obvious. The two of them shared a look I couldn't quite decipher, but my imagination is doing a decent job of filling in the blanks.

After folding up our mess of blankets, I head to my room for a quick shower. It's gloomy out, so I opt for a sweatshirt, leggings, and my favorite pair of fuzzy socks. The guys are already waiting at the dining table, so I take my seat and smile gratefully at the plate of pancakes Havok hands me. It's almost noon, so our breakfast is more of a brunch, but I love our morning ritual of eating together. Sometimes it's chaos, and others, like today, we're too tired to talk and the silent company is enough. Stuffed and unable to force down another bite, I give my unfinished food to Kash and rest my head on his shoulder.

"I'm bored," he mumbles, shoving the last of my leftovers in his mouth.

"You've been awake for half an hour." Lochlan stares at his phone, refusing to entertain Kash's whining. "Would you like to inventory the arms room? I'm sure we're due for a resupply of ammo."

"Hard pass." Kash cuts his hand through the air, completely dismissing the idea. The man is way too much of a busybody to sit still for very long. Menial tasks like that would drive him crazy in a matter of minutes. If it's not a movie or game he's invested in, Kash drifts, quickly moving to the next thing that tickles his fancy. Makes me wonder how he spent hours behind his computer, searching for me and probing the darkest corners of the internet for victims of human trafficking. Kash has barely worked since I've been here. I just hope that's by choice, and not because he thinks I need to be entertained twenty-four-seven.

I'm about to suggest a movie or boardgame when the lights flicker. A loud boom of thunder makes me jump, followed shortly by a streak of lightning cracking across the sky. The power goes out, blanketing us in darkness. My hackles rise immediately. I've come pretty far with most things, but the dark is still a trigger. Instinctively, I grapple for Lochlan's hand, my brain reverting back to that moment in the hospital, when he so easily offered his touch to keep me grounded.

He picks up on my slight distress without me

needing to say a word. Using his foot, Lochlan snags the leg of my chair and tugs me closer. Secure on his lap and tucked against his chest, I take a few calming breaths and let the anxiety fade away. It's not even that dark, now that my eyes have adjusted. The tint is off on the slider, allowing the gray-tinged sky to shed some light on the situation. My fear isn't nearly as debilitating as it was, but I hate that it's there at all.

"I've got it!" Kash snaps his fingers excitedly. "How about strip poker?" Roan's glare makes me smile. He struggles to take a joke, while Kash doesn't know when to not make one. The combination typically results in someone getting smacked in the head. *Kash is the someone.*

"Kidding," he placates. "I actually have a legit idea to help us pass the time. But I need you to trust me, sweetness. Can you do that?" His shift in tone makes my spine straighten. Anytime Kash grows serious, I make it a point to give him my full attention.

"The last time you asked me that, you carted me off—kicking and screaming, I might add—into shark infested waters. Which clearly have more *Jaws* types than Bruce, who thinks fish are friends, not food. Mr. Shit for Luck, God rest his soul, is a testament to the savagery living in those inky blue depths."

Havok sighs in exasperation. "Are you happy? Now you've got Say buying into your crazy, waxing poetic about a goddamn beach chicken."

Kash grins at me while casually giving Havok his middle finger. "No risk of life, I promise."

"Okay." I nod my agreement, hoping like hell I won't come to regret that decision in just a few short minutes.

"You heard her, boys. To the war room! It's time for some tactical catch and release," Kash proclaims with a fist pump to the air.

"Oh, hell yes." Havok surges to his feet, his grin boyish and giddy. I watch in amusement as the others join him, their eyes lit with excitement, an extra pep in their steps as they head for the lower level. Their smiles are contagious, but I'm so confused. Kash takes my hand and pulls me to my feet once we're alone. Our chests are flush as he stares down at me tenderly.

"It's time to face another fear, babe." My pulse kicks up a notch as he tucks a piece of hair behind my ear. Unfortunately, I don't think it's his touch that has my stomach dipping and swirling with nerves. "Remember the words I told you that day? We've got you. *Always*. Trust that above anything else. I'd never put you in danger, and neither would my brothers." I inhale deeply and dip my chin in acquiescence.

Kash twines our fingers together and leads me down the stairs. The flashlight on his phone illuminates our way, but I still squeeze his hand, reassuring myself that despite the cover of black surrounding us, it's not the same stale air of Liam's storm cellar. I'm nowhere near that place, and I'll never have to be ever again. The guys are waiting for us just inside the firing range, the glow of their own phones lighting the space tremendously. The arms room is open, revealing Roan crouched down and digging through a metal wall locker.

"I think the small will work, but it'll still be a little big on her." He stands, gripping some sort of vest in his hand. Roan erases the few feet between us and slips it over my head. It's not very heavy, but it's got some weight to it. It hangs loosely, so he readjusts the placement and tightens the straps along my sides.

"Watch the boobs," I grunt, wincing at the pressure on my chest. It fits just fine circumference wise, but the vest was clearly meant for someone with a longer torso. As it stands, the shoulder pads are practically touching my ears, and the bottom part has to be left unbuckled if I plan to walk without restriction.

"Oh, I'm watchin' 'em, baby girl." Roan winks, giving the breast plate from hell a quick tug to ensure it's nice and secure. His fingers slip beneath the fabric, purposefully grazing my nipples as he performs his fit check. I narrow my eyes, trying my hardest not to smile at the hungry gleam he flashes back at me. Whatever his plan was, I think it backfired. Roan clears his throat and steps away.

"A *ra-ta-ta* for you," Kash sings, shoving a rifle in my arms. "And a *ra-ta-ta* for me." I ease it away from me, blinking furiously at the scary looking hunk of metal. Weird time to discover that they're absolutely insane, but okay.

"Relax, love." Lochlan smiles, tapping a black square on the front of my vest. It lights up, revealing a miniature, tablet-like screen. "It's a laser gun." My head snaps up, surprise washing over me as I glance around to see the others smirking at my not so hidden thoughts.

"Well, it looks real," I snark, trying to compensate for my gross inaccuracy. What was I supposed to think, when they failed to explain that beforehand?

"Because it's supposed to," Krew states. "This isn't run-of-the-mill laser tag equipment. It's sold specifically to companies that require tactical training, therefore simulating the firearms someone in our line of work would actually use." He takes a handgun for himself and passes another to Lochlan. "We usually plan out specific scenarios, utilizing the outside space as well, but today is meant for fun."

"We'll work in teams. Saylor's with me," Lochlan rushes, gripping the back of my vest possessively. Kash swears and pokes his bottom lip out, but Boss Man is undeterred. "Chest shots are kill shots, so if you start vibrating, you're down. No bloody cheating." He stares at the twins pointedly. "Any questions, sweetheart?"

"Um," I start, realizing the whole point of laser tag is that it's meant to be played in the dark. I look to Kash in understanding. This is the fear he wants me to face. He gives me a reassuring smile as Havok tosses him a pair of goggles.

"Be brave, babe," Kash whispers, dropping a kiss to the tip of my nose. He slips the eyewear over my head as Roan steps behind me and ties my hair into a ponytail. "When you're ready, we'll turn the lights off. The specs will automatically switch to night vision. With the exception of being tinted green, you'll be able to see just fine. Think you can handle that?" Kash cups my cheeks and patiently waits for me to answer.

I swallow thickly, but nod with determination.

"Good girl," Roan praises, placing a kiss just below my ear. "You look hot as fuck, by the way."

"Like a tiny GI Jane," Havok chimes in. I laugh and shake my head, knowing good and well I look ridiculous.

"Alright, let's scramble. Set your stopwatches for three minutes. When it zeros out, the game is in play." The guys pull their goggles on and get their timers ready. The twins are paired together, leaving Havok and Roan on a team. Poor Lochlan chose wrong. He must've not seen the mangled sheet of paper from my abysmal attempt at target practice. He'll see the error in his judgement soon enough. Kash waits for my nod before they click off their flashlights. I blink, slightly weirded out by the color of everything.

"You good, Say Baby?" Havok questions as Lochlan slips his hand in mine.

"It's like St. Patrick's Day threw up on everything," I answer absently, pinging my gaze around the room. The guys laugh at my response.

"Ready?" Roan asks, hovering his thumb over the start button on his clock app. I grin at how cute they look, wearing matching expressions of seriousness as they holster their weapons. "*Go.*" The second the countdown begins, we scatter. Lochlan grips my hand tightly as we beeline for the main level. Footsteps sound behind us, but I pay no mind to where the others are headed. It feels like cheating if we know where to start our search.

We burst through the door, stopping to tint the

slider, and then lie low in the pantry. Lochlan leaves it cracked, watching the others come in behind us a few moments later. When they split apart, he glances at the remaining time displayed on his phone. One minute and forty-two seconds. He spins and cages me against the wall, sandwiching my gun between us.

"So cute," Lochlan whispers, ghosting his lips over mine. When he pulls away, my body follows unconsciously, making me stumble forward. He chuckles quietly, earning himself a glare. Deciding to partake in Havok's '*take what I want*' mentality, I sling my gun over my shoulder and grip Lochlan's vest, slamming my mouth against his. Our goggles smack together, so I push them up and out of the way before slipping my tongue between his lips. The bravery I called on downstairs must be leaking over, because our kiss is far from sweet. Lochlan groans, reaching around to grab my ass. He lifts me, wedges a leg between my thighs, then slides me back down.

I'm on my tiptoes, and every time I shift or give him more of my weight, his jean-clad thigh grinds against my clit deliciously. I swivel my hips in search of friction as Lochlan keeps a firm hold on my backside. The tips of his fingers dip low, adding a hint of pressure. These leggings are thin enough I can actually feel him rim my entrance, teasing me from both sides. My head falls back with an audible *thunk* as I tangle my fingers through his hair.

"You need to come, sweetheart?" Lochlan prods softly, his warm breath fanning across my flesh. He sweetly kisses my closed eyes before taking my mouth, tugging my bottom lip between his teeth.

"Ride me. Work these sexy fucking hips and get yourself off." Lochlan guides my movement, helping me find the perfect rhythm. It doesn't take long before I'm seeing sounds and hearing colors, panting and pleading for him to make me come. He pulls me down hard, refusing to let up as he works my clit, rocking my body in short, powerful strokes.

I slap a hand over my mouth at the last second, biting back a scream as I tremble from the force of my orgasm. I can't see straight, much less walk or stand. Slumping forward, I let Lochlan catch me, knowing he'll hold me until I've gone through a proper reboot. His fingers dance along my spine, content to give me all the time I need. Unfortunately, not everyone is of the same mindset. The door flies open, revealing Havok, an all-too-knowing grin stretched across his face with his rifle pointed at us. I scream, having completely forgotten about our game of laser tag, and scramble to get away.

"You dirty little birdy." Havok grins wickedly. I'm not proud of what I do next, but I'm going to chalk it up to fight or flight. I shove Lochlan in front of me, using his body as a *literal* human shield, just as Havok presses his finger to the trigger. I don't even give the man a fighting chance. His goggles are still askew, and there's a definite bulge tenting the front of his jeans. He grunts when the shot rings true and his vest vibrates.

Thinking on my feet, I push him forward like a piece of riot gear. Havok stumbles back and lands on his ass when I ram him with Lochlan. It's a love tap, really. I pull my gun around and step out, hovering above the dazed man on the kitchen floor. I grin and pull the trigger, squealing when the target on his chest goes off with a buzz. I'm barely two feet from him, so it would've been embarrassing if I missed. Havok gapes at me, his icy blue eyes round as saucers.

"Fuck, I love you," he whispers in awe. "That was savage, baby. Never been harder than I am right now." I grin, high on adrenaline and victory. A sound from the hallway has me ready and waiting for whoever's attempting to sneak up on us. Kash saunters out a second later, munching on a bag of chips. He raises an eyebrow at the three of us, holding up his free hand in surrender.

"I'm dead. Roan's big dumb ass took me out in five point two seconds." Kash licks the Cheeto dust from his fingers, then goes back in for more.

"Me and Loch are out too." Havok grunts and groans as he climbs to his feet, happily telling Kash how I wound up being the victor in his ambush.

"Badass." Kash grins and gives me a high-five. "Better beat feet, though. You've got two more assholes to snipe."

"Oh, yes. Run, my love. Please save yourself," Lochlan deadpans, his sarcasm making me giggle.

"Thank you for your sacrifice." I press my lips to his. "I'll make it up to you later." He gives me a '*really?*' look.

"Sweetheart, you and I both know I did no such thing. You straight murdered me." He acts offended, but I see his lip twitch. He pulls me in and speaks quietly against my ear. "You're gonna pay for that over my knee." I meet his honey gaze with a grin. I have no idea if he's serious, but regardless, it's a problem for another day.

"Gotta run."

I kiss Havok and Kash quickly, pull my goggles into place, then bolt for the lower level. Keeping my steps light, I pause at the bottom of the stairs and glance around the corner. The hallway is clear, so I sprint to the media room and slip inside. It's empty as far as I can tell, but they've got to be around here somewhere. Deciding to wait them out, I head for the snack area and wedge myself between the wall and popcorn maker. I nearly fall asleep while I sit there, but a faint noise perks me back up.

"I know you're in here, Tink," Krew taunts as he checks between the recliners. "I can smell you. Ripe and sweet. *Needy*." I still, wondering if that's an actual thing. Surely not. Seeing as my underwear are soaked with my release, I can't say for sure. I'm weighing my options, flip-flopping between making a run for it and surrendering, when Krew pulls his phone from his pocket. He glances from it to something near the ceiling, then back again. I follow the direction of his gaze, finding a camera mounted in the corner of the room. From what I can tell, the angle doesn't show much of the area I'm in, if any. Krew hasn't even bothered to look back here because there's nowhere to hide without being seen. At least not any place *they* could fit.

That lying little cheat.

He knew where to find me because he's been

watching the cameras and tracking our whereabouts. Lochlan's rules clearly don't apply to him, and based on the pointed '*no cheating*' comment, I'm willing to bet this isn't the first time Krew's done this. *Think, Saylor.* I wrack my brain for a way out, knowing I won't have long before he starts a more thorough search. I have the advantage, though. He's in my line of sight and completely unaware. If I can get him to turn around and face me, I might I have a chance.

I carefully pull my hair tie free and use it like a slingshot. It sails past him, but Krew whips around like I knew he would. When the front part of his vest comes into view, I drop forward and pull the trigger. Repeatedly. My aim might not be great, but surely one of those hit home.

"Jesus. The first two were plenty, Tink." Krew laughs as I crawl from my hidey-hole. "You know camping is considered unsportsmanlike, right?"

"Oh, yeah?" I question with a grunt, struggling to pull myself up with all the added bulk I'm carrying. "And cheating is completely acceptable, I'm assuming?" I cock my hip to the side and give his phone a meaningful look.

"I'd be foolish not to use every trick in my arsenal." Krew grins, stepping closer so he can tilt my chin up. "And you would be too. Real life doesn't heed the rules, Tink. The bad guys aren't going to wait around for you to pop off a fair shot before they return the favor. Dirty is the name of the game, so darken that pristine little heart of yours before it's too late." His harsh words drift over my parted lips, spoken so closely I can smell the mint flavored gum on his breath. Krew's voice remains kind throughout his spiel on morality, but the truth of what he's saying still rankles.

Not from naivete or holding on to some misguided notion that the world won't chew you up and spit you back out the first chance it gets. It bothers me that he still sees me as some damsel who can't hold her own. I'm fully aware of my faults; I understand my areas of weakness. But I've also learned from them, and I'm not the same girl who blindly accepted a ride from someone she thought she knew and trusted. This stupid, floating rock we're all stuck on for the foreseeable future is full of people who are ready and eager to take advantage of those perceived as weaker than them.

But how's that saying go? Fool me once, shame on you; fool me twice, shame on me. When you've been burned as badly as I have, your defenses start to mount, and all those people who thought you easy prey become the ones being hunted. We learn and adapt, so we're never again forced into the sort of situation that caused such a fundamental change to begin with. I'll always be kind, that part of me will never change. But I can also wield that sweet demeanor and sunny disposition to my benefit. If there's anything I've learned, it's to use my liabilities against what threatens me.

"I suppose you're right." I lightly trail my finger over the hardness behind Krew's jeans. His face remains stoic, and if not for the slight tic of his jaw, I'd think he was completely unaffected by my touch. As it stands, I've acquainted myself with their tells—just as they have with mine. My connection with Krew might not have been as seamless as the others, but I know enough about him to pick apart his nuances pretty easily. My heart thunders as I grip him fully, applying the tiniest amount of pressure. I've never been this forward, or taken such liberties with another person's body.

"But here's the thing..." I stand on my tiptoes and speak directly against his mouth, assuming the same stance he did with me. "Me and my innocence? We've got you by the literal balls, Krew. And that purity you're so obsessed with and sure of is what landed you here. At *my* mercy. Maybe next time you'll treat me like the threat I can so easily become." I pull the handgun from his back and wrap my foot around one of his. With a quick yank forward and a shove to his chest, Krew loses his footing and falls to his ass. I grin down at him, a mixture of shock and pride filling my chest.

"Holy crap," I giggle, waving a hand at his disheveled form sprawled across the carpet. "I didn't expect that to actually work." I'm not fooling anyone with this five-foot-two body that lacks any real muscle tone, and I doubt my Liam Neeson style warning was very believable or scary, but I did throw him off balance. I'll take my wins where I can, which means Krew and I are a lot more alike than I've given credit to. I reach out to help him up, but the second his hand wraps tightly around mine, I realize my mistake. My chest collides with Krew's as he pulls me down. I laugh, moving to push the hair from my face as I straddle his hips.

"Now you're catching on. Fake it till you make it, Tink. No one has all the answers, all of the time. The key is to feign confidence until a better plan presents itself." I smile at his crazy talk, knowing with absolute certainty that I'll never be able to pull off anything more elaborate than trivial competitiveness. Reality is a completely different beast, and my poker face has never been very great. "Pretty sure Ro is in the arms room. Better get a move on, princess."

My eyes widen as I scramble to my feet. I don't bother sparing Krew a parting glance or goodbye. My mind is already refocused on the game and the last person remaining. I have no idea why I'm so determined to prove my capability, but I think it's more of a mental achievement for myself than to have bragging rights over the guys. Not that I won't parade my victory in their faces, but it's not the driving force behind my need to win. I toss my rifle back, the weight becoming a comfortable accessory at this point, and grip the pistol I lifted off of Krew. Tilting my head around the doorframe of the media room, I peek down the hallway towards the firing range.

The green hue of my goggles reveals no movement, but I bite my lip as I waver indecisively. I've gotten lucky thus far, but that's bound to run out sooner or later. These men are tactically trained. I'm operating on sheer desperation and the disillusion they have that I won't throw them under the bus to save myself. Deciding it's best to regroup, I exit and press my back to the wall—planning to slip upstairs quickly and quietly—but it appears my luck is definitely fleeing on the sooner side.

I freeze as Roan steps out at the same time, but neither of us makes a move toward the other. My side is facing him, so he doesn't have a straight shot at my vest, and we both know my aim isn't good enough to land anything from this far away. We're at a standstill. I feel my heart lodge itself in my throat when his mouth lifts into a wicked grin. To Roan's delight, my brain latches on to the action and declares it a silent threat, sending my '*flight*' response into overdrive. I bolt for the stairs, intent on running away instead of facing him.

"Those little legs can't outrun me, baby girl," Roan chuckles, sounding way closer than he should. I refuse to look back and see how much ground he's gained, knowing it'll cost me precious seconds I don't have. I hit the bottom step but stumble. Throwing my hand out to catch myself, an idea hits me and I play it up, letting my knees slam against the metal slats with a hiss that's, unfortunately, all too real. No pain, no gain, I guess.

"Fuck," Roan swears. Thick, corded arms slip beneath me and roll my body. His worried eyes rake over me, taking in my scraped and irritated skin. His touch is light as he prods the area, making sure the injury isn't anything more than superficial. Guilt weighs heavily as I use his concern to knowingly deceive him. Before I can talk myself out of it, I lift the handgun and press it directly against the target plate on Roan's vest, then pull the trigger. He blinks as the vibration of my hit jolts the both of us, dropping his gaze to take in my backhanded win. For some reason, my eyes sting with tears. Roan sits back with a baffled look on his face, likely realizing he was just hoodwinked.

"I'm sorry," I choke out through a wave of regret. His green eyes snap to mine in alarm.

"What the fuck are you sorry for?" Roan barks in that short and gruff voice of his, brows dipping together in confusion as he crowds me once again.

"That was mean. I made you think I was hurt just to get the upper hand. I don't like this feeling. And despite what Krew thinks, there *are* lines that shouldn't be crossed. That look on your face makes me feel like I'm an inch tall. I shouldn't have used your emotions against you." Roan swipes a stray tear from my cheek.

"You've got it wrong, Little Fighter. I'm not the least bit upset that you used whatever means necessary to come out on top. Honestly, I couldn't be prouder. The look you saw *was* realization, but not in the sense you're thinking. That was me coming to terms with the fact that you, Saylor Radley, are a goddamn weakness. Apparently, all it takes is a skinned knee to render me useless, and that's fucking terrifying. Watching Elira die was the most torturous moment of my life. It wrecked me so profoundly, I'm still trying to recover. But you, baby girl? I'd die if I ever had to witness someone use you as a means to break me. It'd rip my soul straight from my fucking body. There'd be no coming back from that."

Even now, lost to the macabre images plaguing his mind and the very real memories of his sister's murder, Roan holds himself above me, keeping the brunt of his weight from crushing me. I think he does this in all aspects of his life. He treads water, slowly sinking beneath the surface because he's too worried about everyone else to realize that he's the one who's drowning. Roan keeps his demons in check because he doesn't want to burden the rest of us. He's a '*suffer in silence*' type, but that doesn't mean he should do it alone. God as my witness, I'll do everything I can to never leave him to the kind of fate he's so certain of if something were to happen to me.

"We'll never have to find out, Big Guy. No sane person would ever cross you." I smoosh his cheeks together, grinning at the way his lips pucker like a fish's. "You look like a giant leprechaun." I laugh at the green tint of Roan's body, peeling off my goggles and rubbing at my blurred vision.

"This is…disgusting, really. So if the two of you would kindly move, I'd be forever grateful." Krew interrupts, moving from the darkened corner he's been occupying without us even knowing. I press my lips together as Roan rolls his eyes and tilts us to the side, creating a path for him to pass. Just as Krew slips by us, he attempts to pull me free and take me with him. Roan grips the back of his shirt and rips him away, causing Krew to let out a string of curses as he fights for purchase on the stairwell. I'm hoisted up and hugged to Roan's chest as he takes off at a dead sprint.

"They're always after me Lucky Charms," he grumbles against my neck, making me cackle at his play on my leprechaun comment.

If there's anyone who's found an abundance of

luck lately, it's me. And every ounce of it is centered around the five men who've brought me back to life. From the moment I was pulled from that cellar, they've been a constant and vital part of my new normal. I never imagined a life post Liam, but if I had, this would exceed anything I could've dreamt up.

Chapter Forty-Four

Saylor

The power has finally come back on, so we stumble into the main room with all eyes on us. Krew follows a few seconds later, going on and on about how cut-throat I was, taking no prisoners in my quest to win. By his words, no cost is too high. I pin him with a glare and make sure to reiterate that sometimes, it's better to have a clear conscious than a victory under your belt. And then I commence my gloating. Somehow, I managed to take out four of them—though Lochlan was an indirect casualty—despite the fact my aim is horrendous and I've never played laser tag a day in my life.

The guys pick at one another, joking about who I like least based on their '*deaths*'. Sadly, Lochlan comes out the winner of that argument. Roan and Krew take our discarded equipment back downstairs as the rest of us discuss dinner plans. The downpour has halted, but it looks temporary based on the dark clouds still hovering. We all agree it's best not to chance cooking in case there's another power outage while we're in the thick of it. Lochlan suggests we fix our own, so I grab a box of Lucky Charms and get to it. Running around, combined with the orgasm I was gifted in the pantry, has my stomach growling for sustenance.

Roan stands across from me, giving my choice of dinner a once over. He does a doubletake when he catches the joke. I smirk at the cocked eyebrow he gives me, shoving a bite in my mouth with a groan of approval. He drops a scoop of protein powder in his shaker cup, nearly spilling the milk he adds as he splits his attention between measuring his drink and the explicit way I lick my spoon. There's a thrill that comes with being the sole focus of someone who's so overwhelmingly gorgeous.

But the Saylor from *before*? She would balk at my forwardness. I wouldn't say the girl I used to be was a prude, but she certainly didn't lap up affection the way I do now. That girl was sweet and innocent and thrived on approval. She was kind to a fault, and barely stood up for herself. In a lot of ways, I miss her. But I can also appreciate the growth I've experienced in her absence. I'll likely never know the woman I could have been without the interruption of Liam. Maybe I would've been meek and reserved, content to live in a shell of my own making. But that's irrelevant now. My pain and loss have made me who I am, and despite the heartache it took to get here, I happen to like her. This version has the best parts of the old me—her kindness and forgiving nature—mixed with the hardened bits that can only be achieved through tough life lessons.

"Mmmm. They're magically delicious," I moan

around my food, which quickly turns into a sputtering cough as I laugh at the feral gleam in Roan's eyes. His pupils are blown so wide, there's barely any iris left. He slams his shake down and vaults across the counter.

I squeal as I stumble off my stool, searching for someone to save me. I glance at Lochlan just as his phone rings. He gives me an apologetic look—which somehow feels like payback for sacrificing him earlier—before stepping through the slider so he can take the call without distraction. Kash is playing *Candy Crush*, completely oblivious to everything around him, so I sprint across the room and take cover behind Havok. I leap on his back, making him scramble to grip me before we both fall, demanding he keep me safe from the big bad storming after me.

"Give her to me, Kade," Roan demands, his voice sounding strained and gritty. "She wants to play games, so let's fucking play, baby girl." I swallow thickly, keeping my eyes trained on the wall of muscle who has his sights locked on me.

"Did you poke the sexually frustrated bear, Say Baby?" Havok squeezes my thigh, backing us towards the other side of the couch as Roan continues to advance.

"Maybe?" I answer, but we both know I did. I jump as someone grips my hair and tilts my head back.

"Know what I think?" Krew questions seductively, speaking low enough for only the three of us to hear. "I think Tink likes being chased. She enjoys driving us mad with this tight little body of hers. Pushing us to the point we snap and let our dicks lead the charge." I shift against Havok as my breathing grows heavier.

"Is that right, pretty girl? Do you want us so lost in our need for you that we can't think straight unless we're inside of you?" Havok's question goes unanswered, because I honestly don't know. *Do I?* He steps back, fitting me between him and Krew without an inch of wiggle room. My gaze clashes with Roan's, worried he's going to fly off the handle at the position they've put me in, with him front and center to witness. My thoughts vacate as Kash leap frogs over the sectional, effectively dividing the standoff we have going on.

"I love a good round of keep-away-from-Ro," Kash states, rubbing his hands together while sporting a maniacal grin. I have no idea why I ever thought he was in his own world and unaware of us. It's clear by how up to speed he is that he hasn't missed a thing. "Toss her to me, little brother." Kash motions for his twin to hand me over, the two of them communicating silently while the rest of us wait with bated breath for whatever they're planning.

I stiffen as Krew plucks me off of Havok's back, fully anticipating the sinking feeling of being thrown through the air to wash over me, but instead I'm met with the soft cushions of the couch. It doesn't last long, though. Kash pounces on me—screeching about '*protecting the asset*'—then barrel rolls us both over the back of it. He lands first, taking the full brunt of our three-foot fall. I've barely caught my breath when he flies to his feet and hoists me over his shoulder. The world blurs as Kash spins us, making me regret my choice of dinner. A smile spreads across my face as I catch a glimpse of Roan. Krew and Havok have one arm each, holding him back as he spews a colorful array of all the ways he's planning to make them regret their choices.

"For someone who sleeps so fucking heavy, you've got a lot of nerve, Kade. I'm going to paint your ugly ass in peanut butter and duck-tape you to the bed. Just as you wake, I'll crack open that ant farm experiment Kash has stored in the bottom of Loch's safe and let 'em have at it. A high stake, all-you-can-eat buffet. One accidental bite and it's anaphylaxis for you."

"Jesus. That's morbid, dude," Krew admonishes, looking at Roan with feigned horror.

"You have an ant farm?" I try to lift my body so I can address Kash properly, but my arms shake from the effort it takes to hold myself up. I flop back down, waiting for his response. I'm aware of Havok's allergy to the insect. He sat on a whole bed of them in elementary school and had welts all over his legs within minutes.

"Don't remind me," Kash answers with a shiver. "It was a failed attempt at overcoming my fear of the crawly types. I swear I could feel them plotting their escape while I slept, forming a tiny, militant ant-army so they could get revenge for their unjust incarceration. But I can't let them go, because they might find their way back and take me out when I least expect it. So, Loch's safe is the next best thing."

I close my eyes and take a deep breath, willing myself not to outright laugh at his lunacy, but it's a vain attempt.

I'm giggling so hard I hiccup. Kash flips me over and drops me on my feet so abruptly, it makes the room spin. When my eyes refocus, I find him glaring at me, arms crossed and a put-out expression on his face. I press my lips together as the slider opens and Lochlan rejoins the band of crazy he's amassed. A quick glance in his direction has my shoulders tensing. The levity and joking disappear as I take in the odd look he's wearing. The guys follow my line of sight, quickly picking up on the same unease as me.

"What's wrong?" I question, moving around Kash to draw closer to Lochlan. His eyes follow me until I'm just a few feet away. I watch his throat bob as he swallows nervously, but he still doesn't speak. He's uncharacteristically detached as he looks beyond me, like he's not really seeing me at all. "Lochlan?" I try again, starting to panic from his lack of response.

"That was Denvers," he finally answers. "He called to let us know they found Liam. He's dead."

Dead. Liam's *dead*.

Those two little words reverberate inside my head, filling it with so many emotions, I can't tell what I'm actually feeling. They mix together, making my knees weak as I attempt to sort my thoughts. Relief. Anger. Excitement. They're all present and warring for dominance. And I'm left reeling, desperate for solid ground. Just as I think it, the guys close ranks behind me, offering their silent support as I work through the news.

"He's gone?" I question, my voice imploring and full of disbelief. "I can stop hiding now?" Tears streak my cheeks, but I have no idea when I even started crying. It feels like someone's lifted a weight from my chest, but I never realized how heavy it was. How much space it was occupying or the dent it was making. I'm smiling from ear to ear as the reality of what this mean hits me full force. Kash lifts me off my feet, hugging me tightly as our laughter mixes together, creating the sweetest sound I've ever heard.

"Saylor," Lochlan calls out to me, demanding my attention. I shake my head, covering my ears and closing my eyes, refusing to listen to the cause of his worry. We can stop right here, enjoy the moment and celebrate the freedom that comes with Liam's permanent removal from my life. Because I know whatever he needs to tell me is going to eradicate the happiness I'm feeling. It's the reason Lochlan's so on edge, when he should be overjoyed. My gut is warning me, and this time I won't ignore it. "Look at me, love." He pries my hands away and cups my cheeks, urging me to open my eyes.

"Please don't," I beg, finally caving and meeting his gaze, my heart flayed open and vulnerable. "Just leave it. *Please*."

"I can't do that, sweetheart." His thumbs catch my tears as they continue to fall. I nod, knowing he's going to drop another bomb, but this one is going to be far more destructive when it hits. The only thing I can do is grip his wrists, and brace for impact.

"What the fuck is happening right now?" Roan demands, pressing his front to my back as I sway unsteadily. "What's she talking about, Loch?"

"Liam was pulled from the wreckage of his vehicle, which was discovered by a local group of fishers at the bottom of Catalina Lake. It's a private hunting lodge, roughly two hundred and twenty miles from Baton Rouge, Louisiana." Lochlan speaks directly to me, completely ignoring the mountain of rage simmering behind me. "The coroner estimates he's been dead for quite some time. Well past the month mark."

And just like that, the weight is back. I stumble, palming the spot on my chest that expands with pressure so rapidly, it knocks the breath out of me. This can't be right. Their estimation has to be off. Surely being under water factors into the speed of deterioration. I'm vaguely aware of the guys voicing my thoughts, but even as we scramble for any other answer—aside from the blatantly obvious one—I know it's fruitless. Lochlan's already asked them, and likely a dozen more that we haven't thought of yet. He knows they've made no mistake in their findings, or he never would have told me.

Liam has *been* dead.

He's not the one sending me postcards.

He hasn't murdered three innocent women.

As terrifying as it was, Liam was a known threat. We at least had a description to go off of and could point him out in a crowd. Whoever's orchestrating this cat and mouse game we've been unwilling participants in is an entirely new variable. It could be anyone, but I suppose the escalation in Liam's behavior makes a lot more sense now. It was never him. The assumptions we made and the thought processes we used were absolutely pointless. We know nothing. Not the race or gender of the person taunting me, their motivations or reasoning. We're not just at a disadvantage, we're well and truly fucked.

"I need a minute," I state emphatically, my soft words somehow cutting through the chaos ensuing all around me. The guys are arguing, their own panic and frustration leaking over into their conversations with one another. I'm sure they're dead set against letting me out of their sights, but no one moves to stop me as I exit the slider and step onto the deck. The humid air hits me, but I breathe through the thickness and head for the stairs. I have no specific destination in mind, just the urge to move. When the faint whisper of waves greets me, I sigh in relief. Like a tether, I feel the draw of the ocean and my feet move towards it without command. Operating on autopilot, I stumble down the access path without much thought to how far I'm going or the worry it'll cause the guys.

As soon as the shore comes into focus, my toes dig beneath the sand. Just looking at the inky, never-ending surface isn't enough today. I need to touch it. To be a part of the vastness, so I don't feel so speck-like in comparison. I rush toward the water, tripping in my haste to get there as quickly as I can, terrified it's going to vanish before I can reach it. When I finally collide with the rough waves, a sob cracks my chest wide open.

I scream and curse, venting my frustration and hurt. Why me? Why now? Just...*why*?! I let the tide tug me out, wishing it could cleanse me of the horrors I've been subjected to. Praying to whoever might be listening that they'll grant it the ability to right my wrongs, and give me back the innocence that's been so savagely taken from me. Every angry wave that crashes over me beckons me to let go. To slip below the surface, allowing the ocean to sweep me away. Just like that, the pain and fear would be gone.

I can already imagine the relief I'd feel from no longer being weighed down by those debilitating emotions. It'd be fitting, to cease my existence in the same place my father lost his own life. What a way to face my fears of the unknown, forever resting in the depths of the thing that terrifies me, but has also given me the best memories of my life. I could never do it, though. My heart is tattered and bruised, but it's still beating. I've been given a glimpse of my future, and I want it. *Desperately*. No one—known or unknown—is going to stand in the way of that. People care about me now. They'd miss me. And I'll never leave them willingly.

"What the fuck is wrong with you?!" Roan screams, ripping me from the water as it continues to batter the shoreline. Sounds filter back in as the fog is lifted from my mind. Thunder rumbles through the noise accosting me from every direction, snapping my attention to the storm I've been oblivious to. Lightning lights the dark sky, striking too close for comfort. Roan hugs me to his chest and sprints for the house, cursing the heavy rain that soaks us to the bone in a matter of seconds. Someone opens the slider as we approach, but Roan carries me straight to his room without uttering a word.

I grunt from the force of being pinned to the wall, but his anger is understandable, and I know he'd never hurt me. At least not physically. His words, on the other hand, might be pretty scathing, if the look he's spearing me with is any indication of his current feelings.

All signs point to Roan being very, *very* pissed at me.

Chapter Forty-Five

Roan

I took my eyes off of Saylor for five fucking seconds and she disappeared. She was just there, on the other side of the slider. Her arms were clutched around her middle as she stared blankly into the distance, but I could see her. If Lochlan's bomb hadn't been enough to send her running, the influx of testosterone definitely did the trick. Our panic and worry were causing us to snap at each other, instead of addressing the situation like goddamn adults. But it was impossible for me to think with a level head when I couldn't grasp any one thought for more than a millisecond.

As soon as I realized that Saylor was gone, I bolted from the house and took the deck stairs two at a time. I've never—not once— questioned our ability to keep her safe. Mine maybe, because of my own bullshit, but never the team's as a whole. But I was also under the impression that we knew who we were looking for. For nearly two months, I've kept my eyes peeled and ears to the ground, waiting for Liam to crawl out from whatever rock he's been hiding under.

Only to find out that it's not even him we're searching for. Of all the variables we've done our best to account for, this outcome never registered as a possibility.

I think I'm pretty self-aware—enough to admit that we've been overbearing assholes. If I could bubble wrap Saylor and confine her to a quadrant of space that no harm could penetrate, I fucking would. But it'd come at the cost of clipping her wings, and she's barely gotten a chance to spread them. I'd never want to stunt her healing, but *fuck*. This feeling…this sick to my stomach, knee-weakening pit that's gaping inside of me makes me question how far I'd be willing to push her.

I can faintly hear the guys still yelling over one another, but my entire focus is on finding Saylor. My mind is conjuring up every worst-case scenario imaginable. That this unknown threat has somehow slipped past our defenses and gotten to our girl. I've seen firsthand how quickly things can go south, and I'll be damned if sit back and watch it play out in real-time with someone else I love.

My chest burns from how long I've been holding my breath, silently praying I'll catch sight of her. Those little legs couldn't have carried her too far, so every minute that passes makes my worry ratchet up even more. When her small frame finally comes into view, a mixture of emotions pummels me so forcefully, it almost knocks me on my ass. I'm relieved as fuck that I've found her, but there's an undercurrent of anger and indignation fighting for first place.

Saylor's standing waist-deep amongst the

crush of waves, her small body swaying as the storm picks back up. My vision tunnels as I erase the few yards between us. She's completely despondent, but I yell at her anyway. Partly to bring her back to the present, but mostly because I'm mad as hell and her zoned-out expression is doing absolutely nothing to lessen that. Lightning and thunder accompany the downpour as I hug Saylor's shivering body to my chest.

Fuck, baby girl. What the hell were you thinking?

I barely remember coming through the slider. Once I've got her in my room, I pin her to the wall. My chest is heaving, jaw clenched painfully to keep myself from saying something I might regret. She starts to slide, so I press my hips forward to hold her in place. My cock thickens from the contact, but I pay it no mind.

"Care to explain why you decided to take a dip in the ocean mid thunderstorm?" I grind out. Saylor bites her lip, but doesn't offer me any sort of explanation. Her gaze cuts behind me, and that just pisses me off even more. I grip her jaw and bring her attention back to me. "I'm right here, Little Fighter. Eyes on me."

"Ro," Loch calls out, a clear warning in his voice.

"Fuck off," I spit, never breaking contact with Saylor. "This is between her and me."

"You're pushing. Possibly too far." My lip lifts in a snarl at the passive accusation. I'd never hurt Saylor. We both know that. And nothing about her current body language indicates that I should take a step back.

"Maybe that's exactly what she needs. A push." I tighten my fingers the slightest bit. "Why were you in the goddamn water, Saylor?" For a moment, memories of my sister sneak in. Her mangled body lying on the floor. Blood—*so much blood*—pooled on the tiles beneath her as those lifeless eyes stared back at me. I shake my head, desperate to banish the images. Saylor *isn't* Elira, but for a moment, they were one and the same.

"To feel." She whispers the words so softly, I barely hear them. But it's enough to bring me back.

"You want to feel, baby girl?" I lock my eyes on hers, noting every micro-expression. Searching for any sign of distress. I track her nod, stroking my thumb over the pulse point on her neck. "Then I'll make you feel. Better than the goddamned waves ever could." I slip my wallet from my back pocket and tug out a condom. Tossing the piece of leather aside, I spare my brother a glance before issuing a warning of my own.

"You might want to leave now." I look away from where Loch's perched by the door—hands in his pockets, eyebrows drawn together in worry—and refocus on my girl. "You want this?" I dip my voice, keeping my words between the two of us.

"Yes." Her answer is instant, head nodding eagerly as she tightens her fingers around the wet fabric of my shirt. I doubt consent gets much clearer than that. I place the foil packet between my teeth and use my free hand to undo my belt. It takes some effort to get the drenched fabric off, but I've never been more grateful for my underwear preference—or lack thereof. Saylor watches with rapt attention as I rip the wrapper open and roll the condom on. I stroke my cock a few times, making sure the rubber's snug.

"You ready, baby girl?" My words are gritty, voice slightly breathless as I wait on pins and fucking needles for her to give me the go ahead. Saylor licks her lips and nods, her throat flexing as she swallows nervously. As she should be. Our sizes are comical in comparison, but when you think about the logistics of us joining together like *this*...I almost feel bad for the beating her pretty little pussy is going to take.

I don't bother asking her a second time. I trust her judgment, and if she wants my cock, I'm more than happy to give it to her. First, I lift the sopping sweatshirt from her body, groaning when I find her bare underneath. I can't contain my appreciation at the sight of her tits. Unable to help myself, I lick the valley between them before sucking on her nipple. Saylor inhales sharply, making me grin as I release the hardened bud with an audible pop. Next, I slip her leggings off, close to ripping the damn things in my hurry to get inside her.

"Damn, Little Fighter," I pant, tilting back just the slightest so I can drink my fill of her, in nothing but black scraps of cotton. "I can't wait to be inside of you." As if feeling my same sense of urgency, her hips cant forward. I grunt, fisting my dick roughly. It's been a *long* goddamn time since I've been with a woman. The fact that it's Saylor wedged between me and the *hopefully* sturdy drywall has my balls drawing up painfully with the need to come.

Impatient as fuck, I push her underwear to the side and stroke my fingers through the bare lips of her pussy. I sigh, wondering if this is what actual fucking heaven feels like. She's wet, and not from her impromptu swim. No, the slickness of her arousal is all for me. A reaction *I* earned. I push two fingers in, watching in fascination as her lips part. She digs her nails into my sides, but I welcome the marks she'll leave. Done with nice and easy, I line my cock up and grip Saylor's hips. I surge forward at the same time I yank her down, entering her tight pussy in one hard stroke.

"Roan!" she squeals, attempting to shimmy up the wall to get away from the sudden intrusion. I hold her in place, refusing to let her gain an inch of separation.

"You wanted to feel, baby girl. *So fucking feel me*," I groan, trying to keep still so Saylor can adjust, but it's akin to torture. She has me in a goddamn vice grip, and if she so much as breathes too harshly, I'll nut. I look between us, to where my cock is stuffed inside of her, that pink flesh stretched around me so fucking beautifully. I'm transfixed by the sight, desperate to move and watch the way her body takes me, but also wanting to freeze this moment and revel at the feel of her wrapped around me.

I let a string of spit fall to her clit, peering up at Saylor from beneath my lashes as I do, wanting to gauge her reaction to something she might find degrading. Thankfully, all I find are blown pupils and a flushed chest, both of which I can work with. I stroke my thumb over that bundle of nerves. Her eyes flutter, body going lax at the pleasure humming through her veins. I take the opening and start to move, easing out before surging back in. Over and over.

Every mewl and cry Saylor makes only spurs me on. I fuck her harder, cradling her head so it doesn't smack the wall from the intensity of my thrusts. I want every inch of her body, which is why I don't pull back when my cock bumps against her cervix. I just keep fucking her, urged on by the string of '*yeses*' and pleas begging me not to stop, despite the tears streaming down her face. Because right here and now, the two of us have never been more connected. Even with Loch still present, watching me crack the wall from the force of our fucking.

Maybe he wanted to make sure Saylor was okay, that she wasn't biting off more than she could chew. But I'd be willing to wager he's just a horny old fuck who's more than happy to watch our girl come on my cock. And if her heated gaze in his direction is anything to go by, Saylor has no issue with having a spectator. Her bright blue eyes land on mine, making my rhythm stutter. I'm so fucking gone for this girl. We stare at one another as I clench my jaw and wrap my hand in her hair. I tug her head back, exposing her neck so I can sink my teeth into it.

Saylor screams, rocking her hips forward, but I hold her steady. I rut myself inside her, so goddamn lost that I resort to animalistic behavior. This is what she does to me. Makes me forget everything but her, until I'm singularly focused and itching to touch and taste every part of her. Her clit is pressed to my pubic bone, getting worked angrily as I dig my fingers into the flesh of her ass.

"Take me, baby girl," I whisper hoarsely, trying my hardest to stave off my release. "Need you to come." Just as I give voice to the thought, Saylor tightens around me, making me choke back a curse. The walls of her pussy start contracting, setting off my own orgasm. I groan, long and loud, drawing out a few shallow strokes to prolong the pleasure.

We're both panting by the time I come to a stop. Saylor's limp in my arms, relaxed and sated, her mind completely blanked of everything else. An almost indiscernible click sounds behind us from my door being shut. Guess Loch decided to head out now that the show is over. I slide my cock out, hissing at the loss, and tug the condom off. I walk us both to the bathroom and toss it in the trash, then start the shower. Saylor's eyes are barely open, so as soon as the water's warm, I step in.

I soap my girl up, being extra gentle when I clean between her legs. She doesn't seem bothered, though. Just rests her head on my chest and lets me do as I please. We both needed this. To come together and feel. And fuck, did I feel. She's everything. My entire goddamn world, and I refuse to lose her to some nobody who's too chicken shit to show his face. No one is going to take her from us. Certainly not a coward who preys on innocent women under the cloak of anonymity.

We'll never let it happen, and even if I have to remind myself a thousand times, I *will* fucking believe in our ability to keep Saylor safe. The moment I start questioning our competence, I might as well take myself off the case. Because at the end of the day, she's more than our girlfriend. The stakes might be higher because of who Saylor is to us, but we're still qualified to protect and defend her if the need arises. I have to trust my training, and right now it's obsessing over how I found her halfway out to fucking sea.

"You hate the ocean," I mumble, resting my chin on her head. Saylor stiffens, but I keep running my fingers over the bumps of her spine. The last thing I want is for her to feel like this is an interrogation. But as much as I have to trust myself and the guys, I need to trust her as well. We can't protect her if she's hellbent on putting herself in jeopardy. Aside from going in the water and the danger that entailed, Saylor running off like that was reckless in its own right. There are too many unknowns for her to be going anywhere—two feet or fifty yards—without one of us tagging along.

"I'm sorry," she whispers, hugging me a little tighter.

"I don't need your apologies, Little Fighter." I peel Saylor away from me so I can look her in the eye. "You can't do that to me ever again. To us. I know how strong that urge can be to run away from everything, but I need you to fight it. If you need space, head downstairs or take a room. It doesn't even have to be yours. Just don't split and leave us wondering where the hell you went." I brush the wet hair from her face and kiss the tip of her nose.

"Promise," Saylor sighs, leaning up to peck my lips. I flip the shower off and grab a towel to wrap around her. She's dragging, emotionally and physically spent. When she's nice and dry, I head to the closet to get us some clothes. I dress Saylor in one of my t-shirts, then place her on the counter. I kiss her cute little toes before slipping on some socks, knowing how easily her feet get cold. Once we're both dressed, I carry her to bed. She gets comfortable, patting the spot beside her. I slide in, a pleased smile on my face as I tug her closer.

"I love you," Saylor voices, twirling a wet strand of my hair as she drifts off to sleep. It's the perfect fucking metaphor for how wrapped around her finger I am.

"I love you too, baby girl." I kiss the top of her head and close my eyes, allowing myself to breathe fully for the first time since Loch relayed Denvers call. We've still got a shitstorm waiting for us, but for now, my girl is safe and in my arms.

Chapter Forty-Six

Saylor

The following days are nothing short of hell. I've regressed back to the frightened girl who awoke in the hospital, surrounded by people, yet still feeling utterly alone. The gamut of emotions I go through from one minute to the next is torturous. Danielle has cleared her schedule twice now to help me through a spontaneous breakdown, and the guys are walking around on eggshells, at a loss for what to say or do to make any of this right.

I've spent the last hour detailing my latest nightmare. A faceless, shadowed image of a man lurking out of focus, his cold eyes boring into me. I can't see them clearly, but the eerie sense of foreboding it leaves me with tells me all I need to know. It unnerved me so badly, I bolted from sleep. My body started moving without me being awake, desperate to escape the feel of being watched and preyed upon.

After replaying the entire ordeal, listening to Danielle attempt to rationalize the tricks my mind is intent on playing, I'm left feeling drained and nauseated. I've never felt like she used psychobabble with me, but my nerves are frayed, and every bit of '*insight*' she's offering is rubbing me the wrong way. I normally appreciate the steps we go through, the breakdowns and explanations for why I'm feeling a certain way or responding abnormally, but it's too much today.

There's no reprieve—not in consciousness or sleep. All I can think about is how blissfully ignorant I've been. And now the curtain's been pulled back, opening my eyes to the truth, and I can't go back to before. I actually believed this was coming to a close. That the five-year stint of misery I was subjected to would soon be buried, left to rot and fade into a distant memory that didn't plague my every waking moment. It's pathetic, really, how naïve I still am. You'd think after everything I've been through, I would know by now to expect the unexpected.

"For what it's worth—I'm so sorry, Saylor," Danielle laments, interrupting my derailed thoughts. Her face stares back at me through the screen, her eyes awash with pity. I nod, unable to formulate a better response, and avert my gaze. She goes over the same spiel that concludes every session we've had thus far —*call me if you need me, day or night, otherwise, we'll talk next week*. I agree and quickly end the call. The lack of sound makes my shoulders sag.

After taking a few minutes to myself, I head for living room. I feel like I've been on autopilot since finding out about Liam. I'm just going through the motions, doing the things I normally would, but zombified. My movement feels stiff and choreographed, but maybe if I keep at it, I'll start to feel like me again. When the room comes into view, I find the guys positioned in various spots along the sectional, their handsome faces pinched with worry.

"Hey, love," Lochlan greets me, standing to meet me halfway. He takes my hand and guides me to an empty space on the couch. "We're waiting on a call from Denvers. He sent a message about twenty minutes ago, saying he has an update. We asked him to give us some time so you could be here too." I squeeze Lochlan's hand in appreciation, both eager and dreading to hear what the FBI has managed to dig up. His phone rings, leaving me no time to mentally prepare.

"Denvers," Lochlan answers. "You're on speaker and everyone's present."

"I'll get right to it, then," Denvers states. "Liam Price's death has been ruled a homicide, cause of death is strangulation. Looks like someone got the jump on him from the backseat, using a heavy-duty fishing line to wrap around his neck. Timeline is roughly the same, though it's hard to say for sure due to the body being submerged for so long." I have no idea how to feel about that statement, so I push it to the back of my mind for the time being.

"A laptop was found in a storage compartment beneath the passenger seat." Krew perks up, his eyes laser focused on the phone. He's mentioned how hopeful he is that further evidence might be recovered, explaining that even though anything electronic would be waterlogged and fried, the data itself is stored magnetically. "We have a team combing through it, but so far, we've gathered some pretty damning information. Saylor, honey, are you sure you want to hear all of this right now?" The soft tone of his voice has me questioning my mental capacity for any more revelations, but I know I need to hear it. So, like a big girl, I rip the metaphorical band-aid off, quickly agreeing before I change my mind.

"Yes, please."

Denvers sighs, but doesn't disregard my choice. "Liam has been in contact with an unknown individual for years. Thirteen at least, possibly longer than that. These operations work on a trading system —you gotta give three, to get three. It seems that Liam used his standing and position to exploit numerous children, using every opportunity to his advantage. We've unearthed photographs from various sporting events at the Laiken County Recreation Department. Girls and boys changing, for instance. It's a small relief, but we've cleared the rest of his staff. There's no indication that Liam had any of his deputies aiding him."

My fingers shake as I press them against my lips. The guys don't look surprised, so I'm guessing Denvers is explaining the ins-and-outs of child pornography for my benefit. These sick assholes trade our pictures like they're Pokémon cards. But we're *kids*. Innocent, naïve little children who don't deserve to be exploited so heinously.

"The person Liam was working with took a particular liking to Saylor." Denvers pauses, giving his words time to register. There's a visible shift in the guys, an air of anger and protectiveness wafting off of them. "They struck a deal—Liam would take her until the other male could arrange retrieval. There were set guidelines. Liam was encouraged to break her will, so she'd be compliant and receptive, but under no circumstance was he to violate Saylor." The tremble in my hand has worked its way through my entire body. Lochlan pulls me closer, the warmth of his skin helping chase away the sudden chill that's causing my teeth to chatter.

"For whatever reason, Liam went off script." *Yes, he most certainly did.* "Despite the massive sum of money he was given for his troubles, he still deviated from the original plan. We can't say for sure, but we believe the mastermind behind this entire thing is the unidentified male. He's smart—scarily so—and we haven't been able to track him back to a legitimate IP address. He's the one who orchestrated the photo that circulated the auctions, making it look like Saylor was trafficked. We don't know everything yet, but we've got a hell of lot more information than we did."

"The twins are great at what they do, but this guy is fucking extraordinary. How the hell are we supposed to find someone who's managed to be a ghost for this long?" Havok questions, his hands clenching into fists as he works his jaw back and forth.

"We keep doing what we're doing—taking it one day at a time. This isn't a crime show, kid. Cases don't get solved in an hour-long episode." Havok huffs in annoyance, rolling his icy blue eyes as he flops back against the couch. "Until then, I'm arranging a new safe house for Saylor. Once I have confirmation, we'll discuss extraction."

"Wait…what?" Kash leans forward, his gaze bouncing between the others.

"We agreed that she would stay there as long as it made sense. And now it doesn't. We have every reason to believe this guy knows her approximate location, and we have no physical descriptors to identify him by. Moving Saylor is the best thing we can do to keep her safe," Denvers answers, his stern tone leaving no room for argument. Kash shoots me a panicked look, his puppy dog eyes making my chest twinge painfully.

"Understood," Lochlan interrupts, placating Denvers while earning himself four angry glares of betrayal. "Give us a call when you know more." They end the conversation, blanketing the room in silence. I'd been grateful for the quiet when I ended my video chat with Danielle, but this feels like the calm before a storm. There's so much tension swirling around, I could choke on it.

"He can't take her," Kash rushes out, jumping to his feet anxiously. He starts to pace, babbling to himself, his words nonsensical and verging on hysteric. "She's safe with us, not some random team of agents he throws together at the last minute. We care about *her*, not the accolades of a job well done. *She's ours, damnit!*" He yells the last part, successfully cracking my heart in two. Krew hurries to his brother, gripping his face between his hands as he whispers softly, doing his best to talk him down.

It's not working, though. He can't catch his breath as the panic takes over. Our eyes meet, mine blurring with tears as I watch him fall apart before me. *Because of me*. He slaps Krew's hands away and stumbles toward me, dropping to his knees at my feet. Kash lays his head on my lap and wraps his arms around my middle.

"You can't leave," he mumbles, his hands fisting the back of my sweatshirt as he hugs me tighter. Tears spill down my cheeks as I watch Kash crumble. With my vision bleary, I don't even register what's happening when Roan eases in behind him. Not until he sticks him with a needle. In slow motion, Kash looks down at the point of entry, a sad smile curving his lips.

"Can't sleep without you, sweetness." His voice is disjointed as the drug works its way through his system. It only takes a minute, a few slow blinks, for it to fully take effect. Kash slumps over, his weight resting against me.

"Fuck!" Krew roars, slamming his fist through the wall. I understand his anger. His frustration. I hate that Roan did this to him, but he was manic. Kash himself stressed to me how necessary it was for him to be taken out of commission if he was too far gone. Doesn't mean I have to like it.

"Let's put him in Saylor's room," Lochlan instructs. Krew and Havok peel Kash off of me and carry him down the hall. I glance back, watching Roan's head hang as he braces his hands on the counter. *Always taking on the tough jobs*. I'm too emotionally depleted to offer him any comfort, so I let Lochlan lead me to my room. The guys place Kash on my bed, tugging his boots off before covering him up.

"You okay, sweetheart?" Lochlan asks, gripping my chin between his thumb and forefinger, forcing me to look at him.

"Yeah," I choke out, but we both know I'm not.

"Want one of us to stay?"

"No, I'll be fine." I wave him off, stepping back to sever the contact. Lochlan's eye narrow at my blatant dismissal, but he doesn't question me. "I think I'll rest with Kash. It's been a long day." He watches me closely, then relents with a nod.

"Alright, love. Yell if you need us." Lochlan kisses my forehead and turns to leave.

"Love you, pretty girl." Havok pauses on his way out to give me a hug.

"Love you too." I feel the burn of fresh tears, but force them back.

"Take care of my brother, Tink," Krew pleads, pulling me in for a kiss. His lips are soft and warm against mine, momentarily distracting me from the shitshow we're wading through. "I'll check in later."

And then they're gone. I stand there, just inside my door, and stare at the man lying on my bed. He's beautifully broken, but he's mine. I hate what this is doing to him. My arrival in their lives shouldn't be causing this much of a disruption. Significant others are supposed to better you, not make you worse. Right now, I'm struggling to see what I offer that could possibly be considered an improvement.

I slide in next Kash and rest my head on his chest. For someone who's so active and present, it's disconcerting to see him like this. Still and lifeless. If I couldn't hear his heart thumping steadily beneath my ear, I'd start to worry. Try as I might, I can't seem to doze off. I'm restless, anxiety causing me to toss and turn. I finally give up and slip off the bed. A bath might help relax me, but for some reason, my feet carry me to the closet.

I walk to the back, pausing as I bend to pick up the box containing my mother's things. I slump down the wall, tugging it across my lap. My brain is still working to catch up, but it's clear what my heart needs—the comfort of my mom. I slowly pull the lid off, exhaling audibly as the contents come into view. I doubt I'll ever be able to look at this stuff without feeling the unfair loss of her. I was robbed of so many years. We both were.

At the bottom of the box, I find the letter she wrote me. Her '*one day*' hopes, all wrapped up in a small white envelope. My fingers hover above it as I swallow nervously. I can feel sweat dampening my palms, because I know what I'm about to do. I'm going to read it, and that makes me eager and devastated simultaneously. Carefully, I pull the paper out and unfold it. Tears come hot and heavy from the first line alone.

My Dearest Saylor,

It's strange, to be unsure of what you hope for in regard to your child's life. If you're no longer alive, I pray your death was quick and painless. I find peace in knowing your father would have been waiting for you. You might not remember him, but I have zero doubts you'll know him one day. To experience his love is like nothing I've ever known. Your heart has always reminded me of him. I'm ashamed to admit this, but a part of me —the selfish, heartbroken mother—hopes when I die, you'll be waiting for me. I miss you so much I can't breathe some days. How do parents do this? I'm not alone in my grief. The loss of a child is not singular to me, but I can't fathom how they go on. You're a part of me, Saylor Elise. A part I cannot live without. I carried you inside me, endured hours of unmedicated labor. Becoming a mother was the scariest, most gratifying thing I've ever done. I don't know how to exist outside of that. You can't turn it off. But someone took that away from me. They ripped my heart from my body and I've been hemorrhaging ever since.

I press a hand to my mouth and bite back a sob. Tears flood my eyes, streaking down my cheeks in rivers. *Oh, God*. This is torture. Each word I read, leaves one less remaining. Soon, there won't be anything left. As much as I want to stuff it back in the box and save the rest for another day, I can't stop myself from finishing it.

If you are still alive, I need you to fight. If you're reading this, then you've made it home. Whatever you've gone through, it won't just disappear. That beautiful, smart mind of yours will try to turn against you, but you have to be stronger than that. Don't let them win. Whoever did this to us will pay, but not at the expense of your peace. Get help, sweet girl. Live for the both of us. I'm so sorry I won't be there to witness your comeback. Be brave and take control of the life you have left. You're so much stronger than you know, and even if you can't see me, I promise I'll always be watching. Be kind to yourself, and do what makes you happy. I love you now and forever. No matter what awaits me, you are and always will be my greatest joy.

Love,

Mama

I pull a hoodie from the hanger above me and press it to my face. My anguished scream is muffled by the dense fabric, but I vent my hurt—over and over—until my throat is raw and my tears have run dry. That's all of it. Her very last thoughts. I needed them today, but I'm not ready to lose this thread still connecting us. I have no idea how long I've been sitting on the floor, but everything is numb. My heart especially. I stare at the wall in front of me, concerned by the nothingness filling my insides. I think I'm so overwhelmed by everything that's happened, my mind is shutting down. Like it's switched into preservation mode.

I've always felt too much, so it's alarming. I'm sure Danielle would call it a coping mechanism. I did the same thing on the beach. After my angry outburst and berating them for thinking I'd do something dumb and dangerous if I knew about the postcards, I did exactly that. I lost all sense of reality, drifting away to a place the hurt couldn't reach. The only thing to make me feel like me again, was Roan. I've been too in my head to give much thought to what happened between us. The things he did, the way he touched me, all while Lochlan watched. It was impossible to *not* be present. I want that again. To be consumed so entirely, there's no space for anything else. I *need* to fill this void.

With my mind made up, I wipe my face and put the box back together. Once everything is stored properly, I leave the closet. On my way out the door, I stop by the bed and place a kiss on Kash's lips. I can almost taste the sucker he had in his mouth this morning. I should crawl back in beside him, try to sleep off my lack of feeling. Instead, I throw caution to the wind.

I doubt this is what my mom had in mind when she told me to be brave.

Chapter Forty-Seven

Saylor

After searching his office and coming up empty, I slip inside the twins' room and quietly shut the door behind me. I lean my back against it as Krew exits the bathroom, steam billowing around him from the shower he just finished. I feel like we've been here before. He's wearing nothing but a towel, his cut stomach on glorious display. My eyes drink him in as he comes to a stop a few feet in front of me. His head cocks to the side as he assesses me, likely wondering what I'm up to. With deft fingers, I flip the lock on the door. Krew's eyebrow arches at the sound.

"You sure you want this, Tink?" Krew questions, taking slow, measured steps towards me. He pulls the towel from his waist to dry his hair, leaving him completely bare. My gaze drops automatically, taking in the parts of him I've never seen. My throat tightens as I fixate on his cock. There's a barbell piercing through the tip of it, and the longer I stare, the harder it gets. "I won't fuck you nice and slow. In fact, it's going to feel like torture by the time you're begging me to let you come." I shift from one foot to the other, affected by his words alone.

"You won't hurt me." My voice is quiet, but filled with surety.

"Even if I do, you'll like it," Krew retorts smugly, erasing the last few inches between us. His fingers twine around the ends of my hair, gripping it tightly so he can tilt my head back. "By the time I'm done with you, this pussy will be dripping, desperate for my cock to fill it. You want that, princess?" He punctuates the question with another tug, teasing me with his free hand. I hesitate, embarrassed by his words more than anything. I might be unsure of what he plans to do or the experience he has, but I'm certain I want him. I nod my agreement, but he's not satisfied with my nonverbal answer.

"Say it," Krew demands. "Say you want my cock."

"I want your cock," I whisper shakily. Krew groans, his eyes rolling back as he licks his lips.

"Strip," he instructs, stepping back to watch me. I swallow nervously, but face the awkwardness head on. With a deep breath, I lift my sweatshirt over my head. I'm braless underneath, and Krew's eyes hone in on my exposed flesh immediately. Next, I shimmy out of my leggings and panties, discarding them at the same time. We're both naked as the day we were born, drinking each other in.

"Fucking hell," Krew mumbles to himself. "Come here." He lifts his chin, gesturing for me to come closer. I obey, my pulse thundering as I stop in front of him. "You trust me?" he asks.

"Yes."

"Good." Krew leads me to his bed, guiding me down until I'm flat on my back and he's hovering beside me. He pulls something from the nightstand, but I focus on him, willing my nerves to calm. With slow, deliberate movements, Krew places a kiss on each of my wrists. His watchful gaze never leaves mine as he eases my arms above me. A second later, the silky feel of fabric binds my hands to his headboard. Panic shoots through me like a lightning bolt, and I jerk to try and pull them free.

"Stop," Krew demands, his tone firm, but not unkind. "You're okay. Focus on me and nothing else." A whimper escapes me as my heart seizes and struggles to find the right rhythm. My mind latches on to the last time I was restrained, the scent of mildew and dirt making me woozy. "I told you I'd push you past your limit. You'll hate me before this is over, but I promise to kiss it better."

Krew brushes his lips over mine, the contact a sweet juxtaposition to the turmoil he's causing. He gives me little time to voice my acquiescence or objection. His tongue invades my mouth, leaving no room for thoughts outside of him. We're both breathless when he pulls away, a smug grin quirking his lips. With a look of sheer determination, he spreads my thighs roughly and buries his face between my legs. A strangled sound leaves me at the first brush of his tongue.

He sets a pace I can't predict. One minute

it's soft and languorous, the next he's eating me so forcefully, it borders on painful. Every time I climb that peak, he pulls back, switching up his rhythm before I fully crest it. Krew does this repeatedly, working me into such a frenzy, my legs start to shake. I have no idea how long he's been at it when he dips lower, using his hands to spread me open. I squeak at the foreign feel of his mouth in such a private place.

"Be quiet, princess, and let me eat your ass in peace." I sputter indignantly, my eyes pinned to the ceiling as I lie there in shock, but he gets right back to work. Krew licks me from one end to the other, probing that tight ring of muscle with each pass, pushing in a little farther every time. This is, quite possibly, the dirtiest thing I've ever done. But, *God*, it actually feels good. So, *so* good.

"You like that, huh?" I can feel him smiling, and if it wasn't for the way he's using his tongue, I'd squeeze his head between my thighs until it popped like a watermelon. But as it stands, I'm enjoying this far too much to formulate words, much less any sort of aggression. "One day, I'm going to watch my cum drip from this tight little hole."

"Please," I cry hoarsely.

"Please what, Tink?" Krew stops altogether, resting on his heels as he stares down at me. "You need to come? Is that it?" He slips a finger in, making my back arch. "I'll make it better, but first I want you to tell me whose pussy this is. You might be ours, but here and now, you belong to me and me alone. I control your pleasure. Your pain." My lips part, but words evade me. I can't do what he's asking, because I can't think straight.

"Say it," Krew grits out, his own restraint waning after the endless amount of time he's spent driving me to brink of insanity. "Whose is it, princess?" he taunts me, slapping my clit with his cock. I whimper, squirming beneath him as he slides back and forth, rubbing his piercing against me. It's too much, yet not enough.

"Yours," I relent, my voice drenched in desperation, but he continues to keep my release just out of reach. As the first tear slips from my eye, I realize Krew was right. I'm a shaky, strung-out mess, willing to do or say anything to ease the ache.

"Fuck, yes," Krew groans, watching the evidence of my frustration trail down my cheek. I think the sight turns him on even more. He slams inside of me, making me grunt from the force. His thrust is so rough, my body slides up the bed. Krew anchors me, his hands tight on my hips as he starts to fuck me savagely. My mouth falls open, a silent scream on the tip of my tongue as I finally come.

"You feel as good as you taste, princess. But we're far from done." Krew twists me to my side, only pulling out long enough to resituate me. He lifts my leg, turning my body while he keeps the same angle. My hands are still tied to the headboard, the fabric digging in harder without the extra slack. Surprisingly, I relish the hint of pain. I sought Krew out to escape the numbness creeping in. I'm certainly feeling the opposite of nothing right now. The sound our flesh makes as it slaps together is downright vulgar, in the best way. We're drenched in sweat, but the soaked sheet below me isn't from exertion. Krew has edged me for so long, I don't think I can endure any more, but he shows no hint of stopping anytime soon.

"Take it, princess," Krew pants, his thrust slowing just the slightest as he presses a finger against my ass. I'm so keyed up, I don't even flinch. He slips in easily, working me from both ends until I'm nothing more than a wet, writhing mess. "Goddamn, Tink. It won't be long before you're taking two cocks at once." I clench around him, my body on board despite the questions and concerns that scenario conjures.

My orgasm hits out of nowhere, building so quick it makes my vision blur. This must be what people mean by '*seeing stars*'. Krew groans, hissing as he pulls out and rips the condom off. I had no idea he even put one on, which is irresponsible on my part. He strokes his cock, squeezing it angrily till thick, hot spurts of his cum paint my side. I lie there, limp and sated, too exhausted to bother with the clean-up. But, apparently, that's a moot point when Krew isn't finished with me yet. I scream as he drops back down and seals his mouth to my pussy. His tongue spears inside of me, fucking me again. But this tool of choice has the ability to bend and stroke, licking at every spot he can reach. My entire body seizes as I come, gripping chunks of Krew's hair in a vain attempt to pull him off of me.

"You have to stop," I pant. "It's too much. I'm too sensitive, Krew."

"Oh, princess. I'm going to fuck you at least

once more, maybe even twice." I cry at hearing that, my emotional response stemming from the toying way he'll use me. But on the other side of it, pleasure awaits me. He flips me to stomach, instantly covering me with the weight of his body.

"Stay flat and keep your legs pressed together." Krew's breath fans against the side of my face. His cock slides between my ass cheeks, making me tense. "Not today, but real fucking soon," he chuckles, nudging himself in, only using the tip to tease me. Each time, he sinks in a little more, until he bottoms out completely.

"Jesus, Tink." His hand wedges beneath me and grips my throat. He squeezes, just enough to add some panic to the mix, and grinds his dick inside of me. I moan, giving him the go ahead to fuck me as he pleases. And he does. Several times.

Afterwards, Krew stumbles to the bathroom, his balance so off-center he smacks the doorframe with his shoulder. I smile at his muffled curse, halfway to sleep when he finally comes back with a warm washcloth. His brow pinches with annoyance as he wipes his cum away. I sigh when he tosses the soiled rag aside and curls around me. Krew kisses my neck, his arm wedged between my breasts so he can lightly cup my throat. A small part of me questions the silence. My tendency to overthink is warring with what I know to be true. He hasn't voiced his feelings, or given me those three words I long to hear. But I know Krew loves me. He's shown me plenty of times over the past few weeks, whether he realizes it or not.

Proof is in the bathroom light he left on.

~

"You smell like sex and bad decisions," Kash pouts, pressing his face against my neck. The teasing lilt to his voice lets me know he's only joking. I twine my fingers through his curls, happy to hear his voice after the state he was in yesterday.

"That's rich, coming from you." Krew steps from the closet, his bare abdomen disappearing far too quickly behind a fresh shirt. "You good now? Because we've got enough shit on our plate without having to deal with yours too." I glare at Krew, angered on Kash's behalf at his lack of empathy. I know his annoyance stems from seeing his twin suffer through a full-blown meltdown, but that doesn't make it okay. His cruel words are unnecessary.

"All good, little brother," Kash replies easily, appearing unbothered by the obvious dig. They lock gazes, a silent conversation ensuing between them as I watch from the sidelines. Eventually, Krew releases a sigh and saunters closer. He braces his hands on the bed, caging me in and forcing Kash to put some space between us.

"Princess," he greets me softly, a tender smile gracing his lips. "I've got some work to do, but I'll see you later." Krew drops a kiss to my forehead and turns to leave. Just as he reaches the door, he looks back and adds, "Be a good girl. Maybe fill Kash in on that new thing you like?" Krew smirks, his eyes alight with challenge. I flush from head to toe, but the pillow I throw in retaliation only smacks the closed door as he slips from the room. When I turn to face Kash, he has an excited, curious look on his face. I groan and burrow beneath the covers.

"Let's go, stinky," Kash orders, ripping me from the warmth of their bed. He stiff-arms me, holding my body away from his like it's riddled with cooties as he struts toward the bathroom. "You reek of my brother's baby juice," Kash sneers, his nose scrunching in mock disgust. He drops me to my feet so he can turn the shower on, and only then do I realize I'm completely naked. It's a testament to how far I've come—how comfortable I've grown with the guys—that I'm not the least bit bothered by my nudity.

Kash smiles boyishly as I help him undress, his eyebrows wagging comically when I slide his sweats off. I roll my eyes, knowing I'm way too sore to entertain the idea of sex so soon after the wrecked state Krew left me in just a few hours ago. I sigh in relief as we slip in together, letting the hot water ease the tension from my sore, overworked muscles.

Who knew orgasm deprivation could be so straining?

I spin to face Kash, using my soaped-up hands to clean his body. I trace the dips and valleys along his stomach, marveling at the definition. It amazes me how toned he is, especially with his diet consisting of mostly sugar and carbs. Yet he rarely works out. God really does have favorites. His eyes are still heavy, a side effect from the medication, I'm sure, but it does nothing to dampen his beauty. I lift his arm and brush my finger across the faint bruise, then press my lips to it. If I could, I'd take away his suffering in a heartbeat.

It's painful to know that my involvement with Kash is causing him such distress, he's needed to be heavily medicated. Love shouldn't hurt like that, but I know I'll never give him up. He wouldn't let me if I tried.

"I'll take you with me," I insist, standing on my tiptoes so I can reach his lips. "We'll hide you in a suitcase if we have to, but I won't let Denvers separate us." Kash's shoulders sag as soon as the words leave my mouth. That oppressive weight of fear eases up, allowing him to breathe a little easier. But we both know it's unlikely. If the FBI wants me moved, nothing and no one can stop them. This awful sense of doom hangs over me, taunting me with what-ifs. Should Denvers choose to take me from the guys, it could very well be the final nail in the coffin of my psyche. I'm only doing as well as I am because of them.

"I do travel well." Kash rocks his head from side to side, staring off speculatively. "Shelf-stable and pretty low maintenance." I scoff at the outright lie. His sucker addiction alone would require its own set of luggage.

"Thank God you're pretty," I tease with a pat to Kash's chest.

"Yeah?"

"Mmhmm," I force out, my eyes closing as he toys with my nipple. "And sweet." I slip lower, trailing kisses down his body as I make my descent. When I hit my knees, I look up, finding Kash's gaze intent on me through the spray of water. My hair is stuck to my skin, but the sight I make must please him. His breath stutters as he grips himself and traces my mouth with his cock. I lick my lips instinctively, tasting the salty drop of precum he smears across them.

"So sweet," I add, making him groan appreciatively. I open, allowing him entrance, hoping like hell the learning curve for blowjobs is pretty self-explanatory. I start slow, allowing myself a few seconds to adjust to the foreign feel of something probing the back of my throat. When I look at Kash, the heat in his eyes excites me. To see the affect this is having on him makes it worth it. He chokes back a moan when I grip his ass, urging him to take over.

"Sweetness," Kash says in warning. My response is to swallow, feeling empowered by the way he slaps a hand on the wall to keep himself upright. "*Jesus Christ*. I think you sucked my soul out." I laugh—as much as I can with my mouth full. Only Kash could make light of such an intimate moment.

He peers down at me, bringing his hand up to stroke the side of my face lovingly. I nod, giving him permission to use me how he wants. Kash bites his lip in contemplation, but ultimately gives in. He grips the back of my head, his pace nice and easy, but it's obvious that's for my benefit. His jaw is clenched in concentration, thighs strained from the effort he's exerting to keep his need at bay. I dig my fingers in, encouraging him to let go. Kash thrusts forward, causing me to gag, but I don't pull away.

"Breathe for me," Kash instructs while holding himself still. I take slow, deep breaths through my nose, trying not to panic at the way his cock is constricting my airway. His strokes resume, but it doesn't take long before he's fully fucking my mouth.

He taps my cheek, his movement growing sloppy.

"Gonna come, sweetness." I appreciate the heads up, but I've come this far, might as well finish with a bang. I'd like to know what the big deal is. Kash's next words are cut off by a guttural moan. His head falls back as his release fills my throat. I try—I really do—but there's no way in hell I'm swallowing. It tastes sterile. Like the smell of a hospital.

Oh God, I'm going to vomit.

I pop my mouth free and shuffle toward the shower drain. I spit a few times, then tilt my head back and fill my mouth with water. Wash, rinse, repeat. I can officially mark that off my to-do list, and place it on the never-again side. I flop to my butt and peer back at Kash. He's slumped against the wall, looking happier than a pig in shit. I slide over and straddle his lap, happy to see some life behind his eyes.

"You are, without a doubt, the bestest Best Friend ever." I giggle at his absurdity, but it's quickly cut off when my back hits the floor. "Now it's my turn." Kash grins wickedly as he reaches over and detaches the shower head. With his tool of choice in hand, he makes a game of finding out how many times he can make me come before the water runs cold.

Three—the answer is three.

Chapter Forty-Eight

Kade

"Fuck me, it's hot."

Roan tosses me a bottle of water, aimed straight at my head, in response to my bitching and moaning. I might've grown up in this godforsaken swamp, but that doesn't mean I've gotten used to, nor like, sweating from every pore on my body. I down the drink in two swallows, then use my shirt to wipe my face. We've been at it since the ass crack of dawn, working on getting the house prepared before the latest tropical storm brewing over the Atlantic makes landfall.

You wouldn't know it by the current state of things, but shit can change in an instant around here. It's blue skies as far as the eye can see, a veritable fucking sauna, without even a hint of a breeze. *Florida weather, man.* So far, we've managed to get the grill and patio furniture stored away, and now we're securing the hurricane shutters on the top floor windows. It's been slow-going, but the end's in sight, and staying busy has kept my mind off of Say.

I fell asleep to her screams. Ecstasy driven, but

torturous, nonetheless. I had to lie there, alone in my bed, and listen to Krew push her to the brink, wringing out every ounce of pleasure he could muster from her tiny little body. I wasn't sure if I wanted to beat the ever-loving fuck out of the twisted asshole, or sing his praises. He has peculiar tastes, and if Say can handle the shit he was dishing out, then there's nothing I could do to scare her off. I went to bed with a hard-on and woke just as desperate, especially when her whimpers and moans could be heard from the hallway. By the time she joined us in the kitchen, her face fresh and hair damp, I nearly tossed her on the counter and had her for breakfast. Say has no idea how sexy she is, prancing around the house in one of our shirts. It's a goddamn siren's call, seeing her bare legs disappear beneath the hem of a ratty tee.

Judging by Roan's muttered curses and overall discontent, I'd say his night of audible voyeurism was just as miserable as mine. Every time he positions a shutter, I wince. He's not focused enough to be wielding power tools, so he's in charge of sliding the heavy metal barriers into place, then I come behind him with the drill. I thought that was the best way to avoid injury, but as Ro rams the sheet over the window, he traps my poor pinky finger with it.

"Motherfucker!" I wail, ripping my hand free and taking a chunk of skin off in the process. I grip it to my chest as blood starts to trickle down my arm.

"Shit, man," Ro swears. In a flash, he's right in front of me, grabbing at my battered hand. I attempt to swat him away, my inner child scared as fuck he's gonna hurt the boo-boo even more.

"Fuck off." I twist my torso to keep him out of reach. "You've already cost me one digit, so maybe stop while you're ahead, you Hulk-sized sonofabitch."

"You're a whiny asshole, you know that?" Ro crosses his arms and glares down at me. If he thinks shaming me into '*growing a pair*' will work, he's sorely misjudged how stubborn I can be.

"What the hell are you two going on about?" Krew whisper-yells as he slips out and shuts the slider behind him. "Tink just fell asleep after tossing and turning half the night, so let's cut the shit, huh?" I raise an eyebrow, glancing at Ro as we get our asses chewed out by the last person I would've expected to get up in arms over a girl's beauty rest. Two months ago, I wouldn't have believed Krew capable of caring for someone outside of our ragtag little group. Even then, his feelings for me are touch and go. Yet here he stands, pissed on our girl's behalf.

"Awww," I retort mockingly, walking closer to pinch Krew's cheek. "Our resident ice king is starting to thaw. Won't be long before he's a melted puddle of goo, spouting off soliloquies of love."

"This is why no one likes you," Krew deadpans, spinning on his heel to head back inside. "In fact, I'm almost certain you're Tink's least favorite." His voice drops as we follow behind him, all three of us glancing to the small lump sleeping on the couch. My heart pangs at the sight of Say buried beneath the covers, like she's trying to shield herself from the rest of the world. Her reality has been flipped upside down one too many times, but she's too strong to crack. We won't let this get the best of her. It's a setback, but nothing we can't handle.

"Maybe *someone* shouldn't have kept her up, doing all sorts of ungodly things to her sacred body," I tease, smirking at Krew's unamused glare.

"Children," Loch interrupts, his tone serious but quiet. "Denvers just sent a text. They've secured a new safe house. He thinks Saylor can be moved by Wednesday, at the latest."

Fuck.

That's two days. Two goddamn days to drink my fill of her before she's taken from me. *Again.* I clench my jaw to keep from spewing my refusal. It burns like acid to keep quiet, but my opinion wouldn't matter. Not even Loch can stop the wheels that Denvers has put into motion. While I understand the reasoning, my whole being rejects the notion of separating the six of us. We've created something special. This dependency I feel isn't normal, but our love isn't either and watching her leave will feel like having a limb hacked off with a rusty handsaw.

Agonizing.

I turn toward the kitchen sink and flip the tap on. The throb in my pinky has taken a backseat, my focus remaining on the conversation still taking place behind me. Ro growls and spits his own version of my exact thoughts, but it's more to voice his disapproval than actually believing it'll do anything to change the outcome. By the time I get a bandage wrapped around my finger and face the others, Kash has joined the party, looking more unhinged by the second. He's stress-eating a lollipop, wide brown gaze bouncing from Saylor to Loch, like he's waiting for the '*gotcha*' that's never going to come. None of us are coping very well with the looming deadline, but Kash is especially fucked up about it. He's edging toward the business end of another sedative if those crazy eyes continue to hang around.

Despite knowing this is a temporary separation, his mind is struggling to wrap itself around the idea of being without Say at all. Sadly, trauma like his and Krew's can last a lifetime. They deal with it differently, but their connection to Say is steeped with underlying issues they're still trying to work past. Shit, I think we're all drawn to the calmness we feel whenever she's close. Without saying a word, Kash walks off. He stops next to Say and pulls the covers back, then climbs in beside her. After a few more hushed whispers, we break apart, isolating like we do best when we start to feel too much. I drop to the empty spot near Say's head and gently run my fingers through her hair. My nose curls as I glance at Kash, finding that stupid fucking sucker still shoved in his mouth. I let my head fall back, giving in to the exhaustion I feel from working in the hot sun all day.

As my eyes close, that pit in my stomach starts to open. Dread builds rapidly as I envision the moment a blacked-out SUV will drive away with our girl, taking her to some unknown location for an indeterminate amount of time. I push it away, refusing to give it any room to grow. Say's still here. I can feel her glossy blonde strands beneath my hand, hear the soft puffs of air leaving her slightly parted lips. For now, I have her. And no matter how long it takes, I'll have her again.

~

The first thing to penetrate my sleep is a whimper, followed closely by a sharp pain in my arm. My eyes snap open, instantly focused on the last place Say had been when I passed out. She's now huddled against my side, nails buried in my flesh as she grips it like her life depends on it. Those blue eyes are fixated on the slider as she trembles from head to toe.

"Say Baby," I call out softly, inching my fingers below hers. "What's wrong?" She turns slowly, but her eyes stay glued to the deck. The sun has set, making it virtually impossible to see outside.

"Someone's out there," she whispers, her hand squeezing mine as she continues to shake. My brows dip together as I search for any sign of life, but there's nothing. The motion lights are off, and even if something was out there, she couldn't have seen it. It's too dark.

"Get that look off your face right now," she growls. My mouth opens to argue, but whatever I'd been gearing up to say evaporates the second I get a good look at her. She's furious, beautifully so, but there's something else flashing brighter than indignation in those heated blue depths.

Fear.

"Hey," I offer placatingly, but she backs away from me, shaking her head profusely at my silent denial.

"What's going on?" Kash croaks, choosing the perfect moment to wake his lazy ass up and offer some assistance. The last time Say got panicky, she took off and nearly drowned herself in the goddamn ocean. I'd like to avoid a repeat.

"I saw someone. On the deck." Kash spins around so quickly, he almost topples off the couch.

"What? When?!"

"Just a minute ago," she stammers out. "I *felt* them."

My shoulders slump. As much as I hate to admit it, there's a good chance her mind is playing tricks on her. She likely had a nightmare, and wasn't fully awake. It's easy to convince yourself you see something that's not really there when things are still playing out in a dreamlike state. I've done it several times, certain there were spiders crawling up my wall.

"Stop doing that!" Say screams, her shrill pitch making my eyes widen. Ro comes barreling down the hall, on high alert at hearing the incensed tone our girl is using. "I know I've been a basket case, but I'm not crazy. I know what I saw!" Ro looks between us, trying to figure out what the hell is going on without pissing Say off even more.

"Tell me." She slumps over, curling in on herself as Ro draws closer. "What'd you see, Little Fighter?"

"I woke up feeling funny. Like someone was watching me. After seeing Kash and Havok, I thought it might've been one of them, but it was pretty obvious they were both fast asleep. I glanced at the slider and saw eyes. Someone had their hands pressed to the glass so they could peer in. The rest of their body was shrouded, maybe from the dark or their choice in clothes; I don't know. But they *were* there."

The base of my spine prickles as I listen to Say explain her version of events. It sounds farfetched, but something makes my feet move towards the door. Aside from recent events, she's always been levelheaded. More than most would be after going through everything she has. As I stop in front of the slider, my eyes hone in on the smudge of a handprint. Numbness bleeds through my extremities, rendering me completely immobile as I stare at my worst fear come to life.

Someone was here, despite the security measures we have in place.

I reach for my phone, slipping it from my pocket with shaky fingers. As I pull up the cam feeds, my heart sinks to the soles of my feet. Gray, fuzzy screens stare back at me, devoid of any life. They're all offline, yet there's no alert blaring or notification signaling that there's been a malfunction.

"Say Baby," I choke out, refusing to give my back to the door. "I need you to head downstairs."

"What? Why?" she squeaks out as Ro pushes past me, trying to figure out why I'm so goddamned spooked. He swears when he sees the same distinct outline, yelling for Loch as he sprints for the safe we keep in the pantry. My brain finally snaps to attention as I spin and grab Say's hand, forcing her to move despite her dragging her feet and screaming at me for answers.

"Stop!" I grip her upper arms, hoping to shake some sense into her. Say freezes, her fight getting replaced by a look of hurt. "I need you to listen, pretty girl. You can be angry at me all you want, but you have to be alive in order to put me in my place. And I promise, once this is all over, you can read me the fucking riot act. But right now, I need you to go downstairs and stay there."

"You're scaring me," she sputters, gripping the front of my shirt.

"I'm sorry, baby." I shove the door open and frame her face, needing her complete focus as I dish out instructions. "You remember the panel on the wall that locks the door at the base of the steps?" I wait for her to nod her head before continuing. "Good. Place your hand on the scanner and listen for the beep. Once it's engaged, head to the arms room. Stay there until one of us comes for you. Under no circumstance do you leave the safety of that room. Do you understand?" Another nod as tears fill her eyes.

"I love you. So fucking much, Say." I pull her mouth to mine, committing her taste to memory and kissing her like it's the last time I might get the chance to, just in case shit goes sideways. The second I close the door, relief washes over me. As much as I want to yank it back open and keep her close, I know the safest place she can be is far away from us. Whoever this deranged fucker is, he chose the wrong girl. He's clearly underestimated the lengths we'll go to in order to protect the woman we love.

"Talk to me," Loch orders, looking like he just woke up. He's wearing nothing but pajama bottoms, his hair mussed but eyes alert and assessing. He takes the gun Ro offers as he waits for me to explain.

"Say saw someone on the deck. There's a handprint on the glass." Short and to the point. We've wasted enough time already. Christ, I treated my girl like she was seeing shit, when she might the only reason we got a heads up on the situation. "Cams are down, but no alert came through."

"The fuck?" Krew mutters, tapping away on his laptop. I tint the slider as we wait for answers. I want to know what the hell is happening and why our equipment is failing. "He's hacked our feed. I can get in, but he has control." We share a quiet, weighted look. This is it. The inevitable standoff. I think we all knew this day would come, but having Saylor here—just feet away from danger—makes me wholly unprepared to face this asshole. He's been outsmarting us from the get-go, and we can't afford to give him the upper hand now, not when it really counts.

"Holy shit." I stumble back as realization sets in. "It was him—the downed cams. He's been watching, using the cover of other shit to fuck with our stuff. He waited for the guy on the lawnmower to pass, using the shredded frisbee to take out the front feed, then the suicidal bird to mess with the back." I have no idea how I know it, but I *do*. It's been him the whole damn time.

"Why not strike then? If it was him all along, why wait?" Kash questions, looking perturbed but curious.

"He was learning the system. Cataloguing our response time," Krew answers distractedly, still searching for a way in.

I should've picked up on the weird occurrences sooner. We've never had cams go down like that, one after another. But the reasons were pretty believable, which makes me nervous to find out who this twisted, too smart fuckwad is. He used real-life circumstances to his benefit, not once alerting us to his presence. For fucking weeks. I grip the back of my neck and start to pace, needing an outlet for the panic threatening my ability to think straight. We promised her, swore up and down that no one could get to her here. In no realm of possibility did I think that someone would be able to sneak onto the property undetected, much less hack our fucking security system.

"*Saylooooor*," a slick, nasally voice sounds from the speaker in the main room. I stop dead in my tracks, staring at the device anchored to the wall like it's the offending asshole himself. He doesn't deserve to speak her fucking name.

"He's broadcasting throughout the house," Krew rushes out. Which means Say can hear him.

Fuck, baby. Please don't do anything stupid.

"Come on out, darling. It's time to go home."

Red tints my vision. I blackout completely, unaware of what I've done until the bat slips through my fingers and clangs against the tile floor. Our poor, eighty-five-inch flatscreen dangles from the wall, broken bits of LCD scattered at my feet. An innocent bystander, caught in the crossfire of my rage.

"Our equipment needs an exorcism, brother. And quick, before it meets the same fate as the TV."

Chapter Forty-Nine

Saylor

For the third time in my rather short life, I experience that same out-of-body sensation I first felt on the day of my and mom's wreck. Disbelief keeps me frozen as I replay the last few minutes. The nightmare that woke me, followed closely by the vivid image of someone peering through the slider. My skin crawls just thinking about the person behind that chilling stare.

It takes longer than I care to admit for my body and brain to get with the program. I turn and take off down the stairs, barely making contact with each step. The moment my feet hit the floor, I slam my hand against the security panel, shifting impatiently as I wait for the system to recognize me. A flash of red illuminates the screen, echoed by a buzzing sound. My heart drops as I read the '*access denied*' prompt staring at back at me.

I try again and again, but it never changes. I'm shaking like a leaf, my gaze flying around the darkened space, waiting for the moment something jumps out at me. With no other option, I make my way to the media room and power on the projector screen. After several cursed missteps, I finally find the cam feed. I sag in relief as I watch the guys prowl around the living room. They're safe and free of any obvious injuries, but all five of them are armed to the teeth, anticipating the worst.

"Sayloooor."

Goosebumps pebble my skin at the crackle-y voice calling out for me. They keep talking, but my eyes stay fixed on the screen, noting the shock and rage on each of the guys' faces. Par the course for his temper, Havok explodes, taking out the TV with a few well-placed hits. My knees weaken as I realize how truly fucked we are. I can't engage the vault door. Whoever this person is—the man responsible for every awful thing that's happened to me—he has control over the security system.

We're at the whim of a madman.

My eyes fly to the camera mounted by the ceiling. If I had to gamble with whether or not I was being watched, I'd place my bets on the absolutely side. Thinking on my feet, I head toward the snack area. There's no mop or broom in sight for me to poke it with, so I grab a few cans of soda from the fridge. Hugging them to my chest, I ignore the stinging cold seeping through my thin t-shirt, and glare at the camera.

With my free hand fisted, I pour every ounce of the fury I've been stockpiling into that one look, hoping like hell he sees me in all my unbroken glory. And then I launch can after can, venting my frustration with a drawn-out scream. A few go wide, but eventually my aim rings true. I'm fighting for breath by the time it clatters to the floor, landing amongst the sticky, busted mess of coke and sprite. In the grand scheme of things, I've likely only pissed him off. But at least he can't see me. It's quiet—*too quiet*—after giving my nutjob stalker the metaphorical middle finger. It's quick, but I don't miss the pleased smirk Krew flashes.

"That wasn't very nice, darling. I'd hate to punish you on our first night together, but I bet you scream so pretty."

That disembodied voice disrupts the silence, making chills wash over me. I shiver in disgust at what this man has planned for me. I'd rather die than give him the satisfaction of playing out his twisted fantasies. I'm watching the guys intently, looking for any hint or indication of what I should do. It feels wrong to leave them up there, fighting off an enemy I brought to their door. If it wasn't for my watchful eye, I would've missed the shadow creeping from the hallway. Not one of the guys is facing that direction, feeling secure enough to give it their backs, because there's no reason to believe anyone could've breached the house from a top floor window. That would have been difficult on a good day, but I clearly remember the storm shutters getting bolted on earlier.

"Roan!" The glint of a gun makes me lightheaded, but my warning comes a second too late. Not that anyone could've heard me from this far away. He's the closest, directly in the line of fire, and there's nothing I can do to prevent the inevitable from happening. I don't hear the gunshot, but the flinch that rocks Roan's body is unmistakable.

Almost instantly, the lights cut out, leaving me alone in the dark, clueless as to what's happening above me. I wait, my breaths growing choppier as I debate what to do. He's hurt, and every second that passes could be detrimental to whether or not he's okay. My heart seizes painfully at the thought of this ending in tragedy. It can't. It just can't. I need him—need all of them. The screen flickers back to life, but the sight that greets me makes my knees buckle. I hit the floor hard, but the pain barely registers.

Roan stares back at me, his position a mirror image of my own. There's one glaring difference, though. Behind him stands a hooded figure, his frame much smaller in comparison, but the gun pressed to Roan's temple gives him the upper hand. Bile burns my throat, but I push it back, afraid to take my eyes off the man I love.

"Now, now. We can do this the easy way, or we can do it the hard way." My living nightmare emphasizes his point by digging the barrel of the gun into Roan's head. One slip of his finger is all it would take to send my world crumbling. "It's past time for us to be going. Come on out and we'll see about leaving your friends in one piece. Five minutes, darling. Clock is ticking."

My body burns with anger, yet my blood runs ice cold. My hands began to shake, palms pooling with sweat. Roan glares at the camera, his eyes speaking volumes without a single word breaching his lips. *Don't you fucking dare*. But he knows I'll never sit back and do nothing. I did that for far too long, and I have no intention of letting him die. I'd be signing my own death warrant. It'd kill me to have his blood on my hands.

I drag in a deep breath and leave my illusion of safety. I'll have to risk being seen, but there's no way in hell I'm walking in there without some form of protection. I don't think there are any other cameras down here, but who knows what this man has rigged up. I skirt the walls as I head for the arms room, making myself as small as possible. I squeeze through the door, tears springing to my eyes when I realize the panel on the wall isn't going to grant me access. We've been locked out of everything. I backtrack, wracking my brain for a plan B. In a sudden lightbulb moment, I remember that the guys have a knack for hiding weapons around the house. I rush back to the media room and scour every inch I can think of, but nothing turns up.

I'm skirting defeat when I shove my hand between the cushions, searching the leather seats. In my last-ditch effort, I trace every inch, shocked when my fingers graze something hard. There, wedged between the chair and wall, I find a gun. It's secured in a holster, but I quickly rip it free, my nerves skyrocketing as I grip the handle. It's unfamiliar, bulkier than the one Roan taught me to shoot, but beggars can't be choosers. I double check the safety and slip it in the back of my leggings.

A welcome numbness blankets me as I ascend the stairs. Whatever happens, it won't be a result of me caving and handing myself over. I've come way too far to burrow back into that shell of a girl I was, too scared to fight but desperate to live. He won't take another day of my life from me, much less years. As my fingers grip the doorknob and start to twist, I straighten my spine, mentally bracing myself for what needs to be done.

The first thing I see is Krew, his deep brown eyes chastising my choice to walk right into the lion's den, but there's also a hint of understanding. If our roles were reversed, they'd do the same for me. I note the rest of the guys in my peripheral, but my attention is drawn to Roan. He looks pissed, his massive form vibrating with anger. I smile at the big man, my eyes brimming with tears.

In no scenario should someone as strong as him be brought to their knees. I have a sinking suspicion that he's more concerned about what his death would do to me, rather than the possibility of actually dying. If I wasn't a factor, he would've risked it all by now. I raise my hands in a show of surrender, willing to do whatever it takes to get that gun off of Roan.

"I'm here," I choke out, the words tasting like ash.

"That you are."

I can feel the heated once over he gives me, making my lip curl involuntarily. Slowly, he slips the hood from his head, revealing a gaunt looking face. He's balding, his hairline practically nonexistent. Wire-rimmed glasses are perched on a beak-like nose. Distractedly, I notice his nostrils are bigger than most, giving him a cartoonish appearance. Everything about this man screams meek and subordinate. A rule-follower to the highest extent. But I've learned the hard way how deceiving looks can be.

"I've dreamt of this moment a thousand times," he groans, pressing his free hand over the crotch of his pants. *Gross.* "We're going to have so much fun together." The wide, grotesque smile that stretches across his face makes my insides twist. He's certifiable if he thinks the two of us will be doing anything enjoyable.

"Let Roan go so we can leave." A snarl sounds behind me, a vehement display of '*I think the fuck not*' from one of the guys. My chest warms at the love I feel emanating from each of them. This is going to go horrifically wrong. I was a fool to think they'd ever go along with letting me leave here with this deranged pedophile, even if it meant saving their brother.

"Oh?" Roan grunts, swaying side to side as the asshole behind him slams the butt of the gun against his temple. "On second thought, I think he should pay for his transgressions."

"What does that even mean?" I scoff indignantly, my brain struggling to wrap itself around the audacity he's exuding.

"Did you really think I'd allow this cretin to touch what's mine?" His posturing and bravado give way to something dark and sinister. "I've watched him put his filthy paws all over you, on several occasions, tainting your purity. Who gave him the right?!" Spittle flies from his mouth, each word growing more incensed than the last. Something strange comes over me. This wave of hysteria that can't be contained, no matter how hard I try to stave it off. A laugh bubbles out of me, sounding hollow and crazed.

"You've gotta be shitting me." I wipe the tears from my face, the atmosphere in the room growing infinitely tenser in a matter of seconds. Maybe he's broken me. After all this time, all the hell I've been through, this is what causes me to crack. I'm split wide open, my wounds and damage on display for all to see. My fear dissipates, leaving rage in its wake. It's the driving force behind my actions, the anchor I cling to and pull from for bravery as I face the man that ruined my life.

"My purity went out the window when you hired Liam Price to kidnap me. He held me prisoner for five years in an old, dilapidated storm cellar. Five fucking years!" Tears flood my face, but I draw on the guys' presence, knowing they have my back, regardless of how this pans out. "If you think he didn't hurt and abuse me, you're not nearly as smart as you think you are."

"You're lying." The gun wavers, ripping the air from my lungs. I don't dare move or breathe, fearful the smallest flinch might push him over the edge. "Liam wouldn't have disregarded a direct order like that."

"Yeah?" I whisper, darting my eyes between Roan and the weapon he's at the mercy of. "He backed out in the end, right? Didn't follow through on the delivery portion of your deal. That's a blatant show of disrespect if I've ever seen one. What makes you think he had any loyalty to you?"

"You're wrong!" He rips the gun away from Roan and aims it at me. A smile of relief graces my lips, giving me the first bout of hope I've had since walking in here. "And I can prove it. Should I take you here? Make your boyfriend watch? I'll stretch every hole you've got, for no other reason than I can. You. Are. *Mine.*"

"Like hell I am," I grit out. "It'll be a cold day in Hell before you lay so much as a finger on me. I'm not scared of you. *Do you hear me?* You no longer have a hold over me. You're nothing but a twig of man, washed up and so desperate for attention that you sought it out in a child. You're sick. A disgusting waste of space who will *never* know what it's like to have me. Want to know why?" I taunt, taking a step closer.

"Saylor," Lochlan warns, but I brush it aside, intent on voicing my thoughts.

"You can't take something that no longer exists. Any part of me that remained pure after Liam was finished, has been well and truly extinguished by one of these men. They've all had me, in one way or another. I'll never be yours, because I belong to them."

"Shit," Kash murmurs, fidgeting behind me as my ears start to ring. I've gone too far, pushed the crazy man past his detonation point, but I don't regret it. It's eerily silent, an eternity passing in the span of a few seconds. I watch in horror as Roan jerks back, anticipating the psychopath's next move before I can even blink. The gun goes off, a spray of blood coating the back of the couch as I lose all sense of sanity.

"Nooo!" I fling myself forward, barreling headfirst into the man still armed with a weapon, my own safety flying clear out the window as I watch Roan slump forward. Chaos breaks out around me, but I'm determined to cause as much damage as possible. I kick and scratch, using every tool at my disposal to hurt the sonofabitch who continues to rip my life apart.

He wrestles me to the ground, the pressure of his body lying on top of mine making me gag. Fortunately for me, we're pretty evenly matched. He has nothing on Liam height and weight wise, and I went toe-to-toe with him several times. His grimy hands encase my throat, depriving me of oxygen. I buck and twist, but he doesn't let up. The sharp pinch in my back reminds of the gun I stashed in my waistband. With a little effort, I manage to wiggle my arm beneath me. Just as I get it between us, Kash is there, his forearm wrapped around my attacker's throat.

With my last bit of consciousness, I feel for the safety, flick it off, and pull the trigger. My body jolts from the force of it going off in such close proximity. It takes a minute for sound to filter back in, but once it does, I'm met with a flurry of panicked yells. I sputter and cough, drawing in some much needed air. The dead weight holding me down is pulled away, easing my breathing even more.

"Say Baby," Havok's worried voice calls out, his hands roving over my body, eyes wide and terrified. I glance down, seeing my shirt drenched in blood. I push him aside and pat my torso, relieved to find it isn't mine.

"I'm fine," I grunt, rolling to my knees as I try to shake the fuzzy feeling from my head. My eyes land on the dead body next to me. A stranger, for all intents and purposes. I don't even know his name. He destroyed my childhood, and I have no idea who he is. I avert my gaze, not needing to relish in the fact that he's finally gone. For good this time.

"Roan?" Panic swells inside of me as I watch Lochlan press a towel to the wound on his neck. It's gushing blood, a crimson pool of it surrounding his prone body. I scramble over, barely keeping upright in my rush to get to him. His gorgeous green eyes lock with mine, full of acceptance and all the things we haven't gotten a chance to say. He's already checked out. Thrown in the towel and resigned himself to the end. Well, I refuse to accept that.

"You're okay," I sob, brushing the loose hair from his face. "When this is over, and you're all better, I need you to train me more. Not just the firing range, though. I need help in all areas. I'm woefully unprepared in hand-to-hand combat. So you have to hold on, okay?" I use my shoulder to wipe the snot from my face.

"Damn right, you do. She's a horrible shot," Kash grunts in agreement. I turn to glare at him, but it quickly gives way to horror as I watch Krew wrap his brother's arm in gauze. *Oh, God. I shot him too.* "Get that look off your face, sweetness. It's just a graze. I'm more worried about that asshole's blood mixing with mine. Through-and-throughs are nasty little buggers.

Do you think insanity is contagious?" Kash questions his twin, his voice tight with worry.

What the hell is happening right now? How are they behaving so blasé when their friend is bleeding out on the kitchen floor? Indignation washes over me, but I keep my focus on Roan. His blinks are growing slower and farther apart. I can't lose him. None of this will be worth it if he's no longer here. I'd live in fear forever, constantly looking over my shoulder, if it meant he's happy and healthy.

"Hang tight, brother. Help's almost here." Lochlan keeps pressure on the wound, sparing me a quick glance of reassurance. No sooner do the words leave his mouth and the door is kicked open. I scream, shuffling backwards as agents flood the room. The moment I recognize Denvers, a weight is lifted off of me. The cavalry's here. He's going to make everything okay.

"Calloway." He nods in greeting, gesturing toward the paramedics entering through the slider, a stretcher ready and waiting to get Roan out of here. I press a kiss to his lips, wishing I could stay by his side, but knowing the best thing I can do for him is get out of the way and let the professionals get to work.

"I've got you," Lochlan whispers, encircling my waist as we watch from the sidelines. I lean back, needing his support more than ever. A man we both love is hanging on by a thread, and there's not a damn thing either of us can do about it. Helplessness has to be the worst feeling in the world, second only to guilt.

It's a flurry of activity as they whisk Roan

away, and bag the body I can't spare a moment of grief over. I took a man's life tonight, but I feel no remorse. I fought for myself, for the men I love. I will *always* choose us, over anyone or anything. Denvers has a ton of questions, as expected, but I'm useless at the moment. The last bit of brain power I have left is reserved for Roan. Worry for his wellbeing trumps everything else.

By the time we reach the hospital he was transported to, it's more than an hour later. The charge nurse directs us to a private waiting area, informing us he's currently in the OR and she'll report any updates as she receives them. And so begins the longest night of my life, surpassing all the sleepless ones I spent in that cellar, my empty stomach clenching around absolutely nothing. I can't help but wonder if this is how Roan and Lochlan felt as they waited for any word on my condition and prognosis.

As I've come to learn, loving someone makes you vulnerable in a way that nothing else can.

Chapter Fifty

Lochlan

We're nearing the forty-eight-hour mark since Roan made it out of surgery, and every minute has been spent impatiently waiting for him to finally wake up. It feels all too familiar. Too soon. Night one was touch and go, but he pulled through. The first bullet grazed his thigh, but the last one nicked his carotid, causing him to lose more than half his blood volume. He's tough, though. If Roan wasn't trained to read high intensity situations so well, he would've been done for. If he had moved a second later, we'd be planning his funeral instead. The thought alone makes my gut churn. As close as I am with the guys, I've known Roan the longest. I'm connected to him in a way that I'm not with the others. We share everything but blood. At least, until two nights ago, when I donated a shit ton of it to keep the bastard alive.

Tension hangs thick and heavy between us as we do nothing more than stare at the clock, willing time to speed up. We've been taking turns, swapping out who sleeps in Roan's room and who takes a hard ass chair in the waiting area, but Saylor has refused to leave his side. She's floundering from one emotion to the next. Crying one second, then snapping at Kash for his insensitivity back at the house. We all know she doesn't mean it, but that doesn't make it any easier to watch.

Kash has been downcast ever since, walking around like a kicked puppy, trying his best not to let Saylor see how hurtful her words were. When the dust has settled and we've come out the other end of this, she'll realize he was only coping the best way he knew how to. Krew, on the other hand, is out of his mind with the need for answers. He can't figure out how the piece of shit cracked our security system. He's barely slept, working himself to the bone to ensure something like this never happens again. To make matters worse, the coffee here tastes like burnt asshole, and the food is rubbish. I'd kill for a nice bed to stretch out on, but there's no chance I'm leaving this sterilized hellhole until my brother can too.

"Mr. Calloway?" I stop my pacing and face the elderly woman approaching me. "I know it's not much, but I was able to wrangle you boys an extra room. It's a few doors down—number 2208. The sheets are clean and I stocked the bathroom with some toiletries."

"Thank you," I reply sincerely, grateful to have somewhere to wash the filth from my body, if nothing else. "It's more than you realize." She nods, giving me a tired smile as she heads back to work. I lean against the wall, enjoying the brief moment of quiet. I've been eager for space, some time to myself. It's hard to process everything that's happened when I'm constantly worried about everyone else. But it's my job to be the strong one. Not only that, we're a family, and I need them as much as they need me.

Roan's door cracks open, revealing Denvers a second later. I straighten, ready to have this whole ordeal behind us. We've each been questioned about the events that led up to this—one man dead and another fighting for his life. He's just wrapped up his interview with Saylor, saving her for last, and I'm eager to hear where we stand.

"That girl's a fighter," Denvers huffs with a shake of his head. "Proud of her. Seems fitting that she was the one to take the bastard out."

"Yeah? At what cost?" I cross my arms defensively. Am I proud of Saylor? Fuck yes, I am. But that doesn't negate the worry I feel. Regardless of how deserved it was, she still took a life. That sort of trauma tends to linger, and she already has plenty.

"One day, you're going to stop underestimating her." Denvers mirrors my stance and cocks an eyebrow. "Let's hope it's sooner, rather than later. I'd hate to see that sweet woman angry." I snort and fight back a smirk. He has no idea. "As far as repercussions go, you're all in the clear. It was never a concern, but you know how it goes. Paperwork is a bitch and I wanted this done by the book."

I nod in understanding. "So now what?"

"Now," he clamps a hand on my shoulder, giving it a reassuring squeeze, "you live your lives in peace. However that looks. Just make her happy,

Calloway."

Bloody hell, we're transparent as fuck.

"She won't know a day more of misery if I have anything to say about it." I lock eyes with the man who's aided us the entire way, promising to do right by the woman we both fought to save. He holds my gaze for a minute longer, letting the enormity of the moment build between us. We fucking did it. *She* did it. Denvers nods and takes a step back, a pleased smile adding a few more wrinkles to his weathered face.

"Take care, kid. I'll be in touch." He dips his chin and turns to leave. I watch him go, refusing to pull my eyes away until he rounds the corner. His exit feels like an ending. A chapter of our lives being wrapped up and put to rest. From here on out, the future is a blank slate. Fuck, that's a nice thought.

I push through the door, needing to lay eyes on my girl. My good mood slips as I find her curled up next to Roan, her eyes puffy and rimmed in dark circles. I come to a stop beside them, sighing as I take in the way Saylor clings to his burly ass, even in her sleep. She's been terrified to rest, fearing he'll wake and she won't be there to witness it. The two of them might be the most stubborn people I know, but no one loves like them either. Carefully, I pick Saylor up and walk us to room 2208.

"Lochlan?" She stirs, her blue eyes blinking up at me inquisitively. "What's happening?"

"Thought you'd like a hot shower." I step inside the bathroom, hugging her against me as I get the water turned on.

"What? No. I can't be away from Roan that long." She tries to push away, but I hold her tighter.

"You're burnt out, love. You're no good to him like this. You need to recharge. When he comes around—and he will—he's going to need you alert and fully present. I have a feeling you're in for a mighty ass chewing." Saylor gives me a watery smile, not bothering to protest any further.

I place her on her feet and help her out of the borrowed scrubs she was given when we first got here. Aside from the quick rinse she took to get the blood off, she hasn't so much as changed her clothes. Not that we have any extras lying about. It wasn't that long ago that she was sporting a different set of hand-me-down hospital garb. I'll be right as rain if I never have to see her in this washed-out blue color ever again. I ease her top up and toss it to the side. I'm no spring chicken, rearing to go at the first sight of tits and ass, but Saylor isn't just anyone. It's been a long time since I've enjoyed the company of a woman, but I know any prior trysts I've partaken in will pale in comparison to being with her. She smiles shyly and proceeds to return the favor, undressing me with the same methodical precision.

I catch a glance of myself in the mirror behind her, surprisingly unbothered by my unkempt state. I'm always put together, presentable and ready at a moment's notice. It's a product of my raising. Calloway men are taught to be polished and reserved. Even my Nan—God rest her soul—was a bloody stickler in regard to appearance. She always stressed the importance of a good suit and a winning personality. But Saylor makes me forget about all the bullshit that was instilled in me. I let go when I'm around her. The pomp and circumstance feel so unnecessary, and I get to be *me*. As an only child, I craved my parents' acceptance. It took me a long time to realize I'd never get it, no matter how hard I tried. Maybe that's why this situation works for us. We've been eager for approval, and that's exactly what we found in our relationship with Saylor.

I link my fingers with hers and guide us under the water. I groan, my head falling back as Saylor slides her arms around my middle. Her cheek rests against my chest as I run my fingers through her hair, gently working out the tangles. We stay wrapped in one another, taking turns with the soap and shampoo. It's a far cry from the expensive shit she's grown used to, but at least we're clean. As the last bit of suds fade from her long blonde strands, I frame her face and bring her lips to mine.

"I love you," I mouth. Her shoulders start to shake as she pulls away to meet my gaze.

"I'm sorry," Saylor hiccups around a sob.

"Sorry for what, love?" My brows dip in concern as she fights to voice her feelings.

"It's my fault he's here. I knew it was dangerous to anger *him* like that, but once I started, I couldn't stop. It felt like I was purging myself of any part of him. I *needed* him to know those things, but not at the expense of Roan's life. What if he...what if he d-d-doesn't wake up?" Her stuttered wails break my fucking heart. Cleave the organ clear in two.

"I promise you'll never have to know. Ro's a fighter, sweetheart. Just like you. He's going to pull through this and go right back to being the overbearing wanker he's always been." I run my thumbs beneath her red-rimmed eyes, wishing I could speed up the process and lessen her pain. I'm going to beat his ass when he's back to fighting form for making Saylor worry so goddamn much.

Using my foot, I kick the handicap bench down and take a seat, pulling her with me. Her thighs straddle my lap as I run my hand up and down her spine, swearing at every shaky inhale that wracks her body. My eyes close as I breathe in her familiar scent, something sweet and solely exclusive to Saylor. Even the cheap hospital soap can't mask it. I'm not sure how it starts, but slowly, her hips begin to rock back and forth. This is very much not the time nor the place, but this is what I mean. I completely lose my head with her. The slick feel of her pussy makes my dick harden instantly. I clamp a hand around her hip, trying to stop this before we get too carried away.

"Sweetheart, I'm not sure that our first time should be in a shower stall at Pickler Med. You deserve more than that." My voice is drenched with need, a fact she doesn't miss.

"What I need, is you. The when and where are inconsequential, as long you're present."

Fuck.

"You want this?" I grip the back of her neck, needing to see her eyes when she answers. Those big blue pools sparkle as she nods, brimming with lust and need. "Then take it, love. Whatever you want, it's yours. But you're in control, not me." I hand Saylor the reins, allowing her to choose how far this goes. To my shock and absolute glee, she angles her body forward, lines my cock up, and drops back down. In one bliss-fueled downstroke, I'm fully seated inside of her. Saylor whimpers at the invasion, but makes no move to pop off.

"Slow," I direct, tightening my hold on her sides to help guide her movement. She's so desperate for sensation she can't stay still. But I want her to enjoy this. I refuse to give her a quick fuck in the middle of the ICU. I'm going to love her—deep and hard—enjoying every moan and sigh along the way. "Ride me. Nice and easy, love." And Christ, does she. We fuck for so long, the water runs cold. I've pushed back my release too many times to count, so caught up in how good she feels I don't want it to end. I'm teetering at my limit, though. I thrust up, catching Saylor off guard. Her thighs are shaking, spent and overworked, but she's too blissed-out to stop. I hold her in place and take over, pistoning my hips forward.

"Lochlan!" Saylor squeals, clutching my shoulders as she fights to stay balanced. Her pussy pulses as she orgasms, her hot little pants tickling my neck as she squirms from the overstimulation.

"Bloody hell, love." I jerk my cock free at the last second, letting my cum splash across the tile floor. One day, I'll paint her fucking insides, but not yet. "*Home*. You're home for me, Saylor." I press my forehead to her stomach as she sways in front of me, both of us dead on our feet. Once we're dried off and donning a fresh set of scrubs, we crowd the too-small bed with an exhausted sigh. She plants a half-assed, barely coherent kiss on my lips and passes out immediately. I laugh and hug her tighter, grateful that she's here. Grateful she's ours.

At some point, sleep claims me too. I have no idea how long I'm out for, but I wake up alone and the room is dark. A quick peek at my phone shows that it's just after 6pm. I scrub a hand down my face, stretching my back out as I slide my glasses on and head for Roan's room. There's a noticeable shift as I push through the door, a familiar, watery giggle greeting me as I round the privacy curtain. Ro is perched up on a stack of pillows, his hand gripping Saylor's as his morphine-d ass attempts to focus his gaze on her. That unbearable weight of worry falls away at seeing my brother awake. He's groggy and in desperate need of a bath, but he's okay.

Goddamn him for kissing death like that.

"If you needed some time off, all you had to do was ask. Seems a bit much to go to such lengths just to get some PTO, don't you think?" I stop beside his bed, paying no mind to the annoyed look Saylor shoots me. My eyes rake over Ro, pleased to see he has more color than he did. "That gray pallor you were rocking isn't very fashion-forward. Happy to see you've gotten rid of it." He smirks at my pathetic attempt at levity.

"Since when did you and Kash switch places? Dark humor is typically his MO." Ro winces from the effort it takes to speak, but telling him to shut the hell up wouldn't do me any favors. It'd only piss Saylor off, and he wouldn't listen anyway.

"Glad to see you breathing, brother." I squeeze his thigh—the uninjured one—and bend down to speak against his ear. "But mark my words, I will beat your ass—embarrassingly bad, I might add—if you ever pull some shit like that again. Got it?" Ro scoffs, knowing damn well I couldn't harm a hair on his stupidly handsome head, even if I wanted to.

"I hear ya loud and clear, Boss Man," he slurs, the drugs pumping through his body causing him to fade away. "No more playing tag with danger pellets." Ro knocks out, his sleep so instant and heavy that he starts to snore. I grin at Saylor, the pressure on my chest all but gone.

"What'd I say?" I cock my head to the side, enjoying the sweet, carefree smile she gives me in return. "Let's go spread the good news." I hold my hand out for her to take, giddy as a fucking preteen at the slightest contact.

"You were right," Saylor states as we make our way to the waiting area.

"About?"

"The first thing out of Roan's mouth was a lecture on de-escalation. Apparently, I did a stellar job of the exact opposite." My laughter echoes through the quiet hallway as the guys come into view. Kade is star-fished on the 1970's, germ-filled carpet, while the other two are shoulder-to-shoulder, braced against each other for support as they try and sleep through the noise filtering in from the emergency room. I kick the bottom of Kade's shoe, causing him to bolt up, his eyes wide and bloodshot.

"The fuck?" His silver hair is pointed in every direction, looking ratty and gross.

"Sleeping beauty is awake. Time to go." I lift my chin at Krew, knowing he'll have Ro discharged in no time, releasing him to the care of a private physician. I'd be okay with staying put and giving his body a chance to heal, but God knows he'll never go for that. The next time his eyes pop open, he'll be demanding we leave.

"Halle-fucking-lujah. I've got swamp ass and my nuts stink." Saylor's nose scrunches at the imagery Kade's just given her. *Dumbass.* "I'll get his feet. You two limp dicks get his head."

"Absolutely *not,*" Saylor sputters indignantly. "Roan will be leaving here in a wheelchair, or not at all." Silence greets her declaration, followed closely by Kash doubling over, laughing his ass off.

"This is going to be good," Kade ribs, rubbing his hands together giddily. Oh, ye of little faith. If there's anyone who can get Ro to do their bidding, it's the five-foot-two spitfire stomping away, looking for someone in charge to give her marching orders to.

And like the good little soldiers we are, we'll fall in line without complaint.

Chapter Fifty-One

Saylor

Sometimes, it feels like that night just happened, and other times, it seems like ages ago. It's Thanksgiving and the guys have gone all out to make this day special. Kade pulled out Mom's cookbook, pouring over every detail of her dressing recipe. He's been at it for hours, determined to perfect my favorite dish. The only person who's let me help is Kash, and I'd barely call it that. I got to pick out the place settings and point to where I wanted them. It's sweet, but I'm starting to feel useless.

Like it frequently does, the spot Roan nearly lost his life catches my eye. At first, I couldn't be in here without having a flashback. His blood was scrubbed from the tile before we ever came home, but I can still see it when I close my eyes. Even now, I get queasy when I think about how much he lost. He pushed through his healing quicker than he should have, to absolutely no one's surprise. But that puckered scar on his neck serves as a reminder of what could have been. Today would look a lot different without him.

I spent a lot of time afterwards on video calls with Danielle, trying to work through what I was feeling. It didn't take long for Denvers to piece together a complete file on my tormentor. Jeremiah Cartwright, much like Liam, hid his depravity in plain sight. He was an eighth-grade robotics teacher who saw a few pictures of my adolescent, underdeveloped body and decided I was his. Simple as that. In his fucked-up mind, I was ownable. A thing he could claim and store away for safekeeping.

That level of insanity is terrifying. He risked everything—his career and family—to see through some half-cocked plan to retrieve his long-awaited prize. He cashed in his retirement to pay Liam off, arranging for him to keep me until his own children were grown and off to college. For whatever reason, Liam stopped sending the scheduled updates they'd agreed to. Maybe he didn't want to part with his toy after having me at his disposal for so long, but Jeremiah had no intention of letting that stand.

The FBI hasn't been able to prove it, but they're fairly certainly Liam's death was ordered by Jeremiah. Some low life, hired help who was all too happy to oblige in the death of another human for the right amount of money. I'm not sad over it, but it does bother me that we never had our day in court. I didn't get to say my piece to him the way I did with Jeremiah. Liam might not have been the mastermind, but he allowed his strings to be pulled and manipulated. And then he went completely off-script and hurt me in ways I'll never fully heal from.

In possibly the biggest plot twist yet, Jeremiah's

family reached out shortly after he was put to rest. The burial was private, his wife and kids refusing to attend. In the end, he had no one. The greedy man who thought it was okay to steal a child was left with nothing. His gravestone is free of filler words, simply stating his date of birth and death. As much as the people he left behind don't deserve to bear his shame, I haven't come to terms with facing them quite yet.

His wife wrote to me, explaining how sorry she was. How guilty they all feel for not picking up on anything off about Jeremiah. They lived with the man, clueless to how evil he was. I'd like to say it makes no sense, but what I went through opened my eyes to how easily we trust the picture presented to us. I hold no grudge towards them, and maybe one day I'll be ready to meet with them. But at present, and for the sake of my own mental health, I'm not on board with any sort of connection to Jeremiah.

"Hey." Roan tilts my chin up, effectively breaking the stare-off I'd been engaged in with the tile.

"Hi," I respond hoarsely, taking a second to clear my throat. If it only it was that easy to wipe away my memories as well.

"I'm okay, baby girl." My eyes flash to his scar, wishing I could erase the imperfection from his sun-kissed skin. "In fact, I'm happy to demonstrate just how okay I really am. Give me three minutes in the laundry room. You, me, a heavy load of towels in the dryer, working in tandem to get you off as I eat your pussy like a French delicacy." I slap his chest with the back of my hand, rolling my eyes at the ridiculous suggestion.

"Turkey is done!" Kash hollers, his tongue poking out as he concentrates extra hard on pulling it from the oven.

"You drop that bird and we're throwing hands." I step away from Roan, winking as I glance back over my shoulder. "I'm dessert, Big Guy, not the main course." Kade snorts, smacking my butt as I walk past him.

The table is set, our plates perfectly placed and food presented beautifully. I bite back a smile, knowing they planned this just in case today's the day I woke up and decided to become one of those Instagram girls. They want me to test the waters, try out everything I can think of to figure out who I am. Who I want to be. But I'm just me. Simple, boyfriend hoarding Saylor who loves five men without an ounce of shame.

"I love it." I give them each a grateful smile, sliding out a chair so we can get this show on the road. "Which one of you is going to carve the turkey?" Who knew a simple question could lead to such male posturing? Like primed peacocks fluffing their feathers, they puff out their chests, arguing over who's earned the right to knife duty. Playing dirty but smart, Roan uses his forever get-out-of-jail-free card, tossing out the near-death experience he endured.

Dinner is everything I dreamed of one day having. A table full of food, surrounded by people I love. I wouldn't want to spend it with anyone else. The only person missing is Mom, but Kade nailed the dressing. It would've been great to have her here, holding my hand along the way as I navigate life outside of Liam and Jeremiah, but I know she's watching over us. It hasn't been easy, though.

It's hard to let go of the fear that's been a constant for so long. The first time we ventured into town, I had a panic attack. I didn't know what was happening until it was too late. My gaze kept tracking every person we passed, watching the way they'd stare and whisper. I couldn't tell if it was because I was holding the hands of two men, or if they somehow recognized me from the news reports making their rounds across the country. My face was plastered on every media outlet imaginable, so the idea wasn't improbable.

That worry quickly morphed into the realization that I'll never truly know the thoughts and intentions of a stranger. As I've come to learn, sociopaths excel in mimicking normalcy. Most people aren't ever aware that they've come into contact with someone presenting markers for antisocial personality disorder. And I somehow encountered *two* in the first fourteen years of my life. If that's not character building, I don't know what is.

After our failed outing, I stuck close to home. I took comfort in the beach and my guys, content to spend all my time with them. But I know they're worried. I've overheard Lochlan speaking to Denvers, questioning my inability to feel guilt over killing someone. Out of everything I've struggled with, taking Jeremiah's life has never been a problem for me. I understand the difference between malicious harm and self-defense. He doesn't get to live rent free in my head any longer.

"Fuck, that was good," Roan groans, leaning back to pat his stomach. "Not it for cleanup." He touches the tip of his nose with his finger, reverting back to the prepubescent way of settling things. Lochlan and I are the only two who don't rush to join in, both of us shaking our heads at their immaturity. Honestly, though, I wouldn't have them any other way.

We clean the table off together, joking about the leftovers we'll be eating for days. As soon as I swipe the last bit of crumbs from the counter, Lochlan takes my hand and spins me. Softly, a Christmas song starts to play. I laugh as he dances us around the kitchen, my steps faltering when I glance toward the living room and find it filled with boxes and storage totes.

"What's all this?" I take in the bins, looking from one guy to the next as I wait for an explanation.

"Duh, it's Christmas now. Time to decorate the tree!" Kash launches himself over the couch and plucks me clear off my feet. I laugh as he lifts me, holding on for dear life as he rushes for the nearest box. He rights me, holding my arms until I'm steady, then proceeds to rip tree parts out like a manic little elf. His excitement is borderline scary.

"Kash goes a bit feral when it comes to decorating," Kade comments from behind me, like he's using my body as a shield from the crazy.

"You don't say," I reply dryly, watching in disbelief as tinsel and garland get added to the mix. By the time the containers are empty, it looks like the

North Pole threw up in our living room.

"Let the games begin!" Kash claps his hands together excitedly, the megawatt grin he's sporting infectious.

"Games?" I whisper in confusion.

"Yeah," Lochlan answers while handing me a mug of hot chocolate. I moan at the first sip, popping a few marshmallows in my mouth. *Pure, milky heaven.* "Kash likes to make it a competition to see who can decorate the best, but he's really only competing with himself. If we try to do anything, he panics and takes over, convinced we won't do it right." I bite back a smile, in awe of how sweet he is.

Maybe it's not obvious to the others, but I can see how eager Kash is to make everything perfect. For someone who lacked warmth growing up, he wants to fill his own home up until it's overflowing. All the things Kash longed for as a kid, he recreates for his new family. Tears prick the backs of my eyes as I watch him flutter about, tripping every few feet on the mess of Christmas décor he's pulled out. He's like a holiday fairy, spreading cheer everywhere he goes.

My mouth waters just thinking of all the sugary treats he's bound to make. Setting my cup aside, I jump in, determined to be a part of this. Kash halts his frenzied movements as I stop beside him, his brown eyes meeting mine. We share a silent moment of understanding before he pulls me in for a kiss. He takes his time, tasting me thoroughly, unbothered by the audience we have. I laugh as I pull away, shaking my head at the dirty wink he gives me.

“Put me to work, Santa.” I bat my eyes and wait for his instruction.

“Oh, I’ve got some work you could do.” Kash waggles his eyebrows, wincing as Roan smacks the back of his head. “Fun police,” he snarks, sticking out his tongue.

It’s well past midnight when we finally finish. There was a brief intermission for a second helping of pie, but other than that, Kash kept us on track, barking out tasks left and right. Roan lifts me up and sets me on his shoulders so I can put the star on the tree. As soon as the last piece is in place, we all crash on the couch, my body wedged between the twins as they snore soundly. This is just the beginning. We’ve got years ahead of us, and so many memories to make. With that in mind, I fall asleep with my heart and belly full, ready to face the next chapter head on.

Epilogue

Saylor

"Happy Birthday to you."

A sing-song-y voice brushes the edge of my consciousness, but the soft, fuzzy blanket I'm buried beneath feels way too good to vacate.

"Happy Birthday to you." That incessant tone prods at my brain once again, accompanied by a faint tickle to my side. "Happy Birthday, Dear Sayloooor. Happy Birthday to you!"

I gasp as someone rips the covers away and rolls me to my back. Before I can blink through the fogginess, my nipple is wrapped in a hot, wet mouth. I jerk up, bracing myself on my forearms as I stare at Kash above me, a delighted grin stretched across his handsome face. I'm completely naked, having spent half the night wrapped in Roan. He wanted to be the first to wish me a Happy Birthday, so as soon as the clock struck midnight, he proceeded to celebrate my twenty-third year around the sun with back-to-back orgasms. My lack of clothing is certainly working to Kash's benefit.

"Would the Birthday Girl like her first surprise?" Kash's low, sleep roughened voice is intoxicating. Despite the ache between my thighs, I'm eager to find out where this is headed.

"First?" I question curiously, but the years I've had with these men, learning everything there is to know about them, should clue me in that they'll never do anything half-assed.

"Oh, sweetness." The look Kash gives me causes my heart to beat faster, throbbing in tune with the need he's expertly stoking. I watch in fascination as he lifts a tub of frosting in one hand, and a jar of sprinkles in the other. Quicker than I can track, he plops a spoonful on my breast and tops it with the tiny candies. I fall back on a giggle, shaking my head at how fitting this is for my sugar fiend.

"I think this is what they meant by having your cake, and eating it too." I jerk my attention to the doorway, finding Krew braced against the wall as he watches his brother lick me clean. My back arches, lips parting on a pant as he tugs my nipple between his teeth. There's not a trace of frosting left by the time Kash starts in on the other side. I'm a flustered, needy mess when the others finally join us. There's only one person missing. We've toyed with the group aspect, but Roan's held firm on his wishes. He can handle the two of us being watched, but not the other way around. I've respected his boundaries; he's more than enough all on his own. Last night wasn't the first time he's kept me awake till morning, and I'm certain it won't be the last.

It hasn't always been this easy. Naturally, the

guys have struggled with jealousy from time to time, but we've adapted. We communicated and worked through the tough parts. And lying here, the feel of their hungry gazes licking fire across my skin, makes all the rough patches worth it. We've found our sweet spot, an arrangement that works for everyone. Even still, having the four of them here, their sole focus on me, is a treat we don't partake in very often. But the infrequency makes it all the more special when we do come together like this.

"Let's celebrate our girl properly. Move aside, shithead," Havok teases, shoving Kash away so he can take his place. His clothes are thrown off in the next breath, his colorful, toned body making my mouth water. "Come here, Say Baby." Havok scoops me up and falls to his back.

I straddle his lap, rocking my hips back and forth, desperate for friction. I'm keyed up, the anticipation of what's to come making my body thrum with excitement. Havok groans, his bright blue eyes falling closed as my wetness coats his cock. Using the brief distraction to my advantage, I tilt forward, giving him the perfect angle to slip inside of me. These days, I take what I want. And right now, I want the men I love to work me over so thoroughly, I won't be able to walk right for a week.

"Goddamn," Havok grunts, his hips punching forward reflexively. "So tight, pretty girl." I smile, preening at every stuttered breath I draw from him.

"It's about to get a lot tighter," Krew comments, placing a firm hand between my shoulder blades. "Ease forward, Tink." I do as I'm told, too focused on my impending release to pay him any mind. When the frosting makes a reappearance, I falter, my mouth popping open as Krew spreads my ass cheeks. Kash lathers me with it, then backs away, giving his brother the space he needs to tongue it off. I whimper at the dual sensation of being fucked and ate at the same time.

"Please," I beg, the shame I used to feel for wanting them like this a thing of the past.

"You want my cock too? Is that what you need?" Krew prods my ass with his finger, slipping in easily. The timing of Havok's next thrust is so perfect, it makes me come. I cry out at the rush of pleasure, my body going slack as Krew adds another, stretching me gently. It took us a while to work up to this. Lochlan was insistent we start with plugs. I've had them separately, but never two at once. A hint of fear niggles at me, but I want this too much to shy away now. I push back, giving Krew my answer. He pops open a bottle of lube and coats my opening. At the first press of his cock, I start to tense up. Havok slows his movement, dropping a hand between us so he can stroke my clit.

"Relax," Krew instructs, slowly pushing past that tight ring of muscle. I wince at the intrusion, trying to squirm away from the pressure.

"Fuck, Say. I'm gonna nut if you keep moving like that." I snort at Havok's strained expression, trying to breathe through the pain as Krew fills me completely. They start slow, taking turns as they rock into me. Their strokes are shallow, but as the first pleasure-filled sigh escapes me, they pick up speed. It doesn't take long before they're fucking me in unison, slamming in at the same time. Incoherent nonsense slips out of me, my body and brain overrun with sensation.

"Open up, sweetheart." Lochlan taps my lips with his cock. I oblige happily, stroking my tongue over the thick, throbbing vein causing his tip to leak with precum. He doesn't give me a chance to take things at my own pace. He surges forward, making me choke as the heavy weight of him hits the back of my throat. He fucks my mouth, his head falling back in ecstasy. Tears stream down my face as I'm filled from every end by the men I love.

Kash stands beside us, his hand gripping his dick firmly as he watches. I wrap my fingers around his, my coordination somewhat disjointed, but he doesn't seem to mind. I've got four cocks ravaging my body, drowning me in pleasure, and I've never felt more empowered than I do right now. Krew tweaks my nipple, the hint of pain drawing another orgasm from me. It hits like a freight train. I can feel every twitch and drag of their cocks, and it makes my toes curl from how intense it is. Thoughts fail me as Lochlan pulls out and coats my back with his release. Havok grunts beneath me, the hot spray of his cum painting my insides a second later. I'm floating on a cloud when Krew finishes, his hands gripping my hips so tightly, I'll have bruises come tomorrow. He rams forward, burying himself so deep it hurts. I flinch, but he doesn't let up.

"I told you this ass would drip." Krew's hot breath tickles my ear as he slowly pulls out of me. I whimper at the loss, causing Havok's still-hard dick to twitch. "Even hours from now, you'll still feel me." Krew strokes his fingers through the mess he's made, using them to push his cum back inside of me.

"Fuck," Havok swears. "I can feel you." His face contorts, like he's angry that Krew is practically touching his dick, the thin barrier between my ass and pussy not offering much protection. Keen on getting a rise from him, Krew keeps fingering me, pressing down just right to make Havok come again. His mouth falls open, indignation washing over him as he realizes who's technically responsible for his pleasure. Krew laughs and slides his fingers out, hurrying to move away before Havok can retaliate.

"Asshole," he swears, leaning up to kiss me before sprinting after a naked Krew. I fall back, my body spent and sated. Just as my eyes close, Lochlan leans down and strokes his thumb over my cheek.

"Happy Birthday, love." I smile, my heart warming at the adoration shining back at me. "Breakfast in twenty." After another slow, sweet kiss, Lochlan leaves too.

"Finally," Kash huffs, gripping my ankles so he can tug me to the bottom of the bed. "You're mine now, sweetness." In one quick thrust, he's inside of me. His pace is set to brutal, and I'm perfectly fine with that. He pushes my thighs back, spreading me apart so he can fuck me deeper. I swear, my nails clawing at Kash's back as he pistons his hips exquisitely.

"You know why you're mine?" He pulls out and

flips me over, shoving me face first into the mattress so that my ass is at the perfect angle for him to plunge back in. I cry out, the mix of pain and pleasure nearly too much. “Because one of these long blonde strands I love so much was wrapped around my left nut this morning. That’s practically a marriage proposal, Best Friend." I laugh and moan at the same time, my back arching as he fists my hair and tilts my head. His other hand slips between my legs, roughly working my clit until I come with a scream.

“Kash!”

“Fuck yes,” he sighs, his release mixing with Havok’s as he peppers my neck with kisses. If I thought I was tired before, I’m dead on my feet now. I’m a sticky mess in desperate need of a shower, but Kash still pulls me close, both of us taking a few minutes to lie together as we attempt to catch our breath. Thank God we got the birth control situation sorted out a while back, but the sheer amount of cum leaking out me makes me question how effective it might be against so many swimmers. Eventually, Kash carries me to the bathroom, whispering how much he loves me as we clean each other up.

It’s been a lot longer than twenty minutes by the time we finish and join the others. The dining table is full, piled high with all my favorite breakfast foods. Roan snags me around the waist, dropping me on his lap and refusing to let me move. As the guys take their seats, Roan traps my legs on the outside of his. His thick fingers edge beneath my tiny lounge shorts, slowly stroking my sex as the others chatter amongst themselves. I freeze, my breaths growing harsher as he toys with me in secret. I'm dripping wet in a matter of seconds, pushing against the hard bulge of his cock.

Meanwhile, everyone else is oblivious to what Roan is doing to me. He slides two fingers in, fucking me for so long, I start to sweat. Someone asks me a question, but I'm too lost to comprehend what they're actually saying. There's a chuckle, followed by a groan. When he flicks my clit, I detonate, coming apart at the damn dining table. As Roan eases out of me, my eyes land on Lochlan's. He smirks, winking at the dazed look I give him. I happily take the donut he offers, pretending none of that just happened. A few minutes later, he swoops in to kiss away the lingering icing left behind. We eat and laugh, and just like all my other birthdays I've spent with them, it's one for the books.

Two Years Later

I married five men today.

Not legally, of course, but we stood on our private stretch of beach and committed the rest of our lives to one another. It wasn't necessary, but it felt right. With or without the public display, I've always known they're my forever. They brought me back to life in a way that nothing else ever could. As fulfilled as I am, everything I've accomplished would mean nothing if I didn't have them to share it with.

Our guest list included a whopping two people: Denvers and Nurse Karley. The decorated FBI Agent walked me through the sand and hand delivered me to my guys. I think our relationship is a head-scratcher for him, but he respects us all too much to chime in about it. Karley cried, gushing over how beautiful I looked and how proud my mom would be. I considered inviting Danielle, but we've kept our lines strictly professional. She's been my sounding board for years now, and it helps to have a degree of separation between us. We've never discussed my personal relationship with the guys.

I have no idea if keeping those details to myself has hurt or hindered my progress, but I'm content with my decision to leave my love life off the table. We have plenty of talking points without adding that to the mix. I think a part of me has always worried she might make light of it. That she'd classify the rapid rate at which I jumped headfirst into not only one, but five relationships, as a trauma response. And maybe I did come to grips with our dynamic rather quickly, but I'm not ashamed of what we have. It's not for everyone, but it's right for us. The realest thing I've ever felt. Danielle laid the groundwork and gave me the tools I needed to move past my kidnapping, but my real healing happened because of them. It's *still* happening. Every touch and kiss affords me a measure of peace I never anticipated having.

It's been five years since I was freed from that cellar—the same amount of time I spent thinking I'd never see the light of day. I've done so much, seen so much, with the extra time I've been given. Because that's what it is: a bonus. This is the icing on top of the cake. A second lease on life I never thought I'd get, and I've damn sure made the most of it. Our second

Christmas together was spent in Washington, while the guys had the kitchen remodeled at the Florida house. Roan was sick to death of the vacant look I'd get every time that patch of tile caught my eye. We even toyed with moving, but the idea of leaving the beach was unthinkable. So, they hatched a plan to fix it the only way they knew how, and it looked nothing like the space it once did by the time they were finished.

Krew's spent years designing his own security software, determined to build something impenetrable. He still blames himself for Jeremiah hacking the cams that day. For weeks, he had promised me it wasn't possible for someone to breach the property, but it was. I've never once put that burden on him, for the way things went down or the promises he couldn't keep. He's human. Mistakes were made, and it's helped each of us become more conscious of the fact that nothing is ever absolute. We had no idea who we were dealing with, and Jeremiah's background in robotics gave him a leg up we hadn't expected. Thankfully, as soon as the new system was up and running, Krew calmed down a bit.

We've vacationed all over the state, even going to Disney. It had barely been on my list for a full day when the guys started making arrangements. Kash bounced around the parks like a strung-out toddler, while Roan squeezed his massive body into every ride that caught my eye without complaint. I got my GED and went on to earn a degree in psychology, though I don't use it traditionally. Several times a year, I guest speak at seminars for lost and exploited children. It hurts to dredge up old wounds, but if my story can help even one person, an hour-long speech about what I went through is worth it. Outside of that, I help the guys run SOTERIA. We've grown even bigger, my case bringing more attention to the labor of love they created through years of hard work. It can be difficult, but I've learned my limits. I know when to take a step back if a client's situation becomes too triggering.

I'm happy.

So happy it's unreal. I'm filled with hope and excitement for all the years ahead, and I'll never again take those emotions for granted. Life can change in the blink of an eye—for better or for worse. And sometimes, you have to endure hell to reach heaven. It just might take some time to get there.

I'm pleased to report that I've arrived.

I finally found my happy ending, and with any luck, Liam and Jeremiah have front row seats for the encore performance.

I win, assholes.

The End

Acknowledgement

These characters have been stuck in my head for years now. I've second-guessed myself a thousand times while writing this, but I'm so happy to finally have their story finished. I hope you loved them as much as I do! Thanks for reading!

Xo,
MK

For the most up-to-date information on current and future works, please join M.K. Harper's Readers on Facebook.

Made in the USA
Middletown, DE
11 September 2024

60792782R00399